DISCARD

The Ways We Live Now

THE WAYS
WE LIVE NOW

Contemporary Short Fiction
from The Ontario Review

edited by
Raymond J. Smith

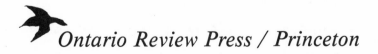Ontario Review Press / Princeton

Library of Congress Cataloging-in-Publication Data

The Ways we live now.

1. Short stories.   2. Fiction—20th century.
I. Smith, Raymond J.   II. Ontario review (Windsor, Ont.)
PN6120.2.W39   1986   808.83'1   86-12468
ISBN 0-86538-054-6
ISBN 0-86538-055-4 (pbk.)

Distributed by Persea Books, Inc.
225 Lafayette St.
New York, NY 10012

"Molly's Dog" by Alice Adams, *OR* 21. Copyright © 1984 by Alice Adams. Reprinted from *Return Trips* by Alice Adams, by permission of Alfred A. Knopf, Inc.

"The Man from Mars" by Margaret Atwood, *OR* 6. Copyright © 1977, 1982 by O. W. Toad, Ltd. Reprinted from *Dancing Girls and Other Stories* by Margaret Atwood, by permission of Simon & Schuster, Inc.

"Saving the Boat People" by Joe David Bellamy, *OR* 21. Copyright © 1984 by Joe David Bellamy. Reprinted by permission of the author.

"Town Smokes" by Pinckney Benedict, *OR* 25. Copyright © 1986 by Pinckney Benedict. Reprinted by permission of the author.

"My Life as a West African Gray Parrot" by Leigh Buchanan Bienen, *OR* 15. Copyright© 1981 by Leigh Buchanan Bienen. Reprinted by permission of the author.

"At the Krungthep Plaza" by Paul Bowles, *OR* 13. Copyright © 1981 by Paul Bowles. Reprinted from *Midnight Mass* with the permission of Black Sparrow Press.

"The Black Queen" by Barry Callaghan, *OR* 13. Copyright © 1982 by Barry Callaghan. Reprinted from *The Black Queen Stories* by Barry Callaghan with permission of the author and Ontario Review Press.

"Homework" by Margaret Drabble, *OR* 7. Copyright © 1977 by Margaret Drabble. Reprinted by permission of the author.

"Death's Midwives" by Margareta Ekström (translated by Linda Schenck), *OR* 20. English translation copyright © 1984 by The O.R. Press, Inc. Reprinted by permission.

"Fruit of the Month" by Abby Frucht, *OR* 20. Copyright © 1984 by Abby Frucht. Reprinted by permission of the author.

"A Pure Soul" by Carlos Fuentes (translated by Margaret S. Peden), *OR* 12. Reprinted from *Burnt Water* by Carlos Fuentes. English translation copyright © 1969, 1974, 1978, 1979, 1980 by Farrar, Straus and Giroux, Inc. Reprinted by permission of Farrar, Straus and Giroux, Inc.

"The Harvest" by Tess Gallagher, *OR* 19. Copyright © 1983 by Tess Gallagher. Reprinted by permission of the author.

"Some Gifts" by Reginald Gibbons, *OR* 5. Copyright © 1976 by Reginald Gibbons. Reprinted by permission of the author.

CONTENTS

Preface

Is THE AMERICAN short story truly undergoing a renaissance, as many observers have noted?—or is it more likely the case that readers are discovering, in ever greater numbers, the high quality of the short fiction currently being published? Certainly the 1980's has been a time of particular richness in both prose and poetry: *The Ontario Review*, like many other literary journals, commonly receives far more publishable material than it can use. Out of more than 8,000 short stories considered since our inception in 1974, we printed a spare 80; out of these 80, a yet more spare 28 have been selected—indeed, handpicked—for this anthology. That much excellent work has had to be eliminated is unfortunate but attests, we think, to the high quality of the volume in hand.

Our theme of contemporaneity apart, the stories in *The Ways We Live Now* are remarkably various. They range from the graphic colloquialism of William Heyen's "Any Sport" to the haunting lyricism of "Mourning" by Robert Taylor, Jr.; from the forthright realism of Lynne Sharon Schwartz's "Rough Strife" to the surrealistic—yet no less plausible—"My Life as a West African Gray Parrot" by Leigh Buchanan Bienen. The Oedipus myth is wittily re-examined by Daniel Stern in "The Interpretation of Dreams by Sigmund Freud: A Story," and the Frankenstein legend is given an eerie recasting by Joyce Carol Oates in "Baby." Maxine Kumin's "On This Short Day of Frost and Sun" is a love story of delicate proportions, while Greg Johnson's "A Metamorphosis" presents the final night of a female impersonator who is devoured by his/her fans. And Carlos Fuentes's "A Pure Soul" and Abby Frucht's "Fruit of the Month" might be seen as love stories as well, of very different kinds.

More than most contemporary fiction, the stories published in *The Ontario Review* tend to deal with cultural conflict of one kind or another. There are no overtly political stories in the volume but there are several in which politics plays a crucial, if not tragic, role in the lives of fairly ordinary individuals—among them Margaret Atwood's "The Man From Mars," Josephine Jacobsen's "The Mango Community," and Paul Bowles's characteristically enigmatic "At the Krungthep Plaza." Joe David Bellamy's "Saving the Boat People" is concerned with post-war Vietnamese refugees

who ironically provide refuge for their beleaguered patroness; Gloria
Whelan's "A Lesson in the Classics" is the story of an American classics
professor who is seduced by the island of Crete—until he discovers the
meaning of the adage "Beware of Greeks bearing gifts." Sarah Rossiter's
"Tea Party," in which the young wife of an American teacher in Wales tries
to befriend a Welsh farmwife, is a comic but moving treatment of this theme.
"Black Cotton" by the late William Goyen is a tale of the East Texas oil
boom of the early part of the twentieth century, deftly and memorably told.
And John Updike's delicately corrosive "Interviews with Insufficiently
Famous Americans" is anthropology at home.

Also distinctive are Margareta Ekström's "Death's Midwives," in which
a terminally ill woman's last days are flooded with poignant and sustaining
memories of giving birth, and Barry Callaghan's "The Black Queen,"
which tersely dramatizes a pair of aging homosexuals' Mother's Day party.
Tess Gallagher skillfully blends humor and pathos in a story about teaching
a blind man to "see," while Reginald Gibbons's "Some Gifts" is a sharply
observed, unsentimental depiction of an elderly violin maker, deserted on
Christmas Eve by all but his art. In Alice Adam's "Molly's Dog," the loss
of a dog becomes symbolic of life's other losses for the protagonist, and in
Elizabeth Spencer's "The Girl Who Loved Horses," a woman regains her
confidence after thwarting a rapist. Margaret Drabble's "Homework" and
Bette Pesetsky's "Confessions of a Bad Girl" offer wry domestic comedy.

Like most of our colleagues, the editors of *The Ontario Review* are
particularly proud to have published work by new, unknown, and in some
cases previously unpublished writers. Among the younger contributors to
The Ways We Live Now are Jeanne Schinto, Abby Frucht, and Pinckney
Benedict (whose "Town Smokes" is his first nationally published story).
We are proud too to have had a number of stories cited for honorable
mention or reprinted in *The O. Henry Awards, The Best American Short
Stories*, and *The Pushcart Prize*; and recorded for *Choice Magazine
Listening*.

I have read each of these stories many times in the process of helping to
select them for the magazine and again while editing this anthology, and
have found that each reading, far from diminishing the story, enhances it
with the discovery of previously unregistered nuances of style or character-
ization or meaning. And this, I think, is the true test of literary value.

—RAYMOND J. SMITH

Molly's Dog

ALICE ADAMS

ACCUSTOMED TO EXTREMES of mood, which she experienced less as 'swings' than as plunges, or more rarely as soarings, Molly Harper, a newly retired screenwriter, was nevertheless quite overwhelmed by the blackness—the horror, really, with which, one dark pre-dawn hour, she viewed a minor trip, a jaunt from San Francisco to Carmel, to which she had very much looked forward. It was to be a weekend, simply, at an inn where in fact she had often stayed before, with various lovers (Molly's emotional past had been strenuous). This time she was to travel with Sandy Norris, an old non-lover friend, who owned a bookstore. (Sandy usually had at least a part-time lover of his own, one in a series of nice young men.)

Before her film job, and her move to Los Angeles, Molly had been a poet, a good one—even, one year, a Yale Younger Poet. But she was living, then, from hand to mouth, from one idiot job to another. (Sandy was a friend from that era; they began as neighbors in a shabby North Beach apartment building, long since demolished.) As she had approached middle age, though, being broke all the time seemed undignified, if not downright scary. It wore her down, and she grabbed at the film work and moved down to L.A. Some years of that life were wearing in another way, she found, and she moved from Malibu back up to San Francisco, with a little saved money, and her three beautiful, cross old cats. And hopes for a new and calmer life. She meant to start seriously writing again.

In her pre-trip waking nightmare, though, which was convincing in the way that such an hour's imaginings always are (one sees the truth, and sees that any sunnier ideas are chimerical, delusions) at three, or four a.m., Molly pictured the two of them, as they would be in tawdry, ridiculous Carmel: herself, a scrawny sun-dried older woman, and Sandy, her wheezing, chain-smoking fat queer friend. There would be some silly awkwardness about sleeping arrangements, and instead of making love they would drink too much.

And, fatally, she thought of another weekend, in that same inn, years back: she remembered entering one of the cabins with a lover, and as soon as he, the lover, had closed the door they had turned to each other and kissed, had laughed and hurried off to bed. Contrast enough to make her nearly weep—and she knew, too, at four in the morning, that her cherished view of a meadow, and the river, the sea, would now be blocked by condominiums, or something.

This trip, she realized too late, at dawn, was to represent a serious error in judgment, one more in a lifetime of dark mistakes. It would weigh down and quite possibly sink her friendship with Sandy, and she put a high value on friendship. Their one previous lapse, hers and Sandy's, which occurred when she stoppped smoking and he did not (according to Sandy she had been most unpleasant about it, and perhaps she had been), had made Molly extremely unhappy.

But, good friends as she and Sandy were, why on earth a weekend together? The very frivolousness with which this plan had been hit upon seemed ominous; simply, Sandy had said that funnily enough he had never been to Carmel, and Molly had said that she knew a nifty place to stay. And so, why not? they said. A long time ago, when they both were poor, either of them would have given anything for such a weekend (though not with each other) and perhaps that was how things should be, Molly judged, at almost five. And she thought of all the poor lovers, who could never go anywhere at all, who quarrel from sheer claustrophobia.

Not surprisingly, the next morning Molly felt considerably better, although imperfectly rested. But with almost her accustomed daytime energy she set about getting ready for the trip, doing several things simultaneously, as was her tendency: packing clothes and breakfast food (the cabins were equipped with little kitchens, she remembered), straightening up her flat and arranging the cats' quarters on her porch.

By two in the afternoon, the hour established for their departure, Molly was ready to go, if a little sleepy; fatigue had begun to cut into her energy. Well, she was not twenty any more, or thirty or forty, even, she told herself, tolerantly.

Sandy telephoned at two-fifteen. In his raspy voice he apologized; his assistant had been late getting in, he still had a couple of things to do. He would pick her up at three, three-thirty at the latest.

Irritating: Molly had sometimes thought that Sandy's habitual lateness was his way of establishing control; at other times she thought that he was simply tardy, as she herself was punctual (but why?). However, wanting a good start to their weekend, she told him that was really okay; it did not matter what time they got to Carmel, did it?

She had begun a rereading of *Howards End*, which she planned to take along, and now she found that the book was even better than she remembered it as being, from the wonderful assurance of the first sentence, "We may as well begin with Helen's letter to her sister—" Sitting in her sunny window, with her sleeping cats, Molly managed to be wholly absorbed in her reading—not in waiting for Sandy, nor in thinking, especially, of Carmel.

Just past four he arrived at her door: Sandy, in his pressed blue blazer, thin hair combed flat, his reddish face bright. Letting him in, brushing cheeks in the kiss of friends, Molly thought how nice he looked, after all: his kind blue eyes, sad witty mouth.

He apologized for lateness. "I absolutely had to take a shower," he said, with his just-crooked smile.

"Well, it's really all right. I'd begun *Howards End* again. I'd forgotten how wonderful it is."

"Oh well. *Forster.*"

Thus began one of the rambling conversations, more bookish gossip than 'literary,' which formed, perhaps, the core of their friendship, its reliable staple. In a scattered way they ran about, conversationally, among favorite old novels, discussing characters not quite as intimates but certainly as contemporaries, as alive. *Was* Margaret Schlegel somewhat prudish? Sandy felt that she was; Molly took a more sympathetic view of her shyness. Such talk, highly pleasurable and reassuring to them both, carried Molly and Sandy, in his small green car, past the dull first half of their trip: down the Bayshore Highway, past San Jose and Gilroy, and took them to where (Molly well remembered) it all became beautiful. Broad stretches of bright green early summer fields; distant hills, grayish blue; and then islands of sweeping dark live oaks.

At the outskirts of Carmel itself a little of her pre-dawn apprehension came back to Molly, as they drove past those imitation Cotswold cottages, fake-Spanish haciendas, or bright little gingerbread houses. And the main drag, Ocean Avenue, with its shops, shops—all that tweed and pewter, 'imported' jams and tea. More tourists than ever before, of course, in their bright synthetic tourist clothes, their bulging shopping bags—Japanese, French, German, English tourists, taking home their awful wares.

"You turn left next, on Dolores," Molly instructed, and then heard herself begin nervously to babble. "Of course if the place has really been wrecked we don't have to stay for two nights, do we. We could go on down to Big Sur, or just go home, for heaven's sake."

"In any case, sweetie, if they've wrecked it, it won't be your fault." Sandy laughed, and wheezed, and coughed. He had been smoking all the way down, which Molly had succeeded in not mentioning.

Before them, then, was their destination: the Inn, with its clump of white cottages. And the meadow. So far, nothing that Molly could see had changed. No condominiums. Everything as remembered.

They were given the cabin farthest from the central office, the one nearest the meadow, and the river and the sea. A small bedroom, smaller kitchen, and in the living room a studio couch. Big windows, and that view.

"Obviously, the bedroom is yours," Sandy magnanimously declared, plunking down his bag on the studio couch.

"*Well*," was all for the moment that Molly could say, as she put her small bag down in the bedroom, and went into the kitchen with the sack of breakfast things. From the little window she looked out to the meadow, saw that it was pink now with wildflowers, in the early June dusk. Three large brown cows were grazing out there, near where the river must be. Farther out she could see the wide, gray-white strip of beach, and the dark blue, turbulent sea. On the other side of the meadow were soft green hills, on which—yes, one might have known—new houses had arisen. But somehow inoffensively; they blended. And beyond the beach was the sharp, rocky silhouette of Point Lobos, crashing waves, leaping foam. All blindingly undiminished: a miraculous gift.

Sandy came into the kitchen, bearing bottles. Beaming Sandy, saying, "Mol, this is the most divine place. We must celebrate your choice. Immediately."

They settled in the living room with their drinks, with that view before them; the almost imperceptibly graying sky, the meadow, band of sand, the sea.

And, as she found that she often did, with Sandy, Molly began to say what had just come into her mind. "You wouldn't believe how stupid I was, as a very young woman," she prefaced, laughing a little. "Once I came down here with a lawyer, from San Francisco, terribly rich. Quite famous, actually." (The same man with whom she had so quickly rushed off to bed, on their arrival—as she did not tell Sandy.) "Married, of course. The first part of my foolishness. And I was really broke at the time—*broke*, I was poor as hell, being a typist to support my poetry habit. You remember. But I absolutely insisted on bringing all the food for that stolen, illicit weekend, can you imagine? What on earth was I trying to prove? Casseroles of crabmeat, endive for salads. Honestly, how crazy I was!"

Sandy laughed agreeably, and remarked a little plaintively that for him she had only brought breakfast food. But he was not especially interested in that old, nutty view of her, Molly saw—and resolved that that would be her last 'past' story. Customarily they did not discuss their love affairs.

She asked, "Shall we walk out on the beach tomorrow?"

"But of course."

Later they drove to a good French restaurant, where they drank a little too much wine, but they did not get drunk. And their two reflections, seen in a big mirror across the tiny room, looked perfectly all right: Molly, gray-haired, dark-eyed and thin, in her nice flowered silk dress; and Sandy, tidy and alert, a small plump man, in a neat navy blazer.

After dinner they drove along the beach, the cold white sand ghostly in the moonlight. Past enormous millionaire houses, and blackened windbent cypresses. Past the broad sloping river beach, and then back to their cabin, with its huge view of stars.

In her narrow bed, in the very small but private bedroom, Molly thought again, for a little while, of that very silly early self of hers: how eagerly self-defeating she had been—how foolish, in love. But she felt a certain tolerance now for that young person, herself, and she even smiled as she thought of all that intensity, that driven waste of emotion. In many ways middle age is preferable, she thought.

In the morning, they met the dog.

After breakfast they had decided to walk on the river beach, partly since Molly remembered that beach as being far less populated than the main beach was. Local families brought their children there. Or their dogs, or both.

Despite its visibility from their cabin, the river beach was actually a fair distance off, and so instead of walking there they drove, for maybe three or four miles. They parked and got out, and were pleased to see that no one else was there. Just a couple of dogs, who seemed not to be there together: a plumy, oversized friendly Irish setter, who ran right over to Molly and Sandy; and a smaller, long-legged, thin-tailed dark gray dog, with very tall ears—a shy young dog, who kept her distance, running a wide circle around them, after the setter had ambled off somewhere else. As they neared the water, the gray dog sidled over to sniff at them, her ears flattened, seeming to indicate a lowering of suspicion. She allowed herself to be patted, briefly; she seemed to smile.

Molly and Sandy walked near the edge of the water; the dog ran ahead of them.

The day was glorious, windy, bright blue, and perfectly clear; they could see the small pines and cypresses that struggled to grow from the steep sharp rocks of Point Lobos, could see fishing boats far out on the deep azure ocean. From time to time the dog would run back in their direction, and then she would rush toward a receding wave, chasing it backwards in a seeming happy frenzy. Assuming her (then) to live nearby, Molly almost enviously wondered at her sheer delight in what must be familiar. The dog barked at each wave, and ran after every one as though it were something new and marvelous.

Sandy picked up a stick and threw it forward. The dog ran after the stick, picked it up and shook it several times, and then, in a tentative way, she carried it back toward Sandy and Molly—not dropping it, though. Sandy had to take it from her mouth. He threw it again, and the dog ran off in that direction.

The wind from the sea was strong, and fairly chilling. Molly wished she had a warmer sweater, and she chided herself: she could have remembered that Carmel was cold, along with her less practical memories. She noted that Sandy's ears were red, and saw him rub his hands together. But she thought, I hope he won't want to leave soon, it's so beautiful. And such a nice dog. (Just that, at that moment: a very nice dog.)

The dog, seeming for the moment to have abandoned the stick game, rushed at a just-alighted flock of seagulls, who then rose from the wet waves' edge sand with what must have been (to a dog) a most gratifying flapping of wings, with cluckings of alarm.

Molly and Sandy were now close to the mouth of the river, the gorge cut into the beach, as water emptied into the sea. Impossible to cross—although Molly could remember when one could, when she and whatever companion had jumped easily over some water, and had then walked much farther down the beach. Now she and Sandy simply stopped there, and regarded the newish houses that were built up on the nearby hills. And they said to each other:

"What a view those people must have!"

"Actually the houses aren't too bad."

"There must be some sort of design control."

"I'm sure."

"Shall we buy a couple? A few million should take care of it."

"Oh sure, let's."

They laughed.

They turned around to find the dog waiting for them, in a dog's classic pose of readiness: her forelegs outstretched in the sand, rump and tail up in the air. Her eyes brown and intelligent, appraising, perhaps affectionate.

"Sandy, throw her another stick."

"You do it this time."

"Well, I don't throw awfully well."

"Honestly, Mol, she won't mind."

Molly poked through a brown tangle of seaweed and small broken sticks, somewhat back from the waves. The only stick that would do was too long, but she picked it up and threw it anyway. It was true that she did not throw very well, and the wind made a poor throw worse: the stick landed only a few feet away. But the dog ran after it, and then ran about with the stick in her mouth, shaking it, holding it high up as she ran, like a trophy.

Sandy and Molly walked more slowly now, against the wind. To their right was the meadow, across which they could just make out the cottages where they were staying. Ahead was a cluster of large, many-windowed ocean-front houses—in one of which, presumably, their dog lived.

Once their walk was over, they had planned to go into Carmel and buy some wine and picnic things, and to drive out into the valley for lunch. They began to talk about this now, and then Sandy said that first he would like to go by the Mission. "I've never seen it," he explained.

"Oh well, sure."

From time to time on that return walk one or the other of them would pick up a stick and throw it for the dog, who sometimes lost a stick and then looked back to them for another. Who stayed fairly near them but maintained, still, a certain shy independence.

She was wearing a collar (Molly and Sandy were later to reassure each other as to this) but at that time, on the beach, neither of them saw any reason to examine it. Besides, the dog never came quite that close. It would have somehow seemed presumptuous to grab her and read her collar's inscription.

In a grateful way Molly was thinking, again, how reliable the beauty of that place had turned out to be: their meadow view, and now the river beach.

They neared the parking lot, and Sandy's small green car.

An older woman, heavy and rather bent, was just coming into the lot, walking her toy poodle, on a leash. *Their* dog ran over for a restrained sniff, and then ambled back to where Molly and Sandy were getting into the car.

"Pretty dog!" the woman called out to them. "I never saw one with such long ears!"

"Yes—she's not ours."

"She isn't lost, is she?"

"Oh no, she has a collar."

Sandy started up the car; he backed up and out of the parking lot, slowly. Glancing back, Molly saw that the dog seemed to be leaving too, heading home, probably.

But a few blocks later—by then Sandy was driving somewhat faster—for some reason Molly looked back again, and there was the dog. Still. Racing. Following them.

She looked over to Sandy and saw that he too had seen the dog, in the rear-view mirror.

Feeling her glance, apparently, he frowned. "She'll go on home in a minute," he said.

Molly closed her eyes, aware of violent feelings within herself, somewhere: anguish? dread? She could no more name them than she could locate the emotion.

She looked back again, and there was the dog, although she was now much farther—hopelessly far behind them. A small gray dot. Racing. Still.

Sandy turned right in the direction of the Mission, as they had planned. They drove past placid houses with their beds of too-bright, unnatural flowers, too yellow or too pink. Clean glass windows, neat shingles. Trim lawns. Many houses, all much alike, and roads, and turns in roads.

As they reached the Mission, its parking area was crowded with tour busses, campers, vans and ordinary cars.

There was no dog behind them.

"You go on in," Molly said. "I've seen it pretty often. I'll wait out here in the sun."

She seated herself on a stone bench near the edge of the parking area—in the sun, beside a bright clump of bougainvillea, and she told herself that by now surely the dog had turned around and gone on home, or back to the beach. And that even if she and Sandy had turned and gone back to her, or stopped and waited for her, eventually they would have had to leave her, somewhere.

Sandy came out, unenthusiastic about the church, and they drove into town to buy sandwiches and wine.

In the grocery store, where everything took a very long time, it occurred to Molly that probably they should have checked back along the river beach road, just to make sure that the dog was no longer there. But by then it was too late.

They drove out into the valley; they found a nice sunny place for a picnic, next to the river, the river that ran on to their beach, and the sea. After a glass of wine Molly was able to ask, "You don't really think she was lost, do you?"

But why would Sandy know, any more than she herself did? At that moment Molly hated her habit of dependence on men for knowledge—any knowledge, any man. But at least, for the moment, he was kind. "Oh, I really don't think so," he said. "She's probably home by now." And he mentioned the collar.

Late that afternoon, in the deepening, cooling June dusk, the river beach was diminishingly visible from their cabin, where Molly and Sandy sat with their pre-dinner drinks. At first, from time to time, it was possible to see people walking out there: small stick figures, against a mild pink sunset sky. Once, Molly was sure that one of the walkers had a dog along. But it was impossible, at that distance, and in the receding light, to identify an animal's markings, or the shape of its ears.

They had dinner in the inn's long dining room, from which it was by then too dark to see the beach. They drank too much, and they had a silly outworn argument about Sandy's smoking, during which he accused her of being bossy; she said that he was inconsiderate.

Waking at some time in the night, from a shallow, winy sleep, Molly thought of the dog out there on the beach, how cold it must be, by now—the hard chilled sand and stinging waves. From her bed she could hear the sea's relentless crash.

The pain that she experienced then was as familiar as it was acute.

They had said that they would leave fairly early on Sunday morning and go home by way of Santa Cruz: a look at the town, maybe lunch, and a brief tour of the university there. And so, after breakfast, Molly and Sandy began to pull their belongings together.

Tentatively (but was there a shade of mischief, of teasing in his voice? could he sense what she was feeling?) Sandy asked, "I guess we won't go by the river beach?"

"No."

They drove out from the inn, up and onto the highway; they left Carmel. But as soon as they were passing Monterey, Pacific Grove, it began to seem intolerable to Molly that they had not gone back to the beach. Although she realized that either seeing or *not* seeing the dog would have been terrible.

If she now demanded that Sandy turn around and go back, would he do it? Probably not, she concluded; his face had a set, stubborn look. But Molly wondered about that, off and on, all the way to Santa Cruz.

For lunch they had sandwiches in a rather scruffy, open-air place; they drove up to and in and around the handsome, almost deserted university; and then, anxious not to return to the freeway, they took off on a road whose sign listed, among other destinations, San Francisco.

Wild Country: thickly wooded, steeply mountainous. Occasionally through an opening in the trees they could glimpse some sheer cliff, gray sharp rocks; once a distant small green secret meadow. A proper habitat for mountain lions, Molly thought, or deer, at least, and huge black birds. "It reminds me of something," she told Sandy, disconsolately. "Maybe even someplace I've only read about."

"Or a movie," he agreed. "God knows it's melodramatic."

Then Molly remembered: it was indeed a movie that this savage scenery made her think of, and a movie that she herself had done the screenplay for. About a quarrelling alcoholic couple, Americans, who were lost in wild Mexican mountains. As she had originally written it, they remained lost, presumably to die there. Only, the producer saw fit to change all that, and he had them romantically rescued by some good-natured Mexican bandits.

They had reached a crossroads, where there were no signs at all. The narrow, white roads all led off into the woods. To Molly, the one on the right looked most logical, as a choice, and she said so, but Sandy took the middle one. "You really like to be in charge, don't you," he rather unpleasantly remarked, lighting a cigarette.

There had been a lot of news in the local papers about a murderer who attacked and then horribly killed hikers and campers, in those very Santa Cruz mountains, Molly suddenly thought. She rolled up her window and locked the door, and she thought again of the ending of her movie. She tended to believe that one's fate, or doom, had a certain logic to it; even, that it was probably written out somewhere, even if by one's self. Most lives, including their endings, made a certain sort of sense, she thought.

The gray dog then came back powerfully, vividly to her mind: the small heart pounding in that thin, narrow rib cage, as she ran, ran after their car. Unbearable: Molly's own heart hurt, as she closed her eyes and tightened her hands into fists.

"Well, Christ," exploded Sandy, at that moment. "We've come to a dead end. Look!"

They had; the road ended abruptly, it simply stopped, in a heavy grove of cypresses and redwoods. There was barely space to turn around.

Not saying, Why didn't you take the other road, Molly instead cried out, uncontrollably, "But why didn't we go back for the dog?"

"Jesus, Molly." Red-faced with the effort he was making, Sandy glared. "That's what we most need right now. Some stray bitch in the car with us."

"What do you mean, stray bitch? She chose us—she wanted to come with us."

"How stupid you are! I had no idea."

"You're so selfish!" she shouted.

Totally silent, then, in the finally righted but possibly still lost car, they stared at each other: a moment of pure dislike.

And then, "Three mangy cats, and now you want a dog," Sandy muttered. He started off, too fast, in the direction of the crossroads. At which they made another turn.

Silently they travelled through more woods, past more steep gorges and ravines, on the road that Molly had thought they should have taken in the first place.

She had been right; they soon came to a group of signs which said that they were heading toward Saratoga. They were neither to die in the woods nor to be rescued by bandits. Nor murdered. And, some miles past Saratoga, Molly apologized. "Actually I have a sort of headache," she lied.

"I'm sorry, too, Mol. And you know I like your cats." Which was quite possibly also a lie.

* * *

They got home safely, of course.

But somehow, after that trip, their friendship, Molly and Sandy's, either 'lapsed' again, or perhaps it was permanently diminished; Molly was not sure. One or the other of them would forget to call, until days or weeks had gone by, and then their conversation would be guilty, apologetic.

And at first, back in town, despite the familiar and comforting presences of her cats, Molly continued to think with a painful obsessiveness of that beach dog, especially in early hours of sleeplessness. She imagined going back to Carmel alone to look for her; of advertising in the Carmel paper, describing a young female with gray markings. Tall ears.

However she did none of those things. She simply went on with her calm new life, as before, with her cats. She wrote some poems.

But, although she had ceased to be plagued by her vision of the dog (running, endlessly running, growing smaller in the distance) she did not forget her.

And she thought of Carmel, now, in a vaguely painful way, as a place where she had lost, or left something of infinite value. A place to which she would not go back.

The Man from Mars

MARGARET ATWOOD

A LONG TIME AGO Christine was walking through the park. She was still wearing her tennis dress; she hadn't had time to shower and change, and her hair was held back with an elastic band. Her chunky reddish face, exposed with no softening fringe, looked like a Russian peasant's, but without the elastic band the hair got in her eyes. The afternoon was too hot for April; the indoor courts had been steaming, her skin felt poached.

The sun had brought the old men out from wherever they spent the winter: she had read a story recently about one who lived for three years in a manhole. They sat weedishly on the benches or lay on the grass with their heads on squares of used newspaper. As she passed, their wrinkled toadstool faces drifted towards her, drawn by the movement of her body, then floated away again, uninterested.

The squirrels were out too, foraging; two or three of them moved towards her in darts and pauses, eyes fixed on her expectantly, mouths with the rat-like receding chins open to show the yellowed front teeth. Christine walked faster, she had nothing to give them. People shouldn't feed them, she thought, it makes them anxious and they get mangy.

Halfway across the park she stopped to take off her cardigan. As she bent over to pick up her tennis racquet again someone touched her on her freshly bared arm. Christine seldom screamed; she straightened up suddenly, gripping the handle of her racquet. It was not one of the old men, however: it was a dark-haired boy of twelve or so.

"Excuse me," he said, "I search for Economics Building. It is there?" He motioned towards the west.

Christine looked at him more closely. She had been mistaken: he was not young, just short. He came a little above her shoulder, but then, she was above the average height; "statuesque," her mother called it when she was straining. He was also what was referred to in their family as "a person from another culture": oriental without a doubt, though perhaps not Chinese. Christine judged he must be a foreign student and gave him her official welcoming smile. In high school she had been President of the United

Nations Club; that year her school had been picked to represent the Egyptian delegation at the Mock Assembly. It had been an unpopular assignment—nobody wanted to be the Arabs—but she had seen it through. She had made rather a good speech about the Palestinian refugees.

"Yes," she said, "that's it over there. The one with the flat roof. See it?"

The man had been smiling nervously at her the whole time. He was wearing glasses with transparent plastic rims, through which his eyes bulged up at her as though through a goldfish bowl. He had not followed where she was pointing. Instead he thrust towards her a small pad of green paper and a ballpoint pen.

"You make map," he said.

Christine set down her tennis racquet and drew a careful map. "We are here," she said, pronouncing distinctly. "You go this way. The building is here." She indicated the route with a dotted line and an X. The man leaned close to her, watching the progress of the map attentively; he smelled of cooked cauliflower and an unfamiliar brand of hair grease. When she had finished Christine handed the paper and pen back to him with a terminal smile.

"Wait," the man said. He tore the piece of paper with the map off the pad, folded it carefully and put it in his jacket pocket; the jacket sleeves came down over his wrists and had threads at the edges. He began to write something; she noticed with a slight feeling of revulsion that his nails and the ends of his fingertips were so badly bitten they seemed almost deformed. Several of his fingers were blue from the leaky ballpoint.

"Here is my name," he said, holding the pad out to her.

Christine read an odd assemblage of G's, Y's and N's, neatly printed in block letters. "Thank you," she said.

"You now write *your* name," he said, extending the pen.

Christine hesitated. If this had been a person from her own culture she would have thought he was trying to pick her up. But then, people from her own culture never tried to pick her up: she was too big. The only one who had made the attempt was the Moroccan waiter at the beer parlour where they sometimes went after meetings, and he had been direct. He had just intercepted her on the way to the Ladies' Room and asked and she said no; that had been that. This man was not a waiter though but a student; she didn't want to offend him. In his culture, whatever it was, this exchange of names on pieces of paper was probably a formal politeness, like saying Thank You. She took the pen from him.

"That is a very pleasant name," he said. He folded the paper and placed it in his jacket pocket with the map.

Christine felt she had done her duty. "Well, goodbye," she said. "It was nice to have met you." She bent for her tennis racquet but he had already stooped and retrieved it and was holding it with both hands in front of him, like a captured banner.

"I carry this for you."

"Oh no, please. Don't bother, I am in a hurry," she said, articulating clearly. Deprived of her tennis racquet she felt weaponless. He started to saunter along the path; he was not nervous at all now, he seemed completely at ease.

"Vous parlez français?" he asked conversationally.

"Oui, un petit peu," she said. "Not very well." How am I going to get my racquet away from him without being rude? she was wondering.

"Mais vous avez un bel accent." His eyes goggled at her through the glasses: was he being flirtatious? She was well aware that her accent was wretched.

"Look," she said, for the first time letting her impatience show, "I really have to go. Give me my racquet, please."

He quickened his pace but gave no sign of returning the racquet. "Where you are going?"

"Home," she said. "My house."

"I go with you now," he said hopefully.

"*No,*" she said: she would have to be firm with him. She made a lunge and got a grip on her racquet; after a brief tug of war it came free.

"Goodbye," she said, turning away from his puzzled face and setting off at what she hoped was a discouraging jog-trot. It was like walking away from a growling dog, you shouldn't let on you were frightened. Why should she be frightened anyway? He was only half her size and she had the tennis racquet, there was nothing he could do to her.

Although she did not look back she could tell he was still following. Let there be a streetcar, she thought, and there was one, but it was far down the line, stuck behind a red light. He appeared at her side, breathing audibly, a moment after she reached the stop. She gazed ahead, rigid.

"You are my friend," he said tentatively.

Christine relented: he hadn't been trying to pick her up after all, he was a stranger, he just wanted to meet some of the local people; in his place she would have wanted the same thing.

"Yes," she said, doling him out a smile.

"That is good," he said. "My country is very far."

Christine couldn't think of an apt reply. "That's interesting," she said. "Très interessant." The streetcar was coming at last; she opened her purse and got out a ticket.

"I go with you now," he said. His hand clamped on her arm above the elbow.

"You . . . stay . . . *here,*" Christine said, resisting the impulse to shout but pausing between each word as though for a deaf person. She detached his hand—his hold was quite feeble and could not compete with her tennis biceps—and leapt off the curb and up the streetcar steps, hearing with relief the doors grind shut behind her. Inside the car and a block away she permitted herself a glance out a side window. He was standing where she had left him; he seemed to be writing something on his little pad of paper.

When she reached home she had only time for a snack, and even then she was almost late for the Debating Society. The topic was, "Resolved: That War Is Obsolete." Her team took the affirmative, and won.

Christine came out of her last examination feeling depressed. It was not the exam that depressed her but the fact it was the last one: it meant the end of the school year. She dropped into the coffee shop as usual, then went home early because there didn't seem to be anything else to do.

"Is that you, dear?" her mother called from the living room. She must have heard the front door close. Christine went in and flopped on the sofa, disturbing the neat pattern of the cushions.

"How was your exam, dear?" her mother asked.

"Fine," said Christine flatly. It had been fine, she had passed. She was not a brilliant student, she knew that, but she was conscientious. Her professors always wrote things like "A serious attempt" and "Well thought out but perhaps lacking in *élan*" on her term papers; they gave her B's, the occasional B+. She was taking Political Science and Economics, and hoped for a job with the Government after she graduated; with her father's connections she had a good chance.

"That's nice."

Christine felt, resentfully, that her mother had only a hazy idea of what an exam was. She was arranging gladioli in a vase; she had rubber gloves on to protect her hands as she always did when engaged in what she called "housework." As far as Christine could tell her housework consisted of arranging flowers in vases: daffodils and tulips and hyacinths through gladioli, iris and roses, all the way to asters and mums. Sometimes she cooked, elegantly and with chafing dishes, but she thought of it as a hobby. The girl did everything else. Christine thought it faintly sinful to have a girl. The only ones available now were either foreign or pregnant; their expressions usually suggested they were being taken advantage of somehow. But her mother asked what they would do otherwise, they'd either have to go into a Home or stay in their own countries, and Christine had to agree this was probably true. It was hard anyway to argue with her mother, she was so delicate, so preserved-looking, a harsh breath would scratch the finish.

"An interesting young man phoned today," her mother said. She had finished the gladioli and was taking off her rubber gloves. "He asked to speak with you and when I said you weren't in we had quite a little chat. You didn't tell me about him, dear." She put on the glasses which she wore on a decorative chain around her neck, a signal that she was in her modern, intelligent mood rather than her old-fashioned whimsical one.

"Did he leave his name?" Christine asked. She knew a lot of young men but they didn't often call her, they conducted their business with her in the coffee shop or after meetings.

"He's a person from another culture. He said he would call back later."

Christine had to think a moment. She was vaguely acquainted with several people from other cultures, Britain mostly; they belonged to the Debating Society.

"He's studying Philosophy in Montreal," her mother prompted. "He sounded French."

Christine began to remember the man in the park. "I don't think he's French, exactly," she said.

Her mother had taken off her glasses again and was poking absent-mindedly at a bent gladiolus. "Well, he sounded French." She meditated, flowery sceptre in hand. "I think it would be nice if you had him to tea."

Christine's mother did her best. She had two other daughters, both of whom took after her. They were beautiful, one was well married already and the other would clearly have no trouble. Her friends consoled her about Christine by saying, "She's not fat, she's just big-boned, it's the father's side," and "Christine is so healthy." Her other daughters had never gotten involved in activities when they were at school, but since Christine could not possibly ever be beautiful even if she took off weight, it was just as well she was so athletic and political, it was a good thing she had interests. Christine's mother tried to encourage her interests whenever possible. Christine could tell when she was making an extra effort, there was a reproachful edge to her voice.

She knew her mother expected enthusiasm but she could not supply it. "I don't know, I'll have to see," she said dubiously.

"You look tired, darling," said her mother. "Perhaps you'd like a glass of milk."

Christine was in the bathtub when the phone rang. She was not prone to fantasy but when she was in the bathtub she often pretended she was a dolphin, a game left over from one of the girls who used to bathe her when she was small. Her mother was being bell-voiced and gracious in the hall; then there was a tap at the door.

"It's that nice young French student, Christine," her mother said.

"Tell him I'm in the bathtub," Christine said, louder than necessary. "He isn't French."

She could hear her mother frowning. "That wouldn't be very polite,

Christine. I don't think he'd understand."

"Oh all right," Christine said. She heaved herself out of the bathtub, swathed her pink bulk in a towel and splattered to the phone.

"Hello," she said gruffly. At a distance he was not pathetic, he was a nuisance. She could not imagine how he had tracked her down: most likely he went through the phone book, calling all the numbers with her last name until he hit on the right one.

"It is your friend."

"I know," she said. "How are you?"

"I am very fine." There was a long pause, during which Christine had a vicious urge to say, "Well, goodbye then," and hang up; but she was aware of her mother poised figurine-like in her bedroom doorway. Then he said, "I hope you also are very fine."

"Yes," said Christine. She wasn't going to participate.

"I come to tea," he said.

This took Christine by surprise. "You do?"

"Your pleasant mother ask me. I come Thursday, four o'clock."

"Oh," Christine said, ungraciously.

"See you then," he said, with the conscious pride of one who has mastered a difficult idiom.

Christine set down the phone and went along the hall. Her mother was in her study, sitting innocently at her writing desk.

"Did you ask him to tea on Thursday?"

"Not exactly, dear," her mother said. "I did mention he might come round to tea *some*time, though."

"Well, he's coming Thursday. Four o'clock."

"What's wrong with that?" her mother said serenely. "I think it's a very nice gesture for us to make. I do think you might try to be a little more cooperative." She was pleased with herself.

"Since you invited him," said Christine, "you can bloody well stick around and help me entertain him. I don't want to be left making nice gestures all by myself."

"Christine *dear*," her mother said, above being shocked. "You ought to put on your dressing gown, you'll catch a chill."

After sulking for an hour Christine tried to think of the tea as a cross between an examination and an executive meeting: not enjoyable, certainly, but to be got through as tactfully as possible. And it *was* a nice gesture. When the cakes her mother had ordered arrived from *The Patisserie* on Thursday morning she began to feel slightly festive; she even resolved to put on a dress, a good one, instead of a skirt and blouse. After all, she had nothing against him, except the memory of the way he had grabbed her tennis racquet and then her arm. She suppressed a quick impossible vision of herself pursued around the living room, fending him off with thrown sofa cushions and vases of gladioli; nevertheless she told the girl they would have tea in the garden. It would be a treat for him, and there was more space outdoors.

She had suspected her mother would dodge the tea, would contrive to be going out just as he was arriving: that way she could size him up and then leave them alone together. She had done things like that to Christine before; the excuse this time was the Symphony Committee. Sure enough, her mother carefully mislaid her gloves and located them with a faked murmur of joy when the doorbell rang. Christine relished for weeks afterwards the image of her mother's dropped jaw and flawless recovery when he was introduced: he wasn't quite the foreign potentate her optimistic, veil-fragile mind had concocted.

He was prepared for celebration. He had slicked on so much hair cream that his head seemed to be covered with a tight black patent-leather cap, and he had cut the threads off his jacket sleeves. His orange tie was overpoweringly splendid. Christine noticed however as he shook her mother's suddenly braced white glove that the ballpoint ink on his fingers was indelible. His face had broken out, possibly in anticipation of the delights in store for him; he had a tiny camera slung over his shoulder and was smoking an exotic-smelling cigarette.

Christine led him through the cool flowery softly padded living room and out by the French doors into the garden. "You sit here," she said. "I will have the girl bring tea."

This girl was from the West Indies: Christine's parents had been enraptured with her when they were down at Christmas and had brought her back with them. Since that time she had become pregnant, but Christine's mother had not dismissed her. She said she was slightly disappointed but what could you expect, and she didn't see any real difference between a girl who was pregnant before you hired her and one who got that way afterwards. She prided herself on her tolerance; also there was a scarcity of girls. Strangely enough, the girl became progressively less easy to get along with. Either she did not share Christine's mother's view of her own generosity, or she felt she had gotten away with something and was therefore free to indulge in contempt. At first Christine had tried to treat her as an equal. "Don't call me 'Miss Christine,' " she had said with an imitation of light, comradely laughter. "What you want me to call you then?" the girl had said, scowling. They had begun to have brief, surly arguments in the kitchen, which Christine decided were like the arguments between one servant and another: her mother's attitude towards each of them was similar, they were not altogether satisfactory but they would have to do.

The cakes, glossy with icing, were set out on a plate and the teapot was standing ready; on the counter the electric kettle boiled. Christine headed for it, but the girl, till then sitting with her elbows on the kitchen table and watching her expressionlessly, made a dash and intercepted her. Christine waited until she had poured the water into the pot. Then, "I'll carry it out, Elvira," she said. She had just decided she didn't want the girl to see her visitor's orange tie; already, she knew, her position in the girl's eyes had suffered because no one had yet attempted to get *her* pregnant.

"What you think they pay me for, Miss Christine?" the girl said insolently. She swung towards the garden with the tray; Christine trailed her, feeling lumpish and awkward. The girl was at least as big as she was but she was big in a different way.

"Thank you, Elvira," Christine said when the tray was in place. The girl departed without a word, casting a disdainful backward glance at the frayed jacket sleeves, the stained fingers. Christine was now determined to be especially kind to him.

"You are very rich," he said.

"No," Christine protested, shaking her head; "we're not." She had never thought of her family as rich, it was one of her father's sayings that nobody made any money with the Government.

"Yes," he repeated, "you are very rich." He sat back in his lawn chair, gazing about him as though dazed.

Christine set his cup of tea in front of him. She wasn't in the habit of paying much attention to the house or the garden; they were nothing special, far from being the largest on the street; other people took care of them. But now she looked where he was looking, seeing it all as though from a different height: the long expanses, the border flowers blazing in the early-summer sunlight, the flagged patio and walks, the high walls and the silence.

He came back to her face, sighing a little. "My English is not good," he said, "but I improve."

"You do," Christine said, nodding encouragement.

He took sips of his tea, quickly and tenderly as though afraid of injuring the cup. "I like to stay here."

Christine passed him the cakes. He took only one, making a slight face as he ate it; but he had several more cups of tea while she finished the cakes. She managed to find out from him that he had come over on a Church fellowship—she could not decode the denomination—and was studying Philosophy or Theology, or possibly both. She was feeling well-disposed towards him: he had behaved himself, he had caused her no inconvenience.

The teapot was at last empty. He sat up straight in his chair, as though alerted by a soundless gong. "You look this way, please," he said. Christine saw that he had placed his miniature camera on the stone sundial her mother

[margin note: short signed]

had shipped back from England two years before: he wanted to take her picture. She was flattered, and settled herself to pose, smiling evenly. He took off his glasses and laid them beside his plate. For a moment she saw his myopic, unprotected eyes turned towards her, with something tremulous and confiding in them she wanted to close herself off from knowing about. Then he went over and did something to the camera, his back to her. The next instant he was crouched beside her, his arm around her waist as far as it could reach, his other hand covering her own hands which she had folded in her lap, his cheek jammed up against hers. She was too startled to move. The camera clicked.

He stood up at once and replaced his glasses, which glittered now with a sad triumph. "Thank you, Miss," he said to her. "I go now." He slung the camera back over his shoulder, keeping his hand on it as though to hold the lid on and prevent escape. "I send to my family; they will like."

He was out the gate and gone before Christine had recovered; then she laughed. She had been afraid he would attack her, she could admit it now, and he had; but not in the usual way. He had raped, *rapeo, rapere, rapui, to seize and carry off*, not herself but her celluloid image, and incidently that of the silver tea service, which glinted mockingly at her as the girl bore it away, carrying it regally, the insignia, the official jewels.

Christine spent the summer as she had for the past three years: she was the sailing instructress at an expensive all-girls camp near Algonquin Park. She had been a camper there, everything was familiar to her; she sailed almost better than she played tennis.

The second week she got a letter from him, postmarked Montreal and forwarded from her home address. It was printed in block letters on a piece of green paper, two or three sentences. It began, "I hope you are well," then described the weather in monosyllables and ended, "I am fine." It was signed "Your friend." Each week she got another of these letters, more or less identical. In one of them a colour print was enclosed: himself, slightly cross-eyed and grinning hilariously, even more spindly than she remembered him against her billowing draperies, flowers exploding around them like firecrackers, one of his hands an equivocal blur in her lap, the other out of sight; on her own face, astonishment and outrage, as though he was sticking her in the behind with his hidden thumb.

She answered the first letter, but after that the seniors were in training for the races. At the end of the summer, packing to go home, she threw all the letters away.

When she had been back for several weeks she received another of the green letters. This time there was a return address printed at the top which Christine noted with foreboding was in her own city. Every day she waited for the phone to ring; she was so certain his first attempt at contact would be a disembodied voice that when he came upon her abruptly in mid-campus she was unprepared.

"How are you?"

His smile was the same, but everything else about him had deteriorated. He was, if possible, thinner; his jacket sleeves had sprouted a lush new crop of threads, as though to conceal hands now so badly bitten they appeared to have been gnawed by rodents. His hair fell over his eyes, uncut, ungreased; his eyes in the hollowed face, a delicate triangle of skin stretched on bone, jumped behind his glasses like hooked fish. He had the end of a cigarette in the corner of his mouth and as they walked he lit a new one from it.

"I'm fine," Christine said. She was thinking, I'm not going to get involved again, enough is enough, I've done my bit for internationalism. "How are you?"

"I live here now," he said. "Maybe I study Economics."

"That's nice." He didn't sound as though he was enrolled anywhere.

"I come to see you."

Christine didn't know whether he meant he had left Montreal in order to be near her or just wanted to visit her at her house as he had done in the spring; either way she refused to be implicated. They were outside the Political Science building. "I have a class here," she said. "Goodbye." She was being callous, she realized that, but a quick chop was more merciful in the long run, that was what her beautiful sisters used to say.

Afterwards she decided it had been stupid of her to let him find out where her class was. Though a timetable was posted in each of the colleges: all he had to do was look her up and record her every probable movement in block letters on his green notepad. After that day he never left her alone.

Initially he waited outside the lecture rooms for her to come out. She said Hello to him curtly at first and kept on going, but this didn't work; he followed her at a distance, smiling his changeless smile. Then she stopped speaking altogether and pretended to ignore him, but it made no difference, he followed her anyway. The fact that she was in some way afraid of him— or was it just embarrassment?—seemed only to encourage him. Her friends started to notice, asking her who he was and why he was tagging along behind her; she could hardly answer because she hardly knew.

As the weekdays passed and he showed no signs of letting up, she began to jog-trot between classes, finally to run. He was tireless, and had an amazing wind for one who smoked so heavily: he would speed along behind her, keeping the distance between them the same, as though he was a pull-toy attached to her by a string. She was aware of the ridiculous spectacle they must make, galloping across campus, something out of a cartoon short, a lumbering elephant stampeded by a smiling, emaciated mouse, both of them locked in the classic pattern of comic pursuit and flight; but she found that to race made her less nervous than to walk sedately, the skin on the back of her neck crawling with the feel of his eyes on it. At least she could use her muscles. She worked out routines, escapes: she would dash in the front door of the Ladies' Room in the coffee shop and out the back door, and he would lose the trail, until he discovered the other entrance. She would try to shake him by detours through baffling archways and corridors, but he seemed as familiar with the architectural mazes as she was herself. As a last refuge she could head for the women's dormitory and watch from safety as he was skidded to a halt by the receptionist's austere voice: men were not allowed past the entrance.

Lunch became difficult. She would be sitting, usually with other members of the Debating Society, just digging nicely into a sandwich, when he would appear suddenly as though he'd come up through an unseen manhole. She then had the choice of barging out through the crowded cafeteria, sandwich half-eaten, or finishing her lunch with him standing behind her chair, everyone at the table acutely aware of him, the conversation stilting and dwindling. Her friends learned to spot him from a distance; they posted lookouts. "Here he comes," they would whisper, helping her collect her belongings for the sprint they knew would follow.

Several times she got tired of running and turned to confront him. "What do you want?" she would ask, glowering belligerently down at him, almost clenching her fists; she felt like shaking him, hitting him.

"I wish to talk with you."

"Well, here I am," she would say. "What do you want to talk about?"

But he would say nothing; he would stand in front of her, shifting his feet, smiling perhaps apologetically (though she could never pinpoint the exact tone of that smile, chewed lips stretched apart over the nicotine-yellowed teeth, rising at the corners, flesh held stiffly in place for an invisible photographer), his eyes jerking from one part of her face to another as though he saw her in fragments.

Annoying and tedious though it was, his pursuit of her had an odd result: mysterious in itself, it rendered her equally mysterious. No-one had ever found Christine mysterious before. To her parents she was a beefy heavyweight, a plodder, lacking in flair, ordinary as bread. To her sisters she was the plain one, treated with an indulgence they did not give to each other: they did not fear her as a rival. To her male friends she was the one who could be relied on. She was helpful and a hard worker, always good for a game of tennis with the athletes among them. They invited her along to drink beer with them so they could get into the cleaner, more desirable Ladies and Escorts side of the beer parlour, taking it for granted she would buy her share of the rounds. In moments of stress they confided to her their problems with women. There was nothing devious about her and nothing interesting.

Christine had always agreed with these estimates of herself. In childhood she had identified with the False Bride or the ugly sister; whenever a story had begun, "Once there was a maiden as beautiful as she was good," she had known it wasn't her. That was just how it was, but it wasn't so bad. Her parents never expected her to be a brilliant social success and weren't overly disappointed when she wasn't. She was spared the maneuvering and anxiety she witnessed among others her age, and she even had a kind of special position among men: she was an exception, she fitted none of the categories they commonly used when talking about girls, she wasn't a cock-teaser, a cold fish, an easy lay or a snarky bitch; she was an honorary person. She had grown to share their contempt for most women.

Now however there was something abut her that could not be explained. A man was chasing her, a peculiar sort of man, granted, but still a man, and he was without doubt attracted to her, he couldn't leave her alone. Other men examined her more closely than they ever had, appraising her, trying to find out what it was those twitching bespectacled eyes saw in her. They started to ask her out, though they returned from these excursions with their curiosity unsatisfied, the secret of her charm still intact. Her opaque dumpling face, her solid bear-shaped body became for them parts of a riddle no-one could solve. Christine knew this and began to use it. In the bathtub she no longer imagined she was a dolphin; instead she imagined she was an elusive water-nixie, or sometimes, in moments of audacity, Marilyn Monroe. The daily chase was becoming a habit; she even looked forward to it. In addition to its other benefits she was losing weight.

All those weeks he had never phoned her or turned up at the house. He must have decided however that his tactics were not having the desired result, or perhaps he sensed she was becoming bored. The phone began to ring in the early morning or late at night when he could be sure she would be there. Sometimes he would simply breathe (she could recognize, or thought she could, the quality of his breathing), in which case she would hang up. Occasionally he would say again that he wanted to talk to her, but even when she gave him lots of time nothing else would follow. Then he extended his range: she would see him on her streetcar, smiling at her silently from a seat never closer than three away; she could feel him tracking her down her own street, though when she would break her resolve to pay no attention and would glance back he would be invisible or in the act of hiding behind a tree or hedge.

Among crowds of people and in daylight she had not really been afraid of him; she was stronger than he was and he had made no recent attempt to touch her. But the days were growing shorter and colder, it was almost

November, often she was arriving home in twilight or a darkness broken only by the feeble orange streetlamps. She brooded over the possibility of razors, knives, guns; by acquiring a weapon he could quickly turn the odds against her. She avoided wearing scarves, remembering the newspaper stories about girls who had been strangled by them. Putting on her nylons in the morning gave her a funny feeling. Her body seemed to have diminished, to have become smaller than his.

Was he deranged, was he a sex maniac? He seemed so harmless, yet it was that kind who often went berserk in the end. She pictured those ragged fingers at her throat, tearing at her clothes, though she could not think of herself as screaming. Parked cars, the shrubberies near her house, the driveways on either side of it, changed as she passed them from unnoticed background to sinisterly shadowed foreground, every detail distinct and harsh: they were places a man might crouch, leap out from. Yet every time she saw him in the clear light of morning or afternoon (for he still continued his old methods of pursuit), his aging jacket and jittery eyes convinced her that it was she herself who was the tormentor, the persecutor. She was in some sense responsible; from the folds and crevices of the body she had treated for so long as a reliable machine was emanating, against her will, some potent invisible odour, like a dog's in heat or a female moth's, that made him unable to stop following her.

Her mother, who had been too preoccupied with the unavoidable fall entertaining to pay much attention to the number of phone calls Christine was getting or to the hired girl's complaints of a man who hung up without speaking, announced that she was flying down to New York for the weekend; her father decided to go too. Christine panicked: she saw herself in the bathtub with her throat slit, the blood drooling out of her neck and running in a little spiral down the drain (for by this time she believed he could walk through walls, could be everywhere at once). The girl would do nothing to help; she might even stand in the bathroom door with her arms folded, watching. Christine arranged to spend the weekend at her married sister's.

When she arrived back Sunday evening she found the girl close to hysterics. She said that on Saturday she had gone to pull the curtains across the French doors at dusk and had found a strangely contorted face, a man's face, pressed against the glass, staring in at her from the garden. She claimed she had fainted and had almost had her baby a month too early right there on the living-room carpet. Then she had called the police. He was gone by the time they got there but she had recognized him from the afternoon of the tea; she had informed them he was a friend of Christine's.

They called Monday evening to investigate, two of them; they were very polite, they knew who Christine's father was. Her father greeted them heartily; her mother hovered in the background, fidgeting with her porcelain hands, letting them see how frail and worried she was. She didn't like having them in the living room but they were necessary.

Christine had to admit he'd been following her around. She was relieved he'd been discovered, relieved also that she hadn't been the one to tell, though if he'd been a citizen of the country she would have called the police a long time ago. She insisted he was not dangerous, he had never hurt her.

"That kind don't hurt you," one of the policemen said. "They just kill you. You're lucky you aren't dead."

"Nut cases," the other one said.

Her mother volunteered that the thing about people from another culture was that you could never tell whether they were insane or not because their ways were so different. The policeman agreed with her, deferential but also condescending, as though she was a royal halfwit who had to be humoured.

"You know where he lives?" the first policeman asked. Christine had long ago torn up the letter with his address on it; she shook her head.

"We'll have to pick him up tomorrow then," he said. "Think you can keep him talking outside your class if he's waiting for you?"

After questioning her they held a murmured conversation with her father in the front hall. The girl, clearing away the coffee cups, said if they didn't lock him up she was leaving, she wasn't going to be scared half out of her skin like that again.

Next day when Christine came out of her Modern History lecture he was there, right on schedule. He seemed puzzled when she did not begin to run. She approached him, her heart thumping with treachery and the prospect of freedom. Her body was back to its usual size; she felt herself a giantess, self-controlled, invulnerable.

"How are you?" she asked, smiling brightly.

He looked at her with distrust.

"How have you been?" she ventured again. His own perennial smile faded; he took a step back from her.

"This the one?" said the policeman, popping out from behind a notice board like a Keystone Cop and laying a competent hand on the worn jacket shoulder. The other policeman lounged in the background; force would not be required.

"Don't *do* anything to him," she pleaded as they took him away. They nodded and grinned, respectful, scornful. He seemed to know perfectly well who they were and what they wanted.

The first policeman phoned that evening to make his report. Her father talked with him, jovial and managing. She herself was now out of the picture; she had been protected, her function was over.

"What did they *do* to him?" she asked anxiously as he came back into the living room. She was not sure what went on in police stations.

"They didn't do anything to him," he said, amused by her concern. "They could have booked him for Watching and Besetting, they wanted to know if I'd like to press charges. But it's not worth a court case: he's got a visa that says he's only allowed in the country as long as he studies in Montreal, so I told them to just ship him up there. If he turns up here again they'll deport him. They went around to his rooming house, his rent's two weeks overdue; the landlady said she was on the point of kicking him out. He seems happy enough to be getting his back rent paid and a free train ticket to Montreal." He paused. "They couldn't get anything out of him though."

"*Out* of him?" Christine asked.

"They tried to find out why he was doing it; following you, I mean." Her father's eyes swept her as though it was a riddle to him also. "They said when they asked him about that he just clammed up. Pretended he didn't understand English. He understood well enough, but he wasn't answering."

Christine thought it was the end, but somehow between his arrest and the departure of the train he managed to elude his escort long enough for one more phone call.

"I see you again," he said. He didn't wait for her to hang up.

Now that he was no longer an embarrassing present reality he could be talked about, he could become an amusing story. In fact he was the only amusing story Christine had to tell, and telling it preserved both for herself and for others the aura of her strange allure. Her friends and the men who continued to ask her out speculated about his motives. One suggested he had wanted to marry her so he could remain in the country; another said that oriental men were fond of well-built women: "It's your Rubens quality."

Christine thought about him a lot. She had not been attracted to him, rather the reverse, but as an idea only he was a romantic figure, the one man who had found her irresistible; though she often wondered, inspecting her unchanged pink face and hefty body in her full-length mirror, just what it was about her that had done it. She avoided whenever it was proposed the theory of his insanity: it was only that there was more than one way of being sane.

But a new acquaintance, hearing the story for the first time, had a different explanation. "So he got you too," he said, laughing. "That has to be the same guy who was hanging around our day camp a year ago this summer. He followed all the girls like that. A short guy, Japanese or something, glasses, smiling all the time."

"Maybe it was another one," Christine said.

"There couldn't be two of them, everything fits. This was a pretty weird guy."

"What . . . *kind* of girls did he follow?" Christine asked.

"Oh, just anyone who happed to be around. But if they paid any attention to him at first, if they were nice to him or anything, he was unshakeable. He was a bit of a pest, but harmless."

Christine ceased to tell her amusing story. She had been one among many, then. She went back to playing tennis, she had been neglecting her game.

A few months later the policeman who had been in charge of the case telephoned her again.

"Like you to know, Miss, that fellow you were having the trouble with was sent back to his own country. Deported."

"What for?" Christine asked. "Did he try to come back here?" Maybe she had been special after all, maybe he had dared everything for her.

"Nothing like it," the policeman said. "He was up to the same tricks in Montreal but he really picked the wrong woman this time—a Mother Superior of a convent. They don't stand for things like that in Quebec—had him out of here before he knew what happened. I guess he'll be better off in his own place."

"How old was she?" Christine asked, after a silence.

"Oh, around sixty, I guess."

"Thank you very much for letting me know," Christine said in her best official manner. "It's such a relief." She wondered if the policeman had called to make fun of her.

She was almost crying when she put down the phone. What *had* he wanted from her then? A Mother Superior. Did she really look sixty, did she look like a mother? What did convents mean? Comfort, charity? Refuge? Was it that something had happened to him, some intolerable strain just from being in this country; her tennis dress and exposed legs too much for him, flesh and money seemingly available everywhere but withheld from him wherever he turned, the nun the symbol of some final distortion, the robe and the veil reminiscent to his nearsighted eyes of the women of his homeland, the ones he was able to understand? But he was back in his own country, remote from her as another planet; she would never know.

He hadn't forgotten her though. In the spring she got a postcard with a foreign stamp and the familiar block-letter writing. On the front was a picture of a temple. He was fine, he hoped she was fine also, he was her friend. A month later another print of the picture he had taken in the garden arrived, in a sealed manila envelope otherwise empty.

Christine's aura of mystery soon faded away; anyway, she herself no longer believed in it. Life became again what she had always expected. She graduated with mediocre grades and went into the Department of Health and Welfare; she did a good job, and was seldom discriminated against for being a woman because nobody thought of her as one. She could afford a pleasant-sized apartment, though she did not put much energy into decorating it. She played less and less tennis; what had been muscle with a light coating of fat turned gradually to fat with a thin substratum of muscle. She began to get headaches.

As the years were used up and the war began to fill the newspapers and magazines, she realized which eastern country he had actually been from. She had known the name but it hadn't registered at the time, it was such a minor place; she could never keep them separate in her mind.

But though she tried, she couldn't remember the name of the city, and the postcard was long gone—had he been from the North or the South, was he near the battle zone or safely from it? Obsessively she bought the magazines and poured over the available photographs, dead villagers, soldiers on the march, colour blow-ups of frightened or angry faces, spies being executed; she studied maps, she watched the late-night newscasts, the distant country and terrain becoming almost more familiar to her than her own. Once or twice she thought she could recognize him but it was no use, they all looked like him.

Finally she had to stop looking at the pictures. It bothered her too much, it was bad for her; she was beginning to have nightmares in which he was coming through the French doors of her mother's house in his shabby jacket, carrying a packsack and a rifle and a huge bouquet of richly-coloured flowers. He was smiling in the same way but with blood streaked over his face, partly blotting out the features. She gave her television set away and took to reading nineteenth century novels instead; Trollope and Galsworthy were her favourites. When, despite herself, she would think about him, she would tell herself that he had been crafty and agile-minded enough to survive, more or less, in her country, so surely he would be able to do it in his own, where he knew the language. She could not see him in the army, on either side; he wasn't the type, and to her knowledge he had not believed in any particular ideology. He would be something nondescript, something in the background, like herself; perhaps he had become an interpreter.

Saving the Boat People

JOE DAVID BELLAMY

*L*ESLIE'S JOURNAL—*Nov. 23rd—Arrival*

The Lieus, a Cambodian family, emerged from the Air North commuter, slowly, timidly, all wearing the same Army surplus T-shirts and enormous yellow numbered badges on their shoulders and backs. They must have been sorted out and numbered like cattle in the refugee camps. Now they looked like figures from some absurd game of human bingo, which, in a sense, they were, numbered not for the slaughter but for the opportunity to begin new lives; and, pathetically, the four children were barefoot and the adults, Mr. and Mrs. Lieu and the elderly grandmother, wore only cheap thongs on their feet, though the temperature hovered in the mid-forties.

The small welcoming group—Mr. Kennedy, the Methodist minister, the three other concerned village women, and I, clucking and smiling and making every effort to communicate welcome and brotherhood—quickly engulfed them and ushered the Lieus into the satisfactory heat of the waiting van.

Saang

The metallic craft brought them to the earth again and through the plastic curtain she glimpsed a barren, desolate landscape more terrifying than any dream and all the color of death. The humans also were the color of death, the most hideous beings she had ever seen, like large pale slugs walking upright, waving their swollen limbs, and baring their teeth strangely, as if upset or in pain. Surrounded by the giant pale-people, who resembled the enemy who had killed them and killed them, they were miserably frightened; and the landscape also was a horrible disappointment. The white air hurt their skins it was so white. How such creatures could feed their bodies from the dry, hard land was a mystery to her. They seemed peaceful, but whenever they approached them, they showed their teeth like sick dogs and spoke an ugly language at them and one to another. "If the great fat male seizes my arm," she told herself, "I must not cry out." The baby began to wail uncontrollably as soon as he set eyes on the crowd of deathly faces hovering above him.

Leslie
She does her stretching on the porch, laying her heel on the snow-scalloped railing and reaching for her pointed toe, then the other leg. Then the quads—catching her foot from behind, pushing it up her back. Bouncing on her toes, leaving a filigree of Nike tread-marks pressed into the powdery floorboards like the fossilized track of some as-yet-undiscovered species.

Out into the quiet snowy street, taking short quick easy steps, as unobtrusive as a fox, just any middle-aged woman out jogging, correctly dressed, easily identifiable as—a jogger. Nothing desperate, sexual, or escapist about this, not at all. What could be a more socially sanctioned activity—twenty million people out here on the roads and walkways of the nation running off the pounds, thinning out the blood; and she is a part of it, the great running craze. A still living representative of all those people from previous generations who used to carry the load of heavy physical labor in the culture, all the really good fieldhands and cartwrights and farmers and lumberjacks, the ones who were in some way sustained by the daily sweat and toil and fatigue of it and had passed on their genes to her—they were causing it, their instincts, their inheritance, their needs, finding expression through her body.

Beyond the rows of houses, she cuts down the familiar rutted country road, blue with snow and etched with the narrow runnels of cross-country ski-blades. In the fall, this trail was thick with ragweed and goldenrod and Queen Anne's lace, the air spicy with the scents of pollen and newmown hay. Now it is overlaid with white, the brownish stalks poking out above the crust, the only visible remnants of the dense vegetable spawning; and the air pinches the nostrils and nearly takes her breath away.

Her accident was . . . two years ago this fall, and she would never be the same. Tears spread back across her temples like the feathers on a bird's wing. No snow then—cars splashing trails of mist, slick asphalt, bubbles of drops clinging to the thick roadside grass like a coating of jewels, the rusty pickup perpetually zooming down upon her like an avenging beast, the two unknown distorted faces gaping in the windshield. They had actually driven off the road to hit her. It had happened so suddenly she couldn't remember or hadn't seen what their faces might have revealed of their motives—contempt for joggers, hatred of women, random homicidal idiocy, drunken frenzy, or merely a slip of the wheel—she guessed she would never know, though she could never stop thinking about it. No motive—no motive at all—seemed plausible to her.

The blow spun her against the cab, where she struck the crown of her head, and then flipped her into the mushy loam of a cornfield, where, when she awoke, she was staring up from the base of several gigantic stalks and the tassles overhead seemed to race across the sky like the traffic above an airport. Her rescuers carried her for miles, it seemed, up a cliff of pastureland toward the glowing lights of a dairy barn. She could neither walk nor speak and, by then, the pickup was long gone. She thinks she remembers all of this exactly, but it may have been a dream—she lay in critical condition in a coma for four weeks and three operations, including brain surgery. She was to become a statistic, an official victim, and the subject of a stern editorial in the local paper about the need for additional caution among both joggers and motorists if such tragic accidents were not to become commonplace. She recovered, more or less, but the process was slow and painful, and the accident left her with a minor speech defect, not an easy thing to accept for someone with her previous verbal skills and energies. It is this incident, and its aftermath, her husband Jerry says, that give Leslie such a "unique capacity to emphathize with suffering humanity, with victims of every sort."

Another mile or so and she will have exhaled as much of Jerry's Benson & Hedges pollution as she is likely to get rid of in one day's struggling, the superficial layers only, and already she is imagining with powerful vividness the desperate little alveoli in her lung tissue, each like a small choking mouth gasping for air and slowly, inexorably, filling up with a pool of tar like a dark tear.

Saang

The larger woman has eaten the food of many people; yet, she seems not to be troubled by this. Her arms are as thick as four arms, perhaps five arms. And there are others like her, many others. Where would they find the harvests, the abundance for such heavy eating in this barren land? Where do they find the food to fatten even their dogs? Each family in the village keeps a fattened dog as if to boast of their excesses. My very dog is fatter than your very dog. What can this mean?

Yesterday, we were taken to a building called the Supper-Market, where they had piled food to the ceilings in every row. So many little colored boxes, and bright lights shining from every corner of the room. Huge tables covered with slabs of red meat many layers together, enough to feed us all for months! As quickly as the people remove the goods from the shelf or table, men in white gowns rush forward from behind the butcher-door to replenish those very items. At first I thought they must have a very huge warehouse in back of the butcher-door, but if so, it is nowhere visible from the exterior. I often worry about what may be behind the butcher-door at the Supper-Market.

We have brought home so many sacks of food, it required two of the wire carts to transport them to the Ford. We have taken perhaps too much for our share and the people might realize now that we eat too much and send us back to the Thai camps. I cannot comprehend why they would want to give us so much food at once right at the beginning before they have seen us work. I sometimes have a very deep fear that they are fattening us all up for some purpose I do not wish to think of.

Leslie
In the early stages of her negotiations with the church, Leslie received an anonymous phone call during which she was told that if she insisted on pursuing her idea about bringing refugees to the village, one day she might come home and find a pile of charred rubble where her house used to be.

"First it was the Blacks in this country, wanting a free ride, now the Cubans and Mexicans and Chinks. Every refugee you bring in, it takes a job away from a legalized citizen. Don't you do-gooders understand that?" He hung up before she had a chance to reply—just some miserable and ignorant hungover man who wanted to express an opinion. She wasn't ready to take his threat seriously, but it did make her more sensitive about public opinion and her obligation to pursuade people of the rightness of what she was doing. One day in the grocery store she overheard someone in the next aisle saying, "Why can't we just send the money to the refugees and let them stay in their own country? For God's sake, why do we have to bring them over here? This is too far north for them. They'll never fit in here." Leslie hurried around the row of shelving and confronted the two women: "Look," she said, "they've la-la-lost their country. Th-th-th-there's no place but here for them to go." On her way home, she passed a pickup with a gun rack across the back window and a bumper sticker that read: "Hungry—eat your foreign car." It was a bad day.

She knows the unspeakable, the unarguable, the crushing fact is—Jerry no longer finds her sexually attractive since the accident. He no longer sleeps with her. Lately, he has begun discussing the social and philosophical merits of open marriage. The sense of alienation is almost palpable and getting worse, and she doesn't know why this has happened. She is the same person, isn't she? He seems upset by her running, by her refugee project, by everything that gives meaning to her life. He disguises his contempt for her under a cloud of solicitous concern. "Hadn't you better just take it easy for a while longer?" "Let someone else save the boat people. Why does it have to be us? We have our own problems." Or, after two cocktails, "If you hadn't gone to that silly liberal school, maybe you wouldn't have turned into such an insufferable bleeding heart."

In fact, he is such a prude, he is undoubtedly embarrassed by her running and, also, by the public exposure of her rescue project. He doesn't like the idea of *his* wife appearing all around town in nothing but her sheer nylon running briefs or her wet-look Gortex and sweatband like a savage, ecstatically pumping endorphins. Or maybe he doesn't want her to reveal her sweating thighs or cheeks, in case his golf or drinking buddies might be watering their lawns or shovelling their driveways at a particular hour. But, surely, if he knows *anything* about her, if he has learned one single truth about her character after fifteen years of marriage, he should know that she *must* continue to run, after what has happened to her, she *must* do it, and she must carry her rescue project through to completion. It is not merely the result of "misdirected maternal instinct," as he has claimed, that she feels compelled to contribute to the relief effort. How absurd! The greatest amateur psychologist of our time always has a conveniently pathological explanation these days for all her motives and hopes.

Leslie's Journal, Dec. 1st

Impressions during first few days: The house seemed to please the Lieus, though they are obviously still confused and distracted from their long ordeal. The small, white clapboard house is on a quiet street, Elm Street in the village, and the rental is being supported by donations from the community and the churches, though the churches have been somewhat less helpful than I might have imagined. We have enough to keep the house for only four months—a fact I am keeping to myself—and I am counting heavily on the further generosity of concerned members of the area and the appeal of the Lieus' presence itself to generate other contributions to their overall support. In an emergency, the small side-porch might be rented out as a separate apartment to help defray expenses, though at present it seems best not to complicate the Lieus' adjustment by inviting strangers to live so nearby. These people deserve privacy and quiet and space after the anguish they have endured. Eventually, we must find work for Mr. Lieu. We must find other, better ways to stimulate people's altruistic impulses. This is our personal contribution to the betterment of humanity, an individual, manageable portion of the world's affliction. We must see that these helpless, frightened little people can survive and prosper.

Further impressions: Though the language barrier is such a problem for all of us, we are slowly growing to understand the Lieus. When we returned from the grocery today, for instance, I was especially touched by Mr. Lieu's behavior. The man refused to eat until after all the children had been fed. (I wonder how often he has gone hungry?) We, of course, tried to convince him that there was enough food for everyone. But then we began to see that it was a matter of principle with him. Eventually, he did eat a small portion of Minute Rice.

Later, I was equally surprised by little Koki. When Judy Wheeler and I began to comb the little girl's hair, the hair kept coming out in alarming tufts in the comb. Finally we smoothed it out and clipped it with a small barrette and held Koki up to show her how she looked in the bathroom mirror. I've never seen such a look of astonishment on anyone's face. It was almost as if she had never seen herself in a mirror before that moment. At other times, she has a deep, pensive look, a look too old, too experienced, for her small face. I suppose the most horrible sight that most of the local children have ever seen is, say, a nightcrawler squashed on the sidewalk or something unreal from a horror film. But these Cambodians, those little dark eyes, oh, my!—what *they* have seen! I hate to *think* what they have seen.

Leslie

During her run, Leslie determines to try to improve things with Jerry. She will go by the office, she decides, and make a point of asking what he would like for dinner. She will be wifely and caring and see how he responds. Around five, she jogs to campus and into his building at the top of the quad. The halls are deserted at this hour. The students have wandered off to the dining halls, and the professors have all gone home, except for *her* husband. The fact that he is still here strikes her as additional evidence of his alienation from her rather than as proof of any special resolution on his part or dedication to his work. He doesn't *want* to come home. He would rather be here in this empty building, smoking and grading composition themes or taking a leisurely gander at the *New York Times*, as if the *New York Times* could tell him anything essential about his life or about their lives together. A wave of self-pity bends her mouth as she moves lightly up the steps to the second floor, trying to nurture a sense of buoyancy she does not really feel.

The door to his office is slightly open, and she sees immediately that he is, in fact, not alone. Someone wearing a shapely pair of ankle-strap pumps is sitting across from him, swinging her foot ever so slightly below her crossed legs. Leslie stops abruptly, out of sight, focussing on the arrogance and presumed familiarity of the gesture, puzzled at first, then alarmed that she might be seen, either by Jerry and the girl in the office with him, or by somebody coming unexpectedly down the hall, where she would be seen standing, appearing to eavesdrop. "I'm not taking anything for granted," the girl is saying.

"I'm not either," Jerry says. "I know I *like* having you around, Debbie. If you think I'm going to be turned off by your silly cock-teasing games, you're wrong."

"That wasn't the idea," the girl is saying, "not at all."

Leslie sways quickly back the way she came in and flees softly and quietly down the stairs and out of the building into the chilly anonymous darkness of snowplowed walks, where she pretends to be jogging again with some definite destination in mind, bouncing up and down foolishly like some frisky adolescent, as her pounding heart takes a nose dive. If she runs far enough now, her mind will be a large empty window, a vastness of rolling white like the moonlit fields outside of town at midnight, and she will not have to feel or think anything about what she has just seen and heard. She will not have to feel or think anything at all.

Saang

We grew and harvested acres of rice, but the crop was collected by Pol Pot's soldiers and hauled away. The Kymer Rouge told the people in Siem Reap they were sending the rice to Battambang. But in Battambang they collected the rice and told the people there they were sending it to Siem Reap. We never knew why all the rice had disappeared. Some days we had to divide one cup of rice fragments among a hundred people. We ate grass and roots and mice and insects. We saw which flowers the horses ate—and we ate flowers. We were desperate for food. We ate like animals. Some turned into animals. I know mothers who ate their dead babies. Almost everyone ate human flesh.

There was a madman in the village who always had a secret supply of meat. My mother used to trade tobacco and gold with him for a few pieces of fat to add to our soup. One day Pol Pot's soldiers broke into this man's house. There were more than sixty human corpses inside—some partially carved up and still bloody and covered with flies—and piles of bones stacked around the rooms and an enormous wealth of gold and trade goods. While the children of our village looked on, the Kymer Rouge beat the man to death until his skull was a pulp on the floor. Then they looted the dwelling and burned every trace of it with flame-throwing rifles.

If we had not escaped this madness, we would surely have perished or gone insane. In the darkness of night in the United States, I often remember the small boat that transported us across the Mekong to Nong Khai—its very drift and creak. We had walked for five days and nights. We feared the fisherman would awake and discover us as we pushed his boat into the dark waters. My sister, Vathana, had been shot to death in such a place, her body poured out on the bank of the river, where the family later came to cremate her, chanting somber prayers and weeping. Therefore, Vathana was much in my mind as we floated across the Mekong that night. The body of my small brother Koy, who also tried to leave with Vathana, has never yet been found. I imagined that the face of young Koy was there too beside Vathana's under the current. Other dead bodies were already swimming there and brushed against our low bow, soft and horrible as squid, or perhaps some were only branches or debris in the black waters, though they seemed to be begging to crawl in with us. When the baby began to cry, I stuffed his mouth full of rags to muffle the sound. I hardly recall the landing or how we later came to the camp, only the groaning of the boards of that small, clumsy boat, the mist, and the frightening quiet and the stillness of the souls upon the water.

Later, I learned that—as punishment for our escape—my relatives were killed by the Kymer Rouge, more than forty people—my father and mother, all my remaining sisters and brothers, uncles and cousins. All were murdered or starved to death. I and my children are the only members of my family left in the world.

In the morning light, we left the boat in the tall grass, collected our few belongings, and walked off down the long road. We had eaten nothing in three days, and could barely walk, and were without rice, fish, silk, or gold for trade. As we came near to the Thai camp, we heard shouts in the distance and, slowly ahead, as in a mirage, hordes of men, dressed all in blue jeans and blue-jean jackets and wearing cowboy hats, were yelling excitedly and holding up chickens for sale by their scaly feet and plastic blow-dryers and French perfume bottles and boxes of Thai cigarettes at $20 each pack.

Leslie

Leslie is running quickly along the village streets on this cold, clear night after nine, a slender figure in a dark blue running suit with silver reflective stripes. The points of the heels of her running shoes are also reflective, so that whenever a vehicle approaches within a certain distance of her, its headlights arc back from her moving body and the driver sees a luminescent figure advancing or fading away, its limbs glowing or sparkling eerily, like some heavenly or extraterrestrial visitation.

Leslie's Journal

The children have been sick for several days now, especially little Koki, and I have spent the last two nights looking after them, sleeping on the side-porch and getting up in the wee hours to sponge their foreheads, take temperatures, spoon out medicine, and comfort them. The symptoms are cramps, abdominal upsets, fevers, and sweats. Saang has these same symptoms too, sometimes even more severe, in fact; but, according to Dr. Goldberg, it is nothing but an array of intestinal parasites they most likely picked up in the Thai camps, where the sanitary conditions are so notoriously poor.

Unfortunately, their condition did cause a problem at school. Some of the local children started making fun of Koki and the others when they would double up in agony and run for the restroom. Young children can sometimes be brutally cruel. Several of the teachers were concerned that whatever the Lieu children have might be contagious. Hepatitis and typhoid fever have been mentioned in rumors and have led to a certain amount of pointless hysteria.

Update: Saang and the children have responded well to treatment and are feeling much better now. This will be my last night on the side-porch, and I am almost sorry to leave. Why is it that helping these people seems so important and gratifying to me? Taking the medicine in to Saang last night, as she rose up out of the covers and waited for me to pour the syrup into the spoon, I noticed for the first time really how exceptional her face is, how truly beautiful she might be when her health returns. It is a benign, exotic beauty, like that of some forlorn and forgotten, almond-eyed Asian princess, and almost frightening when one considers how far she has come to this place and under what circumstances and, by contrast, how alien and ugly we must seem to her. What can she possibly think of us?

Leslie's Journal (cont.)

We have been fortunate to secure work for Mr. Lieu—Kyheng—as a dishwasher at the Evergreen Inn. The salary is not much, but it should certainly help; and, more importantly, it should help give the Lieus a greater sense of self-sufficiency and involvement in the life of the community. Also, it will inevitably cause the people of the town to appreciate the sort of industrious, deserving family they have brought into their midst. The Lieus want to make their own way. They have a resilience and determination that is remarkable to behold. I'm sure they will be an asset to the town, and their story might make it easier to resettle other refugees in locations such as ours.

Language is the hardest ongoing problem. Judy Wheeler tutors Mr. Lieu three times a week, but his progress has not been as swift as that of Saang and the children. He is by temperament a very shy, private man. Because of that fact and the nature of his work, he will have little opportunity to practice what he has learned. If he is ever going to find better work, however, which I am sure he is capable of eventually, he will need to know more English.

Leslie

Leslie often spends evenings with the Lieu family. Kyheng, who has spent the day washing dishes at the Evergreen Inn, is now finishing up the dinner dishes. He reminds her of a porpoise—his hands splashing in the water and the dark gleam of his hair. At the same time, the stiff formality of his face and neck is very unlike a porpoise. Once, when she was trying to explain a joke to him, he suddenly understood—either what she was saying or the essence of it—and his face was transformed by crow's-feet into a look of boyish hilarity.

Someone from the Church has donated a small black-and-white television set for the Lieus, saying, "This will help them learn the language and give them quicker insights into American culture." Leslie is not so sure these are insights they wouldn't be better off without, but she has delivered the set and helped show them how to turn it on and adust it. The Lieus seem quite amazed and grateful. Apparently, they had never seen a TV set up close before.

Leslie sits quietly in the darkened living room admiring the little family as they watch their TV set. She has made this possible. They are such innocent, deserving people, and such a close-knit family. Saang and Kyheng are particularly close. Occasionally Leslie has seen the two of them in town, on the street together, has seen the way they have of sharing a look without uttering a word. But, after all, they are strangers in a strange land and have no other face, no other responsible person (except her) to turn to and share a feeling. She can sometimes feel the spirit that must be between them. She envies it. She does not envy them their fates—of course not that—but she does envy them for their closeness and selflessness.

When she leaves, they are watching a rerun of *Jaws*. She hopes it will not give them nightmares. They are so hypnotically involved that they hardly notice she is walking out the door.

Saang

The large fish with many teeth tries to eat the people. The picture of the fish was taken while it was swimming in the Atlantic Ocean. The picture was piped into a tower and propelled out into the air over many miles. The picture slides through the clouds alongside the several airplanes until it arrives into the plastic window of our TV network box. All of the people who swam in the Atlantic Ocean were eaten or killed by the huge fish, which is larger than a boat.

Leslie

After two miles, her legs feel ripe with blood, flushed and taut, and her movement as lubricated and smooth as a well-oiled engine. But she is not an engine. She is flesh and blood, warm, palpable, living. A living thing. A living creature, running now along a country road with a primitive sense of freedom as the wind blows against her face. A person, like any other, somewhat better educated and focussed than most perhaps, somewhat more determined to impose her will upon the world—the inert, blind, stubborn, pitiful world. But *no more deserving* for the luck of possessing brains and an expensive background—not at all. *More responsible*. A duty to serve the good of the species as a whole. "Be ashamed to die until you have won some victory for humanity." She knows the human significance of these words. She understands them at some organic or cellular level. Her life is poised in a precarious balance, waiting to fulfill this particular mission or calling—to perform some act of charity or devotion large enough to qualify as a victory for humanity.

Saang
The sick woman has a pill in her hand, and after eating it she feels much better. Many very happy people drink Coke, and beer delivered by horses with huge feet. Several men like to shave their faces with buffalo curd. Then they run back and forth bouncing a ball and shouting at one another.

Leslie
The waitress takes Leslie's order to the kitchen, where Kyheng is visible behind the counter. He does not notice her in the dining room. He seems to be racing someone to see who can finish the dishes first. Occasionally, he growls sideways, or seems to, though no one is there. Then his eyes return to his hands, bloodless in the scalding water. The boss likes him, the waitress tells Leslie, because, besides being a hard worker, he never complains and never flinches or talks back when being yelled at. The waitress does not know of Leslie's connection to Mr. Lieu. She thinks Leslie is just curious. "Sometimes around happy hour, some of the men get after him," the waitress says. "They call him Small Pot. They don't like it that he has a job and some of them don't. But Lou"—Lou, she calls him—"doesn't pay any attention. He just smiles away and keeps on washing dishes. I think he understands a lot more than people give him credit for," the waitress says. "I think it's a wonderful thing that he came to this country to be free like the rest of us."

After she finishes her lunch, Leslie goes to the kitchen to say hello to Kyheng. She is relieved when he gives her a toothy grin and seems honored to see her. She lays her arm in a maternal way around his shoulders and starts to say something fatuous about the dishes when suddenly she finds she is crying heavily into the moist neck of his shirt and he is clutching a dripping cup against her sweater, blinking in surprise, and trying hastily to back away and detach himself.

Saang
I use a tub and washboard from the church-people to clean our clothes. The water flows from the spigot already hot, and the suds from the box are thick and full of foam. The strange fragrance from the powerful soap hurts the nostrils. My fingers become red in the scalding soapiness. I rush to hang the clothes on the line before darkness enfolds. My hands grow stiff in the white air, pinning up the wash I can barely see. In the morning, when I go out in the yard to collect these very same clothes, I scream. The shirts and dresses and pants have turned to plastic in the night, or perhaps it is white wood. They are glued to the rope, and when I pull them away, the plastic breaks and falls in small knives across my wrists. I run inside sobbing to tell Kyheng that our clothes have been forever ruined.

When Less-lee knocks, I tell her dreadfully of the mishap of the clothesline. She understands and is never angry. It will be all right, Less-lee says. We must take the clothes to a place called the Laundry-mat, she says, in the wintertime. She goes outside to look, and we put the hard clothes into a basket and into the backseat of her Ford.

The Laundry-mat is a large room with rows of white plastic machines and round windows in the walls, like the ones of the airplane, looking out onto a dark hole, and the burning smell of soap, ticklish in my nose. Together, Less-lee and I unsnap the airport window and fold the clothes into what seems a sideways tub. Less-lee puts coins into it, and suddenly the clothes begin to turn and bounce and the machine makes a rumbling. Less-lee squeezes my shoulder and we stand together a long time and watch the hard clothes jump inside the airport door.

Leslie

The doorbell rings and Jerry goes to answer it. He stands for several minutes jawing with someone in the doorway.

"Who is it?" Leslie says, assuming it is one of his students, maybe the girl from his office.

"Old Professor Henry can't find his cat. Have you seen it?"

"No."

"He thought you might have seen it out on the trails somewhere, jogging along."

"Very funny. No, ba-but tell him I'll keep an eye out for it."

He returns to the door and talks further with Mr. Henry. The old man is a retired English professor who lives across the street. He wears a trench coat and a beret and walks his overweight, beige-haired cat on a string and secretly encourages it to defecate in the yards of neighbors who are not at home. When the cat escapes, he hunts for it with desperate determination; but the cat always comes back eventually.

Later that day, Leslie jogs over to Elm Street to visit the Lieus. Her legs are strong and eager and the short run feels good. The sun is out, bright on the fresh snow, and the yards shine as if encrusted with tiny diamonds. The Lieus are bustling about in their kitchen, looking happier than she has seen them in some time. An odd smell fills the house, and Kyheng smilingly shows her some hideous thing, something not-quite-chickenlike roasting in the oven. "Where did you ge-get it?" Leslie says to Kyheng, uneasily. "Where did the meat ca-ca-come from?" Kyheng looks to Saang for help with an answer.

"He catch," Saang says. "Set trap for small animal." Saang points proudly to a curl of bloody beige hair resting in a newspaper on the countertop. The truth of the matter hits Leslie with a sickening sense of certainty.

"Oh, my God," she says.

"We save money," Saang says.

"Oh, no," Leslie says. "This is a mistake. You must not tra-trap animals in town. Ma-many people have small animals as pets. They will not approve of it, and there are laws against tra-tra-trapping in town. This is something Kyheng must not do e-ever again."

"Not in our country," Saang says.

"But in this country it is so. It is believed very strongly. I will have to explain what has ha-happened to the man who owns this cat. He will be very angry."

Saang addresses Kyheng, explaining about the cat. The expression on his face goes from openness to astonishment to abject regret and guilt. He babbles something incomprehensible to Leslie and rushes to the oven, throws open the door, and pulls out the pan with the cat-carcass, burning his hands and slamming it into the counter. The cat rolls out of the pan just as Kyheng releases the hot metal handles and drops everything with a crash in the middle of the kitchen linoleum and then quickly turns and runs cold water over his hands from the nearby spigot. He stands there, shaking his wet hands like fluttering birds over the sink, afraid to look at anything but the cat-carcass and pan in the middle of the floor. He is the picture of a contrite man, and Leslie can't help feeling sorry for him, though she turns away, suddenly queasy in her stomach. Saang, scolding Kyheng loudly in her native language, begins to pick up the mess, carefully using a folded dishrag as she bends to grasp the spongy carcass and place it in the pan and sop up the puddle of grease.

Surely it is her duty to tell Mr. Henry what has happened to his cat. "These people are from a simple agrarian culture," she will tell him. "They are good people. They did not understand what they were doing. They thought they were being thrifty, causing less of a hardship for their sponsors and the town. They acted as they have done before in order to live—by trapping game." But Mr. Henry will not understand. He will be terribly injured by what has happened. The memory of the ugly hulk of the cat's body in the oven keeps passing through her mind. Then she sees it fall sickeningly to the floor. The cat was the old man's only companion. How could he possibly forgive her or the Lieus or anyone for what has happened? It might be more merciful not to tell him. Then he will not have to imagine the horrible sight in the oven. Let him think the cat ran off and died of old age? Was she just being cowardly to think of it this way, just making it easier for herself, or would it, in fact, be more merciful? She imagines Mr. Henry coming again to her front door to inquire about his cat: She says, *I was just this very moment on my way across the street to tell you some very sad news.* Mr. Henry falls heavily to the porch floor and clutches at his heart.

She might tell Jerry about the cat—as a way of helping her decide what to do. He has sometimes joked about the old man walking his cat into their yard whenever they are away, as he does with the other neighbors, joked about the grass being killed by catpiss or coming home after a two-week absence to find the house surrounded by piles of cat feces. Jerry will probably find the situation amusing, or it will make him angry. "Now maybe you'll admit that you've made a horrible mistake in bringing them here," he might say. "Now maybe you'll admit for once that you could have been wrong."

Saang

Many women have trouble with soap in their plastic machines at the Laundry-Mat, and they squirt medicine into their noses and smile. Soldiers are lying in a ditch beside the road with bleeding arms and feet, and one man is missing from his head. Huge airplanes take off on the runway and fly at the sunset.

Leslie

Leslie has a disturbing dream. She and Saang are out for a walk along the jogging trail. She sees a worried expression on Saang's face that bothers her, affects her mood, even under the surface of her consciousness where time is blown up like the microscopic view of a cell or shrunken as in a computerized aerial-photo of the lunar landscape. She sees Saang walking into a web. She can tell that Saang does not know the web is there, whipping around her ankles. Leslie tries to explain it to her, but her voice is like a distant radio signal, fading in and out. Suddenly, the soil around them is dry and rocky and crawling with long-tailed rats. The rats have yellow eyes and ugly jaws and tongues like giant iguanas. Saang's feet drift an inch above their snapping, lecherous faces.

Leslie wakes up in a sweat. She reaches over to Jerry's side of the bed, but the bed is empty, the sheet cold. The digital clock says 1:58.

She gets up and pulls on her bathrobe and wanders down the hall to Jerry's study. No one there. She checks for a light on elsewhere, tiptoeing bare-footed down the cold stairway, feeling her way along the bannister, then, arms outstretched, thin as a ghost in the darkness, reaching for the edges of the woodwork, the edges of the doorframes. But there is nothing but blackness. A car rumbles distantly in the street, and reflected light passes across her face in the shape of a network of warped panes.

She falls asleep again: The asphalt steams in the early morning heat. The road goes on and on, past groves of maples, fields, crossroads, barns with cattle waiting sullenly for release. She passes a farmer's house and strides out into the open country. She is a long way out, perhaps eight miles, cruising steadily on her hot, slick legs. Up ahead, far up the long road, a dark brown pickup turns lazily out of a farmyard and drifts towards her, the profile of its bulbous fenders squaring up with the sloping berm and fence-rows. Then it accelerates furiously, the round lenses of its glassy headlights suddenly bearing down on her like the eyes of some gigantic mythical demon.

A dark cloud moves across the face of the sun, and the wind begins to stir the high grass. She is bounding down the center of the road, and the pavement is clear for miles ahead except for the brutal scarred grille of the pickup, sweeping down upon her. She picks up her pace, sprinting now. She glowers at the faded hood, feels the rush of air, and sees, at the last moment, as the grille is actually striking her, that the driver is only her husband Jerry, and Jerry's eyes look down at her and are full of regret.

When he comes in, she is still there in the darkness, doubled over, crying into the couch cushion, which smells faintly moist and acrid, like coats returned from the dry cleaners on a damp day; and then he is above her, leaning into her, patting her shoulder and crooning endearments into her ear that are nothing but lies, she knows, miserable lies, every one of them. How can he fail to realize that she could never, ever, be deceived by such self-serving, transparent lies?

Leslie

She runs and runs, her feet drumming on the asphalt like pistons, like the metal thrusting parts of an oil rig, something mechanical and inexorable and indestructible. Something unremitting. Or another thing: anesthetized, falling, soaring, diving, like a wounded gull, like a lemming rushing to the sea and diving over the cliffwall. Soaring. The heat rises into her face and back, the flush and swelling of the blood, the sweat breaking out, the sense of timelessness and oneness with the earth. The pain and the absence of pain. She stops suddenly and walks, enters a grove of trees beside the road, far from any house or watching eyes. Some force has taken over her body now. It forces her to stop, to lean against this particular small tree, to press herself forward against its thin, hard living surface, while she tenses the muscles in her legs and buttocks and moves her fingers slowly over the tautness of the sapling and of her body. The oaky smell of the bark is a wildness inside and outside herself, an intoxication that carries her mind and breath away.

Leslie

She cannot live in the same house with him any longer, that much is clear. His presence is suffocating, nauseating. The energy required to deal with his presence, or the threat of his presence, with its stench of cigarette fumes and counterfeit pain, leaves her drained and pale and feeble. She has to find somewhere else to go. She realizes she has been thinking for some time that she might like to settle into the small side-porch next to the Lieus on a more permanent basis. She enjoyed the simplicity of the two rooms, the light from the high windows, the promise of comfortable solitude; and the idea of greater proximity to Saang and the Lieu family seems inviting too. A chaste and sensible existence seems possible there, not to mention the additional appealing fact that the place is empty and available. She could be closer to the children to help mold them, to help teach them the language. . . . She could substitute at the school to contribute to the upkeep of the family. She gets out the Samsonite and begins packing energetically. The sunlight of a surprisingly balmy February day streams in across the bedspread, and she feels almost happy for the first time in weeks.

Saang

Less-lee brought her suitcases and wishes to move onto the side-porch. She asks if this is okay with me. We sit in the bay window and discuss her upset. The lines near Less-lee's mouth are tight and sharp. Her earnest face is very thin. Less-lee's husband was not a good husband for a woman to have. Poor Less-lee is a miserable woman because of this plight. Less-lee cooks tea and we sit for a long time with the teacups and bread. Then Less-lee holds my face in her two hands and cries and places her head in my lap like a small child. We are trying to think of what to do next, sitting in the sunlight in the afternoon in our small house here in the United States of America.

Town Smokes

PINCKNEY BENEDICT

M$_Y$ DADDY been in the ground a couple hours when it starts to rain. Hunter's up on the porch, strippen away at a chunk of soft pine wood with his Kaybar knife, and I'm sitten out in the yard to get away from the sound, chip chip chip like some damn squirrel. Hunter moves in his seat as he whittles, can' sit still.

It's big drops that are comen down, and starten real quick, like you wouldn' of expected it at all. I look up when it comes on to rain, and what I see of sky's just as blue and clear. Happen like that up here sometimes, my daddy's told me, that you get your hard rain and your blue sky, and both together like that. First time I seen it though, that I recall.

You gonna drown out there Hunter says to me, and I can just hardly hear him over the rain pounden into the dirt of the yard and spangen off the tin roof.

What's that I say. He's not more'n ten yard from me but there's rain like a sheet between us, getten in my eyes and my ears and down my collar. I like the way the cool rain feels as it soaks my shirt. I catch a couple drops in my mouth, and they got no taste to them at all. The rain washes the sweat and the dirt off me.

Drown like a turkey in the rain Hunter says. Out there and mouth open. He gets up to go inside, drops the wood and the knife down into the chair. The heavy knife sticks in the seat, blade down. Hunter moves like an old man, older than my daddy, fat and tired. He ran the sweat like a hog when we was diggen before, because the dirt was hard and packed where we put the grave, out behind the house. I thought his heart might vapor-lock on him there for a while, all red and breathen through the mouth as he was.

Hunter slips the straps of his overalls as he goes inside and I know he will spend the rest of the day in his underwear sluggen bourbon and listenen to the radio.

Get in out the rain he says to me back over his shoulder. I stay out in the yard until the door swings shut behind him. The ground is getten soft under my sneakers but I know that is just the top dirt. It hasn' rained for a good long while and the clay dirt has got dry. The rain comes down too fast and hard to soak in. I know it will not get down deep at all.

I go to the door and I can smell the piece of wood Hunter's been cutten on, the sharp pine sap. It's a tooth he's carven out, like a big boar's tusk, all smooth and curved comen out of the rough wood. He carves a lot of things like that.

He's my daddy's brother that lives with us at the camp up on Tree Mountain. He's a big man, has this small head that sits on his body like a busted chimney on a house. He don't talk much. Old Hunter'll surprise you, how good he is with whittlen. He's sold some things in town.

Water rollen off the roof runs deep around the edges of the porch. Out of the rain, my wet clothes are heavy on me. Against my leg, cold in my pockets, I feel the arrowhead I found in my daddy's grave. Flint hunten point with the edges still sharp. It wasn' very far down, only mebbe five inches. I didn' know this's a good place to find arrowheads. I'll dig again later in other spots to look for some more. I lick my lips, want a smoke, a Camel mebbe.

You got a cigarette I say, goen into the house.

Get you fucken shoes off, bringen wet in the house Hunter says. He's standen in the front room in his shorts, and his hair stands up like he's been runnen his hands through it. The radio he keeps back in his room is on to a news station. What's a fourteen-year-old boy want with a cigarette anyway he says.

Fifteen I say. My shoes come off my feet with a wet noise. I got no socks on, and the wood floor is rough. I know to be careful in bare feet or get a sliver.

I ain' got a cigarette he says.

You got a pinch then I say. I know he's got no snuff but I ask anyway.

Hunter sits down. He's got the bottle in his hand. Christ Jesus he says. You visit whores too?

These are things a man does I say. I guess I just feel like a smoke.

I laugh but Hunter don' join in. He looks at me. When I keep my eyes on him he looks away, out the window. The hard rain throws up a spray of mist and you can' see for more than a couple yards. The roof of the camp is fairly new and tight and it don' leak at all. Hunter and my daddy put it on just the last summer before this one and they did a good job. I carried tacks and tin sheets for them, always scared of slippen and fallen off the roof.

Real gulleywasher Hunter says. They got to watch for them flashfloods down to the valley. Farms goen to lose a lot of dirt to the river, this don' let up.

He keeps on looken out the window and all the time the rain is getten harder. It's finally dark out there, clouds coveren the sun. We are high up and it is strange to see it dark in the middle of day. Generally we get hard bright mountain light that makes you squint to look at it.

Your daddy used to make his own smokes Hunter says.

I say I know.

Mebbe you look through his traps, you find you the fixens he says.

That's a thought I say. I don' make any move to the room my daddy and I share, did share. I stand and drip on the floor and listen to the rain. Hunter looks at me like watchen a snake or mebbe a dog that you aren' sure of. The rain outside the windows makes it look like it isn' anyplace in the world but the camp and us in it; we're alone here. I think mebbe the rain won' let up for a while yet.

Hunter says you do what you want. Always done it that way anyhow didn' you.

He stands, works his shoulders back and forth. He is sore from the diggen and would like his muscles rubbed I know. Rain throbs him some these days.

I'm gonna listen to the radio for a time he says.

I make a bet with myself he will be asleep before long.

The door to Hunter's room don' shut just right, so when he closes it I can still get the sound from the radio in his room. It is a station from in the valley. The announcer says to watch for flashfloods in the narrow, highbanked creeks comen down off the mountain. He says it like it is the mountain's fault.

The tower of the radio is on top of a ridge not far from the camp. The place where they put it is a couple hunnerd feet higher than where we are and you can see it from the porch of the camp on a good day. They took out a whole big stand of blue spruce to get it in.

From where we are, the clearen looks smooth and clean and well took care of, like a yard, but I have been up there a couple time—it ain' such a hard climb as it looks, just a couple hours scramble—and it is a mess around the base of that tower. Vines and creepers around the base and grass to your knees. The blue spruce are comen back too and they are fast-growen trees.

Hunter snaps off the radio and I hear him stretch out on to his bed. He keeps moven around like he will never get to sleep.

* * *

My daddy's things is all over the room in no particular order. It is like he is still there, in all them traps, though I know that he is cold and dead and under the earth not a dozen yards away.

These things are mine now I say but it is not like they belong to me at all. Some of them should go to Hunter. I ain' sure that I want that Hunter should have them, though I would be hard put to say why not.

I move the rifle that is layen on my daddy's bed, the heavy lever-action Marlin, and the cartridge belt that is layen there too. My fingers touch the cool blued metal of the barrel and I know I will have to clean the metal where I touched it, rub it down with a patch of oiled cloth. There is nothen that is worse for any good piece of metal than the touch of a man's hand my daddy would always be sayen.

It is two guns that are in my family, both my daddy's, his old Marlin and the single-action Colt .38 that his grandaddy used sometime way back in the Philippine Insurrection. I put the Colt down on the bed next the rifle, fish out a box of rounds for it as well. From the feel, there ain' too many cartridges left to the box, which is tore up and very old. Beside the guns and his clothes, there is not much else of his in the room.

In the top of the old chifferobe I find his little sack for tobacco. There is not much that is left in the sack, and I can bet that it is pretty old and dry. He was not much for a smoker and a sack of tobacco had a long life around him. There is a paper book of matches next the tobacco with all but two of the matches gone. It is from the Pioneer, which is a bar I have seen down to the valley. There is also a couple bills, a five and a one. I pocket the money.

I scratch through the rest of his stuff in the drawer—a dog whistle and a couple loose .410 rounds for a gun that we ain' even got; needles and thread in a sewen kit; some Vietnamese money that he used to keep around for a laugh—and come up with his old Barlow claspknife and his Gideon's. The claspknife I toss down with the rest of the pieces that I figure I might take with me. It clicks off the barrel of the Colt and leaves a mark on the metal. That is one mark that I won' get a hiden for.

The Gideon's is old and slippery in my hand and missen many pages. My daddy has used it for a lot of years. The paper is thin and fine for rollen your own; if you are good you can get two smokes to the page. As I say, he was not a heavy smoker and he is not even gotten up to the New Testament yet, just somewhere in Jeremiah.

I pull out the next page and crease it with my middle finger, tap tobacco onto the paper. The tobacco is crumbly with age and breaks into small pieces; it is very dark brown and cheap-looken. Some of it sticks to my skin. I lay down on the bed and put the home-rolled cigarette in my mouth. Pieces of tobacco stick to my tongue. I spit out, light the smoke.

Christ I say. The cigarette don' taste good at all, like the tobacco has rotted. I flick it out onto the floor and sparks fly off from the lit end. They stick to the wood floor and smolder there, and one by one the sparks burn themselves out.

* * *

I figure I will go into town for a time I say to Hunter's back.

He is face down on the narrow cot in his room and I figure him for asleep.

The bottle is by the bed and it is several fingers down from where it was earlier. Hunter's back is pale and wide, and there is a mole I never took notice of before in the deep track that his backbone makes.

He says Goen where? and rolls over so sudden it startles me. His face is wet with tears and it surprises me that this old man has been cryen. For a minute I can' remember why. The bed sags under him.

Down the mountain I say. Get me some smokes mebbe.

He is wipen at his face with his arm, drunk and embarrassed that I seen him cry. You can cry for your brother I want to say.

You ain' comen back are you Hunter says.

He puts a foot on the floor and the bottle goes over. I pick it up for him, set it back where it was. It is all but empty with haven been dumped out. The floor is damp and the room smells of bourbon. I look out the little window in Hunter's bedroom and the rain has slacked off some. That is a help.

The rifle's in on the bed I say. He would of wanted for you to have it.

I walk out into the front room and Hunter comes after me, walken in his underwear and bare feet. I got the .38 and the claspknife and all in my kit with me, ready to go.

Why is it that you're goen now Hunter says. With the rain and all. It's a bad day to be goen down to the valley.

I think about that. It is not somethen I have thought about much before this. I look at him.

Because I am tired I say. Tired of the mountain and smoken shitty tobacco. Mebbe I just want to smoke a real cigarette for a change.

Want you some town smokes I guess Hunter says.

I say I guess.

Mebbe want to kiss all them pretty girls down to the valley too Hunter says. I don' say anythen.

Yeah he says. Bring me back a bottle when you come.

I'll do that I say. You bet.

I go outside and the air is cool for a day in the middle of summer. The rain has turned the dust to mud and water runs in streams in the yard, has bit into the dirt. A hard rain for just a couple hours I know can raise the creeks and cut right through the banks and dirt levees down below. I wonder what they are doen with all the water down in the town. The air feels damp but the rain is mostly stopped.

Hunter has followed me out into the yard and his feet are all over mud. How you goen down? he says.

Railroad right of way I say. It's the quickest way.

Hunter follows me the next couple of steps and I cut from the yard into the underbrush so he will stop followen. The leaves on the bushes are wet and soak my shirt, my kit. I know the damp will be hard on the gun.

Ought not to of happened to your daddy that way Hunter says. He is looken in the bushes like he can' see where I am at, but he wants me to hear him.

When the tree falls I say best the man that cut it should be out the way. That is hard Hunter says to the bushes. That a boy should say that about his daddy that brought him up and fed him.

I know that Hunter will see me if I keep on talken. I don' want that he should see me. I turn and go, headen toward the right of way down the mountain.

We should of had someone to say the words Hunter calls after me. It ain' right that there wasn' nobody to say the words for him.

I keep goen through the brush. I guess I would of said the words if I knew them. I ain' got the least idee what words he would of wanted though.

***

The last time I seen my daddy he tells me a story. He has the old two-stroke loggen saw over his shoulder and is headed out to where he known there's some trees that has come down, or are ready to come down anyhow. You want some help daddy I ask and he says no.

Then he looks over at where Hunter is sitten on the porch and this time Hunter is carven a great horned owl out of a big piece of oak that would have gone well in the fire in the winter.

Hunter wasn' always so fat and lazy he says loud enough that he knows Hunter can hear him. Hunter don' stir from his carven, usen a chisel instead of the Kaybar knife. That's how he works on the ones he figures to sell.

Nawsir my daddy says, was a time when he and I used to run and raise some hell in these parts. When we was about your age. I 'member one time down to Seldomridge's place, little shorthorn farm next the river. You recall that Hunter?

Hunter keeps quiet, just gouges a long chunk of wood out the owl's back. It kind of ruins how the owl looks I think.

The river was froze over, couple three feet thick out near the banks my daddy says. Ice got all thin and black out toward the middle though where the water's deep and fast.

He shifts the chainsaw from one shoulder to the other and I see where a little gas mixed with oil has leaked onto his shirt. He don' seem to mind.

So Hunter here riles up Seldomridge's cattle and about a dozen shorthorns go plowen out onto the ice daddy says.

My daddy's starten to laugh and there are these tears formen in the corners of his eyes. I can hardly stand to look at him because he thinks the story is so funny and I don' get it at all yet.

And they're shiveren out there my daddy keeps on. Can hardly stand, all spraddle-legged and tryen to stay up on the ice, blowen and snorten, scared

and full of snot and droolen, them whiteface. Hunter's yellen and holleren at
them from the bank, just to keep them on the move, keep them up and off
from the shore. Hunter's voice sounds loud out there with everythen else so
quiet and covered in snow.

Then the first one goes through my daddy says and he can hardly keep the
saw on his shoulders for laughen.

It sounds like a pistol shot when the ice gives and the steer disappears
down and it's just black black water shooten up through the hole in the ice
like a geyser. That sets them off, stompen and bellowen and the next goes
through the ice, skitteren and scrabblen, and the next after that one. Prob'ly
half a dozen, one after the other, they get out on the thin ice in the middle and
don' have time to look surprised 'fore they go down.

And you was laughen Hunter says from behind his carven.

You damn right I was too my daddy says. I was laughen like a son of a
bitch he says and he wheels and heads off into the woods after the tree that
fell on him. As he goes, me and Hunter can hear him in the woods there,
laughen and laughen about the whiteface that went through the ice in the
middle of the river.

Them cattle showed up as far down the river as Teaberry Hunter says
after my daddy is gone.

Drownded I ask.

Dead as hammers he says. You bet.

* * *

About halfway down the mountain a pig runs across the right of way just a
couple of feet in front of me. Scares the bejesus out of me, cutten out of the
brush on one side and nearly steps on me goen past. It gets stuck for a second
goen across the rails and I see that it is young, just a little spotted sucklen
and haven a hard time of it. It is whining a little as it gets over the belly-high
steel rails, tail twitchen like a dog's. When it gets over the far rail it turns
toward me a second and its eyes are rolled way back in its head. Then it gets
into the brush on the other side of the right of way and it's gone.

Two boys come out of the brush after it and they are right on top of me too.
Christ one of them says and shoves at me. He is not very big and I knock him
down with my kit. The other is big and red-haired and carryen a rifle. He
rushes across the right of way and stares into the brush. Goddam it to hell he
says.

He raises the rifle, pointen into the brush after the sucklen, and I think for
a minute that he is goen to let go. Then I realize the pig must be in under cover
now and he'd be a fool to shoot. Still his finger curves on the trigger a second,
tugs and almost fires.

It is a short-barrelled Winchester carbine that he is carryen with a shrouded front sight for brush-beaten. The stock is wrapped around with black electric tape and there is rust all on the receiver. They are rough-looken boys. The big one is about my age and the little one some younger I figure.

The big red-headed one turns around to me and his eyes are cold. I figure he is mad because they lost the pig that they had been tracken. He drops the hammer back into half-cock, holds the rifle easy in the crook of his arm. His clothes are dirty and too small on his big frame.

Le's get a move on Okie the little one says. His teeth are gone rotten on him and make him talk odd, real soft like his mouth pains him. He says mebbe we can still get us that 'ere pig.

You hush Darius the big one says and he is still looken at me. It makes me nervous and I turn to head on down the cinder roadbed. The cinders are soft with the rain. They stick to the bottoms of my shoes, make my feet feel heavy. It is hard to walk on the railroad ties though, because they are too close together to make for an easy stride.

When I look back the big one, Okie, is still staren at me from under the long red hair. He licks his lips.

Hold up there a minute he says.

The little one trots after me a couple steps and I see there is somethen wrong with his legs, how they are too short for the rest of his body is what makes him so small. He is mebbe not so young as I first thought, mebbe older than me or Okie too. The ties are just right for him and he moves from one to the next without any trouble at all. Okie stays where he is.

We lost that 'ere shoat Darius says and he sounds like on the edge of cryen about it. You seen it he says.

Darius is right up on me now where I can smell him and I stop.

You boys want to let me alone I say. I ain' botheren you none.

Who says you was Okie calls out.

He's got the rifle pointen up at the grey sky now, held in both hands. He spits on the cinders, got a pinch of snuff in the right side of his mouth. He comes down the track a way, smilen, and I see his teeth are gone bad on him too. The snuff'll do that to you in time.

What you got Darius is sayen and I catch him looken at my kit. He's got his hands out like a kid asken for a candy. I drop the bag, put it back behind me. Darius is hoppen back and forth from one railroad tie to the other. He's got mud to the knee on his old corduroy pants, but it seems like he don' want to touch foot down on the roadbed.

He don' want you messen with his stuff Okie says to Darius. It is like a man talken to a kid.

He looks at me. You headen down into town he says. You live up on the mountain? He points back up the way I came with the carbine.

Yeah I say.

He looks at Darius and snorts, spits again. Goddam ridge runner he says. Come down from up on top and don' know nothen. Darius laughs.

What you want to go into town for, ridge runner? Okie says. He pokes the rifle barrel into my chest real sudden. It clunks against my ribs and hurts like a son of a bitch. I can hear Darius goen in my kit but I don' look.

Ain' nothen for you there boy Okie says. Best you go on back up the mountain and stay with the rest of the runners.

Just take the whole fucken thing Darius he says, ain' no use to go rooten through there. It don' stop Darius. Okie turns back to me.

You turn out you pockets he says and he taps me with the rifle again. We could do you he says. Kill you just as easy as killen that shoat and nobody to know any differ'nt about it. Who'd care what happens to a ridge runner like you anyhow.

I know I say. We're about fifteen hunnerd feet above the valley and I figure he is right.

You turn out you pockets and keep you mouth shut and you be all right Okie says. Darius is goen through my stuff still and I can hear the Colt clink against somethen. I hate to think of these two with it but there is nothen to do about it. I wish I had left the thing with Hunter.

My daddy's dead I say. I don' know why I say it.

Looky here Darius says and holds up the Barlow knife. He has got it open and the blade looks shiny even under the cloudy sky. He tests it against his hairy forearm. Sharp he says. Okie holds the rifle on me but he is looken off somewheres else, after where the pig went. I dig in after the money I got in my pockets.

Tree fell on him I say. When he was cutten it down.

Okie takes the six dollars from me, shoves it in his pants. I think about what a 30-30 could do to you this close up. I seen one take the whole hind end off a groundhog one time at about two hunnerd yards, just tore it off and threw the 'hog about ten feet. I hold out the arrowhead to him, turn out my pockets so's he can see they ain' nothen in them. He takes the arrowhead, holds it out from him with his left hand, squinten. He knows I ain' goen to give him any trouble.

Leave me some to get a pack of smokes down to the valley I say. And a bottle for my uncle.

Shoot Okie says. He tosses the arrowhead back over his shoulder. It hits the smooth steel rail and gives out a pretty sound, like a note on my daddy's old jew harp. The flint busts into about twenty pieces.

That was a pretty old arrowhead I say. I don' know how old it was but I want to say somethen.

Gimme his shoes Darius says.

He's standen and looken at my feet. His shoes look like bags tied with string or somethen. Mine ain' much but they are better than that, an old pair of sneakers that was my daddy's.

His shoes ain' about to fit you clubfoot Okie says. Darius is bouncen up and down, still standen on a railroad tie. He's got my kit in his hand. He just looks at Okie and sticks his lip out. He is retarded some I see.

Get out your shoes Okie says. He seems like he is tired of the whole thing now. Just go on and get on out of them he says. He ain' even holden the rifle on me now.

I take my shoes off and hand them to Darius. He don' even try to put them on. He just stuffs them in the kit and laughs, sound like a dog barken. The roadbed is cold with the rain and the cinders stick to the soles of my feet, stain them black.

Darius goes to the edge of the right of way, looks off into the brush. Le's see can we get that pig now Okie he says. He goes off into the brush carryen my kit with him. After a minute I can' see him anymore, just hear him crashen around in there.

Okie looks me up and down and his eyes are still hard. The smell of him that close up is greasy, like somethen fat cooked on an open fire.

You go back on up he says. That's best for ridge runners, the top of the mountain.

I'm headed into town I say.

He looks mad at me and I think for a minute he may shoot me, but he don' even bring the gun around to bear. He looks at me some more, then heads on into the brush after Darius.

I wait a minute to see if they're comen back but they're both gone. No use tryen to follow them into the brush with no shoes. I start down the right of way again, on into the valley. The walken is easier without my kit. The rain has started up again, lighter this time. It don' feel like the kind of a rain that goes on for too long.

The cinders make my feet sore and black. I walk that way for a while, then change to walken on the ties. It is strange the small steps you have to take, but easier than stretchen to skip a tie every time. I get used to it.

* * *

When we find my daddy he's been dead for quite a while. The tree just caught him across the chest with one thick branch. He must of been on his way to dodge the fall when it caught him. His face looks surprised; his body don' look like anythen I ever seen before, all a different shape from what it was, crushed ribs and tore cloth, somethen terrible to look at. Hunter covers him with a good thick tarpaulin right after we jack the tree up off of him and I don' have a chance to look at him after that. We bury the tarpaulin along with him.

The loggen saw's down on the ground next to him. It didn' get caught by the tree at all, looks just like it had when he walked out with it. All the gas in it ain' gone so it must of stalled after he got hit. Hunter and me talk about it but can' never figure what it was about that old oak that made it fall the wrong way or why my daddy didn' figure how it was goen to come down. He must of made the cut wrong somehow and just not seen his mistake until it was too late.

* * *

Lot of folks lost everthen says the man who owns the drugstore. He is a heavy man wearen a white apron tied behind his back. Houses, stock, barns, the whole kitten caboodle down the river and on into Monroe County. He is talken to a skinny man in overalls who nods.

You betcha the drugstore man says. We awful lucky to be this high up. He is sweepen at a puddle of water near the door of his store, pushen the water out into the street. He wears glasses and the glass flashes as he moves his head in time with the broom. The bristles of the broom have soaked up a lot of the dirty water and he works like they are heavy.

The town is quiet, like it's a Sunday, and the streets are wet from the rain. When I walk in the store the men look at me. They see I got no shoes on.

Sucked the pilens right out from under the bridge the drugstore man says. Craziest thing you ever saw. Help you he says to me. I got no money so I don' say anythen back.

The Dodge dealership down to the river the skinny man says. You know, Sims'. Say the cars was floaten up near around the ceilen. Water came in so fast nobody had time to move nothen. Earth dam couple miles up let go and that was all she wrote.

Don' I know the drugstore man says. He sweeps some water past my feet, looks at me again. You need somethen he says.

I was looken for some smokes I say. Cigarettes.

We got them the drugstore man says. All kinds. What was you looken for?

Camels I say.

Its a bunch of miles down the mountain and I feel tired, sick. I want to sit down and have a smoke. I wish I had some money. My feet hurt.

Yo Carl the drugstore man says. You want to go in there back of the counter and get a pack of Camels for me.

Sure the skinny man says. He gets the cigarettes and tosses them to me. I catch them against my chest and the pack crushes a little.

I got no money I say.

The drugstore man stops sweepen a minute. Some of the water he just got out the door trickles back in. It's dirty river water, brown on the white tile floor.

Day like today I guess that's all right he says. He grins at me and I know how dirty I am. I know how I look. He figures I got wiped out by the flood.

My daddy's dead I say.

The drugstore owner shakes his head.

What a day Carl says behind the counter. He shakes his head too, snags himself a pack of smokes. What a day. I don' tell them that my daddy was dead before the rain even started.

That's hard son the drugstore man says. Awful goddam hard.

You got to wonder what the Lord is up to the skinny man says. Leave a boy 'thout a father.

I figure that is the nicest thing I ever heard. All I want to do right then is sit down and cry. I tear the wrap off the pack of cigarettes and the drugstore man hands me his lighter, a plastic Cricket. Coleman's Since 1942 it says on the side, the name of his drugstore. I turn the striken wheel with my thumb and the lighter catches, sends up a good strong flame the very first time.

* * *

I suck in the smoke and the third cigarette tastes just as good as the first. There is nothen like a butt that somebody else has rolled in a machine for you and that don' leave pieces of tobacco on your tongue.

I sit out near the end of the bridge that must of used to connected the two parts of the town across the river. It was an old steel bridge that sat up on stone pilens, and the skinny man was right: the supports are clean gone and the span is down by the middle in the dark rushen river. Right near where I sit there's a sign that says Weight Limit 2 Tons.

I pull on the cigarette until it burns down near my fingers. I seen men that smoked so much they built up yellow callous on their thumb and pointer finger, could burn a smoke all the way down if they wanted to and never feel it at all. I can' do that and besides I got a whole pack yet to go. No use to be hard on myself. I flick the butt into the river and it is gone in the fast water almost even before I see it hit.

I have heard that in floods you will sometimes see animals and trees that got caught in the water goen downstream. I have not seen any by this time and figure they must all of been pushed down the river right at first when the water was highest. There probably won' be any again until the next time the river rises.

It is starten the hard rain again, not just the soft drizzle now, and I have to shield the fourth cigarette against the water to get it to light. The lighter catches the first try. I figure the cigarette will burn pretty well in the rain once I manage to start it goen. I am wet again but this time it is not so pleasant as it was this mornen. This time it is cold and nasty. I ain' sure what I will do. It is sure as hell I won' go back up the mountain.

After a while I may go up the river and look for the earth dam that let go and did all the damage. It must look pretty awful, busted open in the middle and oozen the river water over the lip of the hole, brown and thick with bottom mud. Not like the creeks up on the mountain but a real river and comen through just the way it wants with nothen to hold it back. Yessir, that would sure be somethen to see.

My Life as a West African Gray Parrot

LEIGH BUCHANAN BIENEN

I

THE DARK, I am in the dark. They have put the green cloth over my cage. I am in the dark once again. I smell the acrid felt. I smell the green of transitions, the particles of dust in the warp of the fabric which remind me of forests and terror. I am in the dark. I shall never fly again. Even my masterful imitation of the electric pencil sharpener will not pierce the dark. My master and mistress are talking in the corridor. "That will shut it up," she says, knocking the aluminum pan against the porcelain sink and causing me, as she knows, pain.

My cage sits on a squat wooden table in a room facing a kitchen. The smell of roasting pig sickens me, although the odor of tomatoes and basil reminds me of my duty to God. My mistress does not recognize my powers. She calls from the kitchen, "What do you know, plucked chicken?" A visitor thoughtfully suggests the parrot might like the door shut while she sniffles her way through the cutting of onions. Worse, they leave open the water-closet door, shouting things to one another from within. The animal odors do not offend me, but my master sprays a poisonous antiseptic on the fixtures which irritates my sensitive nostrils and threatens my divine coloration. The red of my tail will fade in fumes of ammonia or chlorine.

Like blood, the color of my red tail has its own startling quality. This extraordinary color makes my red feathers magical. The red is a vivid crimson which glows from across the room. The red is the source of my power, my beauty, which I possess only briefly. The red is set off by its contrast to the pearl gray of my breast. The ivory white skin around my eyes, and the gunmetal gray of my chipped beak. The feathers on my back shade to light gray at the root, leaving a line of charcoal along the knife's edge of my wing feathers.

It is difficult to remember how beautiful I once was. The silken gray feathers falling over a young, full breast in layers as delicate as the tracery of a waterfall, each hue of gray, each smudge of crimson in subtle harmony with the rest. Now only the surprising crimson remains, the purest blue-red of my tail and the hints of the same crimson in my remaining wing feathers. Now to my mistress's distress I have plucked my breast almost clean. Pink dots appear where the oval pinfeathers were. Tiny blood flecks materialize from my pores like crimson teardrops, but not like the crimson of my tail. This urge to destroy myself and my unbearable beauty comes over me in spurts and impedes my progress. In a rush I grab five, six or seven feathers and pull them out in a flurry. The pain is delicious. The mistress shrieks at me from the kitchen when she catches me at it: "Stop picking, filthy bird." But she cannot separate me from myself. Only I possess the engine to destroy my own beauty.

My master and mistress purchased me because they had been told I could talk. The owner of the pet store, a fat Indian with one milky blind eye, pulled out my red tailfeathers and sold them one by one. He told my master and mistress I could talk, not because he believed it but because recently I had bitten his finger through to the knuckle. He believed a parrot's bite was a curse. This same fat Indian failed to mention the magical qualities which caused my feathers to be valued by those who bought and sold them in windowless back rooms. My master and mistress praised my beauty with awe while the Indian, slumped in a small wooden chair in the back storeroom, wondered if he would catch a vile infection from my nasty bite.

The master and mistress proudly carried me home and installed me in a large cage on a table in the dining room, on top of a figured blue carpet and beside a tall window which let in the creamy winter light through white silk curtains. The cat came and curled up in a puddle of sunlight beneath my cage. At first the master and mistress fussed continually over my placement by the window. When the sun went down, at a remarkably early hour every afternoon, the master would jump up and pull the curtains shut. "The breeze will kill the bird," he shouted at his wife, as if she were not in the room. In reply she insisted that cold was no worry. She had seen pictures of parrots in the Jardin des Plantes shaking snowflakes off their wings. "But the draft, the draft, there must not be a draft," she shrieked. As the winter days shortened and became increasingly pale, this exchange was repeated. A small machine was installed in the dining room. Its angry red coils created a suffocating dryness which by itself almost catapulted me into my next incarnation. The heat radiating from those disagreeable wires bore no resemblance to the warmth of sunlight in my African jungle.

In those days a perch stood alongside my cage. On some afternoons, at the time when the winter light was strongest, my mistress would open the cage door allowing me to climb out onto the wooden perch, where I could stretch one wing then another slowly downward towards the floor. If the master was out, my mistress would sit down at the dining room table and recite speeches at me. The same sonorous words over and over. Her diction was beyond reproach on these occasions. Once she taped her voice and played it beside my cage for the entire day. I added to my repertoire the sibilant sounds of plastic across metal as the tape rewound itself on the white disc. Instead of her cultured tones I preferred the syncopated accents of the immigrant cleaning lady who muttered lilting obscenities as she scoured a shine into the inlaid tabletops in the living room.

During this early period I often whispered aloud, laughed, or simply whistled. The master and mistress were amazed when my laughter coincided with their amusement. They did not understand that laughter is a form of crying, that we laugh to keep our perception of the world from crumbling. My own laughter is a hollow chuckle, a sinister and frightening sound, recognizable as a laugh by its mirthlessness. When humans laugh they add wheezes and croaks to mask the sadness of laughter. My master and mistress do not yet understand that the highest form of communication is wordless, achieved by a glance upward or a bestial grunt, by the perception of a change in the rhythm of breathing, or by a blink of an eye, in my case the flicker of a brown membrane between lashless lids.

When visitors came into the dining room they used to remark, to the pleasure of my master and mistress: "Look! How it stares back at you." Meaning, they were surprised. My yellow eye pierced through whatever image they had manufactured of themselves, images of purpose and the aura of an imminent, important appointment which was constructed by a high, excited tone of voice. My yellow eyes can see behind a necklace of stones to the throb at the throat, behind thick tweed to the soft folds of the belly, to the dark roots of hair which has been falsely hennaed to a color which is a poor imitation of the red wings of the Amazonian parrot.

The guests were always amazed. At dinner advertising men and women in public relations were encouraged to speculate upon whether my mobile and bony throat (not yet exposed by picking) or my knobby, black tongue produced such extraordinary sounds. The mistress asked pensively: "Imagine how the bird speaks." The master replied with gravity: "The consonance between words and meaning is illusory."

At her urging they called in an expert in the field of Parrot Linguistics, a spectacled man who wore a Russian suit with wide, waving trousers. The mistress served him tea in a glass with a slice of lemon on the saucer. The man removed his thick glasses and examined the white papery skin surrounding my beak and nostrils. My beak was chipped, but he only commented, "I see nothing unusual about the beak or throat of this parrot."

"His tongue," my mistress urged, "look at his tongue. The bird has an exceptionally long and globular black tongue."

The expert had already donned his baggy jacket and removed his spectacles. "Yes," he said, "it is unusual for a bird to encompass such a wide range of laughter."

My imitations of the human voice exactly reproduced individual intonations. The precision of my imitation of the Polish servant rendered my mistress speechless with jealousy. Erroneously, the copywriters concluded mimicry was the source of my magic, and they congratulated my mistress on acquiring such a rare and amusing pet. In those early days of enthusiasm my mistress would wipe her finely manicured fingers upon a paper towel and scratch my skull, murmuring, "Now Polly, poor Polly, here Polly." In those days they both fed me tidbits from their table, corners of toast dripping with honey, a half eaten peach with chunks of amber flesh still clinging to the pit, or the thigh bone of a chicken, a treat of which I remain inordinately fond. I would sidestep over, slide down the metal bars of my cage with my head lowered, and take the tidbit in one curled claw.

The mistress carefully saved all of my red feathers in those days, picking them out from the newspaper shreds with her long red fingernails. She put them in a box of tooled leather and closed the lid so that the incandescence of red would not startle a stranger who happened to walk into the room. Later they became so alienated from the source of my beauty, and so quarrelsome, they no longer took pleasure or strength from the color of my tailfeathers. They even forgot to lock my cage and sometimes carelessly left the door open after shaking a few seeds hastily into my dish. During the earlier phase they were proud to possess me. They purchased bird encyclopedias and left them open on the table turned to pages with pictures of parrots. The painted drawing of the yellow-headed Amazon intrigued me and greatly contributed to my education. Feathers of the palest lemon cascaded down from the top of the head ending in a ring of creamier yellow around the neck. The white cockatoos also inspired envy, especially for the flecks of fine pink and light yellow which tinged their wings. I admired their crests, feathers as a flag to the world, and the white back feathers which had the sheen of ancient silk. Another source of wonder were the many-hued black parrots from South America, so advanced in beauty they are rarely glimpsed even by their own kind.

Now when they stand beside my cage, my master and mistress only discuss the price I will fetch. "Is it eight hundred dollars?" he asks. "The last advertisement in the paper had one listed at eight hundred dollars."

My mistress is greedier, but also more practical. "It will fetch more at an auction," she answers, "when people bid against each other in competition."

The refusal to acknowledge my sexual identity is a special humiliation. I laid an egg to announce my essentially female nature. Now that she hates and fears me, my mistress always refers to me in the impersonal third person. I have long since been moved away from the dining room, into a small dark room no bigger than a closet. The tiny unwashed window faces a bleak, blank wall of brick, and the door to a dark and dusty closet stands open behind my cage. The mistress uses my room for storage. The abandoned wire torso of a dress frame is a cage shaped in the outline of a woman. A broken vacuum cleaner lies coiled in permanent hibernation in one corner. Portraits of forgotten ancestors, who willed their property to other branches of the family, stand facing the wall. My cage is now cleaned only once a week. The room is too mean even to serve as an adequate storage facility. The fat, neutered gray cat no longer likes to visit me because there is no rug on the floor and the room is unheated. She curls herself in front of the refrigerator, where a small warm exhaust is continuously expelled from the motor. We exchange remarks about the deplorable spiritual condition of our custodians. The striped gray cat and I together speculate upon whether or not the master and mistress will in their next incarnation understand the power of red, as distinct from the power of blood, the sole power which now strikes fear in their hearts. Both the master and mistress show a measurable anger when the tiny flecks of blood appear against my gray skin. My blood is either light pink or a droplet of burgundy, both distinct from the singing crimson of my tail. When my mistress concluded that the picking was going to continue she began to think of ways to get rid of me. But she would not consider letting me go at a loss.

II

It is difficult for me to remember the jungle, the sun in Africa, or my days in the dark pet shop owned by the blind-eyed Indian. My journey must be almost finished, for only the young command memories. In my native jungle parrots are caught by blindfolded boys who climb to the tree-tops and rob the nests of their chicks. The mothers swoop down, diving with their gray and white heads tucked under, as they shriek their protests. They will attack and tear the flesh as the bald chicks disappear into a knotted cloth held in the teeth of a boy who shimmies down the trunk as fast as he can. The parrots beat their red-flecked wings around the heads of the nest robbers, biting an ear, frantically flying from branch to branch as they accompany the marauders to the edge of the forest with high-pitched screams. The village boys are blindfolded because they believe they will be struck blind if they look into a parrot's nest. To these people we have long been recognized as magic birds, lucky birds, or birds which carry a curse. And now we are almost extinct.

With six other featherless shivering chicks who died within a week I was brought to a pet shop in the middle of the urban sprawl which constitutes a city outside the jungle. The owner placed me in a cage on top of a teetering pile of small cages. One contained a banded snake with a festering hole in his side, another held a monkey with a crippled arm. There were also green parrots and yellow ones from neighboring forests.

Eventually I became an ornament in the compound of a king, living in a gilded cage on a vast veranda shaded by a roof of woven rattan. Every evening a servant boy peeled me an enormous rainbow-colored mango. My cage was a tall cylinder, large enough to fly across and decorated with tin bells and wooden totems. Visitors came especially to admire me from a distance. They did not press their faces within inches of my nostrils, oppressing me with the odor of skin. They stood back to gaze at my feathers and offered me meat. Like worshippers, they came in formal dress. The women were wrapped in cloth of bright blue, and the men wore flowing gold-embroidered gowns which swayed and brushed the floor as they walked rapidly towards me across the veranda. Another parrot was resident in this royal household. She taught me bearing, demeanor and style. She had been the property of kings through three generations. She remembered kings who had been forgotten by their heirs and successors, and her beautiful piercing whistle caused all those within earshot to stop talking and listen to her call. When she was found dead at the bottom of her cage one morning they buried her with incense and incantations, mourning her loss with ancient, certain ceremonies.

The royal family also had a dog, a brown cur with an extraordinarily long and ugly hairless tail. The dog had to be locked inside the royal compound, or he would have been eaten by the many hungry people outside the walls. The cur was fat, and the urchins who roamed the mud streets in packs would have snatched him for roasting or stewing. The animal was so dispirited and envious of the esteem in which parrots were held that he spent hours lying beside our large golden cage discussing philosophy. The youngest daughter of the king occasionally came barefoot onto the veranda and held his head on her lap while she fed him morsels of goat. Finally he became so fat and arthritic he could not climb the steps to the veranda. His view was that the vicissitudes of fate he suffered in this epoch were haphazard. In the next generation, he expressed this opinion while lying panting on the cool clay floor, it would be dogs with long tails, instead of birds with red feathers, who would be offered raw meat and worshipped for their wisdom. Who knows, he remarked with a supercilious snarl, whether or not the privileges you now enjoy because of your divine coloration will not be given to those with visible ears? He often called attention to his long, bald tail as if the tail by itself should have entitled him to all that he envied. On drowsy tropical afternoons my partner and I humored him by appearing to take these notions seriously.

III

It is true that when I strike I wound. I bit the finger of a small dirty boy to the bone when he poked a yardstick through the bars of my cage. His mother and my mistress were whispering in the kitchen, and they both ignored my shrieks of warning. The boy ran squawking in pain to his mother, and my embarrassed mistress banged the metal bars of my cage with a metal fork, shouting reproaches. The startled mother held her son to her breast and pressed a linen handkerchief of my master's to his limp finger. Furred tentacles of crimson stretched out along threads of cotton and silently eliminated the white between. The sniffling boy looked at me, where I was shivering in the farthest corner of my cage, and signalled his triumph.

I miss the treats, especially the blue-red marrow of chicken bones, which my mistress used to give me in an attempt to make me recite her name. In those days I used to climb upon the back of her hand. She held out her fist with the painted nails curled under, and I could feel her wince when I placed one gray claw and then the other against her skin. I uncoiled my talons to avoid cutting into the flesh of her hand and balanced myself by hooking onto the cage with my beak. She feared I would turn and strike for no reason, and her wrist would stiffen. At such times I was swept away by the sense of her as another living creature, myself at an earlier stage of development. This involuntary response filled me with sadness, for I thought of the generations and generations which remained before her, and I moved away from her hand and huddled on my perch, mourning as she soaped her hands at the kitchen sink. I no longer try to reach her, except with whistles and catcalls, for I know she has come to hate me. Sometimes I receive a reply. She will turn on the radio or rustle the newspaper in an answer.

If nothing else a cage has walls to climb. When my mistress enters the room I take my hooked beak and spill the seeds out of my plastic dish and onto the floor. I can spill almost all of my food in one angry gesture. My beak along the railings makes an insistent, drumming sound which never fails to evoke a click of annoyance from my mistress. When she leaves I slide down the bars and pick out sunflower seeds, the tiny grains of millet, and especially those very small twigs from among the shreds of newspaper. Sometimes my mistress and master discuss my fate in the corridor, using sign language. I can hear the faint rustle of sleeves as they gesture in the hallway. But I rarely listen. I am dreaming of my next life now. The cat curls up in front of the vent of the icebox. We plan together. She licks her paw, passes it over one ear, then her eye, softly.

I can still not resist music, especially the soprano tones. The high notes bring back memories of the sadness of being human. Until the music plays I can convince myself that I have reached a point where memories could no longer overcome me, a point where my feathers offer complete protection. But at the height of a melodic line I hide in the farthest corner of my cage, assaulted by emotions. The beauty of singing strikes home, into the depths of my parrot's heart. I relive my human life, the fears and promises of childhood, the exhilaration of striving, and the limited peace which settles in the breast on rare occasions. I surpass the highest notes with my own high-pitched shriek.

At first my mistress was delighted with these performances, calling the neighbors to witness. Later she shut the door when the radio played music, as if to keep me away from something. The music which I heard faintly from behind the closed door inspired me to dream, and when I sang I swooned, losing my footing on the perch, falling fluttering to the iron grate at the bottom of my cage. The music transported me back to the high trees of the rain forest where parrots flew from limb to limb high above the shrieking of monkeys, never leaving the shadowed protection of branches.

IV

The Attack. It came so startlingly that my screams of pain and fright escaped without thought. A large rat had crawled from the alleyway, through the old crumbling walls of our city house, into a crawlspace in the closet of my dark room. The door of my cage had been carelessly left open. The gray beast with brown ferret eyes slithered his soft fat body up the table leg and into my cage. He stuck his black snout into my food, spilling the seeds, and proceeded to stalk me with a cold-blooded ruthlessness born of generations of experience. In spite of his aged, spoiled softness, the beast struck swiftly, efficiently, with one bite after another, striking my wing, my leg, my throat, then pulling away from my reach. His rat snout twitched and the small dappled spots on his back quivered as he flattened himself to pounce once again at my neck, my throat. Shrieking, bleeding, I beat my wings helplessly against the inside of the cage. Feathers were everywhere. Blood splattered on the unclean walls from a bite on my chest, an open wound in my leg, and from a hole in my wing. In two bites he had pulled out all of my red tailfeathers. Aiming for the eye of the lumbering beast—in spite of his waddling gait, I could not place a fatal blow he was so insulated with fat—I bit the soft rubbery flesh of his nose. I dug my claws into the well-fed muscular shoulder until he turned his head and with bared buck teeth bit off one talon and a large part of the toe above it. Wounded, he went into retreat, his hairless tail threading its way around the door frame of the closet.

The attack must have been brief although my wounds were many. The vision of relentless, reasonless destruction remained: a fat waddling beast baring rodent teeth as he came to trap me in the corner of my cage. Hours later my mistress returned and found me shivering and barely alive, crouched on the bottom of my cage. At the sight of the blood, the scattered red and gray feathers, my mistress was distraught, especially when she realized her personal carelessness had exposed me to a danger which neither of us realized had been ever present.

For days and nights I was only aware of the electric light clicking on and off at intervals. My mistress, perhaps only regretting the loss of her financial investment, sat beside my cage and wept with a depth of feeling which kindled surprise even in my semiconscious state. Other visitors came and peered at me anxiously through the bars. Those who had marvelled at my feats of imitation came now to stand silently in front of my cage, disapprovingly clucking their tongues over the pity of it.

My bite wounds stopped bleeding almost immediately, but the shock to my spirit had been profound. Worse, a silent, raging infection daily gained upon me. Soon I could only rest my beak on the bottom rungs of my cage. Finally I could no longer stand. I simply crouched in a corner at the bottom of my cage and rested my head against the bars cursing the demon beast of destruction. I could no longer sing, speak or whistle. Every red feather was gone, and my wing and chest, where the feathers had been pulled out, were bare and covered with festering sores.

In the middle of the night my mistress took me to the veterinarian's hospital in the heart of the city, a large facility associated with an old and famous zoo. Although I could no longer raise my head, I felt no localized pain. A young man with a beard and a white coat picked me up in a towel, held me under a bright light, and put a stethoscope to my heart. With my last quantum of strength I flapped my mutilated wings in protest. Then the blessed darkness, my cage left on an antiseptic stainless-steel table, as the doctor switched off the bright light overhead behind him.

In the hospital it was impossible to distinguish night from day. The veterinarian in the white coat, his soft black eyes and his black beard made it difficult to determine his age, treated me with injections, ointments, and powerful medicines, monitoring my blood every few days. My leg was put in a splint and photographed. A milky white substance was applied to the open sores on my breast and wings. The veterinarian sat in front of my cage and talked softly to me as he wrote his day's reports in soft, smudgy pencil on a mimeographed form. When he looked up at me, so clinically, after scratching something on a paper attached to a clipboard, the vision of gray destruction was momentarily dispelled. Under his care I slowly began to regain my strength.

My mistress came to visit on occasion, although she hardly spoke or looked at me when she came. While I limped gingerly to the edge of the cage door, she would talk to the young girl whose function it was to inform the doctors of any unexpected events in the ward. In this large acrid room with concrete floors and row after row of cages, crises were frequent. Not all could be saved. My immediate neighbors were a white cat with cancer whose stomach had been shaved bare to expose a line of cross-stitches like teeth marks across her pale, pale pink skin, a dog whose back leg had been amputated so skillfully that if he stood in profile on his good side his silhouette looked whole, and a one-hundred-year-old yellow crested cockatoo whose anemia had been caused by a diet of nothing but sunflower seeds for over fifty years. She had been sent to the zoo for an evaluation by the heirs to an estate when she passed hands after the death of the old couple who bought her on their honeymoon in a pre-war London flea market.

During the latter part of my recuperation I was placed in a green-domed aviary in the zoo along with other tropical birds. The domed enclosure imitated the wild, which did not, I thought, properly prepare the displaced birds for spiritual progression through containment. Their instincts to fly, to be free, were inappropriately encouraged. Attitudes of confinement and limitation, required for passage onwards, were thwarted. In spite of my condition, I myself was overcome with a memory and desire for flight when I entered the dome, even though it had been years since I had been let out of my cage. The memory of flying overcame me with an exhilarating rush of recognition. To fly, to be free, to soar on a current of wind, seductive memories took over before I was able to re-establish the distance I had learned to impose at great cost to my spirit. The sunlight filtered through the green glass dome and through the imported foliage. I was unused to the soft, almost liquid light, unlike the dark chill of my room.

The tropical birds in the zoo immediately recognized that, unlike them, I had not been born in captivity. I was taken from the wild. Some had ancestors who were wild, but most, the exception being one all-black Amazonian parrot, were born in zoos, pet stores, or aviaries. They could not hope to compete with my heritage as the idol of kings. Two other members of my own species displayed themselves on a palm branch near the top of the green glass dome, showing that even in these circumstances they had learned to restrain from flight. One had a fine assortment of red flecks in the wing he stretched downward for my inspection.

I continued to hop away on my good leg, flap my wings and shriek at the touch of a human, but I knew I owed my resuscitation to the skill and expertise of the dark-eyed doctor. Those gentle educated fingers had deduced what was needed to make me well. His knowledge was the opposite of mine, gained measuring things outside of himself, mine the mastery of the mysteries within.

The creamy chill of winter passed into the shy green of spring. The doctor considered me well enough to go home. My mistress came and carefully listened to his instructions. The doctor never commented upon the cause of my injury, but upon arriving back in the apartment I saw the hole in the closet wall had been hastily covered over with a piece of plywood and a few nails.

After my stay in the hospital my mistress began covering my cage at night, perhaps because my laughter in the dark unnerved her, perhaps to protect her investment. Those occasional shrieks at midnight, attempts to discover if there were kindred spirits in the neighborhood, might have been frightening. One evening the mistress bustled into my small room with a large piece of green felt. It was an especially unusual occurrence because she rarely came close to my cage now, asking the master or even a casual visitor to sprinkle a few seeds into my dish. The first time she walked in with the cover she threw it without warning over my cage as I hissed and flapped my wings. Then she slammed the door shut.

My age, my great age weighs heavily upon me when the cover floats down over the cage for the night. The cover stills my voice, blocks out my vision of even this closet where I will be confined for the rest of my parrot life, unless I am rescued by a stroke of fortune or sold again. If another epoch is coming when parrots are worshipped and fed mangoes and red meat, I do not think I will live to see it. My fate will be to die in this tiny cage, surrounded by my own filth, without love, and reliant upon a natural enemy for conversation. The snow outside makes the wall behind my cage as chill as the marble of tombstones, and I long for the damp warmth of the jungle. What joy have I except the joy of my own whistle? Sometimes the city birds answer my imitations of their calls. Soon I shall be beyond the need to communicate, at a level where I recognize that the attempt to pass messages between living things is as foolish as words. In my next life I will live for five hundred years in a form which is incapable of development or destruction. Perhaps then the dog with his long tail will have assumed my position as teacher, scholar and despised pet, and the cat will be left to sleep undisturbed in the limbo of sunlight.

The master and mistress are huddled together in bed now, happy to know I am temporarily silenced. I hear the creak of the springs, a cough, the single click of the light switch, which I answer perfectly. I shut one yellow eye and wait for the morning.

At the Krungthep Plaza

PAUL BOWLES

It WAS THE DAY when the President of the United States was due to arrive with his wife on a visit to the King and Queen. Throughout the preceding afternoon squads of men had been running up and down the boulevard, dragging with them heavy iron stands to be used as barricades along the curbs. Mang Huat rose from his bed sweaty and itching, having slept very little during the night. Ever since he had been advised that the procession would be passing in front of the hotel he had been awaiting the day with mounting dread. The smallest incident could jeopardize his career. it needed only one lunatic with a hand grenade.

With distaste he pulled aside the curtains near his bed and peered out into the light of the inauspicious day. Later, when he had showered, he returned to the window and stood for a long time. Above the city the gray sky was ahum with helicopters; so far none had hit the tops of the highest chedis towering above the temples, but people in the street watched with interest each time an object clattered overhead in the direction of a nearby spire. At times, when a police car was on its way through the quarter, all traffic was suspended, and there would follow an unusual, disturbing hush in which he could hear only the whir of the insects in the trees. Then there would come other sounds of life, farther away: the cries of children and the barking of dogs, and they too were disturbing, these naked noises in place of the unceasing roar of motors.

No one seemed to know when the royal cortege would go by. The radio had announced the time as ten o'clock, but gossip in the lobby downstairs, reportedly straight from police headquarters, fixed the starting hour as noon. Mang Huat decided not to have breakfast, nor indeed to eat at all until the danger had passed and he was free from tension.

He sat behind his desk tapping the point of an eyetooth with his fingernail, and looking thoughtfully across at Miss Pakun as she typed. The magenta silk curtains at his office windows stirred slightly with the breath of an oscillating fan. They gave the room a boudoir glow in which a motion or a posture sometimes could seem strangely ambivalent. Today the phenomenon, rather than stimulating him, merely increased the distrust he had been feeling with regard to his secretary. She was unusually attractive and efficient, but he had to tell himself that this was not the point. He had engaged her in what he considered good faith, assuming that the information she had written on her application form was true. He had chosen her from among several other equally presentable applicants because she bore the stamp of a good bourgeois upbringing.

His equivocal feelings about Miss Pakun dated from the previous week, when his cashier, Udom by name, had reported seeing her walking along the street in an unsanitary and disreputable quarter of Thonburi on the other side of the river. Udom knew the area well; it was a neighborhood of shacks, mounds of garbage, opium houses and brothels. If she lived over there, why had she given the Sukhumvit address? And if not, what legitimate excuse could she have for visiting this unsavory part of the city? He had even wondered if Pakun were her true name.

Mang Huat was proud of his three-room suite at the Krungthep Plaza. At thirty-two he was manager of the hotel, and that pleased him. Through a small window in the wall of his salon he could, if he felt so inclined, look down into the lobby and see what was happening in almost every corner of it. He never used the peephole. It was enough that the staff knew of its existence.

From where he sat he could hear the trickle of the fountain in the next room. A friend, recently removed to Hong Kong, had left it with him, and he had spent a good deal of money getting it installed. Miss Pakun coughed, probably to remind him that he was smoking. She always coughed when he smoked. On a few occasions when she had first come to work for him he had put out his cigarette. Today he was not much concerned with the state of her throat. Nor, he thought, did he care whether she lived at the elegant address in Sukhumvit or in a slum alley of Thonburi. He no longer had any intention of forging an intimate friendship with her.

Late in the morning Udom knocked on his door. Udom was a friend from university days, down on his luck, who had begged for work at the hotel. Mang Huat, persuaded that it was unrealistic to expect any man to possess more than one good quality, had given the job of cashier to Udom, who was unreliable but honest.

Ever since his uncle's partner had placed him in his present exalted position, Mang Huat had experienced the bliss of feeling sheltered from the outside world. Today for the first time that delicious peace of mind was being threatened. It was absurd, he knew; there was little likelihood of an accident, but any situation beyond his control caused him undue anxiety.

Udom came over to the desk and murmured gloomily that the American Security men were downstairs asking for a passkey to the rooms. I told them

I'd have to speak to you, he went on. It's not obligatory, you know. Only the keys of certain specific rooms, if they ask for them.

I know that, said Mang Huat. Give them a passkey.

The guests are going to object.

Mang Huat bridled. What difference does that make? Give them whatever keys they ask for. Just be sure you get them all back.

It scandalized him that anyone should hesitate to accept this added protection, but it was part of Udom's weakness always to create complications and find objections. Mang Huat suspected that he had not entirely outgrown his youthful Marxist sympathies, and sometimes he wondered if it had been wise to take him on to the staff.

Pangs of hunger were making his nervousness more acute. It was twenty-five minutes past one. Miss Pakun had not yet returned from lunch. All at once he realized that a new sound which filled the air outside had been going on for some time. He stepped to the window. The big official cars were rolling past, and at a surprising speed. His eye suddenly caught the two white Bentleys from the palace, enclosed by their escort of motorcycles. He held his breath until they were gone. Even then he listened for a minute before he telephoned to order his lunch.

Late in the afternoon the receptionist rang his office to say that a guest was demanding to see him. Suddenly the threat was there again. I can't see anyone, he said, and hung up.

Five minutes later Udom was on the wire. I was afraid this would happen, he said. An Englishman is complaining that the police searched his room.

Tell him I'm not in my office, said Mang Huat. And to Miss Pakun: No incoming calls. You hear?

Twilight had come down all at once, brought on by a great black cloud that swelled above the city. The thought occurred to him that he could let Miss Pakun go now, before the rain came. He stood at the window staring out. The city sparkled with millions of extra lights; they were looped in fanciful designs through the branches of the trees across the canal. A triumphal arch had been built over the entrance to the bridge, spectacularly floodlighted in red and blue to show a thirty-foot-high face of the visiting president, with appropriate words of welcome beneath, in English and Thai.

The buzzer in the antechamber sounded. Miss Pakun answered it, and a bellboy in scarlet uniform came in with a note on a tray. He's had smallpox, Mang Huat said to himself. Who can have hired him? On his pad he scribbled a reminder to have the boy discharged in the morning, and took the note from him. Udom had written: *The man is in the bar getting the guests to sign a petition. I think you should see him.*

Mang Huat read the note twice in disbelief. Then he pounded the desk once with his fist, and Miss Pakun glanced up. Because he was angry, he reminded himself that above all he must keep his composure. With such malcontents it was imperative to be adamant, and not to allow oneself to be drawn into discussion, much less argument.

The buzzer sounded. Tell him I'll be free in five minutes, he said to Miss Pakun.

There was no longer any question of letting her go before the storm broke. She would simply have to take her shoes off, like other people in that squalid quarter where she surely lived, and wade barefoot through the puddles and ponds, to the end of the alley where a taxi could not take her. In a moment she came back in and sat down, patting her hair and smoothing her skirt. At that moment a police car must have been in the neighborhood, for there was one of the sudden ominous silences outside. While Miss Pakun carefully applied a whole series of cosmetics to her features, he sat in the stillness and heard a gecko chatter beyond the air-conditioning box behind him; the tentative chirruping pierced the slight whir of the motor. And the insects in the trees still droned. He was sorry he had made a time limit. The five minutes of silence seemed like twenty. When the time was up Miss Pakun, resplendent, rose once more and turned to go out. Mang Huat stopped her.

No typing please, while the man is here, he said crisply. Only shorthand. You can do it. (Her face had begun to change its expression.) This is an agitator, he stressed. We must have a record of everything he says.

Miss Pakun always grew timid and claimed insufficient knowledge of English if he asked her to transcribe a conversation in that language. The results of her work, however, were generally successful. Mang Huat glowered. You must get every word. He may threaten me.

The visitor came in, followed by Miss Pakun. He was young, and looked like a university student. With a brief smile he sat down in a chair facing Mang Huat, and said: Thank you for letting me in.

Mang Huat took this as sarcasm. You came to complain?

You see, the young man began, I'm trying to get an extension of my tourist visa without leaving the country.

Mang Huat slapped the desk hard with the flat of his hand. Someone has made a mistake. You are looking for the Immigration Department. My secretary will give you the address.

The young man raised his voice. I was trying to lead up to my complaint. But I'll make it now. It's an affront to your guests to allow the Americans into the rooms.

Ah! Perhaps you should complain to the Thai police, Mang Huat suggested, standing up to show that the meeting was at an end. My secretary can also give you that address.

The young Englishman stared at him for an instant with patent disgust. You're the perfect manager for this abject institution, he muttered. Then, seeing that Miss Pakun had risen and was holding the door open for him, he got up and stalked out, doing his best to slam the outer door of the antechamber behind him. Equipped against such rough treatment, the door merely gave its usual cushioned hiss. Coming at that moment, the sound, which to Mang Huat represented the very soul of luxury, caused him to heave a sigh of pure sensuous pleasure.

That will be all, he told Miss Pakun. She took up her handbag, showed him her most luscious smile for the fraction of a second, and shut the door behind her.

It was now night, and the rain was falling heavily. Miss Pakun would get very wet, he thought, a twinge of pity spicing his satisfaction. He went into the next room and lay back on the divan to watch television for a few minutes. Then he got up. It was the moment to make his evening excursion to the kitchen and, having examined the food, order his dinner. He lighted a cigarette and took the elevator down to the lobby.

In front of the reception desk he frowned with disapproval at the spots left on the carpet by the wet luggage being brought in. At that moment he happened to glance across the crowded lobby, and saw Miss Pakun emerge from the bar, accompanied by the young Englishman. They went directly out into the street. By the time Mang Huat was able to get over to the door, walking at a normal pace, they were climbing into a taxi. He stepped outside, and, sheltered by the marquee, stood watching the cab disappear into the downpour.

On his way to the kitchen he stopped at the cashier's desk, where he recounted to Udom what he had just seen. He also told him to give Miss Pakun her final paycheck in the morning and to see that under no circumstances was she to get upstairs to his office.

A prostitute, he said with bitter indignation. A common prostitute, masquerading as an intelligent, educated girl.

The Black Queen

BARRY CALLAGHAN

HUGHES AND McCRAE were fastidious men who took pride in their old colonial house, the clean simple lines and stucco walls and the painted pale blue picket fence. They were surrounded by houses converted into small warehouses, trucking yards where houses had been torn down, and along the street, a school filled with foreign children, but they didn't mind. It gave them an embattled sense of holding on to something important, a tattered remnant of good taste in an area of waste overrun by rootless olive-skinned children.

McCrae wore his hair a little too long now that he was going grey, and while Hughes with his clipped moustache seemed to be a serious man intent only on his work, which was costume design, McCrae wore Cuban heels and lacquered his nails. When they'd met ten years ago Hughes had said, "You keep walking around like that and you'll need a body to keep you from getting poked in the eye." McCrae did all the cooking and drove the car.

 But they were not getting along these days. Hughes blamed his bursitis but they were both silently unsettled by how old they had suddenly become, how loose in the thighs, and their feet, when they were showering in the morning, seemed bonier, the toes longer, the nails yellow and hard, and what they wanted was tenderness, to be able to yield almost tearfully, full of a pity for themselves that would not be belittled or laughed at, and when they stood alone in their separate bedrooms they wanted that tenderness from each other, but when they were having their bedtime tea in the kitchen, as they had done for years using lovely green and white Limoges cups, if one touched the other's hand then suddenly they both withdrew into an unspoken, smiling aloofness, as if some line of privacy had been crossed. Neither could bear their thinning wrists and the little pouches of darkening flesh under the chin. They spoke of being with younger people and even joked slyly about bringing a young man home, but that seemed such a betrayal of everything that they had believed had set them apart from others, everything they believed had kept them together, that they sulked and nettled away at each other, and though nothing had apparently changed in their lives, they were always on edge, Hughes more than McCrae.

One of their pleasures was collecting stamps, rare and mint-perfect, with no creases or smudges on the gum. Their collection, carefully mounted in a leatherbound blue book with seven little plastic windows per page, was worth several thousand dollars. They had passed many pleasant evenings together on the Directoire settee arranging the old ochre- and carmine-colored stamps. They agreed there was something almost sensual about holding a perfectly preserved piece of the past, unsullied, as if everything didn't have to change, didn't have to end up swamped by decline and decay. They disapproved of the new stamps and dismissed them as crude and wouldn't have them in their book. The pages for the recent years remained empty and they liked that; the emptiness was their statement about themselves and their values, and Hughes, holding a stamp up into the light between his tweezers, would say, "None of that rough trade for us."

One afternoon they went down to the philatelic shops around Adelaide and Richmond Streets and saw a stamp they had been after for a long time, a large and elegant black stamp of Queen Victoria in her widow's weeds. It was rare and expensive, a dead-letter stamp from the turn of the century. They stood side by side over the glass counter-case, admiring it, their hands spread on the glass, but when McCrae, the overhead fluorescent light catching his lacquered nails, said, "Well, I certainly would like that little black sweetheart," the owner, who had sold stamps to them for several years, looked up and smirked, and Hughes suddenly snorted, "You old queen, I mean why don't you just quit wearing those goddamn Cuban heels, eh? I mean why not?" He walked out leaving McCrae embarrassed and hurt and when the owner said, "So what was wrong?" McCrae cried, "Screw you," and strutted out.

Through the rest of the week they were deferential around the house, offering each other every consideration, trying to avoid any squabble before Mother's Day at the end of the week when they were going to hold their annual supper for friends, three other male couples. Over the years it had always been an elegant, slightly mocking evening that often ended bitter-sweetly and left them feeling close, comforting each other.

McCrae, wearing a white linen shirt with starch in the cuffs and mother-of-pearl cuff links, worked all Sunday afternoon in the kitchen and through the window he could see the crab-apple tree in bloom and he thought how in previous years he would have begun planning to put down some jelly in the old pressed glass jars they kept in the cellar, but instead, head down, he went on stuffing and tying the pork loin roast. Then in the early evening he heard Hughes at the door, and there was laughter from the front room and someone cried out, "What do you do with an elephant who has three balls on him . . . you don't know, silly, well you walk him and pitch to the giraffe," and there were howls of laughter and the clinking of glasses. It had been the same every year, eight men sitting down to a fine supper with expensive wines, the table set with their best silver under the antique carved wooden candelabra.

Having prepared all the raw vegetables, the cauliflower and carrots, the avocados and finger-sized miniature corns-on-the-cob, and placed porcelain bowls of homemade dip in the center of a pewter tray, McCrae stared at his reflection for a moment in the window over the kitchen sink and then he took a plastic slipcase out of the knives-and-forks drawer. The case contained the dead-letter stamp. He licked it all over and pasted it on his forehead and then slipped on the jacket of his charcoal-brown crushed velvet suit, took hold of the tray, and stepped out into the front room.

The other men, sitting in a circle around the coffee table, looked up and one of them giggled. Hughes cried, "Oh my God." McCrae, as if nothing were the matter, said, "My dears, time for the crudités." He was in his silk stocking feet, and as he passed the tray he winked at Hughes who sat staring at the black queen.

Homework

MARGARET DRABBLE

I HOPE I don't give the impression that I'm complaining about her behaviour. On the contrary, I know she has always been very good to me, very generous with her time, very friendly and sympathetic—and I can't really expect it, there's absolutely no reason why she should see me at all. She's a very busy woman, I know—I'm always telling her that I realize how busy she is, and that she mustn't let me put her out, that the minute I start boring her with my little worries she must just tell me to pack up and go. And she never does—to do her justice she never does, and even on this last occasion (and I was a little upset)—well, I quite understood how she felt. No, she has always been very generous to me. I always make it perfectly clear to her that all she has to do if she wants to put me off is just give me a ring. I'm always in, I say. You're the busy one, not me, I'm nobody, I always say: just you give me a ring if you can't manage Tuesday, we can easily fix another day. I'm *always* free. But she never does.

So you can imagine how uneasy it made me, to see her treat Damie so badly. It's so unlike her, she's such a patient, generous, understanding person, and that poor little boy—well, he's not so little now, he must be about twelve, I suppose—but he certainly does get the rough end of her tongue. And the other day—I was really shocked. I wanted to say something, but I didn't know how to, and it was hardly my place.

I got there as usual, at about half past five. She always says, come round as soon as you like—I used to get there at about half past six, in time for supper, but lately I've got into the habit of arriving an hour or so earlier, so we can chat over tea. Once I got there about five, and she was on the telephone, and she stayed on it for hours and hardly looked at me once while she was talking—so, I've been careful not to get there before half past, recently. Once, I got to her street so early I had to walk round and round the block to fill in the time, and I met her on one of the rounds; she was rushing down to the butcher, forgotten to buy the mince for supper—funny, how it's usually mince when I go, I can't imagine they have mince every evening—and she said "Whatever are you doing?" and I said "Oh, just walking round the block, I didn't want to bother you by getting there too early—" and she said not to be silly, to come along in at once, so I did. But I still don't really like to get there much before half past five, if I can help it. It doesn't seem fair on her: she always seems to have so much left to do when she gets back from work. Of course, she says she doesn't mind me being there while she's getting supper ready: she likes to have someone to talk to, she says. I always offer to help her, but she says she's not very good at being helped, she'd rather do things herself.

Anyway, on this particular evening I got there at about twenty past five: she was just clearing away the tea things. I thought she looked a bit tired, and I told her so, but she said it wasn't anything particular: she'd had a late night the night before (she tells *me* that she has to be in bed by eleven) and then a long day at the studio: they started work at eight, for some reason. She didn't tell me much about the programme, so I gathered it wasn't going too well, and tactfully kept off the subject. She asked me how I was getting on with Mary (that's the woman I share a flat with), and how my father was, and I told her about them. (My father's in an Old People's Home: I see him at weekends.) I told her about them, while she started chopping up onions and things to go in the mince. (I wish she wouldn't put green pepper in: I've noticed that everyone fishes it out except her.) While I was trying to explain about Mary and how she couldn't go on an Easter holiday with me after all although she'd said she would be free, the phone went three times: two business calls, and one call that she put down *very* sharply, I thought. "Now look," she said, in this very odd tone, "now look, you'll have to ring again later. And mind you do. I'll be very very annoyed with you if you don't ring later." It didn't sound like her at all: I could tell she was irritable, from her voice. I'm glad she doesn't use that tone to me. But I suppose it is annoying, the phone going all the time, and the children running in and out. "Oh, buzz off, Kate," she kept saying to the little girl, who kept coming in to show her things she was making (origami, it was)—"oh, buzz off, Kate, go and watch telly, I'm trying to talk to Meg, can't you see?" She really was a bit sharp, but nothing like as sharp as she was to Damie later. Anyway, I don't think Kate is as sensitive as Damie, she just went whistling back to the television, which they seem to watch all day and night, or at least when I'm there.

I was just explaining about the fact that Mary had already talked me into paying a deposit for the cottage for Easter when there was another interruption: the front door bell, this time, and she gave such a start that she chopped her finger on the chopping knife. *"I'll* answer it," I said, and set off down the corridor, but she wouldn't have that: no, she had to answer it herself, and off she went, dripping blood and sucking her finger. I couldn't quite see who it was: it was a man, I think, delivering something, but she'd put it down by the time she reached the kitchen. She didn't tell me who it was. Then we had ten minutes to ourselves before the phone went again: I knew who it was this time, it was her ex-husband, Tony. She always puts on that special brisk tone when she speaks to him. I know it conceals a lot of pain, but you certainly wouldn't guess it, unless you knew her well, like I do. Obviously he wanted to discuss something to do with one of the children: I could almost hear what he was saying, he's got such a loud voice. They talked for a few minutes, with her trying to put him off: I started to read the paper to show I wasn't listening, and after a while she said firmly, "Now look, Tony, I can't talk now, Meg's here," and he rang off almost at once. I smiled at her as she came back to the chopping block, feeling quite pleased to have fulfilled the humble little function of having helped to get rid of him, but she didn't look too pleased.

Still, I must say she was very nice about Mary. She even offered to lend me the deposit money until I could get it back from the travel agency, if I was hard up. I declined, of course. I don't like borrowing money, even from someone like her who's got plenty of it. And she agreed with me that Mary had behaved very thoughtlessly—people are *so* inconsiderate, we agreed, they never think of the other person's feelings, they never even notice when they're causing inconvenience. Yes, it's amazing how insensitive people can be, she said, when Damie burst in again (I forgot to say, he'd already been in several times)—anyway, he burst in for about the fifth time, this time with some question about his history homework. Now if it had been me, I know I'd have tried to pay the poor boy a little attention, but she snapped at him in a terrible voice, "Oh, for Christ's sake, Damie, bugger off, can't you, can't you see I'm trying to talk to Meg?" To do the child justice, he hardly batted an eyelid. He just pottered off again with his textbook. But one never ought to speak to a child like that, even if one *is* a working mother. Particularly if, like her, you're always trying to put over the image of yourself as a kind of superwoman.

Anyway, by this time she was looking a little flustered, and what with one thing and another she still hadn't got the shepherd's pie in the oven, and it was getting on for half past six. I asked again if I could help, but she said there wasn't anything I could do, unless I wanted to go and get myself and her a drink, from the other room. So I said I would, to humour her, really, because I'm not much of a drinker. (She is, though. I've sometimes been astonished by the amount she puts away. I've seen her get through well over a quarter of a bottle of gin in the evening.) So I went off into the other room to the table where she keeps the drinks: I knew she'd have gin and water (mother's ruin) because she always does, but I thought I'd have a Dubonnet and bitter lemon. There was some Dubonnet left in a very dusty bottle, probably the same bottle that I had some from last time (I don't think she likes it) but I couldn't see any bitter lemon, so I went back into the kitchen and asked her if she'd got any anywhere else. She said she might have got some in the cellar, and I said I'd go down and look for it, but she said better not, I'd never find it, and anyway it was very dark and cobwebby down there and the light was broken. So I said not to bother, I was quite happy to have the Dubonnet by itself or with tonic or soda. But she'd already set off down into the cellar, and I could hear her stumbling around down there. "Don't worry," I shouted, "I don't want to be a nuisance, I'll be perfectly happy with sherry instead"—but I was too late. I heard her swear as she fell over something—she does use bad language, but perhaps everybody does these days—and then she came up with a very old-looking bottle of bitter lemon. "Honestly," I said, "I'd have been *perfectly* happy with something else." "Oh, that's all right," she said, and at last got around to getting the pie in the oven. At this rate, I thought, looking at my watch, we'll be lucky if we eat before half past seven. And I hadn't had anything except a Mars Bar and a ham sandwich since lunch.

One would have thought things would quieten down a little then, and I did hope they would, because I was really looking forward to asking her what she thought about what Dr. Scott had said about trying to reduce my Tranquillex prescription: he thinks that's what's been making me put on so much weight lately. Apparently it's a common side effect. Also, of course, I wanted a chance to hear about her programme. But things didn't turn out that way. No sooner had we sat down at the kitchen table (she poured herself out an enormous tumblerful of gin, at least it looked enormous to *me* but perhaps there was a lot of water in it)—no sooner had we sat down (she was putting a plug on a table lamp that the cat had knocked over and fused, I've often noticed how incapable she is of just sitting down and doing nothing)—no sooner had we sat down, than the twins burst in, dressed in some funny-looking uniform, saying they'd just got back from the Woodcraft Folk meeting. To tell you the truth, I'd hardly noticed they weren't there, the house was already so noisy without them. They really are the sweetest children, and very happy, amazing when you think how little time their mother has for them—anyway, then we had to listen to a long rigmarole about what they'd been up to at the Woodcraft Folk, which they said was a kind of guerrilla warfare training for Marxist boy scouts—very funny, I suppose, though I don't think I'd like eight-year-olds of mine to be quite so precocious. Then they saw that we were having a drink, and began to demand bottles of Coke and crisps and peanuts and something called Corn Crackers. And she found she hadn't any Coke, so she sent them off to the Off-Licence to buy some, and a packet of Corn Crackers each for all the kids, and one for me. (They were quite nice, actually.)

But what with one thing and another, we'd hardly had time to exchange more than two sentences quietly together before the pie was ready and it was supper time. And those two sentences weren't very satisfactory: she said she couldn't possibly advise me about the Tranquillex, not being a qualified doctor, but that if I wanted to lose weight, perhaps I ought to join Weight Watchers. In other words, she missed the point entirely.

The pie was quite nice, and to do her justice I did notice that Damie at least had stopped fishing the green pepper out, so perhaps one can force anyone to like anything in the end. As usual, there wasn't any dessert, only fruit and cheese. She says she hates making puddings, and anyway, she says, they do one no good. Quite right, I suppose.

It was half past eight by the time we had finished, and then, thank goodness, the twins went off to put themselves to bed, and Kate went to watch television, and Damie went off to finish his homework, and I helped with the washing up. At least she thought I was good enough to help with that. So we did have some time to talk. She asked me more about how I was getting on with Mary—really getting on, not just this business about the cottage—and was really sympathetic, as she used to be when I first met her, and not just listening with half an ear, as she is so often these days. And also, she asked me some more about Dr. Scott, and asked if I'd ever thought of having any psychiatric treatment, and told me some story about a friend of hers who was getting remarkable results. I said, however could I afford it, we weren't all as rich as her and her friends, and that anyway I didn't really have much faith in that kind of thing, and she agreed, and put the coffee on, and poured herself another gin. (I didn't know people drank gin *after* dinner. I said I didn't want anything more to drink.)

We had coffee in the kitchen, to avoid disturbing the children in the other room. Damie always does his homework in front of the blaring telly, and how he manages to do so well at school is a mystery to me. Modern children *are* a mystery. She told me a story about a man at work who kept trying to take her out to dinner, and then the phone went—again—it was her sister this time, and they went on for hours, some problem about her sister's baby's nursery school which they both seemed to find extremely amusing, though I couldn't see the joke myself. When she rang off, finally, the phone went again the moment she put it down, and I think it must have been the caller who had annoyed her so much earlier, because she snapped back very abruptly with that same funny note—"Oh, it's you is it, yes, I know I told you to ring again later, but it's not later enough, it's still early—" and then there was a longish silence, while she listened to the other person, and I couldn't hear a word, because unlike her ex-husband Tony the other person was speaking very softly. And then, she said, in a softer tone, but still, I thought, very irritable, "Oh. Oh, yes, I see. Well, that's different, isn't it? Yes, eleven should be all right. About eleven. See you soon." (Hear from you soon, I suppose she meant.) "Till later, then," she said, and rang off.

She seemed in a slightly better temper, oddly enough, after this call, and started to tell me about her ex-husband's new girlfriend, and how well the two of them were getting on, and how she hoped that he would make up his mind to marry her. She puts a brave face on things, I'll say that for her. And, as the atmosphere was a little more peaceful, I thought I'd tell her about Mary's husband and how tiresome he's being over the allowance he's supposed to pay. But just as I embarked on it, Kate came in to say Goodnight, and Damie came in with his homework. He wanted her to help him. It was physics, and she said she'd never been any good at physics, and he said that didn't matter, it was supposed to be just common sense at this stage (they do the Nuffield course, I think), to which she said that she'd never had any common sense either; but she agreed to have a look at it, and I could see her getting cross all over again when she found she couldn't understand it. So I asked her if I could have a look (not that I'm any good at physics either, but two heads are better than one) but she rather childishly said No, she wanted to be able to understand it herself, and that if a child of twelve was supposed to be able to do it surely she could too.

It would have been all right, I suppose, if Damie hadn't leant over the table while he was trying to explain something in the textbook to her, and knocked over the table lamp that she'd just been fixing. And then I really don't know what happened to her. She flew into such a rage, I've never seen anything like it. She picked the lamp up and hurled it at the wall, then she threw the physics textbook at Damie's head and started hurling abuse at the poor boy—such terrible language too, I hope he didn't understand it—and then she picked up her coffee cup and threw that after him, as he retreated down the corridor. I can't tell you how astonished I was. I was really amazed. And this was the capable woman we're all supposed to think is such a model of efficiency and calm. Poor Damie, I didn't know what to do, I could hear him crying in the other room. I didn't know what to say to her either: I said something about how she must be feeling tired after such a long day and not to blame herself too much, but she'd buried her head in her hands and wouldn't answer. I said I'd make her another cup of coffee, but she still said nothing. So I just sat there for a while, then I said, "Shall I go and see how Damie is?" and she muttered that it would be better to leave him alone, and if I didn't mind very much she thought she'd go to bed, perhaps she wasn't feeling too good after all.

So I could hardly stay on after that, could I? I picked up the lamp and put the bits of coffee cup in the bin. It was still only half past nine, and usually I don't leave till eleven, but there didn't seem much point in staying. She didn't seem to want to fix another day to see me: give me a ring, she kept saying. I wonder if she'd had too much to drink.

Anyway, I felt I had to go. I put my head round the sitting room door on my way out, and Damie seemed all right again: he was getting on with the homework as though nothing much had happened. When I got out, though, instead of walking straight to the tube, I walked round the block, thinking I'd look in through the sitting room window on my way back. I was still feeling anxious about Damie, of course. (She never draws the curtains: the whole street can see in.)

And would you believe it, when I got back round the block and looked in, there were she and Damie, sitting on the settee together, hugging each other and laughing their heads off. Laughing, they were. I can't think what at. There didn't seem to be anything to laugh at, to me.

So I went and caught the tube home.

You know, sometimes I think she's a little unbalanced. I wouldn't like to suggest it myself, but I really do think she could do with some kind of treatment.

Death's Midwives

MARGARETA EKSTRÖM

NOT UNTIL she lost her hair did she begin to cry. It fell out in tufts, she held handfuls of it. Bewildered, she ran her hand over the top of her head, feeling its familiar shape. Her ears resisted the pressure of her hand, folded resiliently. Her forehead was damp, her nose pointed. I'm going bald, she thought. Then she began to cry.

She was sixty-four years old and couldn't remember crying for twenty years. Not like this, she thought, when she sat up at last and turned her tear-drenched pillow to the cool side. These were tears not of anger but of total surrender, tears from the very deepest roots of grief. Tears that involved her entire body, leaving her thinner and weaker, ravaged and fragile. Anything could happen to her now. She was defenseless, shaken by forces stronger than those she called upon in moments of anger, indignation, occasional hysteria.

After a brief nap she stared up at the gray ceiling. There was a crack that resembled the Gulf of Finland, a damp spot that was Leningrad. She was around forty and had just come home from a trip there. Museums had unravelled their corridors for her and displayed their paintings. She was only forty and the painful lump in her abdomen was, of course, the child. When she turned her head she had the same view now as she had had then: the tall, candy-pink buildings and beyond them the park, with chestnuts in bloom, green clouds of elm, and maples bursting into leaf, so clear she thought she could smell them. But she had lost the scents long ago. Something was growing and pressing: was she going to give birth through her ear?

The walls were calm and receptive. She had asked to have the picture removed: two red tulips in a clay pot and a black book coquettishly angled in the bottom right-hand corner. Sometimes she looked for the hole where the hook had been. When she had laboriously hunted out her glasses she could see it easily and it became a hook for her to hang her thoughts on. As long as I can see the hole, she would think, imagining how she would fix her eyes on that black spot in her hour of need, finally to be swallowed up by that minute tunnel and enclosed in the wall. Like so many others who began as small floundering bodies and ended up as one single thin trembling sigh, swallowed up by these walls.

"What about some hair tonic for me?" she asked, when the day nurse came in. But she didn't get the joke, unfortunately, and hesitated for one awful moment between a sympathetic smile, astonishment, and something bordering on accusation. All this visibly crossed her familiar, rosy face. The girl was too young. Wouldn't she be frightened later, when the time came?

Finally she pulled herself together and said, "I'll be glad to ask the doctor if you like, Mrs. Malm."

"Never mind. I can do it myself," she said wearily. Her playful urge had passed. First so many lies, and now these ice-cold showers of truth, truth, truth. She could bear no more. It was too late to be stoic.

She hadn't touched her body for a long time now. All she remembered was fruitless rubbing and tickling, hours of work and not even an echo of pleasure. Only the stubborn effort to make something happen so the dry, leathery lips would moisten once more, to feel a smile spread through her diaphragm.

Now she thought of her vagina as an empty inkwell, long-forgotten in an uninhabited cottage. If a penpoint were dipped into it, it would splay, screeching apart against the shiny walls and in the rust colored residue in the corners.

But in moments of anguish she sometimes wound a strand of her thinning hair around her index finger and bit the knuckles of her other hand, as she had done in childhood. The next day the marks, some white and some red and inflamed, spoke the depth of her fear.

"It's all part of the picture," the bold midwife had said, pressing on her stomach. That was her standard expression, her theme song: "It's all part of the picture." The swollen varicose veins, the heartburn, the waters breaking too soon, the literally unbearable pain were all part of the picture. And in the end even the floundering baby boy, dangled by one leg with screams and vernix and umbilical cord and his little red sex, was all part of the picture. Part of the picture was laughter and tears of joy, and the newly bathed infant whimpering beside her, with glittering eyes that charmed her for life.

At the time she had felt more as if she were being born than giving birth. Shut in the tunnel with no going back, that was what she had been. When the pain strained her to the utmost, folding her like a jackknife, and urine sprayed all over the starched hospital gown as she squeezed the container which should have held it with hands that no longer obeyed her, she glanced across at the window. Five flights. A jump.

This time she was in the other wing on the same floor. But the thought of walking over and testing the strength of her fingers on the window latches nauseated her. She wanted to save her strength. She wanted to stay. Despite the pain. Her mind mocked her poor logic, her instinct for self-preservation, and the mocking laugh became a grimace. There was little room for intellect in this sorrowful business. Just as little as there had been when he was being pressed out of her, cut free to look at her at last.

With a few shrewd little movements she managed to reach her handbag and hunt out her diary. After the page where she had noted down the name of the hospital, six weeks ago, there was nothing but blank pages. She had never been very strong on documentation, and now it seemed entirely superfluous. One of the pockets contained her farewell letter to her son. Sometimes she took it out and read it. It made her smile because it was to him, though perhaps she should have cried because she would probably never see him again. She altered a word, added something, something silly that would make him laugh. She remembered her endless love letters to his father, the joy she had taken in writing them and in reading them time and again before mailing them. The joy of expression and awareness. The sense that everything between them had been crystal clear, that there was no need to be on her guard, to interpret looks and gestures. Then, after this enormous, overwhelming effort, there had been a gradual decline, a dilution, a neutralization which seized them both, like a mutual case of consumption. By then, their son was eighteen and there was no need to pretend. They glided apart and their love was lost to both their memories. She tried to remember what it had felt like, but all she could recover was her certainty of his friendship, respect perhaps, and their independence, as complete as if they had been born in different centuries. It was not indifference. They kept in touch. They cared. But nothing mattered any more.

The nurses came and went. The farce of the rounds was pared down to a bare minimum. Most of the time they left her alone. Sometimes she asked for sleeping pills and they gave her a few at a time, overestimating her desire to take a shortcut.

Sometimes one of the nurse's aides was in the mood to talk. She would tell all about her neighbors who did not remove their clogs indoors, foreign families who bought the wrong things at the supermarket, children who complained about their mothers going off to work. And she listened, propped up by two pillows, trying to smile. One girl named Brita lent her a turquoise chiffon scarf to cover her hair. "You look nice!" the girl beamed, but not even the compliment could make her take her mirror out of her handbag.

In pregnancy, too, she had been transformed into an inner being with no external facade. Everything was taking place inside her, in her veins, her womb, her head. She had closed her eyes to keep out the world, mumbling to the midwife: "I'm sorry. I hope you don't mind my not looking." She had wanted to concentrate on what was taking place inside her body, on the child fighting its difficult battle in the narrow tunnel.

Suddenly the oxygen mask was pressed over her mouth, and someone lifted her head: "Breathe deeply! Breathe deeply! Even deeper!"

When she protested no, no she didn't want any help, they told her it was for the baby's sake, not hers. They had fooled her with it recently. She had breathed deeply, thinking of the baby, but they had wheeled her into intensive care, where she awoke full of needles and tubes. Of course, she thought, I must really have known that it wasn't for the baby's sake now, not now—he's over twenty now, he doesn't need my oxygen or my blood. But she had simply obeyed and breathed deeply.

She turned back the pages of her diary. There it was. She had made a mark there with her thumbnail. That was when she had simply obeyed and breathed deeply. If she had not, she wouldn't be here now and her thumbnail would be a speck of ash which annoyingly landed on a white sheet hung out to dry in the neighborhood of the south cemetery.

Not much had happened since then. They had wheeled her back to her room, where her blood count had continued to fall. She knew that because she felt a kind of lethargy more profound than any tiredness she had known in her life. A dullness. An indifference. I'm turning to stone, she thought. The molecules are moving more slowly, forming new constellations. The leap through the window is an impossibility, and even the thought will be soon.

She read *Memoirs of Hadrian* and wondered if Marguerite Yourcenar were still alive or, if not, what her death had been like. When she was younger she had been curious about death. She had never seen a relative die. Never seen the victim of an accident. The blood-stained man in the tobacconist's shop on Tegnér Street might have been dying, but she had had her little boy in the car and had hurried away to spare him the sight—and herself the awkward questions.

She knew nothing of what lay ahead of her, as little as she had known of childbirth the last time she had lain here. A friend had given her a record of relaxation exercises the day before she had gone into labor, that was all. Breathe deeply. Relax. Don't tense up. Make every limb heavy and relaxed. Perhaps she should have listened to it again this time.

She remembered the turbulent waves of contractions. How, as at sea, you could see them approaching from afar, inexorably. She had forced herself to let go, be dull and indifferent, allowing the pain to wash over her, as over a stranger. And she had felt it work, felt everything open up, felt the child come closer to his life. Never before had she been so close to death. Not her own death, not a personal one. But so close to the border between life and death. She had thought quite clearly, now I know more about death than before, while lying there creating life.

The midwives had come and gone. Some went to lunch. Others worked only part time. One nurse's aide had talked about her children's new teacher, about the pleasure of seeing children interact. The real pleasure was when you had two. She had thought about having two men. She had done that once, and before the complications had become too great, it had been a real pleasure. Unusually pleasant. But she hadn't bothered much about how they had interacted.

Right now she thought no more about bodies than necessary. She was pleased to be able to urinate without a catheter. But her saliva had dried up. A damp washcloth at the corners of her mouth and a sip of orange juice to rinse with occasionally and then to spit out obediently. "Like a wine taster," she had tried to say to the consulting physician, but her tongue would not obey her, so she kept it to herself. What did they need her jokes for? Did she really care about making a good impression? Stalwart to the bitter end. You can't imagine how funny she could be, even when she knew she hadn't long to live!

"I can tell you've been here before," said the nurse in the basement room where they had shaved her pubic hair, given her an enema and taken a blood sample that night. She hadn't, of course, but she felt proud to be so bright and composed, so cooperative.

Would she have cried and moaned if she had given birth alone, in a ditch? And now—if she were on a mountain ledge, the victim of a plane crash, with only death and a void ahead . . . what would she do? What gestures and expressions, what screams and curses would she rain down on the grass and the stones and the distant clouds?

The woolly gray clouds arranged themselves like iron filings above the earth, each so full of microscopic iron particles that it was forced to follow the magnetic pattern of the earth. She remembered reading a scientific version of the creation story, and her enormous joy over those poetic facts. Perhaps the rolling rhythm of the earth altered when all the trees in the northern hemisphere burst into leaf at once, increasing the wind resistance. Perhaps its speed increased again in the autumn when there was nothing but bare branches.

This was better than Isis and Osiris, better than Ask and Embla and Ygdrasil—or were both equally far from the truth—the same saga in different costumes?

When she had still been part of life, she had complained each time a day passed without new knowledge, a new idea. Now she wondered dully what the point of it was. More dully than anxiously. A repugnant lethargy. Now even what was feasible became impossible, desire was cut off at the roots.

She tried to remember her child and his father, the bodies she had loved most. Straight shoulders, angular joints, firm jaws, looks of warmth and light. But they seemed unreal. More unreal than the brown medicine bottle and the small rainbow of colored pill containers you could make into long, flexible chains to use as noisemakers when there was nothing good on the radio.

How long would it last? And death as relief—what doesn't exist cannot relieve—and from what?

"I have lived a good life, better than almost any other life I know of, and better than I ever could have hoped for when I was your age," she had written in the letter. But perhaps he would be able to read between the lines that however good it had been, it now seemed terribly irrelevant, the copulation which had created his little body irrelevant, the bearing down irrelevant when he was finally pressed out of her and into life and air and breathing.

No, not that. Having given birth to him, having managed to get him out whole—that would never feel irrelevant. That was where her scepticism ended and she became a common vixen, a natural she-bear, a true-bred female cat. The baby was in her womb and had to come out. The baby had to be licked. The baby needed milk, caresses and warmth, and to lie as close to her as if he were still in the darkness of her womb. That was beyond relevance and irrelevance. It was. It was Being. And she cherished this beloved prejudice and she smoothed down its fur. Sometimes she took out his picture—the one when he was twelve—sexlessly beautiful and mischievous—and held it long in her hand, hoping she could die that way.

She was in the tunnel and there was no return. But they did not put her on a high steel bed with stirrups, and no one listened to the baby's heart with a stethoscope and said comfortingly: "I'll stay here with you until it's over."

Until it's over. Then she would be two people. It had never occurred to her that she might die in childbirth. The child kicked, wanted to come out. She had protected it for nine months, and she would not desert it in the final nine hours. Yet she had never been closer to death, for it was across that boundary the child must travel in order to live. Now it was her turn. And she asked Brita, the girl, what time her shift was over. "At six, as usual," she answered. "See you in the morning."

In the morning? No, oh, no. Was it going to take all that time? But her body wanted it to take all that time, preferably even more.

Now, as then, flowers arrived from her friends. Flowers from the child's father. They glowed in colorful splendor and wilted. And she was glowing with fever, and wilting at the same time. They were alike: cut off from their natural root systems, fed on cold fluids pumped right into their circulatory systems. She saw the tulips stand straight, their stems gorged with water from the vase, knowing they would die. The lilac leaves did not bother to pretend, but their multipetalled blossoms with the sweet drop of nectar in the center bloomed one by one, and she asked the cleaning lady to hand her a few—yes, to pick them—so that she could suck the tiny stems as she had in the summers long ago. She would have liked to ask the consulting physician to blow on a lilac leaf, but he probably wouldn't have known how, and doctors were easily enough embarrassed anyway. She, too, was embarrassed. Confused and shy. How would she meet her death?

She had also felt shy with her little one, newly bathed and swaddled, lying in her arms. She had grimaced ironically at his father and said: "He looks like a baby-powder ad!" She had been wheeled through endless corridors, the little one sleeping in his cocoon in her arms, his wrinkled cheek so close that she could not resist stroking it. It was all so new. And her breasts, which had lain so flat in the bra cups and rested in the hands of young men, were suddenly transformed into troughs for her piglet to slurp from. She had loved nursing him and would certainly have gone on for a year if the threat of DDT hadn't become so acute that mothers were warned not to nurse.

I will fall asleep, she thought. And when I wake up it will be over. Nothing works any more, hardly even the pain. The pain has died before me. Like the scents, the sounds, the sights. I've been left behind. I am last in my own funeral procession.

Until the older night nurse sat down close beside her and said: "Now I'll stay until . . . "

That was it. Some midwives left before life came. Others stayed and held their vigil. Now I will stay until you die, one body says to the other. Then one will get up and smooth her hair and go home to the morning chores, the shopping, the lovemaking, the weeding, the lending library and the envelopes of grocery receipts and the other will stay. Quite still. Entirely alone.

Then she began to talk. In a weak voice, she tried to explain and elucidate. Like a child asking for a better mark, a longer summer vacation. But the stout woman in her forties took out her knitting, and the light shone on her brown hair where an occasional gray strand gleamed.

She tried to read in the pale glow of the night light: "Even water is a pleasure which, since my illness began, I must enjoy sparingly. But even when I am struggling with death and it is mixed with my last bitter medicine, I shall try to feel its fresh tastelessness on my lips."

But the book fell from her hands and she could no longer think—book. A harsh light fell on her closed gray eyelids. Someone removed her turquoise scarf and she whimpered, as if in her sleep. "*Memoirs of Hadrian,*" said a hard, educated voice, and she realized they were putting her belongings away. Entirely naked and nearly bald she would suffer the final contractions.

"A hand to hold when you die," echoed his drunken voice. He had been nineteen and, like her, had just finished high school. They had been hugging and drinking on the couch in her student room and he had executed a death-defying balancing act outside the window in her honor.

No, no hand to hold. She had not wanted the father to be there when the baby was born. "I'd rather be alone with the pain. Then you can come and share the pleasure. No—no—no, it's not for your sake. I am the one who has to go through it. I want to be alone."

Suddenly the bed was so wet. But when she said, "My water!" the stupid nurse just brought her a glass of water. She searched for words, for memories, for signs that would be understood. She was so new at this, so bewildered and belittled. She felt a moment of bitter joy: today had brought some new knowledge, a new idea.

"There, there, keep calm!" And a broad warm hand patted her cheek, stroked the back of her hand.

Now, as then, she was their lawful prey. She remembered strange women patting her big, hard, pregnant belly. She brought back wonderful memories for them. What was the knitter who sat beside her now, and who had reached the armhole, thinking?

"Is he all right?"

"Oh yes, just keep calm, you're doing fine. I can feel eight inches of head here. You're dilated beautifully." A kind Finn dipped his fingers deep into her and reported from the life on the other side of birth.

She had hoped that he would remember, and send Virginia stocks and snapdragons. But a bouquet of them arrived from her colleagues at the university instead. What did they have to do with the birth?

"Red nose. Golden mouth. Fleet foot. Sweet lark. Mamma's little Oedi-puss." And she had promised to marry him soon, as soon as he was a tiny bit bigger. And at the age of three months when he had fallen asleep on her stomach in a wide, sagging bed in England, she had fallen asleep too and dreamed he was inside her, but just with his little tiny penis, and it was a sweet, light union, far distant from incest and pornography. And yet she had never told anyone about it.

The peculiar knitter stuck her needles into her one by one, knit one, purl one, and the knits had thorns. She turned slowly onto her side, but some new tubes stopped her there. A voice in a loudspeaker echoed, and footsteps ran. Footsteps ran off with young bodies, away from her immobility.

At last she made her way up to the surface. She had dived too deeply from the cliff, into the black waters. Her mother and father smiled at her from out of a blue beach robe and the scent of the sun on the stones and tanned skin came to her nose. Her whole body was shivering, and blue with gooseflesh. They had to rub her warm, but could not stop her shaking.

Then she was suddenly in a yard. The book on her lap was *Memoirs of Hadrian*. An oak spread its foliage over her head like a parasol. She could hear his voice through an open window. It chattered and babbled, interpreting and explaining. And he couldn't say his s's. She laboriously stretched her neck and looked diagonally upwards. The sun was shining through the window. The chestnuts on the horizon bowed to an imperceptible breeze. She couldn't smell them from here. The knitter had fallen asleep over her needles. The light angled glaringly off the sterile hospital medicine stand. But all she saw was the sun bouncing through the nursery window, and his voice babbled on, and as she stretched to see his face, the sun struck her with its double-edged axe.

Like dust humming in the wind and music on a keyboard of cotton. Whispers and shuffles, wheeling and covering. Tubes disconnected and clothing removed before the rigor mortis sets in. Like shadow theater, this whole thousand-headed hospital that descends slowly into the darkness of a new day, while a beam of light laughs in a window and a child talks and talks of life.

—translated from the Swedish by Linda Schenck

Fruit of the Month

ABBY FRUCHT

I WENT STRAWBERRY PICKING with June in her pickup truck ten years ago, in May. Late May, in Virginia. June came early, before Jack got home from work, so we left without him. I left a note on the door. When I get back, said the note, I'll make us some strawberry daiquiris and we'll sit together on the porch and drink them all night long, listening to mosquitos. The nature of my notes to him was always, and still is, piquant, because he likes them that way. He is a sentimental man; he keeps my letters in a shoebox tied with string. In the dark interior of the box the ink doesn't fade, nor does the paper deteriorate. Every couple of years he replaces the string, which turns gray from being so often tied and untied.

June said she knew a place where we could get the strawberries free. I said, Illegally, you mean? and she said, Well, yes. If we took the freeway east a couple of miles and then turned off on a dirt road we would come to the edge of a commercial farm surrounded by barbed wire that had been rolled up the way they rolled it in the army during a war, but further on, just where the dirt road ended near a creek, there was a tree you could climb. By climbing this tree and shimmying out along one of its branches you would scale the barbed wire, dropping down just on the other side of it into the strawberry fields. June wore her hair very long at the time, blond and fine with a touch of a ripple, like the stuff you peel off corn ears. Even now, if I am shucking corn, I think of this. How I looked up from the strawberry patch, from my knees where I had landed, and saw June scaling the barbed wire after me, her long bare legs straddling the tree branch, her hair covering her face. It was a hot afternoon, and the scent of greenery was sharp in the air, and I have never forgotten it. We squatted together between the steaming furrows of earth, pinching the berries and eating some. If they don't come off at once in your hand, June said, leave them on the stems to ripen for next time.

We dropped the berries into a book satchel she was wearing on a strap over her shoulder, and after a while the khaki canvas, bulging with fruit, was stained pink. Our fingers were pink, and our knees, and the edges of our mouths. In the distance, across the shimmering acres of strawberry leaves, like water in the sun, we could make out the wide-brimmed hats of the legitimate berry pickers, and beyond them the low flat white building where the bushels were weighed and paid for, and where the cars were parked. Children played and shouted along the perimeter of the farm, and people gathered on the hoods of their cars to talk and sunbathe. We stayed low and quiet, hoping we wouldn't be seen.

I tired quickly. My legs and lower back ached, and my neck and arms stiffened. I blamed my fatigue on the heat and on my period, which had started that morning. I felt heavy and bloated and entirely out of whack. My head hurt. Finally I lay back on my elbows and told June to go right on picking without me; I was perfectly happy simply to be there. I think I fell asleep. Time passed. The sun got low. The crowd thinned out. When I opened my eyes the first thing I saw was a ladybug that had landed on my stomach. It was opening and closing its small spotted wings in a rhythmic way. One two. One two. I thought of the nursery rhyme, and then immediately of Jack, who would be waiting for me, probably standing near an open window with a tall iced glass of water, sipping and watching the road. His lips would be cool, and his eyes troubled. He keeps his anger inside, in what I've begun to call Hot Storage, and allows it to surface only in the face of a more worldly injustice. And by then it has boiled and sweetened and grown thick. Several days after I went strawberry picking he threw our hairbrush at Ronald Reagan, who was president at the time. Reagan was on the news. He was saying he supported the E and the R but not the A of the Equal Rights Amendment, and Jack got mad and threw our brush at the television screen, breaking it. The brush, I mean. I reattached the handle with duct tape, and we still use it.

When the ladybug had flown off I sat up and saw June straddling the branch again and munching on a strawberry. She grinned down at me. I was still exhausted and my only inclination was to lie back down and sleep some more, but I pulled myself up, and let June pull me up into the tree. She had scratched her leg on the barbed wire; there was a thin trickle of blood. We made our way across the tree and back down into the pickup. June turned the radio on. The song was See You in September. June leaned over and took my head in her hands and kissed me, first on the eyes, then full on the mouth. I was surprised. I responded. Then she said, There, I've been wanting to do that, and she drove me home.

I told Jack about this later, over our daiquiris. He was on his third, but I was still toying with my first, because I still felt weak and knew if I drank much more I would get sick. Also, I knew I would be driving out to Norfolk early the next morning to go sailing with June on her brother's boat. Her brother was wealthy and out of town. I told Jack that June's brother's boat was small, big enough only for two. I considered this to be a white lie. I told him also about the kiss, saying how shocked I had been. Jack was entirely silent. He stirred his drink, and watched the moths that were beating against the light bulb, and lifted, by arching his foot, a tennis ball that had rolled out from under his chair. That tennis ball has always been a mystery; neither one of us plays and we've never figured out how it got there. He would straighten his leg, the ball wedged in the arch of his foot, then spread his toes apart and let it fall. He did this over and over until it bounced out of reach. Then he put his drink down on the cement, but gently, so there wasn't a sound, and went inside. I followed, the screen door banging behind me. He filled a teacup with strawberries, sprinkled it with sugar, and carried it upstairs. He put the teacup on the night table. I began to undress him and we showered. Jack said, Your fingers are pink. That was all he said. We toweled ourselves dry and lay down in bed, our arms slung across each other's necks. I watched him sleep, as June had watched me. Jack has remained entirely silent in fact, about all of this, for years.

The drive out to Norfolk was long and agitating, twenty-five miles on the highway stuck behind some drunken slob in a Winnebago. He had opened the back door and stood with one foot on the fender, in a stained tee shirt and shorts, guzzling beer, then tossing the empty cans out onto the highway. All this at fifty-five miles per hour. The beer cans soared crazily in the hot morning light, then veered and bounced off on the shoulder abreast of my car. I was afraid to pass him—What if he fell off?—and I never did get close enough to read the license plate. I slowed to forty, till the Winnebago was a speck in the distance, then sped up till I was close enough to have to slow down again. I hated that man. Eventually I lost him, thank god, and got on my way, but the Hampton Bridge was jammed with traffic, everybody headed for the beach. So it was nearly ten o'clock when I pulled into Norfolk, along a road that skirted the harbor, past the convention center and into the slums where June lived. I had never been there before, and will tell you right now that I never went back. The narrow street was pocked with craters. June's apartment building made me think of the Triangle Shirtwaist Factory, broad and tall, wood frame with row upon row of small windows, some of them broken, the ancient panes warped. I parked across the street, in a lot strewn with rubbish and whiskey bottles, behind a church that looked firebombed. June's truck was there. I hurried across in my clogs and running shorts. I felt like a child in a war zone. The door was locked. A second door was also locked, so I sat down on the hot gritty stoop and waited to be let in. In the ten minutes that passed I thought about getting back into my car and driving home, but the harbor, several blocks up on the other side of the road, was just visible, dotted with sails. Besides, I was hungry. June had promised me breakfast. Strawberry pancakes and coffee, she'd said. Finally a man with a cat in his arms came shuffling up the steps and pulled out a key.

Inside was a wide hallway and three sets of steps, one more dilapidated than the last. I chose the steps with the working light bulb. June lived on the third floor, down a hall lined with green doors and covered with old gray shiny linoleum. The linoleum had buckled, and as I walked along, it made all sorts of obscene noises under my feet. I wondered how June could live in such a place. I hadn't known her very long, having met her through a friend, and that she lived in such a seedy spot excited me. Then, when I knocked and there was no response, I thought perhaps she had mistakenly given me the wrong address, the address of a friend or relative she had been thinking of. I jiggled the door knob. It turned, and the door opened but was blocked after several inches by a chain bolt. I peered inside. The room was in disarray. Books everywhere, and clothes, and a folding table stacked with cardboard boxes, and underneath the table a heap of shoes, including what looked like a snowshoe. There was the sickening odor of propane gas, and another of what I guessed was a kitty litter that hadn't been changed. The gas worried me. I began to knock more vigorously, and even took off my clog and started banging on the door with the wooden sole. Someone in the apartment across the hall opened his door and looked out.

"Are you one of June's friends?" he said. His tone was vaguely sarcastic.

"I guess so," I said.

"She should be out in a minute," he said. "Just keep banging."

At last the chain was unhitched, and there was June, wrapped in a blanket, her beautiful hair fanning over her shoulders. Her face was bleary with sleep but her eyes were wide open. She seemed surprised to see me, as if she had never asked me to come, or, really, as if she had never seen me before in her life.

"Come in," she said.

"I'm sorry I'm late," I said, realizing at once how ridiculous that was. I followed her in, and she stood in the center of the messy room and stared around at the clutter as if looking for someplace to put me. She cleared some books from a chair and sat down in it herself. A door clicked open from a room in the back. "Just a minute," June called, and the door clicked shut. She yawned, and pulled a bare arm out from under the blanket, and found a cigarette on the table and lit it. It was the first time I saw her with a cigarette. Her hand, I noticed, was perfectly steady. She stared at me and let out a stream of smoke. "I think I need to get a little more sleep," she began. "I was up all night. Don't go. There's food . . . " She gestured toward the kitchen. "I'll be up in a while. Not long. I still want to go sailing."

"So do I," I lied. I didn't know if I was angry or hurt or both. Anyway I tried not to show it. She smiled at me weakly and left. For a while I examined the room but there was too much to look at, piles of books and papers, odds and ends, and on the top shelf of the bookcase, sitting all in a row and out of my reach, a bunch of old stuffed animals. On the walls were some charcoal drawings of June, but the likenesses weren't that good and the shading amateur. I had been wrong about the kitty litter. There was a dog mess, on a sheaf of newspaper spread out in one corner of the kitchen. It was a small dog. A Pekinese. I found her asleep in a bread basket on a low shelf of the open cupboard. I lifted her up and carried her over to the window and we stood there and looked out at the back of a building exactly like the one we were in. Staring across at its windows, I expected to see the two of us looking back at ourselves. I held the dog close to my breast, like an infant. She pressed her nose against the pane and left a small moist dot on the glass. The window, I saw, was covered with these spots. After a time she started squirming and I lowered her back into her basket.

I opened the refrigerator. There were two ceramic bowls piled high with strawberries, and a glass jar filled with brown water. I unscrewed the lid and sniffed, apprehensive about what I might find. Spiced tea. I poured myself a glass and sat on the floor in the main room with a bowl of strawberries cradled in my lap, pinching the tops off and popping them into my mouth one after another. I dropped the green leafy tops back into the bowl. I can't tell you how lonely I felt. I was sitting in a square of sunlight, and when it shifted I inched along with it. Someone was moaning at the back of the house, and gasping. It was impossible to know whether the person who was moaning was the same one who was gasping. Then the telephone rang. It was right at my feet but I didn't pick it up. I let it ring. It rang twelve times. The gasping and moaning continued. My mouth began to sting, from the cold tartness of the berries, but I kept on eating. I held each berry whole in my mouth, sucking the juices out, then pressing it up against the roof of my mouth and crushing it under my tongue. My stomach made wet sloshing noises like a washing machine. I picked up the phone and dialed home, wanting suddenly more than anything to talk with Jack, to tell him what a lousy time I was having and that I wished I hadn't come and that I hoped he would forgive me.

"Forgive you for what?" Jack said.

I didn't know how to respond to that. I sat there in silence. The moaning had ceased but the dog was whimpering. Somehow, I had shut the cupboard door and locked it inside. I got up, carrying the phone, and went into the kitchen to free it. With my free hand I stroked the dog's head, tracing the shape of its broad bony skull with my fingers.

"What's that?" said Jack.

"A dog," I said.

"What do you have in your mouth?"

"A strawberry."

"When are you coming home?"

"I don't know," I said. "Tonight. It's a long drive for nothing."

"Mmmm." Jack said. He would be pressing his lips together, turning them under and holding them shut with his teeth. How familiar he was. He is a gentle man; I have never known another man who does that with his teeth.

"I'll have to be going," I said. "This is costing June a lot of money."

"Mmmm," Jack said. He hung up first. He always guesses when I am waiting for him to hang up, and he never makes me wait too long.

June's lover was tall and olive-skinned and had a mustache almost as thick as a man's. She might have taken some pills. She walked with a swagger, in a bleached denim jacket and jeans and square-toed boots, and she had a mole on her face, in precisely the spot where Marilyn Monroe had one. The effect was freakish. Her name was Faye. I thought to myself, Swarthy Faye. Faye the Pirate. Captain Faye and the Sharks. I saw her as the lead singer in a rock band, dressed in cloak and dagger on a darkened stage in a low-ceilinged room, breathing a song. Her voice would be deep and airy like the sound a bottle makes when you blow into it. I can't remember her voice, now. I don't know that I heard it even once. She stayed close to June, like a bodyguard, and gave her looks fraught with meaning that I could not decipher.

June seemed confused. I think she had expected me to leave while they were still in bed, at the same time hoping I would stay. I was determined to go sailing. Otherwise, I told myself, why would I have come? She still looked tired, and she had wrapped her hair in a madras scarf so you couldn't see it. She was smoking again. Faye kept the cigarettes in the breast pocket of her jacket, and every time June wanted a smoke she had to reach in and get one.

"You had a telephone call," I said, in a voice that was too cheerful. I worked as a receptionist at a hotel in town, and that was my receptionist voice.

"Who was it?" asked June, startled.

"No one," I said. "I mean I didn't answer it."

"Thank god," June said. Faye smiled, only barely, and at no one in particular. We drank instant coffee black, because the fake cream was stuck like a rock in the bottom of the jar. June bent a spoon, trying to get it out. We all laughed when she held up the bent spoon, then stopped abruptly when it clattered in the sink. There was no mention of a breakfast more substantial than strawberries and coffee. By then, anway, it was lunchtime. Sun streaming through the windows. June's arms golden in the sunlight. I was wondering whether, had June and I been alone, we would have made pancakes. All at once I remembered the time years ago when, as a teenager,

I spent my first night with a boy, on a mattress in the closet of an empty house on some church grounds. In the morning we went to the house of a friend, a motherly girl in an apron, who cooked a batch of pancakes and left the kitchen while we ate them. Thinking of this, I couldn't recall the boy's name. The sole image I had was of his Adam's apple bobbing up and down above my face, the forlorn, boyish shape of the bone with the skin stretched whitely over it. I remembered I told him his balls looked like plums, and how shocked he looked when I said it.

The noon hour stretched on. Then June stood up suddenly and announced it was time to go sailing. We walked the few blocks to the harbor, June chatting on and off about how rich her brother was. His boat was moored at a dock crowded with other boats. There were hordes of people, tying and untying ropes, having just come in or else preparing to go out into the bay, and some who just lounged around in bathing suits as if they had no intention of going anywhere. I have never familiarized myself with the mechanics of sailing, and sat on the deck, holding my clogs in my lap while June and Faye passed ropes back and forth and hooked and unhooked things. June disappeared below for a minute, and reappeared with three chilled beers that she passed around. Faye popped the tab off and tossed it right into the water, where it floated. I glanced at June, who shrugged sheepishly, and for a moment there was only the two of us, in the boat that was creaking and bobbing. She made a point of sitting near me while applying some tanning lotion. She had stripped down to her swim suit. When there was too much lotion left over on her hands she rubbed it into my neck. Her hands were warm. The scent of coconuts rose around us. I didn't know what to do. Faye stared out at the harbor past a string of boats, drinking her beer very fast. Then, when she was finished, she crushed the can with her boot and threw it with perfect aim into the mouth of a trash can on the dock, disappointing me. June clapped, and Faye came over to join her, and they started the motor and we were off.

It was slow going. The harbor was jammed. I was struck by the camaraderie of boaters; there was much waving and shouting back and forth. Every few yards we had to stop and sit still while the hot smell of gasoline seared the air. I cringed each time Faye lit June's cigarette, half expecting a blast. Faye wouldn't look at me but June smiled each time the sun dipped behind a cloud. There were clouds suddenly, loose black clumps in patches on the hard blue sky, throwing intermittent shadows on the water. You could see, if you looked way into the distance into the bay itself, how the strung sails brightened and then vanished and then brightened again as they traveled through light and darkness.

"Jack would have liked this," I said.

"You should have brought him along," said June.

"You should have told me to," I said. Faye took June's hand and placed
her own long-boned hand on top of it. They nuzzled and sighed.
At the lip of the bay the coast guard stopped us. There was a man with a
megaphone. A storm was approaching. The clouds had clumped overhead
and there was thunder far off. The air had grown thick, and electric. A few
tendrils of hair had escaped from June's scarf; they glowed like filaments.
Goose bumps appeared on our arms, but there was nothing to be frightened
of as long as we turned back. I was relieved. The ocean looked crazy. We
hadn't even put up our sails. The city was still in sunlight, but we knew it
wouldn't last. We shared another beer, not bothering to speak above the
churn of the motors. Docked, we covered the boat with a tarpaulin and
walked home as the rain started falling. I have never seen such large drops of
rain, like grapes. June caught some in her mouth, and then Faye took her
jacket off and lifted it over our heads. More than once I stepped out of my
clogs and they waited for me without turning around. We all smelled by the
time we got home. Salt and sweat. The apartment was stifling and so dark
we were blinded. June sniffed. "I've got to change that newspaper," she
said. "Poor Phyllis." Then she turned to me and touched me very lightly on
the wrist. "Faye and I are taking a shower," she said.

I kissed Phyllis goodbye and grabbed a handful of strawberries and left.
For a while I sat in the car and waited for the rain to let up, and chewed
slowly to ward off my hunger. For days, I felt, I had been eating nothing else,
like someone lost in a forest. I just wanted to get home. I didn't know why I
had come. I didn't want to know. On the highway I took a wrong turn. They
had to turn me around at a toll booth, stopping traffic so I could cut across
the lanes. The man in the booth had a strawberry nose. "Thanks," I said, "I
would have ended up in Florida," but I don't think he heard me.
Jack wasn't home when I got there. He had been busy; the bed was
stacked with laundry. The windows were open, and the floor was streaked
with rain. Summer where we live is the season of mildew, and I could smell
it on the towel as I wiped the perspiration from my face. I was tired, too tired
to undress. I fell among the fresh-washed clothes and slept.
Later that night, Jack came home. He smelled like soap. I have never
asked him where he was and he has never told me. At the time I was too sick
to care. My throat and tongue were parched, and my limbs ached dully. He
helped me out of my clothes, and fed me water and aspirin. He dampened a
washcloth and held it briefly to my face, which he told me was swollen. My
lips felt swollen and tasted of brine. I refused to eat. Jack brought me hot
cups of broth, which cooled before I touched them.
"What could it be?" he said, on the second day, when I was feeling a little
better. I was sitting up in bed, just sitting, still dazed, doing nothing.

"Strawberries," I said. "That has to be it. Look at this rash. What else could it be?"

"Mmmm," Jack said. He was brushing my hair, a lock at a time. His strokes were even and gentle. That was when we turned the television on, and Ronald Reagan said what he said, and Jack threw the brush and hit him in the face and broke it. It fell to the floor in two pieces. I don't remember the rest of the news, if there was any. We just sat very close. I think I told him about the man in the Winnebago, just then remembering him. Then we both went to sleep. Ten years have gone by, and it is suddenly the season, and believe me when I say I haven't touched another strawberry since.

A Pure Soul

CARLOS FUENTES

JUAN LUIS, I am thinking about you as I take my seat on the bus that will carry me to the airport. I came early intentionally. I don't want to see the people who will actually fly with us until the last minute. This is the bus for the Alitalia flight to Milan; it will be an hour before the Air France passengers to Paris, New York and Mexico board their bus. I'm just afraid I will cry or get upset or do something ridiculous, and then have to endure glances and whispers for sixteen hours. There's no reason why anyone has to know anything. You prefer it that way, too, don't you? I shall always believe it was a private act, that you didn't do it because . . . I don't know why I'm thinking these things. I don't have the right to explain anything in your name. Nor, perhaps, in mine either. How will I ever know, Juan Luis? Do you think I am going to insult our memories by affirming or denying that perhaps, at such and such a moment, or over a long period of time—I don't know how or when you decided, possibly when you were a child, why not?—you were motivated by dejection, or sadness, or nostalgia, or hope? It's cold. That icy wind that passes over the city like the breath of death is blowing from the mountains. I half-bury my face in my lapels to retain my body heat, although the bus is heated and now is smoothly pulling away, enveloped in its own vapor. We leave the station at Cornavin through a tunnel and I know I will not see again the lake and bridges of Geneva since the bus emerges onto the highway behind the station and moves always away from Lake Leman on the road to the airport. We are passing through the ugly part of the city where the seasonal workers live who have come from Italy and Germany and France to this paradise where not a single bomb fell, where no one was tortured or assassinated or betrayed. Even the bus adds to the sensation of neatness and order and well-being that so attracted your attention from the moment you arrived, and now as I clean the steamy window with my hand and see these wretched houses I think that, in spite of everything, one mustn't live too badly in them. Switzerland after a while becomes too comfortable, you said in a letter; we lose the sense of extremes that are so visible and so insulting in our country. Juan Luis: in your last letter you didn't need to tell me—I understand without having lived it myself: that was always our bond—that all that external order, the punctuality of the trains, honor in everyday transactions, looking ahead in one's job, and saving all one's life, demanded an internal disorder to balance it. I am laughing, Juan Luis; behind a gimace that struggles to hold back the tears, I begin to laugh, and all the passengers turn to look at me and whisper among themselves; this is what I wanted to avoid; at least these people are going to Milan. I laugh when I think how you left the order of our home in Mexico for the disorder of your freedom in Switzerland. Do you understand? From security in the land of bloody daggers to anarchy in the land of the cuckoo clock. Isn't that funny? I'm sorry. I'm over it now. I try to compose myself by looking at the snow-covered peak of the Jura, that enormous sheer grey cliff that now seeks in vain for its reflection in the lake born of its waters. You wrote me that in summer the lake is the eye of the Alps: it reflects them, but it also transforms them into a vast submerged cathedral, and you said that when you plunged into the water you were diving in search of the mountains. Do you know I have your letters with me? I read them on the plane that brought me from Mexico and, during the days I have been in Geneva, in my free moments. Now I will read them on the return trip. Except that on this crossing you will accompany me.

We have traveled so much together, Juan Luis. As children we went every weekend to Cuernavaca when my parents still had that house covered with bougainvillea. You taught me to swim and to ride a bicycle. On Saturdays we cycled into town where I learned to know everything through your eyes. "Look, Claudia, at the kites; look, Claudia, thousands of birds in the trees; look, Claudia, silver bracelets, fancy sombreros, lemon ice, green statues; come on, Claudia, let's go to the wheel of fortune." And for the New Year's festivities, they took us to Acapulco and you awakened me very early in the morning and we ran to Hornos Beach because you knew that the sea was at its best at that hour: that was the only time the snails and octopi, the dark sculptured driftwood, the old bottles appeared, hurled by the tide, and together we gathered all we could, even though we knew that later they wouldn't allow us to carry it back to Mexico City, and truly, all those useless objects would never have gone in the car. It's strange that every time I try to remember what you were like at ten, at thirteen, at fifteen, I immediately think of Acapulco. It must be because during the rest of the year each of us went to his own school, and only at the shore and precisely as we were celebrating the turning of one year to another, were all the hours of the day ours. We played wonderful games there. On the rock castles where I was a prisoner of the ogres and you scaled the walls with a wooden sword in your hand, yelling and dueling with imaginary monsters to free me. In the pirate galleons—a skiff—where terrified I waited for you to end the struggle in the sea with the sharks that menaced me. In the dense jungles of Pie de la Cuesta, where we advanced hand in hand in search of the secret treasure marked on the map we found in a bottle. You accompanied your actions humming background music invented at the moment: dramatic, in perpetual climax. Captain Blood, Sandokan, Ivanhoe: *your* personality changed with every adventure; I was always the embattled princess, nameless, identical to her nebulous prototype.

There was only one empty time: when you were fifteen and I was only twelve and you were embarrassed to be seen with me. I didn't understand, because you looked the same as always to me: slim, strong, tanned, your curly chestnut hair reddened by the sun. But we came together again the next year, going everywhere together, no longer picking up shells or inventing adventures, but seeking now to prolong a day that began to seem too short and a night forbidden to us, a night that became our temptation, a symbol of the new possibilities in a recently discovered, recently begun, life. We walked along the rocky Farallon after dinner, holding hands, silent, not looking at the groups who were playing guitars around the bonfires or the couples kissing among the rocks. We didn't have to say how painful it was to be around anyone else. As we didn't need to say that the best thing in the world was to walk together at night, holding hands, silent, silently communicating that code, that enigma, that between us was never, never occasion for a joke or a pedantic comment. We were serious but never solemn, remember? And possibly we were good for each other without knowing it, in a way I've never been able to explain exactly, but that had to do with the warm sand beneath our bare feet, with the silence of the sea in the night, of the brushing of our thighs as we walked together, you in your new long white pants, I in my full red skirt. We had changed our way of dressing and had escaped the jokes, the embarrassment, and the violence of our friends. You know, Juan Luis, that most of them still act as if they were fourteen—the kind of fourteen-year-olds we never were. *Machismo* is being fourteen all one's life; it is cruel fear. You know, because you weren't able to avoid it either. Actually, to the degree we left our childhood behind and you tried all the experiences common to your age, you tried to avoid me. That's why I understood when after years of hardly speaking to me (but I spied on you from the window, I watched you go out in a convertible filled with friends and come back late and feeling sick), when I entered Arts and Science and you, Business, you sought me, not at home, which would have been the natural thing to do, but at my college, and you invited me to have a cup of coffee one afternoon in the Mascarones cellar cafe, hot and packed with students.

You stroked my hand and said: "Forgive me, Claudia."

I smiled and thought that all the moments of our childhood were suddenly returning, not to be prolonged, but rather to be brought to an end, to a kind of recognition that would at the same time dissipate those years forever.

"For what?" I answered. "I'm happy we can talk again. That's all I want. We've seen each other every day, but each time it was as if the other weren't there. Now I'm happy we can be friends again, like before."

"We're more than friends, Claudia. We're brother and sister."

"Yes, but that's an accident. You see, because we are brother and sister we loved each other very much when we were children, but we've hardly spoken to each other since."

"I'm going to go away, Claudia. I've already told my father. He doesn't agree. He thinks I ought to finish my degree. But I need to go away."

"Where?"

"I've got a job with the United Nations in Geneva. I can continue my studies there."

"You're doing the right thing, Juan Luis."

You told me what I already knew. You told me you couldn't stand the whorehouses any longer, having to learn everything by rote, the obligation to be *macho*, patriotism, lip-service religion, the lack of good films, the lack of real women, girls your own age you could live with. . . . It was quite a speech, spoken quietly across that table in the Mascarones cafe.

"It's not possible to live here. I mean it. I don't want to serve either God or the Devil; I want to burn the candle at *both* ends. And you can't do it here, Claudia. Just wanting to *live* makes you a potential traitor; here you're obliged to serve, to take a position; it's a country that won't let you be yourself. I don't want to be 'decent.' I don't want to be courteous, a liar, *muy macho*, an ass-kisser, refined and clever. *There's no country like Mexico . . .* thank God! I don't want to go from brothel to brothel. When you do that then all your life you have to treat women with a kind of brutal and domineering sentimentality because you never learned to really understand them. I don't want that."

"And what does Mother say?"

"She'll cry. It doesn't matter. She cries about everything, what else would you expect?"

"And what about me, Juan Luis?"

He smiled childishly: "You'll come to visit me, Claudia. Swear you'll come see me?"

I not only came to see you. I came to look for you, to take you back to Mexico. And four years ago, when we said goodbye, the only thing I said was:

"Think about me. Look for a way to be with me always."

Yes, you wrote me begging me to visit you; I have your letters. You found a room with bath and kitchen in the most beautiful spot in Geneva, the Place

Carlos Fuentes

du Bourg-de-Four. You wrote that it was on the fifth floor, in the center of the old part of the city, where you could see steep roofs, church towers, small windows and narrow skylights, and in the distance the lake fading from sight towards Vevey and Montreux and Chillon. Your letters were filled with the joy of independence. You had to make your bed and clean and get your own breakfast and go down to the dairy next door for milk. And you had your drinks in the cafe on the plaza. You talked so much about that cafe. It is called La Clémence and it has an awning with green and white fringe and anyone who *is* anyone in Geneva comes there. It's very small, barely six tables facing a bar where waitresses dressed in black serve cassis and say "M'sieudame" to everyone. I sat there yesterday to have a cup of coffee and there I was looking at all those students in their long mufflers and University caps, at Hindu girls with their saris askew under their winter coats, at diplomats with rosettes in their lapels, at the actors who flee from taxes and take refuge in chalets on the lakeshore, at the young Germans, Chileans, Belgians, and Tunisians who work at the OIT. You wrote that there were two Genevas. The ordered conventional city that Stendhal described as a flower without perfume; that's the one where the Swiss live, the backdrop for the other, the city of transients and exiles, a foreign city of chance encounters, of glances and sudden conversations, without the standards the Swiss have imposed upon themselves in order to free their guests. You were twenty-three when you arrived here, and I can imagine your enthusiasm.

"But enough of that (you wrote). I must tell you that I am taking a course in French literature and that there I met. . . . Claudia, I can't explain what I feel and I won't even try, because you have always understood me without needing words. Her name is Irene and you can't imagine how beautiful and clever, how *nice* she is. She is studying literature here, and she is French; strange that she is studying the same things you are. Maybe that's why I liked her immediately. Ha-ha." I think it lasted a month. I don't remember. It was four years ago. "Marie-José talks too much, but she amuses me. We spent the weekend at Davos and she made me look ridiculous because she is a formidable skier and I'm not worth a damn. They say you have to learn as a child. I confess I got a little uptight and the two of us returned to Geneva Monday as we had left Friday, except that I had a sprained ankle. Isn't that a laugh?" Then spring came. "Doris is English and she paints. I think she has real talent. We took advantage of the Easter holidays to go to Wengen. She says she makes love to stimulate her subconscious, and she leaps out of bed to paint her gouaches with the white peaks of the Jungfrau before her. She opens the windows and takes deep breaths and paints in the nude while I tremble with cold. She laughs a lot and says that I am a tropical creature with arrested development, and serves me kirsch to warm me up." I laughed at Doris the whole year they were seeing each other. "I miss her gaiety, but she decided that one year in Switzerland was enough and she left with her paintboxes and her easels to live on the island of Mykonos. So much the better. She amused me, but the kind of woman who interests me is not a woman like Doris." One went to Greece and another arrived from Greece. "Sophia is the most beautiful woman I have ever known, I swear it. I know it's a commonplace, but she looks like one of the Caryatids. Although not in the common sense. She is a statue because she can be observed from all angles; I make her turn around, nude, in the center of the room. But the important thing is the air that surrounds her, the space around the statue, do you understand? The space she *occupies* that permits her to be beautiful. She is dark, she has very thick eyebrows, and tomorrow, Claudia, she is leaving with some rich guy for the Côte d'Azur. Desolate, but satisfied, your brother who loves you, Juan Luis."

And Christine, Consuelo, Sonali, Marie-France, Ingrid. . . . The references were ever more brief, ever more disinterested. You became preoccupied with your work and with talking a lot about your friends there, about their national idiosyncracies, their dealings with you, with the subject of meetings and salaries and trips and even retirement pensions. You didn't want to tell me how that place, like all places, finally creates its own quiet conventions and that you were falling into the pattern of an international official. Until a postcard arrived with a view of Montreux and your cramped writing telling about a meal in a fabulous restaurant, and lamenting my absence, signed with two signatures, your scrawl, and an illegible—but carefully copied below—Claire.

Oh, yes. You were gauging this one carefully. You didn't present her like the others. First it was a new job you were going to be recommended for. Then how it was involved with the next meeting of the Council. Then after that, how you enjoyed working with your new friends but that you missed the old ones. Then that the most difficult thing was getting used to the document officials who didn't know your work habits. Finally that you had had the luck to work with a "compatible" official, and in the next letter: her name is Claire. And three months before you had sent me the postcard from Montreux. Claire, Claire, Claire."

I answered: "Mon ami Pierrot." So you weren't going to be honest with me anymore. How long has it been Claire? I wanted to know everything, I demanded to know everything. Juan Luis, hadn't we been best friends before we were brother and sister? You didn't write for two months. Then came an envelope with a snapshot inside. The two of you with the tall jet of a fountain behind you, and the lake in summertime; you and she leaning against the railing. Your arm around her waist. She, so cute, her arm resting on a flower-filled stone urn. But it wasn't a good snapshot. It was difficult to decide about Claire's face. Slim and smiling, yes, a kind of Marina Vlady, slimmer but with the same smooth long blond hair. Low heels. A sleeveless sweater. Cut low.

You admitted it without explaining anything. First the letters relating facts. She lived in a *pension* on the Rue Emile Jung. Her father was an engineer, a widower, and he worked in Neuchâtel. You and Claire were going swimming together at the beach. You had tea at La Clémence. You saw old French films in a theatre in the Rue Mollard. Saturdays you had dinner at the Plat d'Argent and each of you paid his own bill. During the week, you ate in the cafeteria of the Palace of Nations. Sometimes you took the tram and went to France. Facts and names, names, names, like a guidebook: Quai des Berges, Gran' Rue, Cave à Bob, Gare de Cornavin, Auberge de la Mère Royaume, Champelle, Boulevard des Bastions.

Later conversations. Claire's taste in some films, certain books, the concerts, and more names, that river of nouns in your letters (*Drôle de Drame* and *Les Enfants du Paradis*, Scott Fitzgerald and Raymond Radiguet, Schumann and Brahms) and then Claire says, Claire thinks, Claire feels. Carné's characters live their freedom as if it were a shameful conspiracy. Fitzgerald invented the modes, the gestures, and the disillusion that continue to nourish us. The German Requiem celebrates all profane deaths. Yes, I answered. Orozco has just died, and there is an enormous retrospective of Diego in the Bellas Artes. And in return letters, all of it written out, as I had asked you.

"Every time I listen to you, I say to myself that it's as if we had realized that we need to consecrate everything that has been condemned up till now, Juan Luis; to turn things inside out. Who mutilated us, my love? There's so little time to recover everything that has been stolen from us. No, I'm not suggesting anything, you know. Let's not make plans. I believe as Radiguet does that the unconscious maneuvers of a pure soul are even more singular than all the possible combinations of vice."

What could I answer? Nothing new here, Juan Luis. Papa and Mama are very sad that you won't be here with us for their silver wedding anniversary. Papa has been promoted to Vice President of the insurance company and he says that's his best anniversary present. Mama, poor thing, invents some new illness every day. The first television station is on the air. I'm studying for the final exams of my junior year. I dream a little about everything you're experiencing; I pretend to myself I find it in books. Yesterday I was telling Federico everything you're doing and seeing and reading and hearing, and we think perhaps if we pass our exams we could come visit you. Aren't you planning to come back some day? You could during your next vacation, couldn't you?

You wrote that fall was different now you were with Claire. On Sundays you often went for walks, holding hands, silent; the scent of rotting hya-

cinths still lingered in the parks but now it was the odor of burning leaves
that pursued you during those long walks that reminded you of ours years
ago on the beach, because neither you nor Claire dared break the silence, no
matter what came to your minds, no matter what the enigma of overlapping
seasons with their juxtaposition of jasmine and dead leaves suggested to
you. In the end, silence. Claire, Claire—you wrote me—you have understood everything. I have what I always had. Now I can possess it. I've found
you again, Claire.

I said again in my next letter that Federico and I were studying together
for an exam and that we were going to Acapulco for the last days of the year.
But I crossed that out before I sent you the letter. In yours you never asked
who Federico was—and if you could ask me today, I wouldn't know how to
answer. When vacation came I told them not to accept his calls anymore; I
no longer had to see him at school. I went alone, with my parents, to
Acapulco. I didn't tell you anything about that. I didn't write for several
months, but your letters continued to arrive. That winter, Claire came to
live with you in the room on Bourg-de-Four. Why think about the letters
that came after that? They're here in my purse. "Claire, everything is new.
We had never been together at dawn. Before, those hours meant nothing;
they were a dead part of the day and now they're the ones I wouldn't
exchange for anything. We've always been so close, during our long walks,
in the theatres, in the restaurants, at the beach, making up adventures, but
we always lived in separate rooms. Do you know what I used to do, alone,
thinking about you? Now I don't waste those hours. I spend the whole night
close to you, my arms around your waist, your shoulder pressed to my
chest, waiting for you to wake. You know that and you turn towards me and
smile with your eyes closed, Claire; as I turn back the sheet I forget the places
you have warmed through the night and I ask myself if this isn't what we
always wanted, from the beginning, when we were playing and walking in
silence, holding hands. We *had* to sleep together beneath the same roof, in
our own house, isn't that true? Why don't you write me, Claudia? I love you,
Juan Luis."

Perhaps you remember how I teased you. It wasn't the same thing to
make love on a beach or in a hotel surrounded with lakes and snow as it was
to live together every day. Besides, you were working in the same office.
You'd end up boring each other. The novelty would wear off. Waking up
together. Actually, it wasn't very pleasant. She will see how you brush your
teeth. You will see her take off her make-up, cream her face, put on her
garter belt. . . . I think you've done the wrong thing, Juan Luis. Weren't you
searching for your independence? Why have you taken on such a burden? If
that's what you had in mind, you might as well have stayed in Mexico. But
apparently it's difficult to escape the conventions in which we have been

brought up. In the long run, although you haven't followed the formula completely, you're doing what Mama and Papa and everyone else has always expected of you. You've become a man of routine. After all the good times we had with Doris and Sophia and Marie-José. What a shame.

We didn't write each other for a year and a half. My life didn't change at all. My studies became a little useless, repetitive. How can they *teach* you literature? Once they put me in touch with a few things, I knew that my thing was to go my own way, read and write and study on my own, and I continued going to class only for the sake of discipline, because I had to finish what I had begun. It's so foolish and pedantic when they go on explaining things you already know based on their phony diagrams and illustrations. That's the bad thing about being ahead of your teachers, and they're aware of it, but hide it in order to keep their jobs. We were coming to Romanticism and I was already reading Firbank and Rolfe and I had even discovered William Golding. I had my professors a little scared and my only satisfaction during that time was the praise I received at the college: Claudia has real promise. I spent more and more time locked in my room. I arranged it to my tastes, put my books in order, hung my reproductions, set up my record player, and Mama finally got tired of telling me that I should meet boys and go out dancing. They left me alone. I changed my wardrobe a little, from the cotton prints you knew to white blouses and dark skirts, tailored suits—to things that make me feel a little more serious, more severe, more distant.

It seems we've arrived at the airport. The radar screens are revolving and I stop talking with you. It's going to be an unpleasant moment. The passengers are stirring. I take my handbag and make-up case and my coat. I sit waiting for the others to get off. It's humid and cold and the fog conceals the mountains. It isn't raining, but the air contains millions of unformed, invisible droplets: I feel them against my skin. I smooth my straight blond hair. I enter the building and walk towards the airline company office. I tell my name and the clerk nods silently. He asks me to follow him. We walk along a long well-lighted corridor and then emerge into the icy afternoon. We move across a long strip of pavement that ends at a kind of hangar. I am walking with my fists clenched. The clerk does not attempt to converse with me. He precedes me, a little ceremoniously. We enter the storage room. It smells of damp wood, of straw and pitch. There are many large boxes lined up in orderly fashion as well as rows of barrels and even a small barking dog in a cage. Your box is partly hidden behind some others. The clerk points it out to me, bowing respectfully. I touch the edge of the coffin and for several moments I stand there without speaking. My weeping is buried deep in my belly, but it is as if I were crying. The clerk is waiting and when he thinks it seemly he shows me the various papers I have been negotiating during the last few days, the permits and authorizations from the police, the department of health, the Mexican consulate and the airline company. He asks me to sign the final embarkation documents. I do it, and he licks the gummed back of some labels and affixes them to the coffin, sealing it. I touch the gray lid once more and we return to the central building. The clerk murmurs his condolences and says goodbye.

After clearing the documents with the airline company and the Swiss authorities, I go up to the restaurant, with my boarding pass in my hand and I sit down and order a cup of coffee. I am sitting next to a large window and I can see the planes appearing and disappearing on the runway. They fade into the fog or emerge from it, but the noise of their engines precedes them or lingers behind like the silent wake of a ship. They frighten me. Yes, you know I am deathly afraid of them and I don't want to think what this return trip with you will be like, in the middle of winter, showing in every airport the documents with your name and the permits that allow them to pass you through. They bring my coffee and I take it black; it's what I needed. My hand does not tremble as I drink it.

Nine weeks ago I tore open the envelope of your first letter in a year and a half and spilled my cup of coffee on the rug. I stooped down hurriedly to wipe it up with my skirt, and then I put on a record and wandered around the room looking at book jackets, my arms crossed; I even read a few lines of Garcilaso, slowly, stroking the covers of the book, sure of myself, far removed from your still mysterious letter concealed in the torn envelope lying on the arm of the chair.

> Sweet souvenirs of love now sadly pondered,
> Yes, sweet they seemed when God did so assign,
> In memory joined and bound, mine not to sunder,
> With memory, too, they work my death's design.

"Of course, we've quarreled. She goes out slamming the door behind her and I almost weep with rage. I try to get interested in something but I can't and I go out to look for her. I know where she is. Across the street, at La Clémence, drinking and smoking nervously. I go down the creaking stairs and out into the plaza and she looks at me across the distance and pretends not to notice. I cross the garden and walk slowly up to the highest level of Bourg-de-Four, my fingers brushing the iron bannister; I reach the cafe and sit down beside her in one of the wicker chairs. We are in the open air; in summer the cafe spills out onto the sidewalk and one can hear the music from the carillon of St. Pierre. Claire is talking with the waitress. They are making small talk about the weather in that odious Swiss sing-song. I wait until Claire stubs out her cigarette in the ash tray and I do the same in order to touch her fingers. She looks at me. Do you know how, Claudia? As *you* looked at me, high on the rocks at the beach, waiting for me to save you from the ogre. You had to pretend that you didn't know whether I was coming to save you or to kill you in the name of your jailer. But sometimes you couldn't contain your laughter and the fiction was shattered for an instant. The quarrel began because of my carelessness. Claire accused me of being careless and of creating a moral problem for her. What were we to do? It would have helped even if I had had an immediate answer. But no, I retreated into my shell, silent and uncommunicative, and didn't even try to escape the situation by doing something intelligent. There were books and records in the house, but I dedicated myself to working some crossword puzzles.

"*You* have to decide, Juan Luis. Please."

"I'm thinking."

"Don't be stupid. I'm not referring to that. I'm talking about *everything*. Are we going to spend our whole lives classifying documents for the United Nations? Or are we just living some in-between step that will lead to something better, something we don't know about yet? I'm willing to do anything, Juan Luis, but I can't make the decisions by myself. Tell me our life together and our work is just an adventure, and it will be all right with me. Tell me they're both permanent; that will be all right, too. But we can't act any longer as if our work is transitory and our love permanent, or vice versa, do you understand what I'm saying?"

"How was I going to tell her, Claudia, that her problem was completely beyond my comprehension? Believe me, sitting there in La Clémence, watching the young people riding by on bicycles, listening to the laughter and murmurs of those around us, with the bells of the Cathedral chiming their music, believe me, little sister, I fled from this whole confining world. I closed my eyes and sank into myself, I refined in the darkness of my soul my most secret knowledge; I tuned all the strings of my sensitivity so that the least movement of my soul would set them vibrating; I stretched my perception, my prophecies, the whole trauma of the present, like a bow, so as to shoot into the future, which wounded, would be revealed. The arrow flew from the bow, but there was no bull's eye, Claudia, there was nothing in the future, and all that painful internal construction—my hands felt numb from the effort—tumbled down like sand castles at the first assault of the waves, not lost, but returning to that ocean we call memory; to my childhood, to our games, our beach, to a joy and warmth that everything that followed could only imitate, try to prolong, to fuse with projects for the future and reproduce with present surprise. Yes, I told her it was all right; we would look for a larger apartment. Claire is going to have a baby."

She herself wrote me a letter in that handwriting I had seen only on the postcard from Montreux. "I know how important you are to Juan Luis, how the two of you grew up together, and all the rest. I want very much to see you and I'm sure we will be good friends. Believe me when I say I already know you. Juan Luis talks so much about you that sometimes I get a little jealous. I hope you'll be able to come see us some day. Juan Luis is doing very well in his job and everyone likes him very much. Geneva is small but pleasant. We've become fond of the city for reasons you can guess and here we will make our life. I can still work a few months; I'm only two months pregnant. Your sister, Claire."

And the recent snapshot fell from the envelope. You've gained weight, and you call my attention to it on the back of the photo: "Too much fondue, Sis." And you're getting bald, just like Papa. And she's very beautiful, very Botticelli, with her long blond hair and coquettish beret. Have you gone mad, Juan Luis? You were a handsome young man when you left Mexico. Look at yourself. Have you looked at yourself? Watch your diet. You're only twenty-seven years old and you look forty. And what are you reading, Juan Luis, what interests you? Crossword puzzles? You mustn't betray yourself, please, you know I depend on you, on your growing with me, I can't go ahead without you. You promised you were going to continue studying there; that's what you told Papa. The routine work is tiring you out. All you want to do is get to your apartment and read the newspaper and take off your shoes. Isn't that true? You don't say it, but I know it's true. Don't destroy yourself, please. I have remained faithful. I'm keeping our childhood alive. It doesn't matter to me that you're far away. But we must remain united in what matters most, we mustn't concede anything to demands that we be anything other (do you remember?) than love and intelligence and youth and silence. They want to maim us, to make us like themselves; they can't tolerate us. Do not serve them, Juan Luis, I beg you, don't forget what you told me that afternoon in the Mascarones cafe. Once you take the first step in that direction, everything is lost; there is no return. I had to show your letter to our parents. Mama got very sick. High blood pressure. She's in the cardiac ward. I hope not to have to give you bad news in my next letter. I think about you, I remember you, I know you won't fail me.

Two letters arrived. First, the one you sent me, telling me that Claire had had an abortion. Then the one you sent Mama announcing that you were going to marry Claire within the month. You hoped we would all be able to come to the wedding. I asked Mama to let me keep her letter with mine. I put them side by side and studied your handwriting to see if they were both written by the same person.

"It was a rapid decision, Claudia. I told her that it was too soon. We're young and we have the right to live a while longer without responsibilities. Claire said that was fine. I don't know whether she understood everything I said to her. But you do, don't you?"

"I love this girl, I'm sure of it. She's been good and understanding with me even though at times I've made her suffer; neither of you will be ashamed that I would want to make it up to her. Her father is a widower; he is an engineer and lives in Neuchâtel. He approves and will come to the wedding. I hope that you, Papa, and Claudia can be with us. When you know Claire you will love her as much as I, Mama."

Three weeks later Claire committed suicide. One of your friends at work called us; he said that one afternoon she had asked for permission to leave the office; she had a headache; she went to an early movie and you looked for her that night, as always, in the apartment; you waited for her, and then you rushed about the city but you couldn't find her; she was dead in the theatre, she had taken the veronal before she entered and she had sat alone in the first row where no one would bother her; you called Neuchâtel, you wandered through the streets and restaurants again and you sat in La Clémence until they closed. It was the next day before they called you from the morgue and you went to see her. Your friend told us that we ought to come after you, and make you come back to Mexico: you were maddened with grief. I told our parents the truth. I showed them your last letter. They were stunned for a moment and then Papa said he would never allow you in the house again. He shouted that you were a criminal.

I finish my coffee and a waiter points towards where I am seated. A tall man with the lapels of his coat turned up, nods and walks towards me. It is the first time I have seen that tanned face, the blue eyes and the white hair. He asks my permission to sit down and asks me if I am your sister. I tell him yes. He says he is Claire's father. He does not shake hands. I ask him if he wants a cup of coffee. He shakes his head and takes a pack of cigarettes from his overcoat pocket. He offers me one. I tell him I don't smoke. He tries to smile and I put on my dark glasses. He puts his hand in his pocket again and takes out a piece of paper. He places it, folded, on the table.

"I have brought you this letter."

I try to question him with raised eyebrows.

"It's signed by you. It's addressed to my daughter. It was on Juan Luis's pillow the morning they found him dead in his apartment."

"Oh, yes, I wondered what had become of that letter. I looked for it everywhere."

"Yes, I thought you would want to keep it." Now he smiles as if he already knew me. "You're very cynical. Don't worry. Why should you? There's nothing anyone can do now."

He rises without saying goodbye. The blue eyes look at me with sadness and compassion. I try to smile, and I pick up the letter. The loudspeaker:

" . . . le départ de son vol número 707. . . . Paris, Gander, New York et Mexico. . . . priés de se rendre à la porte número 5."

I take my things, adjust my beret, and go down to the departure gate. I am carrying my purse and the make-up case and the boarding pass in my hands, but I manage, between the door and the steps of the airplane, to tear the letter and throw the pieces into the cold wind, into the fog that will perhaps carry them to the lake where you dived, Juan Luis, in search of a mirage.

—translated by Margaret S. Peden from the Spanish

The Harvest

TESS GALLAGHER

MR. G.'s STORY, the patched-up account I'm about to set straight, starts with the arrival of the blind man at my house. But the real story starts further back than that, back in Seattle with days Mr. G. knows nothing about. Days I was typing for Norman, running errands, going through files and reading stuff out-loud to him. Norman and I were working in Research and Development for the SPD. It was a bizarre thing in the first place—a blind man working for the police. But they let us alone, the other researchers and developers. They gave us a little cubicle with no windows, and they shut the door. This was okay with Norman. He liked it fine. I guess I did too.

Norman was a chain smoker. He had an actual little chain he pulled out of his vest pocket and rattled when he broke the news to me. He laughed, then lit up a cigarette. Sometimes the visibility in our cubicle was so bad I could barely make out the silo on the big State Fair calendar behind his desk. But we did okay. We enjoyed working together. We listened to each other's stories. It got to be more than a job. It became a friendship.

We'd kept in touch off and on for years. Once in a while one or the other of us would send a tape, and once in a blue moon there'd be a telephone call. Norman got married and passed through a series of low-grade Federal jobs. Then, with the help of his wife, he'd quit government employment to start his own business. I'd made a few wild swerves myself and had ended up back East working at the gas company and living with Ernest. Ernest was my kind of guy. He understood that your life hadn't started the minute he walked onto the scene. Ernest knew about my friendship with Norman. So when Norman called up to arrange a visit, Ernest didn't make a big deal out of it. He didn't say much. He griped a little, sure. But that's in the nature of things.

Right at the start Mr. G. slips off the track as he tells this whole thing. Gallivan is his real name, and he works with me on the graveyard shift at the gas company. Gallivan is agreeable enough when he wants to be. But at work you can't count on it. On the job he and I share a work area. It's mainly my humming that Mr. G. objects to. I'm also an intermittent whistler. If Mr. G. were doing the work he's paid to do, none of this would be a problem. But most of the time he's hammering away on his novels and stories at the secretary's big Selectric. Nothing he writes gets published, but that doesn't stop him. He says he just hasn't been at it long enough to make a breakthrough with the editors. But if what he did with Norman's visit is any example, he may just type his way to Kingdom Come with only his unfortunate fellow workers to read the stuff. A sinking feeling came to me reading what Gallivan—Mr. G. as I call him—wrote about Norman. It was like looking out over a field of trampled wheat and knowing that this wheat has still got to be harvested.

Gallivan has no respect for facts. But he also can't stay away from what's true. The result is what I call "the marble cake" effect. If he were an out-and-out, honest-to-goodness liar I would have more hope for him. But as it is, he can't imagine anything unless he gouges himself with the truth once in a while, and that's what's so confusing for those of us who have the misfortune to be in his vicinity. Aside from this, he's not an altogether bad guy. As I say, he did invite Norman to dinner that night.

If my blind man, Norman, had not called from the train station a day earlier than he was supposed to have arrived, there's every chance that Mr. G. would never have met him. But as it happened, Ernest and I were just on our way out of the house, heading to Gallivan's for dinner. Believe me, it was a rare occasion to go to Gallivan's for dinner. The phone rang just as we were locking the door. Ernest let go with a few choice words.

"Forget it," he said. "They'll call back if it's important."

"Yes," I said, "they'll call back and I won't be here. Maybe it's my chance in a million." I unlocked the door and went back into the kitchen to pick up the phone. Ernest took this as an opportunity to fix himself a quick drink. It was Norman Roth, the blind man, on the phone. He was at the train station and wondering where I was.

"I'm here in my house," I said.

"Oh dear, am I early?" he said. And I could picture him touching his watch with the days of the week nubbed into it—a watch he no longer owned, as I learned.

"You're a day or so ahead of me, Norman," I said. "But that's fine. No problem," I lied. I tried to act cheerful and eager. "I'll be right down to get you. We were on our way to dinner at a friend's. But it's okay. We'll work something out."

I got off the phone and called Gallivan. He said it would be fine to bring Norman. Of course there'd be enough food. As long as my blind man wasn't Man Mountain Dean, Gallivan said and laughed. I decided to drive to the station by myself. Ernest was beefing up his drink anyway. He huffed into the living room and switched on the TV, then reached for a cushion. He was settling in again.

"Ernest, I've got some things for you to do," I said. "I want you to clear away those keepsakes on the mantle and anything else that might break." I didn't wait for an answer. I lined it up for him. "Don't forget the throw rugs," I said. "Stack them on the back porch. And any electric cords too. Make sure he won't have cords to trip over." I was still thinking of things to tell Ernest as I pulled out of the driveway.

I hadn't seen Norman in years, but I'd spoken with him six months before when his wife passed away. She'd had a cancerous brain tumor which had caused her hospitalization. Months of deterioration followed. Near the end, Norman had called to tell me about it. He said she'd been able to give him little pressure signals on his hand right up to the end—"Yes" and "No" answers to questions he formulated for her.

"Strange, her losing her voice like that," Norman had said. "Oh, she knew everything. She just couldn't talk. Couldn't make a peep. I had to do the talking for us. 'Want to try some physical therapy today?' I'd ask her. 'Okay, sure,' I'd say. 'You'd like that pillow under your shoulders? All right, yes. The window up? How about some fresh air?' "

Norman was standing next to a small black valise in the empty waiting room of the station when I arrived.

"Norman!" I said, locating myself in front of him. We embraced. Then he stepped back, fumbled for my face and planted a kiss on my jaw.

"I'm so humiliated," he said. "You can't know how stupid I feel. A day early! Oh I'm so ashamed, I wish I could evaporate."

"Now, now," I said. I took his arm and picked up the valise. "You're here. That's what matters. I just wish I'd had the whole day to look forward to your coming."

"I have a new watch," Norman said. We'd gone as far as the taxi stand. He stopped, let go of my arm and took an object the size of a deck of cards from his coat pocket. "Look at this. It's computerized. I guess it was misprogrammed on the days. But the hours work fine." He pushed a switch and a voice approximating the human said, "Fi-ive for-ty-ni-en and fif-ty seconds." A little bell tone sounded.

"That's something," I said. "What'll they think of next!" He returned the voice-clock to his pocket, and we made our way to the car.

I situated him in the front seat, then stowed his bag behind the driver's seat. I got in on my side and patted him on the leg.

"Good to see you, Norm!" I said. "Don't you worry about a thing." I assured him he was welcome at my friend's house for dinner.

"Mr. Gallivan's a writer," I told him. "He's written six novels and three books of non-fiction. Nothing's been published yet, but he has hopes. Right now he's suffering writer's block, so he's taking up the slack by entertaining a few people from work tonight."

Norman brought up his recent visit to his dead wife's relatives in Vermont. (Mr. G. places them in Connecticut.) Norman confessed he didn't miss his wife as much as he'd thought he would. "It's a terrible thing to admit," he said. "But it's true." He was fingering my dashboard, trying to figure out what sort of car I had.

"This isn't the same car you had," he said.

"That one bit the dust a long time ago," I said. "This is a Beetle. A 1973 VW Beetle.

Mr. G.'s story begins right here, as we get out of the car and I help Norman up the steps to the house. The narrator for Mr. G.'s story sees his wife gripping the arm of the blind man and guiding him toward the house. He thinks how strange it is to catch a view of his wife in a moment of intimacy with a blind man, a man he's never met and is not eager to meet.

"These steps have an odd slant to them," Norman said. "That one nearly got me." He leaned on my arm. I looked ahead of us to anticipate possible stumbling points. On the porch I held the screen door back and asked him to step inside. I latched the screen and guided him into the living room. I set his valise at the end of the couch. Ernest wasn't around, so I moved some newspapers from his end of the couch and Norman sat down. I went into the kitchen and fixed Norman and myself Bloody Marys. Then we started to reminisce. We sipped our drinks and called up the names of people we'd known together at the Police Department—Barbara Dukes, a woman officer we'd liked—still in the Juvenile Department, then a sergeant in the Bad Checks Department I'd called Smiley.

"Oh you mean Chuckles," Norman said, and laughed. He used to do that a lot, changing things from a sighted way of talking to how he perceived them, by hearing or touching. "Gee, it's so dark in here I can't feel where I'm going," he'd say and laugh his big laugh.

Norman was trying to locate an ashtray on the coffee table in front of him. I carried one over and placed it under his hand. I'd nearly forgotten about Ernest when he came down the stairs and tip-toed across the room to his easy chair. Before he could sit down, I motioned him over.

"Norman," I said, "this is the man I live with. Ernest, this is Norman Roth." Norman got to his feet. His hand came up like a toy pistol, his thumb cocked. Ernest looked at the hand and then he took it. He was not thrilled to have a blind man in the house. Mr. G. has that right.

"Pleased to meet you," Norman said. He pumped Ernest's hand, then reached behind him to locate his place on the couch.

"Yah, me too," Ernest said. "I heard a lot about you."

"Nothing too bad, I hope," Norman said. "How about a light, while you're up?"

Ernest fished for his lighter, then handed it to me. "I'll let her help you," he said. "I'm not too steady today."

I took the lighter, flicked it and reached out to the cigarette Norman was holding. He inhaled and the smoke wafted out into the room. We sat down and took up our drinks again. Ernest had been drinking all afternoon. He retrieved a bourbon he'd left on the coffee table. Ernest watched Norman's every move.

"How was the train ride?" Ernest asked.

"Swell, just swell," Norman said. "Once I got the porter trained to bring me drinks, it was very pleasant." He put a hand into his suit pocket and kept it there. He smiled and nodded and sat there as if waiting for the next question. Then he remembered his cigarette ash and started pinching the air until he'd located the rim of the ashtray again. He knocked off his ash and smiled out into the room, just enjoying the fact that he was on top of things. Then he located his drink and took a long draw on that. I had time to look at him.

He's not blonde as Mr. G. later described him. He's never been blonde. He's bald, except for close-shaven sideburns and a band of hair at the back of his neck. There'd been a few sprouts left on top in the days I'd worked for him, but these had dropped away. Now when he tossed his head, light dodged back and forth on the bare surface of his cranium. I thought he seemed balder than he was because his eyes were clouded over. I'd always felt invisible staring into those eyes. I could stare as long as I wanted to and not be seen.

"Did you ever see one of these?" Norman said, taking his voice-watch out of his coat pocket and holding it out in Ernest's direction. "Little bugger got me here a day early."

Ernest reached across the coffee table and took the watch. He examined it and pushed the switch. "Six-twen-ty-four and ni-en sec-onds," the watch said. A little bell tone sounded.

"Great little gadget," Ernest said. "How much did it set you back?"

"Not much," Norman said. "Got a deal on it from the Bureau for the Handicapped." Norman waited for the watch to touch his hand, then put it back in his pocket.

"Good to see the taxpayer's dollar is helping a few people," Ernest said. I shot him a shut-up-or-I'll-kill-you look. Ernest just grinned at me.

"I think we'd better head over to Gallivan's," I said. I wanted to get Ernest's mouth full of food before he started going on about how he wished a little federal aid would come his way.

We hadn't finished our drinks, so Ernest found a carryout holder. He put our glasses into that. He took them out to the car while I helped Norman down the steps.

"Is your house big?" Norman asked. "It feels like it's big." I looked back at the house, then opened the car door for him.

"Yes, it's big. Two stories and an attic. I'll show you around tomorrow."

On the way over to Mr. G.'s I described the neighborhood so Ernest wouldn't butt in with more cracks on federal aid. I was driving. Norman was in the back seat. "There's a college dormitory in this block with a health-food joint next door," I said.

"Granola," Norman said. "Now that's a triumph of the sixties. Granola and pot. Tell me when you see a shop that sells pot!" He slapped his thigh and rocked back and forth in his seat. Ernest looked at me and then had some of his drink.

Gallivan lives in a brick duplex. The landlord lives in another city. Nobody looks after things. The shrubs crowd over the walkway so that it's hard to push through. But Gallivan has cut a little passageway to his door. The whole neighborhood is a mess, cans and bottles, old newspapers, and some of the yards are knee-high in grass. Naturally Mr. G. does not mention the decrepit condition of his premises in the account he gives of his meeting with the blind man.

Gallivan had on his uniform—a yellow shirt, green tie, dark brown trousers. He always wore these clothes. He'd worn them to his job at the gas works the three years I'd known him. In the months before writer's block had set in, we'd arrive at work, check the gauges to make sure the gas levels were properly regulated, that the gas was feeding out okay. Then we'd decide it was time for a coffee break. After that, Mr. G. would go to the typewriter and begin work on his manuscript. I'd work on my crocheting or talk to my mother long distance on the WATS line.

"Welcome," Mr. G. said to Norman. "A nice accident of events that you could join us." Norman brought his hand up again, and I stood back so he could give Mr. G. one of his eggbeater handshakes.

Ernest squeezed Gallivan's arm as he walked past him into the living room. He nodded to the other two guests, my fellow workers at the gas plant. Mr. G. positioned them in front of Norman. Each of them met his grip and then stepped back. Sal Fischer, the soft-spoken foreman who worked swing shift, was there with his old Labrador, Ripper. Margaret, a secretary who was dating Sal, looked pretty in a blue cotton print dress with tiny red flowers along the hem. Ripper sniffed Norman's pockets and crotch, then allowed himself to be petted by Norman.

"Smell that food, Norm?" Gallivan said. "It won't be long now. We're in the homestretch."

Norman turned his head and sniffed. "I'd know pork roast at fifty paces."
"Amazing," Mr. G. said, and shook his head. "You're close. It's ribs,
back-ribs. I've made my special Texas barbecue sauce."

I situated Norman on a sturdy chair at the center of the room and went
into the kitchen to try and get the meal onto the table as quickly as possible. I
could hear Norman's voice booming out over the other voices. Mr. G. had
begun to question Norman about talking records for the blind.

"My father doesn't read," Mr. G. was saying. "Oh, he *can* read, but he
doesn't. He might listen to something though. If he could just plug in one of
my novels while he shaves or tidies up the kitchen, then he might get through
one of my books. That's all I'm asking. Just a few minutes of his time each
day."

"I'll certainly do what I can, you bet," Norman shouted. "I've had some
dealings with those people. I just might be able to hustle them along."

"Ernest," I called into the living room. "Come here." Ernest came into
the kitchen, a glass in his hand. I gave him the platter of ribs I'd taken up.

"What're you doing," he said. "This isn't your kitchen." His eyes had
that filmy look they get when he's had too much to drink.

"I know that," I said. "But I'm taking charge." I dished up cole slaw and
beans, then followed him into the dining room. The table was set. I filled
water glasses and then went into the living room to announce that we were
ready. By the time the others wandered into the dining room, Ernest was
already seated at the table.

"Here, Norman," Mr. G. said. "You sit next to me. I want to hear more
about your Independent Management Enterprises."

"Oh, that's all finished now," Norman said. "My wife worked with me.
But now that she's gone, I don't have the heart for it."

"I'm sorry, I didn't catch that," Mr. G. said and cocked his head.
"Gone?"

"Gone," Norman said.

I could see then that Gallivan felt he was on the track of something. He
kept his eyes on Norman for a minute. Then he unbuttoned his cuffs, rolled
his sleeves, and forked a stack of ribs onto his plate. He racked another
portion onto Norman's plate. Then he reached across Norman and handed
the platter on to Margaret. He said, "Margaret, help yourself and pass them
along." From the looks of her, Margaret had never sat next to a blind man.
She kept glancing over at me, trying to catch my attention, as though I would
send her silent messages on what to do.

Norman took a row of ribs in his hands and began to gnaw on them. He
leaned over the table to make sure he didn't drop anything onto the floor.
Talk stopped. We got into some serious eating. Norman held his own. His
cheeks were bright orange with the barbecue sauce, and a patch of orange

had somehow reached his forehead. Ernest had not once looked up from his plate. There was the sound of bones clacking as we finished with them and dropped them onto our plates. I imagined Norman must hear that sound as Norman licked the barbecue sauce from his fingers. Then, without warning, he pushed his chair back and stood up from the table.

"Where's the loo, if you'd be so kind?" He said this roughly in the direction of the light fixture, then took a jerky step into the table like one of those TV monsters who can see to kill but that's about it. Margaret looked up at him, alarmed, as if he might stoop and carry her off.

I got up and led Norman down a hallway and left him at the door to the bathroom.

"The facility's just inside, to your right," I said. "I'll wait for you."

From inside the bathroom I heard Norman's watch go off. Then I could hear water running. It seemed to run for a long time. When he didn't come out, I listened harder. I could hear a sobbing noise. I stood there for a while thinking what I should do. I knocked softly and the sobbing stopped. I went back to the table and asked Ernest to go get Norman.

"What'd he do, fall in?" Ernest said. He moved the bones on his plate to one side and helped himself to more ribs. Then he looked wearily at me, pushed his chair back and got up.

In a little while I could hear Ernest and Norman bumping along the hallway. It was then that Ripper broke from under the table. He scrabbled across the hardwood floor and began to tear at Norman's trouser leg, growling and slavering. Sal cursed and jumped up from his chair. He yanked Ripper's collar so hard he fell back with the dog. Norman would have heard all this as a yowl, then a series of thuds and more cursing.

After all this, I could see Norman was in no shape to stay on, so I tried to head us toward home. Ernest was in no hurry. He was standing in the doorway to the kitchen gnawing on a rib. I mentioned a TV special I didn't want to miss. It was on nuclear war, I said. That's when it happened. Gallivan threw down his napkin and stood up.

"I'd love to see that show myself," he said. "My TV's on the fritz. But I want to see that show. We all need to face up to the horror of what could happen. Even if we can't do anything about it."

I got Norman by the sleeve and eased him carefully past Ripper toward the door. Before I knew it, Mr. G. had turned the clean-up duties over to Margaret and Sal and was following us back through the undergrowth to the car.

"I want to hear about your dreams," Gallivan said as he climbed into the back seat beside Norman. "Is it true that if someone were throwing, say, a lemon-meringue pie at you in a dream—you'd first experience the taste sensation 'lemon pie' and then you'd feel the meringue all over your face?"

Norman rocked back and forth on the back seat. "That's about it, kiddo," he said.

None of the dinner scene just described, or the car ride home, makes it into Mr. G.'s version of the story. He also removes himself entirely from the scene which follows. A scene in which, purportedly, the blind man and the husband and wife watch a TV program, and the wife falls asleep.

One thing is true, I did fall asleep. But not before I'd taken Norman and his bag upstairs to the spare room and pulled out the hide-a-bed for him.

"Sleep as late as you want," I told him.

"You know me. The birds get in my ears," Norman said.

I plumped his pillows and helped him locate his ashtray and some towels I'd put on a shelf near the bed. Then he sat down a moment on the bed. He tipped his head back and his blind eyes ranged off toward a Mexican vaquero on a velvet wall hanging—something my brother had bought for me in Juárez.

"Jeannie's mother," he said. "I think I could have gotten through it okay except for her."

"We can talk tomorrow," I said. "We'll have a good long talk like old times." We were facing the Mexican vaquero in his spangled sombrero.

"I just want to tell you this one part," Norman said. His head rolled back. Then he leaned forward and said, "Jeannie's mother kept putting words into Jeannie's mouth. It was after the biofeedback petered out on us. Her mother'd do things like have Jeannie refuse drugs. She was taking the drugs to help with the pain. 'She says she doesn't want those pills,' her mother would say. 'She says she can take it. Can't you honey?' I mean, can you imagine me watching someone else put words into Jeannie's mouth?"

"Let's go downstairs," I said. I stood up and put my hand under Norman's elbow.

"You know me," Norman said as we headed for the hallway. "Jeannie and me, we were close. I convinced her about biofeedback. To try it. It was something to hope for. She had about three more weeks of hope, because I got instructions on how to do it."

I could hear Mr. G.'s and Ernest's voices as we took the first set of stairs to the landing.

"My doctor says fallout shelters won't be any use," Gallivan was saying.

"Doctors won't be any use either," Ernest said. "I'm going to stock in some old Doctor Johnny Walker."

"You're going to have to get some kind of pastime," I said to Norman. He was leaning on the rail. "Something to carry you through."

"I'm taking banjo lessons," Norman said. "I didn't bring my instrument with me, but normally I practice two or three hours a day."

"We'll say good night to Mr. Gallivan. And then we'll turn off the set and call it a night," I said. We took the last of the steps and I coached Norman past my big paradise palm towards the couch.

Mr. G. was adjusting the color on the set. Ernest had his feet up on the coffee table. He looked comfortable. I got Norman seated on the couch and then started straightening the coffee table, clearing away some old newspapers and circulars that had stacked up. Then I told Norman I'd be back. I was just going upstairs to get ready for bed. I glanced over at Ernest who jiggled his eyebrows at me when he heard me say "bed."

In a little while I went back downstairs. Mr. G. was in the kitchen fixing drinks for everyone.

"I don't want anything," I called to him.

"I hear you," he said.

I'd changed into my robe and slippers. I sat down on the other end of the couch from Norman. He'd begun to nod. But I couldn't tell if he was asleep or just agreeing to something he was thinking. Ernest lifted his glass in my direction and gave me the old glitter-eye, so I flipped the robe open quick to give him a peep, hoping it would accelerate our getting upstairs. But the TV was on and Norman suddenly broke out with a question.

"What's he mean 'limited nuclear war'? How limited is it if they obliterate Europe?"

"You got to count from the flash," Ernest said. "You forget to count in this next war and you're fried."

"Or gassed or shot," Norman said. "For once I'm glad I'm not able-bodied."

"If they had a button for you to push, you'd have to push it," Ernest said. "You'd have your orders." His eyes had that wild look they get when he's been on the bourbon.

Mr. G. returned with the drinks. He'd loosened his tie. He was on the scent of "material." I leaned my head back on the couch. My eyes were shutting down on me. An aircraft carrier as big as three hotels moved heavily across the TV screen. I knew I'd be asleep sitting up in no time, but I couldn't seem to move. I could hear the ice cubes clinking in their glasses. Norman hears those ice cubes, clinking, I thought, and I felt close to him in the old ways, those times I'd had to think what he needed when we'd worked together at the police station. The word "capability" occurred several times in the voice coming from the TV. Then I heard Norman ask Ernest to get him a piece of paper and some scissors. I closed my eyes. I must have dozed because when I woke up, my robe had fallen open. Ernest, Mr. G. and Norman were bent over the coffee table. Mr. G. had Norman by the hand and was moving his fingers over a piece of paper. "That's the nose of it right there," Mr. G. was saying. "Feel that?" There were scraps of paper on the rug and on Mr. G.'s trouser legs.

"Ernest, what are you doing?" I said.

"Helping him see what a word means," he said. "Missile. He doesn't know what the word 'missile' means. We cut one out of paper here, and he touched it. Now he knows."

"Flash," Norman said. "That means a sudden burst of light."

"Yah, try cutting one of those out!" Ernest laughed. He shook Gallivan's arm. "Try cutting a flash out."

"But the word 'light.' Does that word make any sense to you?" Mr. G. asked Norman. "I mean, I could say 'a sudden flash of sagebrush' and it would be all the same to you, wouldn't it?"

"A nuclear flash would be blinding," Norman said. "In some things, I'm ahead of the game."

As Mr. G. tells it in his version, the TV program was a film on cancer hot spots in the body, so they weren't examining the drawing of a missile at all, but instead, a drawing of the stomach. Mr. G. ties this in nicely with the death of Norman's wife. I told Gallivan about that later. He ends the piece when the narrator has one of those "recognitions"—what literature types call "epiphanies." The narrator in Mr. G.'s story, an inarticulate sort, had somehow experienced blindness through his blind visitor. Mr. G. says he's considering a new twist, maybe bringing Norman's mother-in-law into it somehow.

What really happened was that I cinched my robe shut, got up and switched the TV off.

"Enough is enough," I said. "Goodbye world. Goodnight Mr. Gallivan," I said. "Ernest?"

I went upstairs and got into the bed, naked. I heard Ernest come up the stairs. But he didn't come into the bedroom. I heard the front door shut. Not long after, I heard voices outside on the lawn. It was summer and the screens were on, so sometimes whole goodnight love scenes would drift in the window.

"Where have you been?" I asked when Ernest finally came into the bedroom. "Did you get Norman to his room?"

"I was smoking a cigarette," he said. "And looking out the window."

"Where's Norman?" I asked him.

"He's out there on the lawn," he said, "with Gallivan." Ernest laughed. Then he undressed, put his pajamas on, and got into bed with me. "Nobody ever told your blind man about constellations, so Gallivan's doing it. Out there telling a blind man the stars."

Ernest reached over and began patting my hair like he does when he wants to get something started. But I was upset.

"How will Norman get back to his room?" I said. I threw the covers back, got up and went over to the window. I raised the shade and looked out. There was Mr. G. holding Norman's arm over his head like the poor man had just won a prize fight.

"Now this here, see this? This here's the Big Dipper," I heard Mr. G. say as he moved Norman's arm around. "That's the handle on the Dipper right along there."

I could see them below in the light from the street lamp. They were drawing something in the air. I couldn't see the stars. The sky was overcast. I don't know much of anything about constellations myself, except that some of them bear the names of animals, and Greek gods and heroes.

"What stars?" I said. "Ernest come here and get a look at this."

Ernest slid over to my side of the bed. He stood up behind me and looked over my shoulder at the two men in our front yard with their right arms raised in the air. There was Mr. G. chanting the names of the stars like a station master.

Ernest cupped his hands around my breasts. We watched as Mr. G. led Norman out into the middle of the street. A siren went off somewhere towards town. How silent the stars are, I thought. How silent and far away. If each star were to make just the smallest noise, what a thronging would be over us! The night was as black as any night I've seen. I could see the tops of the houses across the street and that was about it.

Down there in the street, Mr. G. had turned Norman in another direction entirely. The headlights of a car came up over the hill and beamed down on them a moment, then fell away down another street. We got back into bed, but we could still hear them out there. In a minute, Ernest turned into his sleeping position and began to snore. I wanted to stay awake until Norman came in. But I closed my eyes.

Somewhere in my sleep, I thought I saw Norman still out there in the front yard. He was holding onto a tree as if he were afraid he might be pulled off the face of the earth. I went outside and stood a little way from him. I didn't say anything. All the houses were dark. The trees were making a soft rushing sound above us. I should have been cold, but I wasn't. I was asleep as I watched myself say something and go over to him.

I woke up and listened for a few moments. There was no noise from the street. Everything was quiet. I got out of bed. Ernest kept on sleeping. I went into the hall and turned on the light. The door to the guest room stood open. Norman was on his back, asleep, his blind eyes closed, the covers pulled up to his chin. His pants were folded across the back of a chair, but the rest of his clothes were in a heap on the bureau. In his sleep, he sighed. Maybe he was dreaming. If so, I wondered if he had to touch everything in his dream to know where he was.

I left the door open and turned off the hall light. I started to go back to bed.

But then I turned and felt my way down the stairs, through the darkened living room and onto the front porch. I stood a moment, staring through the porch screen. The image of Norman and me on the lawn came back. Of course, when I looked, there was no one under the tree. But I pushed the screen door open and moved, as I had in my dream, across the yard. The stars were out. The grass was damp under my bare feet. I stood there and looked into the night. I was wide awake. There was nothing stopping me.

Some Gifts

REGINALD GIBBONS

PERHAPS HAVING AGREED between themselves on the hours of their visits, they came dutifully on Thursday, one at three-thirty, the other at six, to stay for a few minutes only. Both of them were balding in an ugly way, gradually exposing that knobby cranium they could not repudiate. It was his, of course. He had given it unconsciously to them, but they could not forgive him for it, just the same, nor for anything else. And he, toothless and stinking, let each enter unheeded through the ragged screen door, without having answered their calls or the knocking of their knuckles on the unpainted wood. Where else would he be but here?

The kitchen door was the only way in. The kitchen table was oily and cluttered with dessicated hunks of cheese and halvah wrapped in coarse waxed paper. The smell of wood glue blended at the door with that of cold broth in a pot on the little stove. Old recipes, old ways—these were what they couldn't stand, the little things they had turned away from in their own lives, with no regret, with a sense of relief. But he held to them stubbornly. He had nothing to change for, no one, no ambition that required it.

He was not working; he had not worked for days, but the excuse he made silently to himself was that he was waiting for the glue in the ukulele to dry fully. Around the room, at eye level dangling from wires stretched from corner to corner like clotheslines against the wall, hung violins and violas, a mandolin or two. Each instrument hung by a small loop of wire wound round the scroll. The violins had not been strung for years. The ebony fingerboard of the ukulele on his worktable was inlaid with an ivory and mother-of-pearl bird.

Two boxes. Each left one on the piles of newspapers that hid the decrepit old sofa. With each, he exchanged the same sort of talk as always, after the customary silence during which each stood gazing sorrowfully and hatefully around his room. Then he lumbered to his chair, and slouched unspeaking, reading a scrap of a magazine, while each guest waited a moment out of habit, then left. He owed the younger one a hundred dollars rent. This was a constant problem. He had not paid the rent for two months. But, he thought, a son should not treat his father as he would any other debtor. Nor a father treat his own son as an ordinary creditor. A hundred dollars. He had a violin to repair by Saturday, and the ukulele, which had been ordered. He would get through this week with the violin, and next, and then think about the hundred dollars. It would take some thinking.

And why not let them take away some of the instruments and sell them where they would? Well, and why not? He could not say, except that to himself he repeated that they were his own, to sell or not to sell as he saw fit. As the chance came to him. If there were few who knew of him, who would come to see his work, what was he to do about it? Buy an advertisement on the damned television stations? He snorted with derision. Even an imbecile—and they abounded—could see that he had made fine, fine instruments. Perhaps he had made better in the past. Some of these were old. But here too he had constructed first-rate violins! Full, three-quarter, half-size fiddles. And he was a poet with ivory and mother-of-pearl. But of course he did not mar violins with such decoration. But on mandolins and ukuleles, the inlay of a mystic! This climate made things so difficult, though. Materials inferior. That was the reason, that and the damp air.

But under the accusatory eyes of his youngest son, his creditor, the row of dark dusty fiddles seemed to shrink, pegs shriveling, f-holes seeming mouths about to cry out.

* * *

He wiped his hands on his pants, leaving glossy streaks of glue on his thighs. He pulled the sleeves of his sweater out of their knots at his elbows and slid them down to cover his bony wrists. Sinking into his armchair among newspapers, he let out a groaning sigh and shivered. But this was nothing compared to many a past winter. Snow and ice seemed to cover every street he could remember. From his childhood, from his miserable job at the bakeries when he was seventeen, to America. And everywhere in between. He had baked a hundred loaves of bread every morning for lieutenants and captains. What he had received in return was a bowl of soup twice a day and leftovers. And lots of bread. At seventeen one can suffer.

The fiddle had been a sort of redemption, for he had played, none too well but enthusiastically, the Ukranian dances and songs those northern officers love to hear. Well he had most likely gotten the best of that bargain. They had probably died in that Japanese war, after he had left, some time after. No doubt of it, really. He had emigrated. But those winters! God Almighty! Gott in Himmel, she used to say, though for her German was an affectation. They spoke Russian, he and she. He too had learned English, later. He could speak some other languages, too, or used to. In English he had bartered oranges for a night's lodging for him and the children in Peking. No, that wasn't right. It was in Russian. They were Russian, the innkeeper and her husband. Lots of Russians there then. None in New Zealand.

It was not real to him anymore. It had no substance, somehow. It did not seem his life that he remembered. The stories that he himself had often told he now recalled as if they had been told by someone else, as if someone else had been born, and lived, and traveled in his place. Who?

* * *

The two presents lay on the sofa. He stared at them without seeing them. His eyes were large, set deep in his enormous bulging skull. He adjusted his spectacles and picked up a scrap of newspaper. His friend Kulakowski still advertised violin lessons. Many instruments repaired for Kulakowski, many. Kulakowski lived in a mobile home. They knew each other since Cleveland.

The grandson had a friend who took lessons from Kulakowski. He had told him that his friend's violin had his label inside, a coincidence. "Repaired—V. Vyazemski—Cleveland 1934." But perhaps not such a coincidence. It must be a good violin. Where had he found it in this city? He certainly had not come here to buy it. No memory of that.

It was time to eat something. It was already dark, had been dark when the second one had come at six, but then he hadn't felt any hunger. He usually cooked beans or boiled a broth with chicken wings or lamb bones, but then he would keep the leftovers too long, forgetting to eat them, forgetting entirely to eat. There would be something. Well, later. When he put on the light, the ukulele shone, the oiled wood and brass frets. He would have to make a trip soon for brass. A pity that he did not need wood as well, so that both could be bought at once. This climate too damp, though, can't keep the wood here in this room. It rains, the wood swells with moisture. Impossible to do decent work. Someone buys a fiddle and carries it with him to desert or mountains and the damn thing probably splinters in his hands.

The scraps of paper on the table were filled with sketches of strange creatures. Arabic numbers metamorphosed into beasts and birds: the three a snake, the four a stork on one leg, the five a scaly dragon. He loved birds best, though most often he drew and inlaid in ebony the same one: the long-legged egret that lay in the fingerboard of the ukulele.

In the black wood, streaked with a dark red grain, the white bird stretched from the second to the sixth fret. Long legs bent slightly at the middle joint, small body with trailing wing plumes and tail, the neck curving up, and the bill—long, pointing back downward. Iridescent mother-of-pearl gleamed uncannily as he turned the instrument in the light—the body of the bird seemed to move while the pale white bill of ivory seemed to thrust and pierce the wood like a blade.

He put the ukulele down. Then he stepped into the kitchen. A noise from outside led him to the door and out onto the tiny landing of the stairway. A damp breeze blew at him darkly from the night, making him shiver. Jays were squawking down below. He usually heard them only during the day. It would be a cat on a predatory outing by the stagnant creek that flowed behind this street of old brick houses. Without a freeway a block away, it would have been a quiet neighborhood, perhaps. Pleasant. He no longer heard the traffic anyway, though when he did, it struck him as unearthly, frightening. He could smell oil, sulfur, and smoke from the ship channel and refineries hidden somewhere in the distance. He had never seen them.

From the landing he watched reflections from his outside light sparkle on the wet grass below, rippling from right to left and back as he moved his head from side to side. It had rained all afternoon; there would be a newspaper, and, he hoped, it would be wrapped in plastic. He might as well get it now; it was, as he thought, the only luxury he allowed himself, though he could not help but think of it as a necessity, such was his passion for reading of events which he enjoyed knowing did not affect him.

He went down the rotting steps slowly. They were like those of a fire escape, and the daddy-longleg spiders under each plank came awake for a moment, then clustered again in clots of tiny bodies surrounded by hundreds of waving legs like stiff threads. He knew they were there. What number, what number, with so many legs, could he make them? He has no interest in Roman numerals.

The newspaper was wet at the open end of the plastic sack. His spindly frame knotted itself and moved with a strange, ungainly gait, as if he were about to tip over, as he picked up the paper and turned back towards the stairs. He walked back cautiously and glanced down the slight slope of the lawn at the dark trees that hid the bayou. The bare bulb overhead cast an unnatural glow on the green and brown foliage, and threw long slim shadows behind each blade of grass. The trees, some twenty yards off, waved in the clammy wind. He thought of the turtles balanced on logs, and of sluggish fish rising to the greeny surface of the water for insects. He would sometimes sit down there near the water, swatting at mosquitos, gauging the slow current. The concrete flagstones which led down to the bank, each a foot wide and surrounded by stiff St. Augustine grass, were painted a bright blue—the blue of the sky of some other place, not the black, green, and gray of this sky. He could never remember where he had seen a sky as blue as the paint on this smooth concrete, but he was sure that he had seen it once or twice. A pity that there was no tree whose wood was of that color!

He put a hand on the wooden railing, clutching the newspaper with his other arm, and went up the steps.

* * *

Once inside, he locked the door and put the paper on the kitchen table. Tomorrow everything would be closed. And probably the day afterward, too, Saturday. So Monday for the brass, and until Monday there was the inlay and the violin to be ready by Saturday morning. He warmed some beans on the stove, and then spooned them in great gobs into his mouth, reading the paper. He noted that it smelled of newsprint and ink. He hardly noticed any smells anymore, much less the smell of himself which he knew repulsed his children. Spoiled food and dust and dirt, and wood and rosin and glue and tarnished metal, his own flatulence—filled the small rooms but meant little to him. The ungratefuls! Let it worry them if it would. They had not even been very decent musicians. Suddenly he realized that he had gotten himself into a fury and was no longer paying attention to the words he was reading. "Houston To Host Space Conference." He looked at the spoon in his hand and saw that he had bent it in two. He placed it gently on the table next to the aluminum pot of beans and sat back in his chair for a moment, breathing quietly.

In his inside shirt he kept the money, and now he pulled it out to count it, to calm himself. He was prodigiously strong, even now that he was so thin. One twenty-dollar bill, which he never spent. Three tens, three fives, and sixteen ones. He would sometimes throw his small change into one of his boxes of foreign coins, without thinking, and later spend hours picking out and eyeing every yen and lira and dinar and grosz that he had ever restrained himself from spending, years ago, in search of an occasional penny or nickel. He kept dimes and quarters—for they were silver—in a leather pouch in his shirt pocket. Hidden in the bathroom he had a tiny box of gold coins. The pouch had been given to him long ago, in Germany. They had said it was the scrotum of a ram. The thoughts of the pouch and of his little gold mingled to give him a sense of vague wonder, and he shook his head.

Again he counted the money. He would buy the brass and this time he would get a few groceries downtown. The Chinese grocer down the street charged him too much. He put the money back into his inside shirt, and scratched his chest through that one and through the undershirt beneath it. As his eyes wandered aimlessly over the table with the subtle pleasure of his scratching, he saw the letter. He started, and leaned forward abruptly to stare at it before picking it up. One of them must have brought it up earlier from the mailbox. Had either said a thing about it? He could not remember,

but he had not, he thought, listened very carefully to what they had said.
What for?

He knew as soon as he saw the handwriting on the envelope who had
written to him. It was from her. Holiday greetings or some such nonsense.
The envelope bore Christmas commemorative stamps, and he tore away
the corner, and, pushing back his chair very deliberately, rose and went to
put them in the top drawer of his bureau. Then he sat in the armchair, whose
worn cushion, resting on useless sagged springs, sank under his weight until
the arms of the chair came nearly to his shoulders. The envelope yielded and
revealed a plain white card. Her hand. The high flowery tops of the h's and
f's, and the straight stabs of the y's. Why she would not write to him in
Russian he did not know. It was so like her. His spectacles slid up his nose as
he pulled at them slightly with the muscles of his large, almost transparent
ears.

Again this year I send you this greeting, out of the sense of human
decency which I at least have preserved through these years. I will be
at Christine's house for the day on Friday, and perhaps on Saturday. I
do not yet know if they are thinking of coming to visit you. In any case,
they may come, but I will not. Again this year I give presents only to
the grandchildren. Changez-vouz la vie et nous nous rencontrons au
ciel.

A.

Her damned French. *Ecrasez la femme* and to hell with her then. He threw
the card away from him with a jerky motion of his arm and shoulder, and
sprang up from the chair as if from the floor. He switched on the makeshift
lamp over his worktable and sat down on his high stool. Taking a piece of
paper from the stack of carefully hoarded clean sheets and scraps, he
sketched with a blue-leaded pencil the curving outline of a serpent's back,
curling, coiling into the number two. A cobra! He had drawn it thoughtlessly,
his hand guiding the pencil of itself, pulling the squared-off point of knife-
trimmed lead across the pale yellow paper. But the hand had its wisdom, did
it not! He dropped the pencil and held up his arms as if playing a violin, and
mimed fast bowing and furious fingering. He chuckled, but then broke off his
soundless musical flourish to stare, amazed, at his own knuckles and nails.

He turned back to the table, picked up the pencil, and quickly began to
finish the drawing. That's what she was and had always been, a cobra! He
should have stayed away the first time he had left her, for good. The neck
flared below the head, and in green ink he added a design of interlocking
diamonds and spots to the poised body. He would put a cobra on a little
rectangular piece of ebony, mother-of-pearl on ebony, framing it with a strip

of brass. And send it to her. As a present. Did he not bring her silk from China? And had he not taught the children, after his own fashion, on their travels? Certainly what they had learned from him they could never have gotten in some American school! Even she scorned the American schools. And always harping on his ignorance. But he was *not* ignorant, he was *not* an uneducated man! He would read tonight, before going to sleep, something good. Enough newspapers! He had his Tolstoy here somewhere. He had not read anything in Russian in a long time, but he would, tonight.

He snorted and turned with fresh energy to the ukulele, after carefully laying to one side his sketch of the snake. But then he thought of the violin, which tomorrow he would have to repair. He inspected the crack. It shot out from under the bridge—a strange failing!—and jutted toward the f-hole, crossing the grain in its way with minute side-to-side jerks, widening as it went. He had taken them around the world! And they hated him for it.

* * *

But there was an answer to that. Did they think that they too would not stink some day, would not pace through rooms they rented from their own children?

He went into the kitchen. With a spoon he skimmed the layer of congealed fat from the cold broth on the stove, and with his free hand pushed open the screen on the window above the sink. They would awaken rudely, indeed! He adroitly flipped the fat from the spoon to the shingles below the window, where the roof of the empty garage jutted some four feet outward. It fell on a slick spot which testified to the many times he had thrown fat or suet there for the birds. He dropped the spoon into the sink and latched the screen. Wiping his hands on his thighs, he returned to the larger room and went dutifully to sit again in his deep chair, clasping the two flat boxes in one hand as he sank backwards into its comfort. One box was bound with a green ribbon, the other with red. He had worn a red ribbon around his head, in the gypsy band. That was what he had called it though of course they weren't gypsies. But they had worn ribbons and scarves and peasant blouses with sleeves that ballooned at the wrist. The pants had been drawn with a rope round the waist. What a joke, a fine joke! She had hated it. Gypsies. Gypsies! She who spoke French as if it made her a daughter of nobility. But voice-lessons and tutors had ended with their marriage. On the other hand, things had not been so bad, at least at first, had they? The trip to Arabia, and then emigration to America. New York, Pittsburgh, then Georgia. That had been a mistake, to be sure. That apple-orchard was probably all American apartment buildings now. It was true, what she had said: he could have been a rich man. But he didn't want to stay there, and she couldn't understand. To travel—anyway, it was all worthless once the Great Depression came. All their money. Or was it? He could not remember any more.

At times he was tortured by the thought that somewhere a bank account which he had opened and then forgotten was waiting for him, bursting with riches after years of neglect. But where? Could he have lost some of the money along the way? Or invested it? Maybe he had invested it.

He stood up again, slowly this time, leaving the unopened boxes balanced across one arm of the chair, and went to the bathroom. The lid of the toilet tank was gone, and the handle as well. But the tiny, dark, dank room served its purpose. He merely parted the zipperless gaps in his two pairs of pants, then pissed, and pushed the cloth back together. He reached into the tank and took hold of the plunger, pulling it up. As the water swirled through the pipes he shuffled wearily back to his worktable. His legs ached, and when he urinated there was a pain.

The pink and white egret still lay in the wood of the ukulele. He held it near his eyes, turning it to catch the light. He had been very well known for this work in Cleveland, too. The rest of the family had left him there, where he worked for ten years without them. No, *he* had left *them* to themselves, and this time they had traveled off and he had stayed behind! They had come here, and later he had followed. They were together against him. But they could not make him do what they wanted.

Starve. They could make him starve, maybe. He chuckled very softly. Maybe they could.

He set the instrument carefully down, and straightened his pile of papers, his bottles of glue and wood-stain and solvent, his paintbrushes and knives. Tomorrow everything would be closed. He turned out the work-lamp. Perhaps it would be clear in the morning, good light. Then the cobra. There is time to make it. Work that is worthy of him. And of her. A present, this year. No, next year. It would take time, it would have to be done properly. How many years in this place—fifteen? Could it be twenty? She would wait one more.

Passing by the chair on his way toward bed, where he would shed his outer layer of clothing and crawl between the blankets, he casually picked up the two presents in one hand and stepped into the closet, where he placed them unopened on a tottering stack of others wrapped identically with green and red.

Black Cotton

WILLIAM GOYEN

Isn't it funny how two things that just come up out of the ground—just crops of the ground's all they are—can reach into a family of humans and turn their whole lives asunder and corrupt the generations? In this way I guess crops of the ground are just as important as humans—*some* crops, anyway. Wonder would turnips have done the same thing, would grief have fallen on the generations because of turnip greens? Well, I don't know about greens, but certainly cotton brought trouble; and oil too. A nasty mixture.

Discovery of oil in the family cottonfields of Calcutta, Texas caused everybody in the Hawkins family to have resentments that they never got over and were handed down from children to grandchildren. There'd been cotton on the Hawkins land in Calcutta for some generations. When Will Hawkins died (young—fifty-one—and probably as an escape from his marriage, some said), his father old Hull Hawkins had planted some cotton and he planted some more—he divided the cottonland into five equal parcels and left in his will one to each of his children Lew, Jake, Hazelruth, and Trixie, and one to his wife Marchetta, who was a good part Cherokee and called Marchetta Granny.

Now the story tells that somebody found a black cottonboll one morning on Hazelruth's parcel and got hold of a wildcatter around there and he come and stuck his funnel into what was a hidden lake worth millions of dollars— and on the spot become what you call an independent oil man. When that oil was found, Hawkins family seemed like was suddenly inhabited by leaping devils. At first the others said that Hazelruth put the wildcatter up to it, that *Hazelruth* was the wildcatter; but later events proved that to be wrong, as you will see. Anyway, there was a long deep black lake of oil hidden under all that sweet white cotton. I'm from that part of the country myself and I can tell you that white cotton seemed in our early days to bless the very fields around us. We felt it was the hand of God that laid out all that white in the moonlight. Seemed like it quietened everything, seemed like nothing could ever happen to any of us long as the white cotton grew and bloomed around us. In those days before trouble there was singing and laughter in the

cottonfields, though God knows we worked to the bone, so tired at night and
sometimes still as tired when we got up in the dark of early morning, sweat of
our brow fell on the cotton, twas not all song and laughter. But what I'm
telling you is that for ages white cotton was the peace of our land. And the
black oil broke it. Some say oil was a curse on the land. That wildcatters
were the Devil's henchmen. That Satan came to Texas in oil.

Ever see black cotton? One drop is all you need to dye a million acres.
Blacken one flower and the field's black. Because you know and I know that
once you get oil on your land you got *oil*. Cotton, oats, the peace of a family,
don't care what, all falls before oil. So what I'm trying to tell you is that once
a drop was found on a cottonboll even those that was in favor of cotton got
oil; couldn't help it. Caused the grief in the Hawkins family that I'm telling
you about. What you going to do if oil just shoots up outa your cotton crop,
walk away from it? This is what Marchetta Granny Hawkins declared when
the family had a meeting that changed the fate of the generations of that
family, caused them to have resentments that they never got over and were
handed down from children to grandchildren. I know because I saw it. If
you're going to have bad feelings of resentment, commented Trixie
Hawkins the wild one of the family, I'd rather have mine riding along in a
Lincoln Continental with the bar open than in a Chevrolet with a can of beer
between my legs. The Hawkins family was mortally divided between those
in favor of drilling for oil and those that wanted to keep the old cotton. In
case you had any doubts, oil won.

Jake, the next to oldest and like his daddy, was for cotton, Lew for oil—he
was greedy even when he didn't have anything—the youngest, Trix, was for
oil of course, would buy her better whiskey; and Hazelruth, the oldest,
cotton and the old way. Marchetta Granny threw the balance. Said at first
that she was all for cotton, that her own father-in-law old Hull Hawkins
(everybody knew that they hated the ground each other walked on, but what
ground! Full of cotton and oil) had planted cotton on land *his* father had
bought when he was a young man, good-for-nothing land that even the wind
wouldn't blow over, wasn't worth its time, just Godforsaken dirt until old
Hull Hawkins planted some cotton in it and it flourished. But Marchetta
Granny had pictures in her mind's eye of silver and gold laid under that
cotton—her Papa-in-law might just as well buried rings of gold and
platinum, candlesticks of purest silver in that ground, and diamonds and
rubies—it was just as though she went out into the field, in her mind's eye,
and dug under the cotton and pulled up golden bracelets and put them on her
arms, because that's what she pictured. Strange crops. So when Marchetta
Granny's mind's eye pictured the oil that she knew would make her one of
the richest women in Texas oozing up luxuries from under that old-time
cotton, she said to drill; and broke the family deadlock. Not only was

Marchetta Granny's mind's eye working overtime but so was her mind's *ear*, because what she kept hearing in her mind was a voice saying this is the way to get back at an old sonofabitch never treated you worth a dime and treated your own daddy who was three-fourths Cherokee Indian like dirt, setting him up to bootleg in his cotton gin and then taking a levy of three-fourths of the profits ("the same percentage as of Cherokee blood you got," said old Hull Hawkins to Marchetta Granny's daddy). Or so it was repeated by those that said they heard it. But eye and ear aside, Marchetta Granny's *mouth*—already primed to paint its lips with expensive (imported from Paris) lipstick to match her glowing fingernails, like the other rich ladies of Texas—announced that she would keep a few acres of the prettiest cotton, as if it was a flowerbed, back in there around her old house (which of course was not hers but her in-laws') for old times' sake and as a memorial. Don't ask me if the American flag still flies over that patch of cotton, put there by "Mrs. W. Wilson Hawkins," as it said on the gold plaque she put on the big flagpole. Marchetta Granny pulled in the Wilson from Grandpa Will's hidden second name nobody ever thought of before, Grandpa Will hated Wilson and dropped it when he was a young man and went by just Will. But Marchetta Granny pulled it back. Mrs. W. Wilson Hawkins!

But it was Hazelruth that everybody put the pressure on because the oil had come up on her parcel of land. And of all of them, she was the one that least cared about it. She nearly went crazy. Her brothers and her sister and her mother began to act like people she never knew. Threatened her in the night and came with presents in the morning. When the drilling began and all the rigging started tearing up the cotton, she moved her family away to Houston. The oil gushed and flowed and Hazelruth was the richest because her one-fifth was the first and biggest producer.

But what nobody knew was that somewhere Hazelruth had given over a big chunk of her oil stock to a Guru. Some Indian nut had turned Hazelruth's head (turned out to be not such a nut), but Hazelruth said give her some of the sweetest peace for the first time in her life (and also kept her from murdering her brothers and sister Trix and particularly Marchetta Granny, because now they were all accusing Hazelruth of draining and sucking oil off their one-fifth and getting richer and richer). Poor Hazelruth just had no peace and went off to India to be consoled by this Guru named Soochamaroojy or Soocharoony, don't know what was his name, but something like that. Anyway, these things of stocks and money don't make much sense to me, I've always worked for a living, *hoed* the cotton. But it turned out that over in India the Guru got more and more power just sitting cross-legged on his behind over in India than all of the shenanigans of the Hawkinses with high-powered lawyers, because he suddenly owned more Hawkins oil than anybody in the Hawkins family. Except Marchetta

Granny who had bought up her son Jake's one-fifth, he was a lot like Hazelruth and wanted out of the scramble. So here they were, the Guru Soochamaroojy or everwhat his name was, that'd suddenly cropped up in Texas, and Marchetta Granny stark face to face at the stockholders' meeting. Granny told the Guru that he was just another person trying to cheat a Cherokee, and that he didn't know oil from his left foot, and the Guru said *Madame* yes I do. And he did. Those two together, two smart Indians, is another story. But back to Hazelruth. To have been so rich and to have renounced riches—well, Hazelruth didn't *renounce* riches, she gave them over to a spiritual leader, she said—and live in plain cotton robes and barefooted, was a kind of a scandal to the Hawkins family—who must have forgotten that their ancestors one generation back walked barefooted, too, some of them, on dirt farms in East Texas, so what *scandal* was there?— and the brothers and sister Trix and their mother seemed ashamed of Hazelruth and just renounced *her*. Said she was a crackpot.

Now it was Hazelruth's poor lonesome husband Clyde that worked for the Southern Pacific in Houston's idea to bring everybody together for Thanksgiving, to try to bring some peace and forgiveness into the family. He'd hoped he could get Hazelruth to come, he told everybody. Sure enough here they all came in their Lincoln Continentals with bars and telephones, and smiles painted on their faces. Marchetta had on a pure silk hat made of silk autumn leaves, *imported*—funny how everything was *imported* suddenly when before all you could see on bumper stickers and in store windows was *Made in Texas for Texans by Texans*. Anyway the Calcutta bunch thought Hazelruth would be there and had an announcement to make that she had renounced the Guru.

They came into a madhouse. Jack, Hazelruth's son, had brought home a damned spreading adder from school and it'd got loose. Jack said the class had elected him to be the one to keep the prized class pet over the Holidays and that was a big honor. He was as puffed up over it as the adder. But just before the Hawkins tribe arrived, the thing escaped from its bowl and hid somewhere in the house. Jack had cried that he'd be ruined at school and that the whole classroom and Miss Muggins, the teacher, too, would be mad at him for the rest of his life and never trust him again. Not to mention the endangered life of the almost sacred spreading adder that the schoolchildren and Miss Muggins considered as almost holy. Jack sobbed and begged everybody please to help him find the precious pet of his schoolroom. So by the time the Hawkinses arrived, the hunt was on. Every room in the house had been turned upside down, stuff in the middle of the floor, and most of the neighborhood was there in a whirlpool of people running and crawling and climbing to try to find the lost spreading adder, they were under beds and clambering over upturned divans and swiping across the tops of cabinets and chinaclosets and bureaus with brooms and mops—and across Marchetta Granny's silk hat because she had been the first, naturally, to step right into the pandemonium, bellowing "Where's Hazelruth? Where's Hazelruth?" And when they yelled that it was an adder that had been lost she answered that she'd come to see her daughter Hazelruth and not a spreading adder. Trixie managed to get clear of the traffic and perch up on the grand piano where she could go on safely drinking. In a nutshell, Thanksgiving was ruined. When the Hawkins could get out, they just went back to the oilfields of Calcutta, mad as hornets. The runaway adder was never found and Jack had had to go back to the schoolroom with the empty bowl that the adder lived in. And that was the last time the family ever tried to get together in peace. Seemed like the spreading adder was just one of the Devil's henchmen to hold a family asunder.

Time went on and seemed like the Guru Soochamaroney and Hazelruth Hawkins just traded places. She became devouter and he became richer. She lived in a little temple and he lived in one of five hotels he owned, in a big suite on a whole top floor of the newest glass building in Houston that he'd bought. He cut his name down to Maroney, began to wear cowboy clothes and joined the oil clubs. While Hazelruth meditated outside of town in a shack in a shawl. When she wasn't secluded in a little temple called an Ashram, in Los Angeles.

Passage of time took away most of that family in what seemed like not much time at all, as you'll see sometimes in rich families: a lot die early and leave only one behind with all the money. Makes you see how mortal we all are, rich or poor. Trixie and her husband died in a flaming car wreck—sudden death, so they didn't have to suffer, it was said; and anyway, Trixie was numb with her whiskey, probably, people said, so she wouldn't have felt anything. Marchetta Granny? She passed on in a final stroke that put her in her grave with her mouth up under her left ear—wonder what she's telling herself, there in the ground. And Hazelruth just vanished into the land of India far away from the whole world. A few said they had word of her whereabouts, for a while, that she was living deep in a hidden vale of India near a great holy man. And then all news stopped, and it seemed like Hazelruth Hawkins just melted into the holy vale of India. But oilwells know not life nor death and they went on pumping money into who-do-you-think's pocket: ex-Guru Maroney's, of course. What Hazelruth had renounced—the strife of money—he took; she was free, in his native land and he was bound, in hers. Isn't it peculiar the way things are sometimes? And money pumped into Jack, Hazelruth's son's pocket, too, because you remember that she left some royalties to him. And he had got hold of Marchetta Granny's when she died, don't ask me how. He was grasping. This brings us to Jack.

All other Hawkinses had been persuaded, by a lot of money, and a soft Guru tongue, to sell out, leaving Jack the only Hawkins to hold any interest in Calcutta Oil. Jack would not sell to Maroney for a long time, but he was not any good at business as he grew older and besides he got tired of fighting the ex-Guru so he finally threw in his towel. A forty-million-dollar towel. Now, people that had always thought that "Calcutta Oil" was an Indian outfit were right.

When Jack came to see me, I saw how money had done a pretty big job on him. Wonder why it made him worse? Looked like money had got hold of his face and dug lines into it and had puffed up his eyes and pulled out a lot of his hair. And made him drink heavy whiskey, even in the morning. Money can be mean. And don't know why he couldn't keep a wife (there'd been three), with all that money, or find some peace in his mind or ever stay very long in any of the houses that he bought or built—one even on a tropical isle; and he owned the isle too.

Anyway, Jack had come back to Houston to get rid of his mother's house and to see if he couldn't do something for his daddy Clyde that was living out at the S.P. home for retired men and seemed content enough. Jack's daddy Clyde wouldn't let him do one thing for him, seemed like he was glad to be clear of the whole mess (that meeting at the S.P. home between father and son must have been something, but I wasn't there so can't tell you what happened). But others said that Clyde just wouldn't take one penny from Jack and said, I've got my S.P. pension. Somehow he seemed the saddest of all because he was a good man come from a poor family back of Calcutta, Texas and married into all the Hawkins trouble. He really worshipped Hazelruth, too. *There's* a story—Clyde Bonner—if somebody could tell it. Oh there's lots of stories.

Anyway, when Jack was going through some packed-away stuff in his mother's closed-up house in Woodland Heights of Houston, he found in a cardboard box of buttons a frail figure of bones. Yes, it was the spreading adder that never got back from Thanksgiving holidays to Travis School long ago. He'd found it at last, but too late. There was a ragged hole where the hunted adder had clawed its way to its tomb. And the buttons that had belonged to people long gone! Saved, surely, by Hazelruth. Some looked like they were from a wedding dress for they were yellowed white satin; some were from a war uniform; there were baby buttons of mother-of-pearl; some sparkling ones, maybe from a party dress; and a few, shaped like red strawberries, that held a misty memory for Jack still lingering in his eyes— they must have been on a dress of his mother's that he'd fingered as a child at her breast. Hunted by crazed humans, in its fear the adder had hidden in a place where no one would have thought to look, and, alone and terrorized, died among the buttons. The spreading adder was, surely, as Miss Muggins the teacher had long ago told Jack's class, of a very old species, coming from an ancient civilization, because now it looked like an ancient fossil come out of the haunted ages. Somehow it got over to Travis Grammar School in the 1930's and lay upon a stone in the Texas morning sunshine until it was found by a squealing girl and captured by a brave boy and brought to Miss Muggins. Miss Muggins at once identified the spreading adder and told that it was of a family a million years old. It had found its tomb among the relics of a troubled family already vanished. Isn't humanity and the story of the world peculiar? Isn't it a wonder? You can't help feeling reverence, the teacher had said. Miss Muggins had made the class feel that feeling, wonder—and reverence—long ago, although it took a lot of years for some of them to find the feeling again, after hurt and disappointment, and Jack felt that old feeling then, when he opened the button box and saw that stark figurine that had come out of the ages and through his hands into the brief quarreling life of one family on just one Thanksgiving Day, was lost, and was found again, years later. Jack wept. He wondered, again, what his life meant.

I know Jack's feelings, because when he came out to Calcutta to see me he brought the button box. Then the whole story that I've told you just a little bit of, came back. Maybe some time I'll tell you the rest. Jack hadn't been back home since his mother and daddy moved to Houston, in his boyhood; Hazelruth would never let him go back into all the Hawkins turmoil of the oilfields. Was the pretty flowerbed of cotton that Marchetta Granny had kept back still there, with the flag flying over it? What do you think? You're right: Calcutta oil flowed under that, too, and they'd dug right after it. Down had gone the flagpole with the Mrs. W. Wilson Hawkins gold plaque on it and down had fallen the flag. Black cotton.

And then Jack went away. That was quite some years ago. Then—I don't know when it was, now—we heard that he'd gone to the land of India to look for Hazelruth his mother. But nobody knows whether he ever found her.

I like to dream that he did and that they're peaceful together deep in a holy vale of India.

Any Sport

WILLIAM HEYEN

I

F OUR MEN in a new Buick LeSabre are driving west on the New York State Thruway from Rochester to Buffalo's Rich Stadium where the Bills are to play the Cleveland Browns in a late-season game. After meeting at a bar in Rochester, they piled into Burke's big car, believing it to be the safest in case of an accident. It was snowing as they left, big flakes down from Lake Ontario in the north, beginning to stick, and now they are doing 25 mph in driving sleet getting icier by the minute, the weather coming at them now from Lake Erie in the west.

"Relax, they'll play," says Burke, checking to make sure he has his lights on. "Rich drains good, the tarp's on. This'll let up. Maybe they'll start late, but they'll get it in. They got to, they can't postpone it, they got to get it in."

From the back seat behind Burke, Squeak hits them with a question. "Who were the starting guards in 1960 for the College All Stars against the Knicks at the Garden?"

"1960, 1960," Jerry says. He's looking out his front-seat window to his right at the sleet slanting into a turf farm near Batavia. A few days before, he saw that same angle of lines on the screen of his new IBM PC as he went through an introductory program. He made the lines move. His wife had just told him she was sick of him. That's what she said, "sick." Now, seeing the broken lines of sleet angle down to the flat land, he is depressed. "1960— West and the 'O'."

"Right," says Squeak.

Jerry feels a little better, an obscure veil dissolving from around his heart.

"Jerry," Russ says from behind, "which Knick did they call 'The Horse'?"

"Shit, I don't know," Jerry says. "He must have picked up splinters. I don't fuck around with bench-warmers." The veil forms again. "Sick" was the word she used.

"Harry Gallatin," Burke says. "I saw that big mother once. He spoke at our senior sports dinner. He was a . . . " Burke's voice trails off as he peers low to see through the splash of sleet thrown up on his windshield by a passing truck.

"If this shit freezes," Russ says, "they'll never get it in."

"If this shit freezes," Jerry says, "they can look for us out here in the morning."

"Who invented the doughnut that replaced lead bats in the on-deck circle?" Russ asks.

The other three are silent, thinking hard. The LeSabre swerves right with other cars into the lane for the Rich Stadium exit. As they leave the Thruway behind them and slow for the toll booth, Russ answers his own question.

"Elston Howard. You guys never give the niggers credit for anything."

"I love the niggers," Burke says. "I just hate the fucking Yankees."

"You and your fucking underdogs," Russ says. "All your life you're betting losers. You'd think you'd get tired of putting my kids through college."

They all laugh. Burke has lost $100 to Russ on last season's NBA playoffs, and the C-note is a delicious bone that Russ keeps chewing.

"What was the name of the Russian who made that basket to beat us in the '76 Olympics?" Squeak asks.

"They never beat us," Russ says. Now he is angry. "You call that game legal? Three plays for the fucking Russians in the last six seconds? Shit, we didn't even bother to pick up the silver at the awards ceremonies. That was bullshit. It was fixed. They'll never beat us. Stop asking asshole questions, Squeak."

Squeak wants to say the name, but knows Russ well enough by now not to. They went to high school together in Rochester. Squeak managed the basketball team for four years while Russ started on the varsity his junior and senior years. Squeak got by, he himself knew, by being quick with his mouth. He was a wise-ass who had hustled water and basketballs and uniforms and orange slices for the section-champion varsity for two years before Russ made it up from jay vees. Russ had always been a hothead. Squeak had seen him kick a cheerleader when untangling himself from the crowd after not quite being able to save a bad pass. Squeak had read a book on Elvis Presley, and Russ reminded him of Red West, one of Elvis's friends, a quick-tempered bodyguard. Russ had red hair, too. So Squeak does not mention the name of the Russian who beat America with that basket, though the diminutive Squeak, out of work from his job in a print shop, somehow cherishes that name as though it were a little prayer, or spell.

Burke presses the lever to roll down his window. At first, ice clutches the window, but the glass breaks free and rolls down. The toll is $2.60. He hands three singles to the woman in the booth and tells her to keep the change.

"Burke," says Jerry, "I never saw anyone tip a fucking toll booth collector before."

"Jerry," Burkes says, "if you'd had a good look at her, as I did, you'd have seen that they were worth twenty cents each."

Jerry is thinking of his wife, thinking of the first time they were in bed together. It was their wedding night. He knelt between her legs and was kissing her belly, his hands on her breasts. She was writhing under him. It was as though, holding her breasts in his palms and fingers . . .

"I knew it," Russ says. The LeSabre is being waved past the Rich Stadium parking lot entrance by red-tipped flashlights held by men in yellow slickers. The sleet is not letting up. It's noon, but visibility is only about a first down in front of them. The LeSabre is sliding in ruts of slush and ice.

"What true-blue All American college did Bevo Francis play for?" Squeak asks.

II

A waitress has just brought a third round of drinks to their booth. "This time I'd bid fifty cents each," Burke says, straight-faced, as he flips a folded buck onto her tray.

"If her husband's as big as her diamond, you'd better watch your ass," Squeak says.

"She's got that available look," Burke says.

Driving away from the stadium, they'd found this place by luck, its blue neon rooftop sign flashing CHEKKO'S—TRUCKERS WELCOME at them just as Burke was wondering where the hell to go, what to do. He pushed the LeSabre as far as he could into a slushbank beside the place, trying to get her ass end out of the way. They've got a corner booth. Waylon Jennings is on the juke, singing about how he loves America.

Shit, Burke was thinking, he'd really wanted to see that football game. He'd *needed* to see it. He'd wanted to sit in their end-zone seats with Jerry and Russ and Squeak and get sloshed, yelling like hell for Cribbs to bust one or for Butler to make assholes out of the Cleveland defense. He wanted to yell all afternoon, watch the scoreboard post other NFL scores, and cheer or moan with the crowd. He wanted to drink stadium beer and his flask of Jack Daniels and sleep in the back seat while one of the others drove back to Rochester. Now he was sitting in a booth at a fucking truck stop. At least he was with his three friends. At least there was that. In about eighteen fucking hours (weather allowing, and it was just his luck it would) he'd be at work at Kodak, busting his ass in the gloom and stink of the silver recovery building. He couldn't wait to retire.

Burke had played some high school football. Chugging half his beer, he imagined the Bills down in their locker room under Rich, some still in pads, some in civvies already and heading home, one or two in whirlpools and glad to rest their injuries, some maybe playing poker. Maybe he and Jerry and Russ and Squeak ought to try to make it back to Rochester and get up a poker game. They could play all night and call in sick in the morning. But the fucking Thruway was probably closed by now. He'd never seen the weather this bad.

Squeak was thinking what Burke was thinking. "Good thing this shithole is open 24 hours," he said.

"Fucking A, Squeak," Russ said, lifting his mug of Bud to Squeak, making amends for his outburst in the car.

"Fucking A," said Jerry, lifting his shot of Seagrams to his friends and then downing it. Who was the bitch to say *he* made *her* sick? She'd gained thirty pounds. Fuck her. Let her go. There were plenty of women around, like this waitress whose buns he'd like to palm. He'd been voted "best looking" in high school, and hadn't lost it. He'd proved that enough times. Fuck her. She made *him* sick.

They took turns walking past the pool table over to the picture window. The stop's parking lot was criss-crossed with vehicles stuck in foot-deep slush, and the weather wasn't letting up—freezing rain, hail.

The place was crowded with truckers and with disappointed football fans like themselves. Every few minutes, the power winked off, but came back on right away.

"Squeak, let's you and me show these assholes how to shoot some pool," Russ said. He got up to put a quarter on the rail of the pool table behind several other quarters. They wouldn't have the table for about a half hour.

"How can a pitcher be both the winning pitcher and the losing pitcher in the same ball game?" Jerry asked. He'd heard this one at the salesroom from old man Wiczorek, who would call tomorrow, Jerry predicted, to buy that clean pickup Jerry had offered him. Jerry could pick up a fast four hundred on that one.

"He can't," Russ said. "Impossible . . . No, wait a fucking minute. What if it was only four innings, and he was winning or losing, and the game was rained out, and he was traded to the other team, and . . ." Russ sold insurance. He unravelled the complicated process by which a pitcher could appear in just one game and end up 1-1.

"Close enough," Jerry said. "You get the idea."

"Jerry, that was a shit question," Russ said, but this time he wasn't angry.

It felt good answering one of those shit questions. Jerry was okay. Old Squeak was okay, too. They were all okay. Squeak couldn't help it if all he could do was carry water.

Jerry said "Fucking A," smiled at Russ, got up to find the john. He passed the register and asked the waitress. She lifted her hand to point. Her bosom rose, swelling her pink satiny blouse toward him. Jerry asked her to do him a favor and serve up another round for his friends back there, and he told her he wished she'd have a drink herself. Jerry noticed that she had some hard miles on her, this woman, and serving this whole truckstop today made her appear as old as she was, about forty, but she had what seemed to be natural honey-blond hair, and good teeth—he wanted to tongue those teeth—and a body that wouldn't quit.

She said she would. She said she'd heard them talking sports back there. She said her favorite baseball player was her namesake, and could Jerry guess? She turned and went to the bar, two or three men calling to her. That's what you call a body, Jerry said to himself.

Standing at the urinal, holding his pecker in his fingertips, Jerry realized he was glad he was here. Even before he was done pissing, thinking of the waitress, he began to get an erection. This was more like it, he said to himself.

The four men drank and smoked. They shot pool. They ate burgers and eggs. They began drinking again. Chekko, jolly at the killing he was making, a Ukie with a thick accent, ordered up a round on the house. "Ve vill trink no more," he shouted, pounding the bar, then waited a second. "But ve vill trink no less," he thundered. Burke kept supplementing bar drinks with jolts from his flask of Lynchburg. Strangers bought one another drinks, swapped life stories.

It was dark out now. A trooper stopped in to tell everybody to stay put. Burke was playing "goalposts" with Squeak and Russ, one holding up fingers while the other tried to flick a pack of matches through. They played "edges," sliding quarters across the table. Waylon and Willy and Dolly and Johnny kept singing to these western New Yorkers, telling them that country is in the heart and you shouldn't raise your sons to be cowboys and you were always on my mind, honey, even when I was drinking in town because we're broke and I can't take it no more and the crops have burned out and the cows need milking. Jerry, car salesman at Rochester Motors, was helping his Rose behind the bar now, touching her when he had a chance, following her into the kitchen and holding her from behind when she went to the bread drawer.

She turned around and faced him squarely. She licked her lips with her tongue and said, "You look like you could swing a mean bat, honey, but we better not, maybe I'll see you later." She turned him around and put her hands on his buttocks and said "Now march." Jerry left the kitchen, following his erection back out to his friends.

Jerry was going to go to bed with this woman even if he had to hitch home a week later. Let his wife think he was lost in Buffalo ice, let his three friends say they got separated in a blizzard and he was probably dead, but he was going to sink into Rose. He went back to the booth to check on his friends.

"Burke," Jerry said, "I don't know if you can take this, but if you're so goddamned smart, what's the record for World Series homers, and who hit them? . . . The *Mick*," Jerry shouted, answering his own question. "Who the fuck else? Your fucking Pirates ain't even been *up* eighteen times. They can't even get it *up*," he shouted. "God made a mistake, and you know it. Clemente should have been a Yankee!"

III

At 4:30 in the morning, sleet has lightened to snow, but the snow is heavy and drifting in this squall area near the lake. No traffic, nothing moving. Russ, Squeak, and Burke are shooting pool. Half the men are still awake, drinking and talking quietly, others are sleeping or trying to sleep, leaning back in corners of the booths or stretched out, chairs extending their beds. The only other woman in the place besides Rose is sleeping in her husband's arms along a wall where he has spread blankets for them. A trucker gets up every five or ten minutes to try to call Detroit, Chicago, New York, but the phone is out. The stop smells of stale beer and cigar smoke.

Squeak banks in the 8-ball. He says he's had enough fucking pool. Russ and Burke throw bills on the table. Squeak, master in the use of the bridge, has won a total of about $200 in about ten games. Burke looks around for the broad or for Chekko, but Chekko is asleep in his trailer out behind the stop, and who knows where the broad is? He wants a poker deck. He's got one out in the LeSabre. "I'll go with you," Russ says, "I need some fucking air." Stuffing the bills into his pocket, Squeak goes back to their booth.

Jerry is with Rose. She is sitting up on a table in the kitchen. The only light is coming in over the half-door from beer signs in the windows out past the bar. Jerry is standing between her legs, feeling a nyloned thigh with each hand, working his thumbs close to her sweet vee. Rose has her arms around his neck, alternately, teasingly, pushing him away and drawing him forward. "Now honey," she is saying, "I like pinch hitters, but not here, we just can't do it here."

"They're all asleep," Jerry is saying, feeling Rose's legs, pressing his erection up against the metal table. He feels like he could split the table.

Burke and Russ are watching their breath steam against the gray morning light. The snow has let up, but they know it's going to be a long time before this parking lot unclogs. They'd pushed their way to the LeSabre through chest-high drifts. Burke liked the way his car waited in the dark for him. It would get him to the next game no matter what. He fishes a deck of cards from his glove compartment.

"Russ," Burke says, "I wanted to see that fucking game. The Bills would've whipped Cleveland's ass, I just knew it."

"So what," Russ says.

"What do you mean so what?"

"Who gives a fuck?" Russ is angry, glaring at Burke. He'd like to hit Burke.

"Russ, it's for the fucking *playoffs,*" Burke says carefully. He knows that Russ hated losing that money to Squeak. Insurance isn't as steady as Kodak checks, and there's all that tuition Russ is paying.

"Fuck the playoffs. Man, Burke, grow up, will you? We're standing in the dark here outside a truck stop and we don't know our asses from a hole in the ground and you're talking about the playoffs. Where's the dough in *your* pocket if they win the fucking Super Bowl? Fuck the Bills. I'm never going to another fucking game."

"I know what you mean," Burke says, though he knows he simply doesn't know what Russ is talking about. The game was for the *playoffs!* The two stand there another ten seconds, scanning the blank gray heavens for a sign of who knows what, then push their way back through their paths through the drifts.

"You know, Russ," Burke says, "we recover twenty-six million ounces of silver a year from old film and shit. That stuff is awfully pretty when you burn it out." Walking behind Burke, Russ thinks of snapping Burke's neck in two and burying Burke in a drift. "Burke, go fuck yourself with your silver," Russ says.

In the kitchen, Jerry has his hands inside Rose's pants. He has buried his nose between those basketballs he's wanted to palm all his life. Then she says it.

"Jerry, honey, maybe we could for a little money." But she's not much of a businesswoman. She has her hands half over Jerry's ears, and he can't quite hear her. Jerry is pulling her panty hose down. Maybe he heard "we could." Whatever. He has pulled her off the table onto him. She didn't want to do this, not without three or five of his twenties to take back to her husband in the trailer—when she does that he does things to her that sometimes make this life worth it—but she's doing it, and it's too late now, too late, and Chekko's a pig next to this Jerry, and this is wonderful, and any sport in a storm, she says to herself, this is wonderful, but in five or ten thrusts Jerry has fucked her, but, damn it, she hasn't come.

Jerry hoists her back up onto the table. "At last," he thinks, "at last, God," he thinks, "Jesus," he thinks, "that was something." Rose sits up, begins putting herself together. She's thinking of her sister, living on a farm out in Kendall with her husband and kids. They plant a whole acre of sunflowers out there every spring. You can stand among them in the summer and almost listen to them. And they bend down those beautiful heads to listen to you, those gold-rimmed heads. You could just stand there for a long time inside those sunflowers, watching the bumblebees in their faces, and the butterflies flutter around them and land on them and open and close their wings. You could just stand there for a long time, "a rose in the sunflowers," her sister said.

Jerry joins his three friends at their booth. He's sitting next to Burke, and sees Burke fold three aces to Russ's two-pair in a game of draw for a good-sized pot. What the fuck is Burke doing, Jerry wonders. Jerry wonders if he should call Wiczorek about that pickup today. He doesn't want to seem to be too anxious, but sometimes you can play too nonchalant.

Morning light begins to fill the stop, washing out the neon beer signs. A plow rumbles along the highway. Jerry sees Chekko in the parking lot with his snowblower, arcing the whitestuff high over the roofs of cars. Jerry thinks his new PC is going to change his life. Maybe his wife had the rag on. She's probably sorry about that word. She's probably worried about him right now.

Squeak is thinking about Gayle Sayers, how a linebacker said that when you tried to tackle him straight on he seemed to divide in half, go around you, and reassemble. You just couldn't lay a hand on him, you were left there with air in your arms. Another defensive back swore that one time he looked behind him after Sayers flew over him and saw wings sprouting between Sayers' shoulders.

Burke hits a flush, and knows he has a winner.

"Who scored six touchdowns against . . . "

"Gayle Sayers, old #38," says Russ, as he rakes in another big pot.

The Mango Community

JOSEPHINE JACOBSEN

THE VICE-CONSUL again looked at his shoes. He appeared not critical but, more annoying, embarrassed.

"Mrs. Jane Megan—yes, and Mr. Henry Sewell." He raised very pale blue eyes to Jane's, dropped them to his toecaps. "And Daniel. Daniel Megan. Fifteen? Is that right?"

"That's right," said Jane. She added, "Mr. Adams."

"And your purpose here was a vacation?" This time he got himself together and looked at her quite hard.

"Work," said Jane. "I'm a painter." His eyes flicked to her fingernails. "It's on my passport. Henry is a writer. A novelist."

If she had looked for him to say, "Oh, *that* Henry Sewell," she was wrong.

"Yes, well," said Mr. Adams moodily. "You see my position," he said rapidly but uncertainly. "I can't actually ask you to leave. I mean, there would have to be actual and manifest danger."

She hoped ardently that Harry would not appear, lugging fish and cristofine. He and Mr. Adams were, temperamentally, unsuited to a dialogue. Soothingly she said, "I think you've been very kind to come all the way out here. And I quite see your point. We'll think about it, we really will. But this business has been going on for weeks and weeks, and we leave, anyway, in a few months."

At last Mr. Adams looked cross. "Mrs. Megan, I've tried to explain that if you do insist on staying on under present circumstances," he stopped and repeated more loudly, "present circumstances, the U.S. government simply cannot be responsible for your safety."

"I know that," she said hastily. "That's perfectly reasonable." (All the same, she thought, your problem is that I know, and I know you know, you'd try.) They had reached an impasse. Would it be like suborning a policeman to offer him a drink? "Could I offer you a cup of tea, or a drink before you leave?" Perhaps the tea decontaminated the invitation.

"You're very kind," he said primly. "I'm going to miss my plane if I'm not careful. Well, the other families in town to whom I've spoken have all agreed on the advisability of leaving." He looked at her, and his general disapproval was just diluted by a flash of friendliness. "I do wish you well, Mrs. Megan. You're really isolated here." ("Oh, there're people next door . . . " she protested; he ignored this.) "Perhaps you'll pass on to Mr. Sewell what I've said. And there's your son to consider."

The implied reproof made her say jauntily, "I'll keep that in mind." She put out her hand, and the Vice-Consul, unable to do less, shook it and restored it to her. "Good-bye, then," he said, and a minute later the jeep started too fast, kicking up sand.

In an attempt to sort out her mind, she sat down on the eroded planks of the porch steps and stared out over the beach to the mad palette of the Caribbean.

She felt she was muttering. When did it all *begin*? She thought that while it had been by laughter that she had first known her husband, it was by a hot and huffy argument, improbably conducted on the fringes of a cocktail party, that the threshold of intimacy has been crossed with Harry. Of all things, the Sermon on the Mount. And hadn't that argument, between a fresh divorcee and a stranger, across a sea and in another world, landed her right here, between Harry and the Vice-Consul?

Isolated by Harry's intensity, they had found themselves on ancient ground: overnight the world could be changed by passive resistance— unflagging, indomitable. To violence, the universal cheek turned, once and for all. In a flash of conviction, that evening Jane had come to believe what she still did, that Harry would let himself, in the proper cause, be martyred without so much as making a fist. Profoundly, this impressed her.

"All *right*," she had said, draining the last drops of her martini, "say you're going to be murdered. You're going to be raped . . . " ("Less likely than you, there," he murmured.) "You turn the other cheek; and you *are*. But what do you do when someone else doesn't *want* to be murdered? Turn their cheeks for them? It never tells you about *that*," she said bitterly.

Not then or later had he answered the question to her satisfaction. Was it unanswerable? He never lost that inner assurance that she could see captivating Dan. Undeviating programs are so dear to the young, she thought meanly. But she knew it was more than that.

It was as though Dan had been waiting for Harry. Disconcertingly, the classic case of preparing an adolescent for a resented stepfather reversed itself. Even early on, Jane became aware of a united front, a sort of silent compact, in which Harry's need to proselytize and Dan's to be stable were locked into a kind of dogged intimacy. Why this should frighten her, she had no idea.

As she stared morosely ahead, here, loping jerk jerk along the beach, came the three-legged dog. That dog. The most enchanting of the children who burst onto the sand even in this remote section, when school was out—a liquid-eyed, gentle-faced charmer with the suavest voice—flung stones at the lame dog. "She ogly! See how she go—so!" And he hobbled, jerking. Entranced, doubled with laughter, the children reached for sand, stones.

Through the sprays of magenta bougainvillea, the sky of Ste. Cecile appeared as a mosaic—blue, green, lilac.

"Did he come?"

It was Harry who had come, noiseless on the sand.

"What kind of fish is *that*?"

"That is a turbot. Did he come?"

"Yes. He came. And went."

'And said?"

"And said we should leave."

"Had to leave?"

"No. He stopped short of that. If we're stuck and a coup breaks out, he can't promise us help. You know, I think we *should* go," she added, surprising herself. Did she think so? Politically, or personally?

Harry disappeared into the shadowy interior; a moment later he was back. He sat down beside her, plucked off a sneaker, knocking out sand.

"What did you tell him?"

"That we'd think about it. That we really would."

"Very diplomatic. His own game."

He looked perfectly beautiful, sitting there pulling off his other sneaker. The idealized beachcomber, the tropical poster.

"Look, Harry," she said, "I think we're getting in awfully deep."

She could feel the tightening. "How so?"

"Well, something *is* going to happen. We both know it; it's just *when*. We're isolated here. We're strangers—*really* strangers, I mean. It wouldn't be malice, but we'd just be in between."

"*You* look, my dear," he said in his inspirational, persuasive teacher's voice, his hand on her bare shoulder. "We came here for a year. The place is beautiful. The people are marvelous. I'm working, you're painting. Dan's happier than I've ever seen him. This guy is going to be thrown out eventually. In the most civilized way we'll ever encounter. That isn't something to make us run away. That's good."

"He's not going to be thrown out without a lot of people getting hurt."

"Jane, do you know, in a way it's the most impressive thing I've ever seen. They've lost their jobs, shut their shops, been spied on, pushed around, jailed, worse, much worse. Thugs in police uniforms have been sent after them, looting and smashing. The Barracudas are holding a cocked gun to their heads—and they *march*! That's what they do! No guns, no machetes—

they just march and chant and pull in their belts!"

"Harry, I live here too."

"Well, sure. You know, too. But you don't seem to realize how amazing it is. They're forcing him out without a shot."

Here came the black-coral boy; heavily lame, he threw out his left leg in an immense arc, lurching. He had fallen from the top of a coconut palm. Jane had a wild vision of the three-legged dog at his heels. The boy had a small waist, broad gleaming shoulders; and an immense smile and lifted a hand to them. Now he angled across toward the Montroses' fence, lurching more heavily in the dry sand. Mrs. Montrose appeared at her gate, and they fell quietly into one of those dialogues of which Jane could not have understood a word. This, although the Montroses, in their sparse conversations with their American neighbors, spoke an English perfectly intelligible, if more musical and differently emphasized. The only time Jane had ever seen Mrs. Montrose laugh was when Jane had asked about "mongeese." But when Mrs. Montrose said "four sheeps" and "three mices," it seemed not so much funny as expressive—more mouse-like, more sheepish.

Far out in the daze of sun, she could see a red object—the sunfish, and two dots, Alexis and Dan.

Harry got up, sneakers in hand. "We're not going to settle it this afternoon," he said. She saw that he had already settled it. Well. She could leave, and take Dan; but there were too many reasons why she would not.

Alone on the porch, she felt a tiny deflection in the heat. The sun had lowered by a fraction; the sunfish, nearer, was defining itself.

Guns cocked at their heads, said Harry. Barracudas, recruited by Him from the dregs of this and other island jails. How men loved the sound of a cocked rifle: Ton-ton Macoute. Ku Klux Klan. Yet when she and Harry argued, in his domain of words she seemed evasive and cynical. I can't bear the writer in him. In his beginning was the word.

She found Harry's work disconcertingly superior to her own, but never, never his medium. On this tiny island she remained amazed at the progressive detail of her own sight; new shades of purple and rose appeared in the noon sea. She was stunned by the varieties of green: the serious glossy green of the breadfruit, the translucent green of the fringed plantain-blades, the trembling play of the flame trees, the palms' hard glitter. Green, what on earth was it? Behind their stilt-house and its path, behind the road, the hill rose in a Rousseau jungle. On its steep garden patches, in violent blues and reds and yellows, the dark distant figures moved in the dawn light when disoriented roosters and insomniac dogs at last fell silent.

Now here came Mr. Montrose out of the house, a hoe in one hand, machete in the other. In the mornings, astride the burro, his buttocks resting just before its tail, the huge balanced milk cans at his knees, he wore one day a yellow, the next a violet shirt and a ravelling straw hat. Now he wore only faded khaki shorts that blended with his identically colored skin.

Seeing her head turned toward him, he raised his machete slightly in a courteous but formal gesture. In six months they had not got much further than that. At first the Montroses had seemed friendly, though baffled and a bit nervous. But in exact proportion as Dan and Alexis had plunged into their intimacy, the Montroses had retreated into a pattern formal as an armor. Always greetings; now and then a sour-sop or a sapadillo from their tree, sent via Alexis; once, some cassava cakes made by Mrs. Montrose. Never an acceptance or an invitation.

Twice Jane, meeting Mrs. Montrose coming home from market, or carrying on her head the big wicker basket of clothes to the line stretched across the dusty yard, had rather timidly suggested a cup of tea. Mrs. Montrose had smiled, her teeth strong and white, while she dropped her eyes, saying nothing whatever. Jane instinctively knew this was not rudeness; it was the dilemma of someone unable to accept and not possessed of the formulas of refusal. Jane had thorough sympathy for this. Was Mrs. Montrose to say that she had an engagement for tea every day for six months?

Jane did not waste much time speculating as to whether all this was Mr. Montrose. But she knew, infallibly, that it had to do with Dan. She could see that Mr. Montrose, no fanatic, could not well forbid his son to associate with a next-door neighbor of almost the same age; but though he treated Dan with the same grave courtesy, Jane knew that he found Dan an extraordinary phenomenon, and feared and disliked the friendship. What was Dan doing here in the first place? Why was he not at school or at work? Why did he call his father Harry? How could his parents (did Mr. Montrose think they *were* his parents?) permit his tone in talking to them? When the Montrose family went to Mass on Sunday—Christabel and Eugenie-Marie in starched dresses and long white socks, Alexis in a crisp short-sleeved shirt, Mrs. Montrose in pond-lilies on red, and Mr. Montrose in dark trousers and a shirt of palmetto palms—their three neighbors could be prone on the beach, practically naked, Dan sulking at Alexis' departure (no cricket); or on the sunfish; or Jane could have set off with her gear and Harry be rattling on his portable, stopping constantly to curse and bemoan his electric typewriter, useless in its corner.

Jane had had a solitary conversation with Mrs. Montrose. It had left her with a curious sense of warmth and communication, though it had led to nothing whatsoever.

Five or six weeks after the ménage's installation, Jane—possibly propelled by an inability to deal with the evasions of tropic green—had been driven in nostalgic defiance to a canvas of snow crystals. Three lit within the limits of the canvas, one disappeared in mid-pattern over the edge. On the black background they looked like stellar intentions.

Coming past in her royal walk, three coconuts in a small basket on her erect head, Mrs. Montrose had unwillingly but helplessly paused.

"What it is?" she said.

"They're snow crystals," said Jane shyly. "Flakes of snow," she added in response to the glance Mrs. Montrose had transferred to her face and back to the canvas.

To this Mrs. Montrose said nothing, and together they stared at the flakes, unmelting in the brutal sun. When Jane thought, we will drown in silence . . . , Mrs. Montrose said, her eyes still on the canvas, "You did see snow?"

"Oh yes. We have it often."

"It is whiter than sand?"

"Oh, much. When it first falls."

"It does lie on the ground? Right on the ground? You have walked on it? Right on over it?"

"Yes," said Jane. Suddenly envious she thought, I've never seen snow!

They stood there for a minute, isolated and intimate. Then Mrs. Montrose gave her a small adventurous smile, bent, and cradled the basket in her arms. She raised one hand in the familiar sidelong gesture and, without looking back, went through her wooden gate, across the bare yard and up the steps into the house.

Jane repeated to herself, I don't think I've ever seen snow . . . , but she felt an exhilaration welling up inside her. She began cleaning her brushes, hissing a little song. Something wonderful had happened. What? Now we can't ever be strangers. She couldn't wait to tell Harry; but she never did. Because peace was his specialty, and she was not sure what kind of peace she had to talk about. Always Harry thought "community," but she knew sadly that he hadn't gained an inch on this sandy strip. "The mango community?" she had jeered once.

The sunfish was right off the beach. It turned over, as usual, and Alexis and Dan, floundering in the water, pushed it in and dragged it up the sand. By now Dan was the same shade as Alexis. Christabel and Eugenie-Marie, like Mrs. Montrose, were mahogany dark.

Jane waved to the boys; they waved hastily back. Already they had the bats and the tennis ball out of the old beached and dissolving rowboat in which they were deposited each morning, shoved down from dogs and other marauders. There had been difficulties over those bats. The boys at first had played, like other children up the beach, with flat pieces of found wood; then one day Harry came back in the minimoke with two cheap cricket bats. At once, Mr. Montrose had jibbed. Finally it had been diplomatically settled that while both bats were Dan's, Alexis had possession of one.

Now down the hard sand Alexis was running, releasing the straight-arm pitch. At first Jane had imagined that it was because Dan thought baseball as Alexis thought cricket, that Dan could never compare. Then, her trained eye taking in the motions, she saw that it would never change. Alexis ran, and pitched, and batted, as he swam, as he climbed a bare bole, as he dove, with a fluid power. Dan said proudly that Alexis was the best cricketer in his school. "He's going to get a scholarship somewhere—maybe Jamaica or Trinidad. He's going to be like V. Richard. He's going to be better," said Dan, carried away.

Oddly, it was Alexis, daily embroiled in their lives, who stopped Jane. She did, and she did not know him. Instantly, she had had sense of almost intimacy—a drawing toward. Was it that of a painter? The marvelous texture of the skin, the head's perfection, the movement as worth watching as a secret dance, the quick deep luminous look? Though he smiled, he never laughed with her; but she could hear him; soft, irresistible convulsions, broken up, falling against the rowboat-skeleton, with Dan's staccato yelps.

After a while she began to understand that, the end of a long year come, she would never know Alexis. Separated, he and Dan would remember each other as part of the sun and sand and salt-wind, as in patches of light and happiness. She—and she thought, Harry—would be to Alexis figures come and gone, strange and not very interesting. She thought of the boys as a frieze against the sea.

As she went into the house, Jane could see through the window the peaceable kingdom: the water picking up red from the sun's angle, the red sailfish on the humped sand; on the gleaming edge, the boys against the sea.

There was Mr. Montrose, calling to Alexis to come now, come; and crossing to the back window she watched as Alexis rounded the house, crossed the lane and shot up the hill. She followed his blue trunks through layers of green; then here he came, the white goat trailing behind, stopping to snatch at a frond and jerking ahead. The green growth hid, revealed, hid, revealed them. The goat, shoved into its shed, let out its stammering vibration.

"What did you say to that guy?" Dan had come up behind her. His hair was still damp from sweat or sea water, the cricket bat was over his shoulder. "We saw his jeep when he left. What did you say to him?"

Conscious of a male alliance, she had begun to feel like a witness under interrogation. "I told him we'd think about what he said."

"Which was?" He had picked up Harry's mannerisms, his inflections.

"Which was that we should get out. Now."

Dan's face darkened, he leaned against the house wall. "Silly wimp," he said. "Petty official."

Amazed, Jane heard herself shouting on behalf of Mr. Adams.

"Dan! Don't be such an idiot! You know absolutely nothing about what's going to happen."

"Neither does he."

"Look, there's no use yelling at each other!" (*I* wasn't yelling . . . " said Dan.) "We'll just have to reach some sort of sensible decision. As a family," she piously added.

"Harry says He can't take the pressure much longer. He'll have to have elections like He promised. Now the teachers are out, they're going to have the kids march too."

She looked at him. "Not unless their parents are crazy. People disappear here, Dan. They just *disappear.*"

"No kid is going to disappear; He's got to pretend."

"All right, no child is going to disappear. But someone is going to get shot in public, not just in private. And when that starts . . . "

"Suppose Gandhi had said that? Suppose the people who lay down on the tracks . . . "

"Oh go and wash *up!*" she said rudely. "I'm tired of being preached at."

A great beginning, she thought, for the family decision-making process. Why did discussions of peace inevitably produce fury? She put her hand on her fist and stared at the low sun; it was the top half of a blood orange, exactly touching sea level.

The first time she had seen Him was at close hand. She was walking down the real road, cautiously on the edge of the jagged cavity of its deep stone gutter, when the black big car, flying its small intense flag, had slid past her. Flanked by two burly figures, the face familiar from posters, under the military cap, the eyes invisible behind the ritual dark glasses, had stared straight ahead. A second car followed closely. That was when He was still playing for respectability, still the emerging statesman, the strong but just father of His island, paternal rather than fascist. There was, in the stance of the rigid chauffeur, the three faces expressionless behind their formality, the middle man's head advanced a little, like a dominant vulture, something which made everything suddenly real. That's what they've all looked like, she had thought, chilled.

She went in to the icebox. It was almost empty. Tomorrow, Saturday, was market day. By thinking of how much chance she would have to be alone tomorrow, she discovered the depth of her uncertainty. Was *she* the wimp? When she had arrived in Ste. Cecile, one question had loomed: marriage. It drew and repelled her. She desired, admired, probably loved Harry; she believed in his toughness, his kindness, the absolute quality of his integrity. Did it really matter that that integrity's expression sometimes frightened and infuriated her? He and Dan. She thought snidely, lucky devils! What bliss total commitment must be. How long was she going on this way, perhaps yes, perhaps no, perhaps leaving, perhaps staying? Alone with Harry the choice would be easy. It was Dan. But how on earth was Dan going to get hurt? Yet in moments she knew he would. He would throw a stone, he will yell at Him.

Then all at once, the thread of patience snapped. Tomorrow, away for hours and hours from the pressure of voices, of presences, for worse or better, she would harden her mushy mind. She felt like the heroine of an opera; she even said aloud, "I *am* Dan's mother . . . "

That evening they played scrabble.

The light from the kerosene lamp enveloped them with—*mollesse*, she thought, a light unknown to the glare of a bulb: cheekbones, eyes, the faded, rather dirty shirts, took on a luminous look so that the three sat—man, woman and boy—untroubled, archetypal, in the light's soft pulse. Outside the sea hissed and hushed, hissed and hushed. A faint indeterminate calypso just touched their ears. The dogs answered each other, near, far up in the hills, bark bark bark. Bark. Bark bark. Already, a manic rooster crowed. This is peace. But she knew it to be armistice.

She was taking the minimoke all the way to Bellemore to paint the new boat; they were building it there. Elevated, the spare ribs were still fresh-cut wood; the shape, bow, prow were there. It went very slowly. Somehow it was wonderful to see tree turn to skeleton, earth-growth to marine intention; the ancient shape, near any sea, always. She must market first; when she came back, all the best fruit and vegetables would be gone. She was alarmed at how delight rose in her at the thought of being alone.

"Q on a triple," said Dan, and his face lit with just his father's look.

The rough sketch was all right, but the rudimentary painting was a disaster. She stopped, wiping her brushes, going into the bush to pee, then sitting on the frame of the inevitable wrecked rowboat, opening her thermos. But even after she decided just what was wrong, the painting balked. The magic of promise in the bare ribs, strong, complex, but still only a shape, was broken. All she had was a mathematical structure. Ah, but she had another structure, complete, in her mind; she knew she could hold to something, once given. She was going to stay.

Everything had been a risk. Mixing her life so deeply with Harry's resolute and single mind; pulling up stakes from friends and the full, competitive world of her work; being remote among people of a different race plunged in their own rough struggle. Either it was worth it or not. The mania that Dan would be shot, would be arrested, would be hurt in some preventable way, left her. Was hero-worship so dangerous? In a world of vicious enmities, was it so perilous if Dan saw Harry as pointing the path to light, to which there was one way only?

Her grandmother had used a palm-leaf fan; she hadn't seen one in years, Jane realized. Why had she thought of that pale yellow shine, so remote from its gusty green? Then her grandmother's dictum came, as though the lacquered fan had wafted it. In the inn of decision, the mind sleeps well. Now she entered, tired, rejoicing.

The nets, fishy-smelling, lay on the sand. Haul over, the racks of tiny fish dried in the sun. There was only an old man, grizzled and small, sitting on a log, his pipe out but clenched, his rheumy eyes meeting hers as she gathered up her load. He smiled. His teeth were intermittent, but from leathery lips he said, with the air of a host, "How are you, Mistress?"

At first she had naively winced at the address, then felt a fool for her assumption, when she discovered it to be pure Elizabethan courtesy, extended to the washerwoman, the goat-tender.

"Well," she said, meaning it. "Thank you, well." She dumped her gear in the minimoke; there was the pile of fruit and vegetables. Uncertain, embarrassed, she lifted a mango.

"May I offer you this?" she formally asked. The old man removed his pipe. Screwing up his eyes, he considered. "What it is?" he asked; then, seeing, "Is it ripe?" he asked with interest. She stepped forward and handed it to him. He took it in his used-up hands, turning it. "It is ripe," he said. "My wife and I will eat it tonight. I will give it to she." He had not thanked her. It was as though they had collaborated on a logical action.

She climbed into the minimoke and turned the key.

"You are from Cal-i-for-nia?" he called, his pipe in the air. They all asked her that. The movie nearest to him was a tin building at the other end of the island. But he asked the same question.

Cutting the wheel, she called back, "No. I come from Baltimore."

Disappointed by the useless name, he put his pipe back in his mouth and juggled the mango a little in his hands. He had lost interest.

The marketplace, when she turned into it, was empty. Boxes, stands deserted; shards of vegetables, a broken crate. Two Barracudas, lounging over rifles. A hot sick pang went through her. She tramped on the brakes and leaned out.

"What's happened to the market?" she called to the nearer policeman. He stared at her, less with hostility than contempt. He hefted his rifle. "That does be closed!" he called back.

"What's happened? Has something happened?" she shouted at him, but he only gave her a wide cold smile.

She saw now that in all directions the streets were empty. Along the sea wall, two more Barracudas strolled. A very old woman, bent, in bright blue, came out of the Catholic church a steep block uphill.

I mustn't drive too fast, she thought. Small pastel houses, wooden shacks shot by. Here came a whole lorry of Barracudas; forced to the edge of the steep stone gutter, she nearly lost control. Now she began to see a few people, in small groups, on the steps of houses, under the high porches.

They'd never do anything to Dan or Harry. Americans. Not unless there was fighting. And there isn't—look, there's a girl driving home two goats. But all the tension of weeks sang in her nerves. On her right she could see the beach flying past her. At the final turn the minimoke rocked precariously, shot down the lane and fetched up in a shower of sand.

There was Harry, on the porch. He had his arms crossed and he stared at her. She could feel her blood drain.

"Where's Dan?"

"He's in his room."

"Is he all right? What's happened?"

"Of course he's all right," said Harry irascibly.

She had been gripping the wheel so hard she could scarcely straighten her fingers. "What's happened?" she said again. She couldn't decide whether Harry looked angry or exalted; at any rate, strange. At the steps, she cried again, "What's happened?"

"All hell," he said. "His goons broke up a march. A man got shot. Where are you going? Dan's door's locked." He grabbed her wrist. "Jane! Just sit down a minute, will you? Just ease off a little. I'll tell you all about everything. Sit *down* a minute."

But she was already knocking lightly at the door.

At once Dan's voice, keyed high, said, "Not now . . . Go away. Please, go away."

Harry had followed her. He passed her; at the cupboard he pulled out a bottle of Mount Gay, gathered two glasses.

"Dan's perfectly all right," he said. "Give him a little time. Come on out on the porch."

Like a knot in her gut, Jane could feel the anger swelling. "I take it there was a march." She followed Harry outside. He poured rum in each glass.

"Yes, there was a march," he said.

"You knew about it ahead of time?"

"Not really. Word gets around fast, you know."

"And I take it you marched?"

He held out the glass to her with a small friendly gesture, and she shook her head. "That's right."

"You took Dan?"

"I didn't 'take' Dan. He'd been planning to go."

"I told him he couldn't."

"Jane, a time comes when you can't make that stick."

Angrily she met his eyes; she saw then how badly he was shaken. Suddenly she felt exhausted. Nothing irrevocable had happened. She was undermined by Harry's face.

She took up the rejected glass and leaned against the rough railing, staring unseeingly at the Montroses' empty yard of dust.

"I can't fight about it now, Harry. But how could you, behind my back? Who was the man? Was he killed?"

"I don't know. Yes. The Barracudas were cracking heads, and he yanked away a police club. It wasn't behind your back. You just weren't here. You couldn't have stopped Dan. He's fifteen.

"*You* could!" she said in a flare of bitterness. She saw in Harry's face an odd mingling of the old stubborn glory and a curious timidity. But he said doggedly, "I wouldn't if I could have. He's old enough to have a conscience and a will, Jane. In three years he could be drafted. He's old enough to know what he believes."

"Was it the shooting?" Jane said uncertainly. "Did he see it?"

Something was unspoken. Harry turned the glass round and round. "No, actually he didn't."

"Then why . . . ?"

To her amazement she saw Harry's eyes blur with pain.

"It's Alexis."

"*Alexis!*"

He looked at her miserably.

"Alexis got hurt."

"*Alexis* was marching?"

"He came with Dan."

"They let him?"

"Mr. Montrose was on his route. I think his mother had walked into town. To the market."

"*You* let him?"

"For God's sake, Jane. I've no earthly power over Alexis. He scarcely believes I exist. I didn't want him to come."

"Wasn't he worth proselytizing?"

Harry did not answer that.

"What happened to him?"

Josephine Jacobsen

"A policeman hit him in the head—but it wasn't that. He was knocked flying down into the gutter. You know what those are. He broke something in his back. We didn't even know. It was a madhouse and we were separated."

"How do you know now?"

"Dan and I went to look for him, and we couldn't find him. After we got back, the police came."

"Here?"

"To tell his parents. Montrose had just got back. He went off with the policeman, to the hospital. Dan tried to go, but Mr. Montrose . . . He was so upset he didn't know what he was saying," said Harry bleakly. "When Mrs. Montrose got back, I tried to drive her to the hospital but—for Christ's sake, Jane, how do you think *I* feel?"

"Well, how *do* you feel?" she said; and then the community of their misery stopped her. "How bad is it?"

"Dan and I went to the hospital. They'd left word we weren't to be allowed to see Alexis. It's pretty bad, I think. Of course, these doctors . . . The back is broken and there are some internal injuries—I don't think they're very positive about anything yet. At least, I don't see how they can be." His face looked pared, polished. Round and round he turned his emptied glass. She reached over and touched his shoulder, and in his eyes tears appeared, for whom she was not sure.

They stayed there, silent. The tide was coming in, pushing the curved bubbling fringe up over the high sand. A way down the beach they could just hear faint thin shouts; tiny shapes ran and pitched. Games had resumed.

At that moment two figures appeared, coming slowly down the path from the road: the Montroses. Ahead walked Mr. Montrose; a few paces behind came his wife. Without hesitation, without a glance, they passed through their gate, across the yard, up the steps to the house.

"I'm going over," said Jane.

"Wait till tomorrow," said Harry quickly. "Don't go right now."

"I *can't* wait," said Jane. "Don't you see? We can't just sit here—us here, them over there. We can't."

"Dan tried to say something to Mr. Montrose. I wish you'd wait."

"I can't." She stood up.

"Look," Harry said in a desperate whisper. "They can't tell really how bad it is yet. But it is bad. Leave them alone."

Jane went down the steps. She thought she had never walked so far as to the Montroses' gate. I won't just keep saying I'm sorry, I'm sorry. The house was silent. A small lizard darted by her toe. The cricket shouts just reached her ears. She knocked at the door.

As if he had been waiting behind it, Mr. Montrose stood before her. Her instant impression was of distance—the fierce remoteness in his gaze paralyzed her.

She said, "Mr. Montrose, I've just heard about Alexis. How bad is it?" she said. From a million miles, from a million years, the eyes watched her. At last he said, "The back is broke up. The hip too." Slowly, impersonally he added, "No way they can fix it right."

"They can't say that!" she cried, terrified. "This is just a tiny hospital. In Trinidad—please, *please* let us send him to Trinidad!"

The face changed so that Jane recoiled.

"You go to hell," said Mr. Montrose very slowly. "Where you is come from. Evil, evil, evil. All of you. Go home—if you do have one."

Behind his shoulder appeared Mrs. Montrose's head; her hand covered her mouth.

I can't move, thought Jane. I am here forever.

"You come here," said Mr. Montrose. "Why? Why you come? You are devils. Go where you come from. You are evil." Then he added with formality, "If you do stay here, you will die."

She couldn't tell if it were a threat or a statement. She looked behind him at Mrs. Montrose's face—it had a strange expression as though it were being pulled apart.

"I'm going," she said to the still figure towering over her. "We're going." With a huge effort she moved, turning. Then she stopped.

"Dan and Alexis are friends," she said.

At that, suddenly Mr. Montrose let out a kind of howl. "*He* should be there, in that place!" he shouted. "Never he should run again! Bad things will come to him, you have done it. You will see. Bad things."

Mrs. Montrose moved suddenly forward, but his right arm shot out pushing her back.

Halfway to her steps, Jane heard the door close.

The next morning while there was dew everywhere and the air was still fresh, Harry drove them to the airport. Dan sat in the back.

He had not spoken since late last night when he had found no shelter.

"I won't go," he said then.

Jane, beyond tact, beyond persuasion, said, "You have to. I'm taking you home."

"I'm staying here," he said. "I'm staying with Harry."

"No, you're not, Dan," said Harry. They were down to raw statement. "I won't have you. You've got to go with your mother now."

"I won't go. How can you make me? Carry me? Call the Barracudas?"

"You can't stay right now, Dan," said Harry more gently. "How could you? Not here, not next door. Where?"

"I'll stay with the Montroses!" he cried. There was a small silence. Dan began to weep. Jane touched his hand but, as though she had burned it, he flinched. He gazed furiously at Harry. "You quit!" he said thickly. "The very first thing, you quit! You give up! You give me up! You tell me something, you make a big deal, and then you quit!"

"What's that?" said Jane quickly. "That was a knock."

"It wasn't a knock," said Harry. "It was someone on the porch."

They listened: dogs, dogs; and the sea. Harry got up and walked over to the door. He said over his shoulder, "If someone's here, just give me a chance to talk to them. Right?" At the door he raised his voice. "Yes?"

No voice answered. Harry turned the brown glazed handle and the door opened on the scented night. As it did so, something fell forward onto the floor and lay there shining a little: a cricket bat. They stared at it, its handle oiled with sweat, soaked in sun and salt. Then Dan darted over and snatched it up. He took it and went into his room. The bolt shot in its slot.

A few miles from the airport, dawn arrived. First the outline of tinged clouds, separate in their drift. Then a sort of enormous renovation of the sky—it cleared, produced a faint pure blue, gradually lit all the greens. On the edges of the road children appeared, with cans or bundles. A man overtaken in his loose barefoot stride raised a machete in greeting.

Jane was transfixed by the dailyness. Light would come just like this through the Montroses' red curtains; over Alexis, asleep or awake, announcing the day of hours, minutes, seconds. Of the first boats, and the sea's colors, and the sand. And in the afternoons, the rich fall of that blood orange, the yells and shouts and flat hard sound of the plank bats. Alexis would indeed remember his neighbors.

At the airport, the waves ran up almost to the runway. The tiny plane already sat there.

At the head of the narrow steps, the tall brown stewardess obstructed them, her voice bored and musical. Of course the cricket bat would not fit under any seat. Forbidden to frown, the stewardess smiled in annoyance. She took the bat gingerly and, carrying it before her, wedged it upright in the coat section.

Dan would not sit with her. But, like a damaging consolation, she knew that already, willing the opposite, he was fleeing—mutinous, looking back—but fleeing something he couldn't bear now, or change, ever.

Harry would be confirmed. Or not. How far he went, to them or from them, what happened, what became of everything, was part of the unfinished. Now he still hoped all things, money, doctors, something. The principle was sacrifice; but what of Harry now that Alexis had stolen it, to carry?

They vibrated violently. The tarmac slid toward them. There was the wheels' *chock*, a wing tilted and the few dark figures fell away.

They were over the sea and through the thick glass she saw the green bright land, valleys, dense hills, falling, falling, bright and small and smaller, in its particular shape, releasing them to the universal sky.

A Metamorphosis

GREG JOHNSON

TINY DISTANT LIGHTS, prickling this soft, uncertain, rumbling darkness —star lights, spot lights! She thinks: here it all begins. He thinks: *here I am, again.* That portentous hush, little flickers of light near the ceiling— wavering, dancing, mocking a night sky to still the waiting hundreds in suspense, to quiet their voices and widen their eyes for *her*. For Lacey. Who also waits, not knowing herself when the tiny ceiling stars will vanish and give way to the light-flood and her own radiant smile and thunderous welcome. She waits, her heart pounding. Everywhere the normal lighting disappeared to prepare for her, voices fell into expectant silence—broken only by scattered whispers, exclamations, giggles—and now she stands onstage, alone. Invisible except for the weak unpredictable lights hovering far above her and reflected by her sequins if she breathes; or the sudden flare of a match being struck, out there; or the faint glimmering of cigarettes in the distance, moving in slight dizzying patterns. When the lights go up she must smile, her eyes cannot scan the audience except in her vast, sweet, impersonal gaze that takes in all of them, loves them all. How she loves them! She thinks: look at them but don't see them, their faces. Don't really see. He thinks: *I am afraid.*

But darkness persists and she sees nothing, no one. How she once revelled in these brief breathless moments just before the lights, the cheers . . . her heart had pounded in excitement, not in fear. Her heart pounds, hammers. What had Teddy said?—"Sweetheart, don't be afraid— it's not the same place anymore, not to worry! This is your homecoming, they all love you, everyone loves you!" "But what if I look out there and see—and see—" "Lacey, don't worry! I'm taking care of you now, nothing should make you afraid anymore—you're well again and beautiful as ever and you're coming home a star—they'll love you, they'll worship you! You're a goddess, Lacey." "But—" "No buts: a goddess."·

Teddy's words are like bits of ice shooting through her veins. The air reeks with Fear and she can smell it. He gave her something: small orange capsules. She took them greedily—two, three, five, she can't remember—so that now she feels the Fear but can't remember why. Something out there, something dangerous, but there is a constant faint buzzing in her head and a slight film over her eyes and she will be all right. When the lights go up she does not want her eyes to flick outward to the crowd as if searching for someone, for one particular face. Nothing is there, nothing her eyes could catch onto. Past is past. Four years have elapsed since she stood here last, since then she has played clubs in every major city in the States and in Europe, she is Lacey Clarke, *Lacey*, a star, the queen of all queens and adored by everyone. They worship me, she thinks.

He thinks: *she is a star and no one can hurt her, not anymore....*

A tradition: walking onstage in silence, in darkness; but they *know*. It excites them, her presence they cannot quite see. Only a teasing flash of sequins, so many minutes of suspense! They sit, trying to catch the scant reflections of her sequins from the tiny teasing bone-white lights above them that are like little stars, little cracks letting the death light through. It doesn't light up anything. But the darkness protects them. Most of them, tonight, have probably never seen her. But they love, adore, worship her. A goddess! They know she began here long ago—in this dingy, smallish club in the seedy section of a middle-sized, crass, unglamorous city—and went on to L.A., Atlanta, New York, Paris Amsterdam London and wowed them all. She didn't have to come back here and so they love her all the more. They remember the cover story in *Newsweek*, what an honor! *Lacey Clarke: Dragging Her Way to Stardom.* Her picture—those wide violet eyes, the blonde flawless waves of hair, that angel mouth!—was placed alongside that of John Wesley Herrington, a nondescript young man in glasses who stared dully out of a black-and-white photo, probably from a high school yearbook. The caption read: "John Wesley Herrington/Lacey Clarke: A Metamorphosis." She remembers how popular it became, putting the pictures side by side. She remembers feature stories in the New York *Times*, the Cleveland *Plain-Dealer*, the Washington *Post*, the Dallas *Times-Herald*, the St. Louis *Post-Dispatch*, even three staidly written columns in *Saturday Review* with the two pictures placed neatly above them, side by side. She read all these stories cynically, her eyes narrowed; or Teddy would read them to her, while someone did her make-up. Together they laughed over all this publicity, since it made them rich and was so absurd . . . and she laughed to herself, privately, because the newspapers and therefore the world would never understand who she was or why she created such love, they could never understand these sweet moments of fear just before the music lights and cheers, their bland mundane perceptions could never sharpen down to moments such as this!

Yes, she thinks, this darkness is pulsing with love—and at once the Fear subsides. Whispered conversations are going on, out there; she senses the excitement in their voices. She can be anyone, her act is carefully planned of course but she can be anyone at all: she can be a goddess of her own making, she can be Diana Lola Barbra Liza, or she can be simply *Lacey* for they will accept even that, she is that big a star. She feels the tension rise, the large room expanding with it in this enveloping darkness pierced by the the tiny star-lights and her sequins and the match-flares, everything hinted at and nothing disclosed, she feels a tingling in the muscles of her thighs, calves, something burns half-pleasurably in her throat and she feels a slight ecstatic stinging in her eyes. Tears. She weeps that such love and excitement and tension can hardly be withstood, it is too rare, too brief, too fleeting—but the past is past, forgotten, she is home again and she is loved and everything is reborn, she feels something like a small exquisite flood deep inside her— only a flood of love!

In an instant music blares and the crowd cheers and her body sparkles in light.

She thinks: I am loved.

He thinks: *I do not exist.*

"God, you were so fine. So beautiful. . . . " For once he isn't screaming: his voice is a reverent whisper.

"Don't call me God," she jokes. "I'm a girl."

Teddy lowers his eyes. "A goddess. A goddess."

"I'm tired, Ted."

"But of course, you worked so hard—a solid hour. Can't you hear them?—they're still cheering, Lace. They love you. They want you."

She sits in a rickety chair before the huge mirror she carries with her everywhere; the mirror is surrounded by light bulbs that make her face eerily bright. The dressing room itself is decrepit, ugly, dirt in all the corners, paint needed everywhere, but she pays no attention to that. She remembers the first night she'd seen this room, four years ago—she'd thought it grand enough. Now she sees only herself and the mirror, they are in love, she has forgotten why she is here. She has forgotten everything.

Teddy hands her something: two orange capsules.

"No more, Ted."

"But the second show isn't for two hours, Lace. You don't want to lose it. Don't forget Amsterdam."

"But I *want* to forget Amsterdam—"

"God, how they loved you. They were so hyped for the second show, I thought they'd tear the place up when you cancelled. I hung around, listening to them, while we were waiting for the ambulance—I thought they'd burn the place down!"

She stares at Teddy: a big man, wearing glasses with heavy black frames that are always sliding down his moist nose. She watches Teddy sweat. He is very excitable and he sweats uncontrollably, he never stops sweating. He manages her tours and promotes her career and soothes her fears and stands just backstage at each of her shows and shouts praise at her constantly and always sweats. He *loves* her. She'd found him in New York, when it looked as if her career might be flagging, he'd fallen in love with her at once and since then they'd spent every moment together. He must be forty-five at least, though she isn't certain. Neither of them asks questions. He's never met John Wesley and he doesn't want to.

"Relax, Ted."

But when she says these words her voice wavers and she wonders if he can tell. She does need the capsules. But no. No. She remembers Amsterdam. Toward the end of the first show, that night, her eyes had suddenly stuck on one of the faces out there, they stuck and could not move: she stared. Stricken, paralyzed. It was him. He wasn't smiling like everyone else. He wasn't swaying with the music or leaning forward eagerly into her magnetic presence onstage or shouting cheers and encouragement like everyone else. He sat back, scowling. He watched her. She froze. She finished the number in her chilled flesh, her eyes slightly widened with terror, her legs stiff as a doll's.

Backstage Teddy said, "Honey, what happened?"

"He's there. He's—out there."

"Baby, *who* is out there? Who is this guy—?"

"I—I—Ted, cancel the second show. I can't—I—"

"Is it somebody you know? Lacey?"

She pushed past him. She locked the door to her dressing room and stood there, panting. Already Teddy was pounding at the door. *Lacey, sweetheart, open up—Lacey, I love you, I—* She tore off her wig and threw it in the corner. That face: sometimes she becomes careless and her eyes flick out among the crowd and one of them catches at her, one particular face. She remembered how he scowled. His mouth a thin dark supple line. That mouth was like a small crack, her eyes had frozen onto it, onto that little dark squiggling line like a dangerous crack of unreason, a dark delicate river that might lead her riveted eyes away from here, out of herself entirely . . . she could not look away. Mechanically, her own mouth had continued moving to the recorded voice blaring out from somewhere but the movements of her body had slowed, weakened, she stared at his dark unsmiling line of a mouth and then, with a quick jerk, glanced back up into his eyes, terrified. They stared. A recognition.

She remembers Teddy's hysterical voice, outside. With a cloth she had wiped off her make-up, pawed at it viciously like a child trying to wipe away dirt; she was careful not to glance into the mirror. Her skin hurt. She ripped off her earrings. *Lacey, Lacey, please unlock the door—please answer me. The crowd loved you, sweetheart—there's no one out there, no one bad—don't be afraid—* She had heard the muffled hammering of her heart.

She hears it now: it is telling her something.

She says to Ted, "I feel like hell. Did you have to bring up Amsterdam?"

"I'm sorry, sweetheart."

She tries to be ironic. "They want to eat me alive, don't they? Don't they want that, Teddy—to eat me up until there's nothing left?"

Teddy snickers.

She thinks about the crowd—usually she doesn't mind them. Most of them are lonely, unbeautiful pricks, she thinks sadly. Most of them would slit their throats if she asked them to. She makes a mental note for her next act: ask one of them to slit his throat, get him onstage, smile, raise a flirtatious eyebrow, hand him a razor blade and say in that sweet simpering voice: *Slit it, honey. Slit it for Lacey.* It would be justice, after all, for she has wasted every night of her adult life in crowds like these, waiting for something, always waiting—even before she became a star. Especially then. She remembers John Wesley at eighteen, searching among those faces every night for the perfect man, an ideal—he was there, of course! Somewhere! It was only a matter of time. Poor John Wesley, just out of high school, sneaking away from the house after his parents had gone to sleep, still wearing a crewcut—hopeless, living on hope. He had wised up, eventually. The faces had turned into fearsome masks, eventually, and he began wearing one himself. John Wesley found four lovers in the crowd and died four separate times and was reborn.

He became acquainted with the Fear.

As a child, he had not known fear—though he had been a disappointment, certainly, that was always made clear. What was it his father called him? "The runt"—of course, he was *the runt of the litter.* Frail, sickly, with that unaccountably girlish face. His older sister, Marcia, had dressed him in her own clothes one rainy summer afternoon and he'd never forgotten it: only ten years old, yet he'd stared into the mirror in fascination at the long pale yellow dress, the pinkened lips, the powdered flawless skin. His eyes had gone wide in disbelief. A transformation. "Johnny, you look just like Marilyn Monroe!" his sister screamed, delighted. He himself had not screamed—he only stared and stared. Years later, when the idea of performing first entered John Wesley's head, his mind had reeled back to that afternoon in his childhood and to Marcia's delighted, half-envious stare. . . .

Onstage at twenty-one, in that seedy ordinary club, her first appearance, she had seen him at last: her eyes had caught on him. . . . But he had changed: there was no love in those eyes. It happened again in New Orleans. And in Denver. In Amsterdam, finally, Teddy had pounded on her door: *Oh sweetheart, why don't you answer, please say you're all right. Who's out there, Lace?—I won't let them hurt you, don't worry—Lacey? Lacey?—Hey! You guys! Somebody do something, help me break down this door—go get somebody, a locksmith—oh my poor Lacey, oh God— please, sweetheart, talk to me—just one word—one syllable—*

She was dazed with fear and she'd made a mistake. Slouched at her dressing table, trying to ignore Teddy, she had glanced for an instant into the mirror. She saw: something horrible, grotesque, freakish, only a mass of smeared blues, pinks, reds like blood dried but still bright, tiny lurid black rivers runnelling down her cheeks. She stayed silent, staring. They looked like tiny cracks in a doll's face, but they moved. She bared her teeth. Her hand reached for something—a bottle of sleeping pills, bought in London at the "chemist's" but still half-full—but she did not move her eyes. She stared. The rivers widened into little faint ribbons as her face got wetter, she heard her own whimpering, a sound that did not seem to be hers at all—a man's unaccustomed, belabored whimpering—and she ignored Teddy's hysterical banging on her door. She swallowed pills without water. Four pills, then four more. Then six. Eight. They were small pills with a slick coating and went down easily, the bottle was soon empty, she let herself slide down into her chair until she could no longer see that face in the mirror and then, somehow, she was on the floor, holding onto the slender delicate legs of her little vanity table, sobbing. . . .

Now she thinks: there is something out there, it wants me, it doesn't love me at all but it wants me—

"Relax, Lace, do you hear? Shouldn't you take something? Lace?"

She stares at Teddy. "No second show," she says coldly.

"But Lacey!"

"No—I can't do it."

"Baby no, you're just upset—I shouldn't have brought up Amsterdam, I'm sorry. Listen Lace, they love you. I love you. Not to worry, Lacey, not to—"

"Call me John," she says.

He stiffens. "Don't lower your voice like that, honey, it's not like you, you're too beautiful for that kind of voice, I can't stand—"

"I'm through with this, Ted," she says. "It scares me. The crowd scares me. There's something they want—I don't know, but sometimes I see one of their faces, accidentally, and I realize what could be out there, that anything at all could be out there, waiting. . . . "

"Honey, I don't understand you."

"Once I thought it was a man out there, a certain man. Love. And I'd find him. I'd be beautiful and he'd see me and we'd find each other."

"But what about me?"

"Then I began to see other things, something in a pair of eyes, or the gesture of a hand, or someone's mouth—sometimes I get so afraid—"

"Lacey, this is nonsense!" Teddy is angry. He stands up and moves around the room, irritated, pacing. He says, "You remember what Dr. Adler said, that time—a neurosis, Lace. It's only a neurosis. You've got to fight it. Now look." He pauses rhetorically, standing over her until she raises her meek eyes. Her brain is blank, she is listening. His long white finger points and nags. "You just look: you don't need this. You don't need to be told anymore—you've beat this once and you'll beat it again. You *know*, intellectually, that no one is out there, that there's nothing to be afraid of, that no one wants to hurt you. So you don't have to let this happen. This is life, Lace: overcoming fear, struggling through this shit. You've got to live your life!"

"But this isn't my life, it isn't real—"

"Of course it's real—you're a star!"

"But I wish—I wish I could give them something—something real. Not Lacey. Not going through someone else's movements and mouthing someone else's words. But I know they wouldn't love me then—they only love Lacey."

"But Lacey, Lacey—that's who you are."

She thinks: no.

He thinks: *you've got to live your life!*

She shakes her head, staring at the floor. There is a silence.

Teddy bends down. "Sweetheart, just take these. They'll help you through. You know the doctor said it's all right—they're just to help you through. Lace—?"

She lets him lay the capsules in her palm.

He smiles. "On with the show?" And when she nods he smiles again, he backs away in deference: "I'll go away for a while, honey, let you get freshened up—take your time, Lace, you've got an hour—call me if you need me. . . . " He backs out the door.

She thinks: bastard. She gets up and goes into the toilet, watches the pills swirl down. Bastard!

He thinks: *I need you. . . .*

Nothing to fear, she thinks. The show is almost over and she writhes in light—the final number! She floats around the stage in white chiffon, yards and yards of it, trailing a white feather boa she uses on the crowd to make them laugh. One moment she is simpering, coy, a tease, the next she opens up and has them on their feet, cheering. Lacey! *Lacey!* They cry out her name, they are frenzied and ecstatic and in love with Lacey. She smiles, feeling her lashes touch the tops of her cheeks, swaying with the music, knowing they are in love with her every movement. When she looks out she can glimpse, far in the distance, posters covering the walls of the club—announcing the homecoming appearance of Lacey Clarke, her name in high, pink, swirling letters! As she passes her sweet vapid stare among the crowd she notices many of them wearing large round buttons, pink letters on a white background: I LOVE LACEY. There is nothing to fear out there, she did not take the pills and is perfectly clear-headed and she even lets her eyes rest upon their faces, their eyes, their smiling mouths, but there is nothing to fear. The number is coming to an end and the lights are hot, bright, glaring, she can scarcely see but knows they have risen to their feet, cheering, stamping, calling her name—

Shouting, *Encore! Encore!*

Of course the show must not end, they want more, more. Always more. She bows and grins, she keeps them in suspense, and finally signals to the rafters: of course she will oblige. It is planned. She senses Teddy in the wings, smiling. The lights grow softer now and the music starts up again and she begins to "sing" in a strident, strong, sarcastic voice: "Free Again." Her favorite song because she never knows if they believe the words.

They are listening but still they seem tense, expectant, barely restrained. She moves, gestures, grimaces. She is giving them everything but still it is not enough. Her heart hammers in glee. They love only the mask of her but that is all right—she is a symbol, an ideal, a star. She knows they too are wearing masks and she has often thought, up here, working her heart out, how necessary are these brash outlandish masks, how indispensable to protect the secret, feeling self. Smiling on stage. Backstage her make-up streaming away in tears, sweat, grimaces of fear.... She understands it now. She is all right. She sings:

> *Free again...*
> *Lucky lucky me, I'm free again...*

But something is happening—the song is winding down, ending, the last song, but they will not let her go. They are chanting something: *We want Lacey! We want Lacey!* Where is the music?—somehow the record is over. It is over too quickly. The crowd cheers, stamps, screams. *We want Lacey!* Yet here she is, in full view. What do they want? She stands there, trying to smile, to make a joke of it—she does a little dance. She rolls her eyes. but this does not appease them. *We want*— Finally her smile vanishes. She stands there awkwardly in the hot lights; she feels a dribbling of sweat down her back. Cold insidious moisture breaks out on her temples. What is happening? Her body seems awkward suddenly, exposed, swaying slightly . . . the violent heat of lights bears down, she breaks into sweat. The crowd is screaming, calling—she can't make out the words. She turns to them, her arms spread wide in a helpless gesture, an appeal. She begins to speak: "Please—I want to say that I love—no, please—please listen—I want—" But from a distance, of course, she appears to be moving her mouth silently, they cannot hear her words; she knows this but keeps on. "Please wait—no, please wait—" They yell, applaud, jeer. She squints out, trying to see past the lights, trying to make contact with something out in the total, restless, wavering darkness. . . . Then there is a throbbing in her temples, making her throat ache with fear and her eyes widen in fear and her bones chill with fear: her eyes stick on something. A smile. His smile.

Behind her she hears a familiar voice, probably Teddy's, stage-whispering her name—somehow she hears it through the crowd. Their cries. Hissing, chanting. *We want—!* She thinks: is this love? He thinks: *is this love?* Music has disappeared, drained away into that little crack between his lips, that blackness, a tiny river . . . she stares, fascinated. The crowd has gotten to their feet but she has no eyes for them. She stares. Somehow they are closer: the darkness, the vast sea of faces, like living pale flares in the darkness, bobbing. The bright lights vanish. She discovers she is no longer onstage but is being sucked down gradually into them, she feels hands upon her, she knows that the minute crack of unreason has ballooned around her—how has this happened? Her eyes are suddenly freed and they dart everywhere, like a frightened bird's.

She imagines herself in the eye of a tornado, feeling nothing. Harsh, high voices all about her, raucous, greedy, a cacophony strangely distant, unreal. She ignores it. She is pushed and turned and mauled. Her eyes rest on nothing, she sets them free. She hears her name in the screaming calls of voices, a frenzy of callings, she feels deft hands paw at her from all sides, pummelling, she sees the white chiffon go drifting across the darkness in shreds, like white delicate birds fleeing a tempest. Hands tear at fragments of the dress that still cling to her body until there is nothing—she feels her wig sucked away, her earrings yanked off, her shoes wrenched from her feet, something twists and tears at her stockings, something yanks at her underwear, something dangles out. She drifts in this dark turbulent sea of noise. Fists appear, pummelling, angry, then retreat dripping red. Stained red. She glimpses a face: its bloodied nose, glasses aslant (broken?) across it, eyes white with terror. "Lace, grab my—" The face dissolves back, disappears. She is pounded, clawed, mauled, hands on all parts of her body, poking, prodding, getting in. . . . Someone's teeth raze her cheek: a bright spurt of blood. She wants to say, to scream: "But I love . . ." but she cannot say these words, they are a lie, all the love is being sucked out of her, drained out, like energy sucked out of stars until they become great black holes, ugly pockets in the universe. Now something flashes before her eyes: a blade, a knife blade rising out of the dark like a silver fin approaching on a black sea.

Teddy's face appears again—strained, contorted. Struggling. He takes her arm. "Lace, hold onto me—" He won't let go, she thinks, won't let me be free. . . . And then she feels it, the harsh bright stab of pain. It spreads downward through her legs and up through her chest, her arms, up her aching throat to her wide, blank, staring eyes. The pain cleanses her—it is pure, absolute, a miracle.

Her eyes roll back into her head.

The crowd sends up a cheer. Something bloody is passed from hand to hand, in triumph.

Teddy holds on, pulls her slowly away. Naked, battered, unhuman, like some hideous plucked chicken, some great bleeding insect—he pulls it away slowly, back toward the stage. And it seems he will pull it free, drag it away and backstage and into hiding, for the crowd does not notice and continues with its festival.

On This Short Day of Frost and Sun

MAXINE KUMIN

CHARLES MAREK stood in the kitchen making shaggy mane soup from mushrooms that had fruited on his front lawn. It was a rainy October Saturday and even the oak leaves were beginning to let go in a gusty west wind. Of course most of them would stand through the winter, purpling the afternoon light so that it suggested the interior of a cathedral, but here and there he could see holes had been torn in the woodlot by their dropping.

It rains a great deal in the Cascades, but Marek, a native Oregonian, was content with the dampness, pragmatically speaking. At the University he had held an endowed chair in mycology for ten years. Although he had something of a reputation as a recluse, serious students from all over the Pacific Northwest flocked to his graduate seminars. He was known as a witty lecturer. Marek's wife, however, could not tolerate her arthritis in a climate so congenial to agarics and boleti and went off to Arizona every September to stay with her sister until April.

The recipe Marek was following was Katey Hallowell's, neatly typed on a 3 x 5 file card. He had never made soup from shaggy manes before. He was not much concerned with the edible properties of mushrooms. Their fascination for him lay under the microscope where, stained with Melzer's solution and fixed on a slide with penetrating oil, the marvelous individuality of their spores stood revealed. He detested having to lead a pack of eager amateurs on a Sunday mushroom hunt along the forest floor. He was an inactive member of the local mycological association and he avoided all cocktail parties where bits of puffballs were served impaled on toothpicks.

When Katey Hallowell came west from Connecticut to give her workshops on Aspects of the Dance in the School of Education, Marek was coerced by Duncan McAllister.

"I'm not just speaking as Chairman of the Department," McAllister said, lighting his pipe and sending up clouds of Balkan Sobranie. "You're such a goddam hermit, Chuck! The lady is famous in her field. We only got her out here because she's a mushroom freak, she wants to go, what does she call it? Foraging. Man to man, Chuck. Help me out. At least come over to the house tonight and meet her."

They were all sitting on the floor when Marek arrived: School of Ed people, the basketball coach, two instructors in the English Department whom he knew and liked, and a sprinkling of students. He accepted a bourbon and soda and stationed himself near the door. The living room was dark, the fireplace smoked, but there was an air of enchantment so pervasive that he soon was drawn into the group.

Katey Hallowell was tiny. Her face was not young. She wore dangling earrings. Her hair was done in a single black braid that hung forward over one shoulder and she was barefoot. As she talked he noticed that her toes worked as expressively as her hands.

"I hate being called a dance therapist," she said. "Because the same principles apply to everyone, not just to exceptional children. The approach is a little slower, a little more basic, not as subtle, but the joy is the same."

"That's the ingredient, isn't it?" McAllister asked. "We say skills, you say joy."

She was firm. "To learn how to use your body, to find your own space and push out into it, that's joy."

When they were introduced on two feet, Marek had literally to lean down to talk to her. Unaccountably, he felt less shy than he had expected. "I hope you don't feel dragooned," she said. "Duncan tells me you're terribly busy. But I came on purpose during the rainy season and there's so much you could teach me."

It amused him to think of this mild October as a rainy season. "Saturday, then? I don't have any classes." He found himself adding, "I'll bring a picnic lunch, we can make a day of it."

"You're an angel," she said. "No, I mean it, you're very kind. I hope you'll come to the workshop tomorrow. It's at two o'clock, in the gym."

He had no intention of going, but he nodded. "I'll try."

At two the next day, as if drawn by some phototropism to an unknown light source, he wandered over to the gym. *Joy*, she had said. It suggested a foreign country. The group was just getting underway. Forty people sat stiffly on the floor, their backs to the wall. Katey Hallowell, barefoot and in a black leotard, squatted in the center. Light glinting from her enormous earrings made her appear even more fragile and childlike than he had remembered.

"Now I want to ask all of you to take off your shoes," she was saying. "And put down your pocketbooks, if you're carrying them. Since most of you are teachers, let me point out to you what is happening. You're all pressed to the security of the wall there. You feel comforted. We're always afraid of putting ourselves into the empty space in the middle."

There was no place to stand without being conspicuous. Marek sat down and took off his shoes. The floor was cold and waxy.

"Come make a circle and hold hands," Katey directed. "You see how uptight we are about using our bodies? The circle is the most natural form for a group to take. In it you can see each other and share with each other."

The hand on his left was young and flaccid. On his right he touched Duncan's tough fingers and was ashamed.

"Divorce yourself from where you've been, from your cars and classrooms. Close your eyes and rub your hands together. Feel the warmth of them? It's energy! Now send that energy around to the hand on your left and the hand on your right. Listen to your own breathing. Let your belly balloon out, pull it in so it empties. Keep your eyes shut, everyone."

He wanted to flee. He wanted the floor to fold under him and let him drop down, out of sight.

They progressed to stretches and warming-up exercises, then to walking out of the circle and in, touching toes barefoot. It was not a solemn occasion.

"You see why you're all giggling," Katey said. "It's the sensuality of touching, you see how we defend ourselves from it. Now we can understand why our kids giggle and squirm."

She had them, oh further embarrassment, lie down on their stomachs. Now her voice descended to his passive body. "This has to do with coming from the earth as an amoebic form," she told the group. "You must push out into space, pull away from gravity—that's it—and let yourselves be pulled back. Wiggle over and touch your partner, wiggle back to your own space. Arch and relax. Now everybody up! Walk as you feel. Find someone whose walk feels good to you, get into couples, move together. Adapt to each other." And she began to tap out a rhythm on a flat leather drum.

Marek, who had felt suffocated on his stomach, began to loosen up. Passing Duncan, he smiled at him, and began a sort of patty-cake gesturing with a plump open-faced girl opposite him.

When he was a child in Klamath he had gone often with his parents to the Grange square dances. The excited rhythm of the fiddle compulsively repeating itself, the heave and jounce of breasts and paunches as farmers' wives and loggers and tradespeople swung in and out of their figures had made him seasick. He had always stayed near the door, ducking out from time to time to take deep breaths of the frosty air. And then the war came and the dances were discontinued and he was already hunched over a microscope. No, he had never been a dancer. And now his pelvis gyrated and his arms swayed; someone else had taken up the drum and he moved in thoughtful undulation face to face with Katey. He felt bound to her not by love but by blood. He felt hopeful, adroit; at the same time he was over-whelmed with lassitude and longed to lie down.

She walked back with him afterwards to his lab, she in her leotard and elfin black slippers, he in the tweed jacket of a tenured professor. Here he prepared a few of the commonest slides—a russula, a clitocybe, an armillaria—for she had, she said, never seen a mushroom spore under magnification. He was touched by how much she knew, even though she mispronounced the Latin names.

"It's because I've never heard them said out loud," she explained. "I only know what I've learned from books. Oh, and six field trips the Connecticut Wildflower Association ran one year."

They progressed to dinner in Eugene, stopping first at her motel so that she could change into what she called city clothes. He waited in the lobby, examining travel brochures that exhorted him to come to Britain, tour Paris or ski at Davos. He could not believe his exotic good fortune and was surprised at the appetite with which he confronted his sirloin steak. It was an old-fashioned kind of restaurant with big glossy photographs of movie stars who had supposedly once eaten there and given this testimonial of their enjoyment. Nostalgia for Clark Gable and Lana Turner, Ida Lupino and Cary Grant loosened their tongues and they exchanged a good deal of biographical information.

Katey Hallowell had been married twice, both times to dear, feckless men. The first one drank and the second one gambled and she still loved them both a little in a detached way. She missed them on wintry Sunday afternoons with *The New York Times* unmussed beside her, or somewhat more acutely at the holiday season. Twice a year—at Christmas and on her birthday—she heard from them and she was grateful that neither bore her any ill will. There had been no children, but her work was child centered and she had five nieces and nephews besides. She was a gourmet wild mushroom cook. Her chanterelles baked in cream were famous all over Connecticut and she had invented a way to prepare coprinus soup—any coprinus, but she favored the shaggy manes—that was marvelous fresh, but would keep for months in the freezer. The only trouble was, she confided, the gray color. "Gray as an elephant's hide," she said. "I've tried a dozen things to change the color, but the trouble is, anything I add adulterates the taste." He pondered this.

He pondered the circle he had sat in touching his cold toes to the toes of perfect strangers, and the lustful gyrations that had seized him, urgent as the drum beat. He, Charles Marek, who had married once in the year of his majority and had fathered upon his suffering wife a son who was a physicist in Texas and a daughter who was away in boarding school. He liked to make furniture in the basement while his wife wintered in Arizona. He had made seven coffee tables and a Spanish settee with carved arms and he knew the names and characteristics of all the trees indigenous to the Northwest.

He slept restlessly that night, mocked by his dreams, rose at seven, breakfasted, and packed a picnic lunch. Katey was waiting in the lobby when he pulled up to the motel entry. They drove almost an hour up the sullen foothills to an overlook. The day was blustery, a water-color sky threatening showers, and he had wisely brought along an exta jacket. It enveloped her like a greatcoat and when she thrust her hands in the pockets he suddenly thought of long lines of refugees, soup kitchens, the solitude of his winters. He rubbed his own hands briskly together before shouldering the pack.

On the way down into the gorge he led, turning from time to time to make sure she was following. She was agile and quick, and bent once to retrieve a pale violet mushroom with violet gills. She brought it to him wordlessly.

"Know what it is?" he asked her.

She held it to her cheek. "I think it's laccaria laccata. See?" And on tiptoe pressed it to his face. "Feel it on your skin. It always feels colder than any other."

It *was* laccaria laccata but he had never heard the folk tale of its lower body temperature. His cheek burned where she had touched it.

Halfway down the steep path he found a scattering of cortinarius collinitus, and presented her with one. She received it gravely, observing the rusty orange cap, the ragged remnants of veil, and paid special attention to the stalk. "Bracelet cortinarius?" she asked.

She was right. He couldn't resist giving her a little pat of approval before they went on.

It was warmer along the creek bed. The water was lively, but narrow enough to crisscross as they moved upstream. Marek thought he would collect some fresh specimens for his lab students while he was about it. He worked methodically, prying fungi loose with a quick twist of the knife, identifying each for her, genus and species, rolling the clusters into small cornucopias of newspaper and settling them in his pack. Katey produced a pad of paper and a pen and took serious notes of their field characteristics as he talked. She was like a bird watcher recording her sightings. He felt beneficent and peaceful and he wished the day would never end.

They ate their bread and cheese on a fallen log. The sun came out briefly and turned the apples golden. Uncapping the thermos of coffee he thought unhappily that he should have brought a bottle of wine, but resourceful Katey produced two miniatures of scotch. They laced their plastic cups with the liquor and drank to new finds.

"What do you want to see that you've never seen before?" he asked her.

"Well, the beefsteak mushroom, for one. Fistulina hepatica. I've looked and looked but I've never found one."

"Neither have I," he had to confess.

"And lactarius deliciosus. I'd know it in a minute if I ever saw it. I mean, I've seen a thousand pictures of it."

"I can't promise," he said. "But I know where to look."

Half a mile upstream the gorge widened into a bowl. They climbed up the north slope, gentler here where hardwoods were mixed among the conifers. He stopped and waited for her to come alongside.

She put both hands to her face in a gesture of what? Dismay? Joy? When she did not move, he went forward a few steps and brought her back the largest specimen. She slit the gills with her thumbnail and watched the orange latex ooze from the green bruise, tested it with her tongue, and still she did not speak. Finally he realized she was crying.

"Oh come on," he said, mortified. "Come on now." And then, feeling awkward as a Boy Scout, he drew her to him and kissed her.

They sat among the lactaria and kissed until the sun disappeared behind the west slope and then they drove back to the motel in Eugene. They were both chilled from their excursion and made love in an awesome tangle of bedclothes. Afterwards, she spread all his mushroom specimens on the bureau to dry and frowning, referring to her notes, identified each one again. Her hair, unbraided now and somewhat tousled, hung down her bare back to the cleft of her buttocks. He was silent. Every comparison for that dark waterfall that came to his mind was banal. She was his naiad; he was bewitched. Later, when Room Service delivered their hamburgers, he was shy as a schoolboy and went and stood in the bathroom until the waiter had gone.

He tried to tell her something of this but he was a man unused to dalliance and he could not find the right words.

"I read something once," she said, trying to make it easier, "something I've never forgotten. It was by Walter Pater."

He was disappointed. "You mean burning with a hard gem-like flame?"

"No. The same man, though. It goes like this." She took his hands and folded them inside hers so that the energy passed left to right and recited: " 'Not to discriminate in every moment some passionate attitude in those about us is, on this short day of frost and sun, to sleep before evening.' "

It was then past midnight. Clearly, they were wide awake.

She was a traveler, Marek thought, a stranger in his bed. Actually, it was her bed, her Holiday Inn, but he had slept alone for so long that he woke every hour to assure himself that she was still there, or rather that he was still here.

In the morning they shared her toothbrush and he took her to the airport.

What could he say? Thank you for the two most quixotic days of my middle age? Thank you for a strange and wonderful time?

"I'll write," she said. "We'll keep in touch. You're a lovely man, Charles."

He watched her disappearing back, her lithe and tough little self as she went down the runway to the plane.

She wrote, as promised. Each time after a decent interval he answered, hoping always that some consultancy would take him East or her West. A year wound down like a clock's hands. Early the following October she sent him the shaggy mane recipe. "After they've all stewed down to an appropriate mess, be sure to buzz them in the blender for a long time. Otherwise the soup will have a disagreeably grainy texture." Then some lines about her new appointment to the Division of Mental Health. Then the news that sank like a stone in his gut: ". . . a widower with two half-grown children. He is a quiet, kind man with the same capacity for joy in his work—he's a mathematician—that so attracted me to you. We're getting married on Saturday in Middletown. Luncheon afterwards with guess what? Shaggy mane soup. Please, Charles, wish me luck this time round. As I wish you, for always."

When the soup was finished, Marek poured it carefully into pint containers, sealed and labeled them and set them aside to cool. Later he would put them in the freezer where, as Katey had assured him, they would keep for months.

Baby

JOYCE CAROL OATES

THE SECOND NIGHT my brother was home I told him, I told him straight out not troubling to lower my voice, Well she's waiting for you in there isn't she, pretending to be asleep with the light out and it's only nine-thirty. I tried to keep my face from going heavy and sullen like it does. I said, You think I'm blind, the way she's been looking at you all day?—it just about makes me sick.

He's my half-brother not my real brother, three years older than me though he has always acted younger, running off to the Merchant Marines when Ma was sick and losing weight so you could see the bones pushing through the skin, somewhere in the Red Sea (wherever that is: I never had time to look it up on a globe of the Earth) when she died and yours truly had to make the arrangements and pay the bills and deal with the funeral parlor crooks who talk like butter wouldn't melt in their mouths. Already him and Etta's girl were probably carrying on behind my back but my brother looked at me all innocent and a little angry, and said he didn't know what the hell I was talking about.

I said again it just about made me sick, the girl was taking after Etta anyway, you couldn't stop that, but under Ma's roof it made me sick, you'd think some people would have shame.

He said again he didn't know what the hell I was talking about but I had better mind my own business, maybe.

I said right back not troubling to lower my voice that I *was* minding my own business, Etta trusted her girl with me after all and I'd be the one blamed, even if the daughter took after the mother (God forgive me for saying so but God knew it was gospel truth) and surely had tainted blood from the father's side (you could see it in that fat lip no matter how light her skin was, and her hair and eyes), and was already causing trouble at school.

How's she causing trouble at school, my brother asked, like he didn't believe me,—she's too simple, they'd slap her down.

Oh no she is *not* simple, I said. That's just one of her tricks.

My brother got a beer from the refrigerator and started drinking it with no mind for his rudeness or the fact that I was still talking. I spoke calm as I always do on the subject of Etta's girl (in which yours truly has become an expert and could straighten out the principal and those psychiatrists or whatever they call them at the school but why should I go down there to be insulted?—I already wrote them a dozen letters), explaining that she only pretends to be simple around the house so she can get away with more tricks. Like she pretends to be smiling all the time and humming under her breath and taking an hour to do the dishes and then not drying half the plates right, or forgetting to scour the coffee pot or the oven, and crying when she wants to, her eyes filling up with tears like somebody on television. I told him Etta's girl had been asking when he was coming home for weeks, maybe for months, and the last few days she'd been acting so strange she didn't mind staying out of school to help with the cleaning, just forgot about school, when other times she's scared somebody will come to the door, or telephone asking where she is. I told him I had to laugh, him pretending he could fool *me*. I told him you'd think he would have some maturity at his age—going on forty wasn't it—no matter if the girl was halfway to being a slut and you could wait till Hell freezes over before Etta was going to admit who the father was.

He said he was going out, not to wait up for him—he had plans until pretty late.

I calculated he had been drinking since ten this morning, one beer and then another, taking it slow but drinking steady the way he learned from his father (who was my father too but belonged more to Etta and him, in my opinion), some of the beer here in the house though he knew I didn't approve, and the rest of it in one or another of his beer joints downtown. He was looking up his pals and making telephone calls and I just had to laugh, he got in such a rotten mood by the time he came home for supper, one of his girl friends moved away or wouldn't see him, that was written all over his face. He thinks he's good-looking because of his curly hair and moustache he keeps trim but from the side his chin just dribbles away, he has to stretch to close his lips over those big front teeth, ten times worse than mine. He thinks he's good-looking because probably one of his girl friends (by which I mean some slut or whore he'd never bring to the house) flattered him to get some cash out of him: they know how to do it. And now Etta's girl, not fourteen years old, mooning over him and staring and stumbling like a baby cow when he's in the room—you can see how a man's head is turned.

I followed him out into the front hall and told him he'd better not make a lot of noise when he came back, and he didn't pay any attention, and outside I could hear him toss the beer can onto the sidewalk,—that's the kind of pig they are, him and Etta both—not caring that it was right in front of the house probably and somebody (yours truly) would have to pick it up next day.

This was going onto ten o'clock and near as I could figure out he didn't get home until early morning—five-thirty, maybe.

I thought,—He won't dare, at first. He'll hold back as long as he can. Which was maybe true, for all I know. He had twenty-one days at home counting the first day and the last.

Or maybe they started in right the next afternoon, when I was away at the doctor's office, first in the waiting room and then in one of his cubicles, all those hours.

Blame it on me for my trusting nature, listening to Etta's lies about when she'd send for her little girl, when she never paid half her share for Ma's funeral or anything else for that matter. (Is this your "little girl," I asked Etta when I saw the child, but she never caught on to my sarcasm or maybe pretended not to hear. I had to laugh, seeing the size of her; and how much she guzzled when you weren't watching.)

First Etta begged, then Etta cried, she promised it wouldn't only be for a few months, until she got settled. I never knew whether there was another man in the picture or not and wouldn't waste my breath asking: there aren't two sisters, half-sisters or whatever, on the face of the Earth more different than Etta and me, praise God. She had the girl, who was eleven at the time, almost pretty except for her small close-set blinking eyes that looked scared all the time, and her mouth that she was in the habit of keeping open (you could hear the poor thing breathe—it was actual panting), and some kind of pimply red skin rash on her arms and neck she couldn't stop scratching. And she had the little boy who was maybe eighteen months old but small for his age, high-spirited and laughing when there wasn't much reason to laugh. Sometimes the girl's daddy and the little boy's daddy was one and the same man (gone out to the State of Washington, going to send for Etta any day), sometimes you got the impression there were two men, two daddies, but I wouldn't lower myself to ask. Etta promised how she'd send money for the girl's room and board (as she called it) and for a few months there was $20 every other week or so, $45, $60 a month, then naturally it tapered off. The last postal money order came from Tampa, Florida, $45 and zero cents, no note enclosed. That was maybe a year ago.

At least the girl could work around the house and do errands in the neighborhood, that was a blessing. Panting like a cow or a sheep or something, and sweating so you could smell it a room away, and talking to herself under her breath when she didn't think I was close by. . . . The neighbors said how good-hearted I was, they pointed out how Ma always claimed her youngest child (which was me) was the only one that ever loved her or showed respect, but anyway the girl could help out with the housecleaning, that was a blessing. Also, she never gave me any sass or ran away when she was being disciplined the way a brighter girl or boy that age would.

I didn't want to tell them that even so I'd have preferred the little boy, if Etta had given me a choice. (Of course she didn't.) He was noisy and made messes but he took to me right away, flailing his fat little hands around and laughing even when I scolded, like he didn't care what my opinion was, he had his own. One day Etta seen me looking at the baby and said with that nasty laugh of hers, He about ripped me in two, that one, took a night and a morning to get himself born, and the way she said it, and the fact she said it so straight out (we were right in the kitchen getting supper) made me sick to my stomach.

After Etta went away taking the baby and leaving the girl behind I sometimes heard the baby's crying, I thought, coming through the walls, or up the heating ducts from the cellar, but the girl never heard anything so I knew it was all in my head. Then later I forgot about him and told myself I'd better forget about Etta, too.

There's one born every minute ain't there, my father used to say, pointing to some fool or idiot in the newspaper that got himself killed, say, for picking up a hitchhiker, or opening the door to a stranger at the wrong time of day.

All these things I explained to Baby when I judged him old enough to comprehend. No matter how ugly the truth is it's still the truth and must be honored, praise God.

How they managed to do their nasty tricks in secret, my brother and that thirteen-year-old slut (and her a niece to us both), I never knew, unless it was when I went Wednesdays and Saturdays to the market, or took to my bed with migraine. Or maybe they arranged to meet outside the house. Etta's girl could cut classes, and my brother could take her somewhere nobody would know about. . . . He was low-minded enough to give some thought to it, and her no better, in spite of pretending to be so simple-minded and sweet like she did.

Even before he shipped out at the end of December the girl was crying a lot and acting strange, but I had my pride about poking my nose where it wasn't wanted, and my dignity. Also, my brother's temper was getting worse and worse like it always does at the end of a visit home, and you'd better watch your lip around him, and feed him when he wants to eat, not too early and not too late; he got it all from our father, it runs in the blood. I wouldn't provoke him by asking questions, I wouldn't lower myself to such filth then or now.

One night he went on a drunken rampage, and me and the girl locked ourselves in the bathroom. He's going to kill us, he's going to kill us, Etta's girl was sobbing like crazy, hot and clumsy as a baby cow but trying to burrow against *me* as if I was her Momma!—so I gave her a slap of my own and said loud enough for him to hear through the door, Anybody lays a hand on anybody else under this roof, the police already know who to arrest,— and that's just the beginning of his troubles.

So my brother pounded on the door a while longer, and said I'd better unlock it, then he gave up and went away, and didn't come home until seven the next morning, sick-drunk and stinking of vomit. If Etta's girl was crying over *him* it serves her right.

Over the winter I saw how she was putting on weight in her belly, and the baby fat around her face became sort of hard and white and shiny, and she'd eat like a pig or maybe eat nothing at all for a day; so I knew the shame that was upon us and took her out of school. I was obliged to whip her a few times, it was my responsibility, but she cried and shrieked so hard my migraine started, and I didn't want to be too rough because something might happen to the baby inside her (who I did not call Baby at the time) and that would be a sin in God's judgment. It was bad enough it would be born a bastard of an unclean union and draw ridicule and scorn upon us throughout the neighborhood.

What did you and him do that I never knew about, I asked Etta's girl, and she bawled and said they never did nothing, she wasn't a bad girl, you could ask Mrs. Cassity (who was in charge of the Special Education students at the school) if she was one of the bad girls, or the good girls, Mrs. Cassity knew them all. Oh yes that's a likely story, I said laughing, I got so angry I was laughing lots of the time that winter and into the spring,—*that's* a likely story, we can tell your mother that can't we.

But I gave up after a while because what was the use?—some people are born too wicked to feel shame.

Etta's girl stayed indoors but, still, around the neighborhood they started in asking,—Who's the father—who's going to own up to it?—looking me square in the face. But I never said a thing, I wouldn't give them the satisfaction. Then they started in asking me where we would place the baby. The Catholic adoption center was just a few blocks away on Grand River Boulevard but if you knew how to go about it there were plenty of couples desperate for babies of their own and they might pay, well, five hundred dollars . . . a thousand dollars. . . .

Yours truly never said a thing.

My plans were: buy myself a plain gold wedding band, and see about renting another house across town where people would mind their own business.

By the middle of the summer Etta's girl had left off crying and just sat around the house, not watching television but only staring out the window into the street (did she think *he* was likely to come back?) or the rear yard. Where before she guzzled everything in the refrigerator if I turned my back for a minute now she wouldn't hardly eat at all. Any kind of gravy made her sick to her stomach, and just the sight of fatty meat, and globules of fat floating in soup. I had a book I was reading on diet during pregnancy but Etta's girl just shrugged her shoulders. Finally I went out in 95° heat to buy a gallon of butternut-ripple ice cream one day to get her eating again. She said she'd be sick at her stomach but I handed her a spoon and that was it: once she got started she couldn't stop.

There were exercises she was supposed to do too, according to this book I had, but she was too lazy to budge. I told myself,—Well, babies get born anyway, they always have.

It was queer how her stomach got—big and round and high, and hard-looking, not like an ordinary fat belly—while the rest of her was pinched and sallow. The baby fat disappeared from her face and her eyes were bruised-looking and old. Once I looked up at her in the kitchen—this was in early August, not long before Baby was born—and thought I wouldn't know who that girl *was*, if she was kin to me or not.

Already Baby was a strong presence in the house, you knew he was there, just waiting. He'd kick and I swear I could feel it across the room!—even before Etta's girl made one of her sharp whining noises like she was being stabbed.

Already you knew he was a *he*. There was never any question of that.

My timing was just right: we moved across town to Union Street, and a few days later Etta's girl went into labor (it lasted fifteen hours but they said that was normal enough) and Baby was born, seven pounds four ounces, no known defects, Caucasian male (as they called him).

It was like the baby book explained: you think they are ugly at first, and their skulls not right, and that flushed skin, and queer blackish hair and blind-looking eyes. . . . Etta's girl laughed and said, *I* don't want it, later on she said (embarrassing me in front of the nurse), I don't know what it is, it isn't mine, I never had anything to do with it.

So I had to take charge immediately, or Baby would have died of neglect. (Later I would think, or God would allow me to think, that Baby should have died right there in the hospital, he should have been born already dead, but of course I couldn't have such knowledge at that time).

When Baby first came home I was frightened to hold him thinking he might slip through my arms, he could squirm and kick so, or he might stop breathing all of a sudden the way they say babies do. But of course nothing happened because he was too strong. He fixed his eyes on me right away and knew who I was.

Etta's girl pretended she was too sick to nurse so yours truly had to take charge as anybody would have predicted. At my age! . . . preparing baby formula, changing diapers (which did not seem so disgusting after the first week or so), giving Baby his bath and laying him down for his nap. In this new house (a duplex—I believe in upstairs and downstairs and having your own front and rear doors) Baby and I were situated upstairs and Etta's girl had a room off the kitchen that the landlord said was a dining room if you wanted one.

Baby's crib was white wicker, old-fashioned and sturdy, that I found in the old cellar when we moved. This was my own crib a long time ago, I told Baby,—so it's right you should have it.

Etta's girl lazed around the house too mean to nurse though you could see the milk staining through her clothes. She watched television now whenever she could get away with it and just laughed when I asked wasn't she going back to school?—she knew from the start how Baby had turned against her and pretended it was *her* doing.

Baby knows who his true mother is, I said, and Etta's girl just laughed, swinging past on her way to the bathroom.

Baby knows who hates him and who loves him, I said. Who his true parent is.

By this time Etta's girl had got so fat and sloppy you could feel the floorboards give a little beneath her bare feet. She had got so mean and lazy she whispered swear words under her breath pretending I wasn't close by.

Once when I was telling her about Baby, and about how he knew more than he let on, she turned to me with an ugly grinning face and said, That baby don't know shit.

And when I went to slap her she dared raise her hand against me—both her hands against me, made into fists—like she was going to hit *me*. And Baby was a witness all along. So I knew I had let things go too far, I would have to notify the health authorities about Etta's girl and get her taken care of properly, as her condition required.

So Etta's girl left, and Baby and I were alone together as God decreed. It was the right thing to do, having Etta's girl taken away, they told me at the county home not to feel bad about it, if I read the newspapers (which in fact I do if I have time) I'd know that more and more young mothers were doing injury to their babies. They were dependent, they told me, on people like myself stepping forward and speaking out.

One of the nurses told me a person like myself wouldn't believe what went on in that housing development on the west side, they were just animals there, if I knew what she meant. I said I did know. She said it made her sick sometimes to be called over into the neighborhood, it made her almost lose faith in the human race, but my niece was not of that category of course.

Well, I said, wiping Baby's mouth with a tissue where he had drooled on himself,—some people *are* animals, after all.

That was our happiest time now I look back on it—three or four months when the house was empty of Etta's girl and Baby had not yet come into his powers.

He learned to crawl, and to walk, and to say things meant to be talking, all earlier than the doctor said to expect, which comforted me in the beginning because it meant that he would not grow up feebleminded like his mother. Even when he was asleep, though, he filled the house upstairs and down, there wasn't a room he wasn't in, I could feel him through the walls. No matter what I was doing—for instance scouring the oven one time—he could summon me to him if he wished without making a sound.

Baby knows who loves him, I would say. Baby knows who his true parent is.

And Baby stared at me understanding every word and smiling for of course he *did* know.

That's a husky baby people said in the neighborhood,—that's a good-looking baby, they would say, fixing their eyes on me and getting ready to ask (I had to laugh, I knew it was coming) where his daddy was. So I said, Well now his *daddy* is halfway around the world but he's good about sending money home, that was one good thing about him, and the way I talked you could tell they were puzzled but they didn't know to ask where his *mommy* was, which was none of their business anyway.

That's certainly a *boy* baby, a woman from across the street said, poking her nose into Baby's face, you wouldn't have any doubt he's a *boy*, she said, meaning to flatter, then smiling a big wide smile and asking what his name was—if I'd told her, she said, she must have forgotten.

Baby is what I call him for right now, I said. Baby is name enough for us both.

Yours truly was *not* rude—but kept the baby buggy moving.

* * *

Just when the Change started in I cannot say, although looking back there were signs all along.

Sometimes Baby would allow me to cuddle him, and rock him, and kiss him, and sometimes he would not—he'd fly into a range and half choke with shrieking. *Like he did not want to be touched.*

Sometimes Baby would eat every spoonful of his food as I fed it to him (his favorite for many months being mashed apricots which I flavored with sweet cream and sugar) but sometimes he would not: he'd spit it out, maybe cough and vomit, and scream and kick and flail about as if someone had hurt him. (Which assuredly I did not—for I knew very well never to put hot food or a hot spoon in Baby's mouth, a common error it is said ignorant young mothers frequently commit.)

Sometimes, also, Baby would sleep peacefully when he was put to bed, but sometimes, what a commotion!—he'd shriek and clamber about in his crib, kicking, and banging his head against the sides, I didn't dare lay a finger on him because he would only get worse, his face all wrinkled and purple and his breath irregular. What if he chokes to death in the blankets, I thought, what if he puts his head through the bars and strangles himself. . . . Next door the neighbors began to knock against the wall in protest and I was sick with shame, that strangers might know of our private business, and talk amongst themselves of Baby and his wildness.

You must learn to be good, I told Baby, half-fainting because my heart beat so, you must obey your Mother, I told him, but he only stared at me cold and insolent like he had never seen me before.

There is nobody on this Earth who loves you as your Mother loves you, I told Baby.

Baby laughed.

You could not doubt but that Baby *was* all boy, however, nothing weak or feeble-minded about him. Thus I praised God as it became clear that his nature had skipped over my brother's and was close to being Baby's grandfather's if I remember correctly. His hair had turned light brown and was very, very fine and curly. His eyes had turned the bluest blue.

Baby must have his way inside the house and out, and his Mother's legs, that have never been strong, cannot keep up. I laughed to myself saying that I had been fool enough to pay $7.50 for a big jar of cod-liver oil tablets sold to me at the door (by a high school girl a stranger to me) when Baby did not need extra help in growing . . . !

There were five hundred tablets in the jar, of which I gave one to Baby before his breakfast each morning, and by the time the jar was emptied the Change was well upon him—though I would not say that the cod-liver oil tablets were to blame.

By this time Baby had long since learned to dress himself and to go about his business as he wished, sometimes very quietly in the morning, so only the creaking of the floorboards alerted me that he was awake. At other times of course Baby romped about, and crashed into things, and chattered to himself as (it is said) small children will do at that age. I pressed my ear against the wall to hear more closely but his words were secret to me.

Baby what are you saying, I whispered through the wall but of course there could be no reply.

How husky he was growing!—as all the neighbors commented, the mothers in particular who were perhaps jealous of Baby. For, by the age of three, Baby stood near to my shoulder (tho' I am not a tall person it must be remembered) and when we were seated, why, I believe we were of a height. Baby used his own spoon now—and his own knife and fork—and often ate with his head lowered to his plate as my brother did (though there could be no influence for Baby had never glimpsed my brother). It was not indifference to his Mother for I believe he loved me, but simply the way he was, thinking his own thoughts and forgetful of my presence.

There was much resistance to his bath now for Baby said he wished to bathe himself (feeling some shame perhaps at his nakedness—for Baby had rapidly matured); but I did not trust him to cleanse all his parts thoroughly. Thus we had frequent disagreements which flared up in quarrels leaving Baby blotched in the face and panting hard, and yours truly half-fainting on the sofa, sick and dizzy with grief. (It is not the place to speak of my health but I am obliged to mention that my Doctor expressed some concern for my blood pressure and an "erratic" heartbeat he detected with his instrument. Since moving to Union Street I have consulted a new doctor who knows me as "Mrs." and respects the ring on my finger and the fact that I am a Mother—altho' I am wise enough never to allow him to examine me down below, as, being a doctor, he would surely note some evidence that *I had not had Baby in any physical manner.*)

When I lay fainting on the sofa Baby would give evidence of remorse but (God forgive him) would not apologize. Doubtless he shed tears in secret—as I did—but his pride was such he could not be humbled.

Also, sometimes when I napped in the late afternoon (for my nerves were such I had begun to tire halfway through the day) Baby would appear silent by my bedside gazing down with no earthly expression on his face. Though my eyelids were closed I could see Baby clearly, as he was in real life yet altered with queer nicks and dents in his cheeks and a tawny glow to his eyes such as you find in the eyes of cats. Baby it is in your power to do great harm, I whispered to him (though my lips could not move), but I pray God you will show mercy to me . . . for I am your dear Mother who loves you above all the world.

Baby did not speak. His eyes were in shadow and his mouth was pinched inward like a fist.

As the months passed, however, the Change grew more and more upon him, and I fell into despair wondering what I must do.

He had begun to stay away long hours from the house despite my pleas; and where he once chattered and babbled happily under my roof now he was silent days at a time. Why do you grieve your Mother, I asked him, but he turned aside as if the question was a shameful one. When I tried to kiss him he went hard as stone or ice shrinking from me in his soul.

Now it happened too that the mothers along Union Street rose up against Baby saying they no longer wanted him to play with their children. Has he injured any of them, I asked, my heart beating so hard I could scarcely breathe. He has not injured anyone yet, one of the women said unkindly. But he speaks to them, he gathers them around him to say such things they will not repeat to us,—and when we approach they run away guilt-faced and laughing.

No, he is not a natural child, another told me, her face contorted with hatred. You must keep him away from our children!

Not a natural child! I exclaimed. How dare you say such things, when you know nothing of us!—And in pride and scorn I turned from them to retreat to my house where Baby hid crouching at the window.

Not a natural child. The words lodged deep in me as a curse.

For Baby had altered to such a degree he was scarce recognizable at times; God was urging him from me whether I would consent or no. If I made to embrace him impulsively, as mothers do, even to stroke him with loving fingers, Baby shrank from me murmuring *Don't touch me! don't touch!* with scarce a movement of his lips. In hurt I cried that he was not a natural child but he laughed and paid no heed.

Not a natural child. But what would God have me do, to make amends?

I wept that my halfbrother, the cause of so much sorrow, had abandoned me to this corrupt offspring, to live out my life in apprehension. For I could not control Baby. I could not control his thoughts nor the wayward movements of his body. One night while bathing him suddenly I summoned all the strength in my frail body to push his head beneath the soapy water and hold it there . . . but of course Baby resisted as of late he resisted my every desire;

and in the end, after much struggle, and kicking, and splashing, and shrieks, I relented and let Baby go: my bosom and skirts soaked, my face wet, pulses beating wild. I relented and let Baby go, to my shame, having not the physical strength nor, it may have been, the moral courage, to continue. For by now Baby had grown husky indeed, his muscles taut as steel seeking to prolong his life.

Afterward he lay gasping and whimpering on the floor, his mouth pursed still like a fish's and his eyes rolled back up in his head. I calmed him; sang softly to him an old lullaby sung to me, many years ago; told him his Mother loved him and would protect him, though his Father had abandoned him long ago. And Baby clutched at my skirts, and sank into sleep in trust of me.

Often now I thought of my brother; and of Etta's girl (who is said to be happy amongst others of her kind in a Home in the country); and of my wicked sister herself (who has not contacted me for many years). I thought of them with some bitterness, yes and some rage hidden in my heart, that they have abandoned me to Baby who watches me so strangly now, his eyes narrowed to slits, and his thoughts so secret and cunning. Now at the age of four he has grown to my height, and a little beyond; which is to say,—for I measured myself against a doorframe—five feet one and a half inches. His hair is of no distinguishable color, and wild and springy; his skin smooth as a true baby's, yet coarsely flushed; his lips oddly full as if heavy with blood. Yet it is those eyes that frighten me, a cat's eyes intense with thought, peering into my very soul. *Yes? What? You? Who are you?*—Baby seems to mock.

I have not described Baby's voice because though he has a voice he rarely allows me to hear it save in shrieks or murmurs. As to *words*,—never does he speak words, to me. (Yet I have seen him many times out in the alley, surrounded by children who listen avidly to his every word: and my heart is torn with affliction,—for what does Baby say? What does he tell them, he will not tell his Mother?)

What would God have me do, I begged nightly. To make amends.

Thus it came about I took Baby into the country one wintry day, telling him it was time now for him to join with his true Mother, who missed him greatly, and was now summoning him to her.

And Father? he inquired in his low hoarse voice I could scarcely hear; a voice, I am sorry to say, quivering in mockery.

Yes: your Father as well, I stoutly replied.

Hastily I dressed him, at dawn, as for a long journey. Took him downtown to the Trailways bus depot where I bought tickets for a village I had located on the map (its precise name need not be recorded) some five or six miles from the Home in which Etta's girl is lodged. The tickets were round-trip for me, one-way for Baby, a melancholy fact he could know nothing of though during the morning's long ride he sat silent and stubborn beside me staring out the window, turned from me as though we were strangers. What is your boy's name? an elderly lady across the aisle inquired of me, rather cheekily I thought, though I answered her politely: His name is Baby, I said, he is not so old as he appears. Oh, said the lady staring, and is he a good boy? He is not always a good boy, I said frankly, hoping Baby would overhear (for he had turned resolutely away as if he knew me not) . . . no he is not always a *good* boy . . . his mother and father abandoned him long ago.

Oh, said the lady again, staring yet more rudely, I'm sorry to hear that. Yes, I said. It is a sorry thing.

At our destination I took Baby firmly by the hand and walked him from the bus depot along a street that dipped to an area of warehouses, vacant lots, cracked and weedy sidewalks. Baby made no resistance. Though I had never set foot in this town before I felt not the slightest hesitation as God was now guiding my every step. At last we came to a deserted park, a playground with three meager swings and two teeter-totters and a drinking fountain damaged by vandals. *Here?* Baby seemed to cry out in his soul. *Here? Is it here?*—Your true Mother is to come for you, sometime before dusk, I said. So you must not despair beforehand. You must not run away.

Baby's face was wet with tears but when I peered closely I could see the pupils of his eyes shrunk to pinpricks. *Don't touch!* Baby whispered; and indeed I did not.

So it was I was forced to leave Baby in the playground and to make my retreat. I too was crying in my heart but I did not slacken, not during the long journey back to my home on the bus, not till I unlocked the door to my house and stepped into the darkness. For it seemed he had preceded me! Baby, I called out blinking,—are you here? Are you here, and hiding?

But Baby was not there, so far as I knew.

In the years following I have heard of certain hideous acts committed in the countryside, yes in the city too, no longer do I dare read the newspaper, for amongst its lies are tales of such peculiar mystery, I am led to believe Baby is the agent; yet I cannot know. And often in passing the playground beyond Union Street I see Baby sitting on one of the swings, idly turning, head bowed, or does he sleep, alone on the swing with no playmates near (for natural children avoid him), turning now from left to right, from right to left, slow and idle as the Earth's turning on its axis, and his old secrecy about him, those cat-eyes narrowed and aslant so that he can watch me pass by hurriedly. *Yes! You! It is you!*—thus his wicked heart calls out but I am not tempted to pause.

Not till I am safely in my house, the door locked against him, do I think of him with regret, and tears, and love; and I bite my lips murmuring Baby if you have come so close to home. . . . But I have not weakened thus far: and God give me strength, that I do not.

Confessions of a Bad Girl

BETTE PESETSKY

M Y GRANDMOTHER WAS BORN near the village of Nowogrodek in Poland, also the birthplace of the poet Mickiewicz. My mother was born in Minneapolis, I think. I know absolutely where I was born, because the proof is staring me in the face. A certificate duly registered with the Bureau of Vital Statistics, Department of Health. Doctor's name Miller. Legitimate checked yes. City, Milwaukee. I fingered the birth certificate, surprised to find it in the lefthand desk drawer. Why wasn't it in the safe-deposit box next to the records of my husband and my daughters? I pushed the paper aside. I can't distract myself from my task. I have been hunting for a misplaced checkbook for three days. On the second day my husband said to me in disgust, "What is it this time? What have you lost?" I shook my head, I denied it. Nothing, I swore. Did he believe me? I immediately became secretive about the search waiting until I was alone before digging under piles of papers, shuffling through miscellany in drawers, examining the contents of closet shelves. When my children were home there was always the thought that they had appropriated the lost item. How often had I replaced a lipstick or purchased a slip certain that one of my daughters had it, and then days later the shiny case that held Revlon's color of the month or the nylon slip with ecru lace would reappear tucked away among my possessions. But the checkbook—this particular checkbook was large. My husband chose the style. We had a businesslike book, three checks across, three down. The dark brown vinyl cover was embossed by machine to look like alligator. And I couldn't find it. I wrote all the checks, kept the household accounts. I had been given as a present a small calculator, but even before its appearance, I had managed, my addition and subtraction were excellent. How could I admit that *I* had lost the checkbook?

Is the ability to lose papers determined at conception?—do zygotes when dividing carelessly drop those cells with the ability to keep everything on tap, in place. Where is it? my mother would say. We didn't know, none of us knew. Never leave anything behind, my mother said. Take everything, every crumb, sweep clean.

I think that when I die someone shall find my love letters and pity me. Couldn't she hold him? They will laugh at my lists. *This*, they will say, she saved. *This* bears witness. The answer to these sweet leavings is that their message is false. These papers were not saved nor pressed nor treasured— they were eaten up by warrens of drawers, stuffed beneath beds, trapped between the covers of books.

Surely the checkbook was somewhere. But when could I look? I had to limit the times of my search to one hour in the morning before I left for work while my husband showered and dressed and in the evening during those moments when he was not aware of my purposes. And all the time I must conduct my affairs, must pretend that this loss did not weigh upon my thoughts, and ordinary life always interrupted.

Suddenly I found my birth certificate again. This time in the closet among a pile of wrinkled receipts, appliance warranties, fat brown envelopes. If the same paper can turn up again—why not the checkbook? One shuffled in a circle through papers like orphan children lost in the woods. See the tree— turn left, turn right—then there it was again. The tree.

My mother had papers too—string-tied packages of political pamphlets, the paper crisping at the edges, and receipts and clippings and notes that begged her to come at once or at the very least to send money. We carried all this with us when we moved. We carried it into the flat on Fon Nur Avenue where we lived for two years.

I paid attention to these papers. I was always sneaking around, looking through holes, hoping to see what was unspeakable, undone buttons, secrets written out. One of the first words I ever looked up was anomie. Did I ever run out of material? No. What I found at one age, I could rediscover later and uncover new meanings. There were certain funny things everywhere. For instance, my mother's parents disowned her—the word was *verleugnen*. The handwriting was heavily slanted, maybe a letter switched, a conjugation misinterpreted, but by and large, the consensus of my translators was that the meaning was disowned. I read my mother's letters. Sometimes friends moved, and letters came back marked address unknown. I'd read these too. Some I forgot about, others I used. In my play entitled "Robin's Home Again" I put in the contents of an entire letter. I switched names just the way I'd seen it done. The names have been changed to protect the innocent. This I printed on the bottom of page one.

We lived at the time above a store. It was a liquor store, it was not dangerous. Every married woman in that neighborhood was fat. The only exceptions were Theresa's mother whose husband drank and two other women whose insides were said to be consuming them. All the rest were fat.

Even my mother, although she was always talcumed and tightly corseted to fit into a white uniform that she wore to pretend to be a doctor's assistant. Just do what I say, he told her. If they call you nurse, don't contradict. The jobs I've held, my mother would say and sigh. But a working girl can always make her way.

I didn't plan to be fat or to wear black crepe in winter or wallpaper prints in summer and puff upstairs with legs wrapped in Ace bandages. I didn't plan to be married. I planned to write plays.

For "Robin's Home Again" I needed costumes. If you're careful, my mother said, you can use the stuff in the boxes. There were three boxes of dresses set aside by my mother, clothes from a different time, she said. For me I selected a dress of dove-gray silk. I had at that time only one friend. It wasn't easy to pick something for Bridgy. Already at age ten her figure was inclined to marriage, and she got cranky if the dress chosen didn't immediately fit. Sometimes she would turn right around and go home. So I hunted through the box. For her I finally selected a loose chemise with a collar lined with sequins. Bridgy liked a touch of glitter.

The play was a romance, but there were no parts for boys. I knew no boys. Bridgy and I would talk about lovers who would themselves never appear in the play. Most of my plays had just two characters.

In front of the mirror in my mother's bedroom, I tried a few of the lines I'd written. I'll cut you dead, I said. I'll never speak to you again. I repeated the lines, my voice grown distant and scornful, my reflection dove gray, my face white. I would do that to Bridgy. I knew that even though it made me shiver to think about it. But yes, some day I would pass her on the street—plump, cranky, grown-up Bridgy—and I would cut her dead.

We presented the play that afternoon in the upstairs back hall, me in dove grey and Bridgy in salmon pink. In my first version I found a letter and was to wonder whether or not to show it to Meg, the character played by Bridgy. If I gave that note to Meg, what would she say? *My God!* I thought she would say. *My God!* Would I be asked to keep a secret? One of my characters says that she never means exactly what she says. That was one of Bridgy's lines. I knew that she wouldn't say it right. No, Bridgy would make the words sound sour like some line in a squabble. Imagine, Meg should say lightly, this old paper, a joke, part of a silly game—forget it. For the actual performance I changed this part, did the letter as my dialogue.

ME: I was married once before—don't you know?—a long time ago.
BRIDGY: No, I never heard about that.
ME: Who did? He was M. K. Gale—a saloonkeeper, a gambler, a dynamite man.
BRIDGY: You never spoke about him.

ME: Because it's done with, Meg, it's finished. No missus in front of my
name anymore. No more Mrs. M. K. Gale. Forget whatever
you've read about him. I'll tell you all next time we meet.

My mother left the kitchen and came into the hall. "What's that?" she
said.
"The play is over," I said.

The letter had been written to Dot, one of the pile of returned letters that I
had steamed open—later Dot sent her new address. But I knew who Dot
was. Dot and my mother graduated from Blewett High School. Dot came
every couple of years all the way from Evanston, Illinois to spend a week
with us. She had married a man who owned a dry cleaning store, and she had
three boys. She had photographs of them, great hulking boys. I hoped never
to meet them. Dot was a great visitor. I'm here to pep up things, she'd say.
She and my mother would giggle, would act silly, would wear fancy
bathrobes and buy liquor and mixes and pour whiskey sours into tall
glasses. Dot would let me sip from her glass, and my mother would laugh
and say, Stop corrupting a child. Dot always had a sore on the corner of her
lower lip that she tried to conceal with lipstick, but it was there, a silvery
glow, a moist patch. I would never let her kiss me.
    You could overhear a lot when Dot visited, if you pretended not to be
listening. What's out there, Dot would say. You wouldn't believe. And his
hand, Dot said, crept, yes crept, right up my leg under the dress to the
garters. Midday, she said. A matinee.
    I went into the bathroom and closed the door and sat on the edge of the tub
so that my hand could creep up the side of my leg—up, up to where a garter
might have been. There was nothing to feel though, just my thin, boney leg.
Dot's garters hung from pink loops firmly sewn to the edges of her girdle.
The dry, rubbery garters were bent and distorted where they had pressed
into the richness of her flesh.

As I searched, a mountain grew behind me of single gloves, beads, scarves,
notes, passports. But I did not find what I was seeking. Some things, I knew,
remain lost forever. A creamy yellow blouse with a scalloped collar, the
directions to a strange and complex game sent to my daughters from
England by their father and the girls wept and accused me, the recipe for a
sauce in which the exact proportions of the ingredients were needed to
create a sharp mustardy flavor. I think I have its essence sometimes, but it
was never right. Who is to say that what is lost is valuable? Only that what is
lost is never forgotten.
    I was not ready to give up. The checkbook must be found. I have dumped

the contents of two drawers from the Empire high chest upon the floor. But it was not among those tumbled sweaters and torn nightgowns. "Cleaning?" my husband said to me suspiciously. "Sorting? Looking for something? What would you do if the IRS wanted to audit us?"

I left everything on the floor and went to call my daughter Elaine and my daughter Audrey and invite them both to dinner on Friday night. It was close to the end of the month, and money was scarce—they both accepted.

I went to my office where I was distracted, answered inappropriately, and was rude to my colleagues. I was firm in my position. I got away with a certain amount of belligerence. "I want," I told my secretary, "the files on Hazelraft and on Kant and on McLowen." "All of that?" she said. "Yes," I ordered.

That evening my husband was late. I have a meeting, he told me. I used the time to unfold the linen. The checkbook could be caught between the sheets. Before I finished, the telephone rang. It was my mother calling from St. Louis. Aunt Arlette has broken her leg. That's no small thing, my mother says. For an eighty-year-old woman that can be the end. In her lobby, my mother continued, a good thing she wasn't alone. Send a card, my mother says. Take down the address. My mother names a hospital near Forest Park, near a wide boulevard. You must send a card, my mother says. Yes, I say. Or else, my mother warns, you have a heart of stone.

I will not send a card, although I have a vision of the old woman slipping on a worn marble floor and sliding and rolling downward—why downward when the floor is level? Let the old woman slit open her other envelopes. Hallmark has lost a customer in me.

They stuck a needle in my arm in the hospital with a fluid that contained a radioisotope. A tag, they said. They could chart the course of that fluid by the presence of that tag.

Everything, I believe, has a tag. Find the tag and chart the course. You run your hand over a particular bit of blue cloth and the roughness on the tip of your finger rasping against the velvet makes you tremble. Your nostrils wrinkle at an unexpected scent and sniff the air. What's that? What's that? Tag.

I was in Aunt Arlette's apartment. What's it to you? Aunt Arlette whispered in my father's ear. He was her brother. Why did you leave Springfield so suddenly? My father shook his head. My father was being sent somewhere to help a good union shop. At least that's what my mother said. Be a good girl, my mother said. See you in apple blossom time. Was I afraid? Did I feel abandoned? Count the days, my mother said and marked important circles on a calendar.

For seven weeks I would stay with Aunt Arlette. And Aunt Arlette would say, This is my brother Ben's child. Yes, she's a big girl. And I would nod and bob. But this was only to her friends. *Landsleit* were different. They rushed at me, no introductions needed. My father's relatives roamed through that apartment in startling numbers. I was from a family of three. We had always lived up north. Names were shoved at me. I was embraced by fierce ladies, and their pins pricked my cheek. Who does she look like? they asked each other.

I had never seen Aunt Arlette before. But, she said, you have. When you were three, she said, and once as a baby. I ate breakfast and lunch in the kitchen with Aunt Arlette and a woman named Rae who did the cleaning.

What happened? All that happened were the holidays. I had never known so many holidays. And for the holidays the dining room doors were pushed back into the walls, then the table was stretched outward with insets of wood. White linen cloths, plates dazzling with painted red flowers entwined with large green leaves. Aunt Arlette would take off her black crepe dress and her gold bracelets and cover her black rayon slip with a long white apron like butchers wore and stand next to Rae in the kitchen and cook. The first course was already on the table when everyone arrived. On small clear glass plates were pale gray fish balls, two on each plate balanced in a cup of lettuce leaves, the balls separated by a pink-toned scraping of horseradish. Never had I eaten such food, how I disgraced myself, gagging on the taste of that fish. The cousins my age, all alien, giggled. She's barfing, one said. My plate was removed. An excuse was made. She is not feeling well. Could this be said every time?

I learned which odors I could not bear, knew when the fish balls were being made. On the stove would be the simmering broth, afloat in the pot the skeletons of fish bobbing to the bubbling motion, fish heads, bits of onion. The smells of oceans blowing through the rooms. Winter carp, whitefish, pike. Rae was sympathetic. Don't worry, she said, gefilte fish is an acquired taste. Buck up, kid.

Was it always a holiday? How often did God rest? It was a holiday. They set the table, ten places down one side, ten places down the other. The gray fish balls in front of each chair. Except for me. Suddenly for me there was a scoop of tuna fish salad cozily placed within its half-circle of lettuce. I didn't mind tuna fish salad. I could always eat tuna fish salad. There, Aunt Arlette said coming up behind me. See what I've done.

They arrived, the people and filled up the rooms. I was all right. I even laughed and spoke to those cousins. It was the first bite. The first forkful of tuna fish salad. There among the pink flakes most cleverly disguised were bits of mashed fish ball. I tasted that, held that in my mouth. There was noise at the table, there was much conversation. I left the table unnoticed. Went to the back of the apartment. Opened the bathroom door. I spit the hated mouthful into the toilet. Aunt Arlette came into the room, did not knock, pushed the door against the wall. She stood there staring at me, a firm woman in black crepe and gold bracelets, and she drummed her long finger-nails against the tile wall. I thought so, she said. I thought so.

I paid our bills on the fifth of each month. The truth of it was that I did not always do this in the same manner. Sometimes I sat at my desk in the bedroom, but sometimes I wrote the checks in the morning while drinking my coffee. And still again I occasionally slipped the checkbook into my briefcase and wrote the checks at work. I could not imagine that checkbook lost. Someone's hands turning back the brown cover and tracing our lives from those stubs. What would they make of us? The purchases at the flower shop, the codes and initials, the rent, the habits of extravagance, our tendencies. I vowed that I would try again to remember what I had done. I concentrated while I made my morning cup of coffee. The brew was strong and as brown as the cover of the checkbook.

My husband came into the room. "This was probably it," he says, "Here you are—the object of all that hustle-bustle searching." He handed me a copy of Updike's *The Witches of Eastwick*. "A fourteen-day library book," he says, "between the folds of the Sunday Travel Section, about to be thrown down the chute. My arms were full of newspapers. The book suddenly fell out. And look at the fine! I bet you owe six dollars."

It is difficult to remove books from a library today unless they have been duly recorded. There are magnetic strips in books or something. Books must be defused before they can be removed. This is a new innovation. I imagine that this must save libraries enormous sums of money. At one time I smuggled books from libraries. Yes, I did. But not with the intention of keeping them or otherwise harming them. But nevertheless I took them. In among the books properly credited to me I would on occasion secrete another book. I was then duly bound to read that book. The idea was Freddy's—oh not to take a book, but to alter my habits, to lift, he said, my limitations. You've read nothing, he accused. I couldn't believe that. I had spent endless hours reading books. Had I done much else? Whatever did they teach you in the prairies, Freddy said. He rattled off names—Cabell, Ford, Canfield, Rolland, Norris, Wetherwax. And no, I had not read them. See, he said.

How to make my choice of a book special? I mean how would I know whether or not I had deliberately picked that book thus ensuring a continuation of my limited experience. Random choice. I decided to snatch my special books from a wooden cart where they were stacked to be reshelved. The books taken this way were not classifiable. I read masonry self-taught, I read a romance about a girl named Denise and a man named Jed who spirited her away to the Isle of Corfu, I read a history of Flemish painting, Oliver Twist, meatless cooking, ten mysteries. I read one hundred and twelve books. I believe that my experience can be equated with that apocryphal story that if a chimpanzee types long enough he will recreate Shakespeare. Never once in my thefts did I encounter anything of Shakespeare's.

I hadn't returned the books. Meant to, but hadn't. They dispersed themselves in the corners of Freddy's apartment. Be a doll, Freddy said to me one morning. Oversee the move will you. I've arranged everything with the movers, and my mother is expecting the load. Isn't it better to sell? I said. Instead of shipping everything to Ohio. Sell? Freddy said. This furniture costs a fortune. What isn't an antique is an original. Okay with me, I said. Freddy kissed my lips. I'm off to Spain, he said and went to Kennedy.

I had to get boxes, I had to defrost the refrigerator. I packed everything. I called Freddy's mother in Cincinnati. She was not happy to hear from me. Of course I have enough room to store everything, she said. Who are you to ask that?

What did I have in Freddy's apartment? Only my clothes and a reading lamp. And, of course, one hundred and twelve library books. Cleaning that apartment had not been easy. I rewarded myself with the mattress to the double bed, one gray chair with lion's claws that gripped the floor, and all the drapes which strangely fit the windows in my new apartment. I could have packed the books in boxes except that packing them seemed to make them permanently mine. So I stacked the books in paper shopping bags, averaging ten to twelve books per bag. Should I take them back where they belonged? Was that dangerous? The books actually came from four different libraries. I borrowed a car from a girl named Sharon who actually liked to lend it. Drive with care, she said, but have a good time. I packed her trunk with the books. At nine p.m. I left the city and drove down the Saw Mill River Parkway. A library is a library after all. I had a map and a county telephone book for addresses. I was looking for libraries with night depositories. If seen, I had stories ready. The neighbors, I would say, left me their books to return before they moved away. The children, I would say, off to camp. The first library was a colonial brick and the night depository, a gray metal mailbox apparatus. *Return Books Here.* Three bags filled it. I saw no loiterers, but I trembled. Two more stops and the books were gone, tumbled into those chutes, a grab bag of words. I drove back to the City, paused beneath the abandoned West Side Highway, and flung those empty shopping bags into the Hudson.

*   *   *

Dot has invited me to visit her in Florida, my mother said on the telephone. Dot's husband had died abruptly one morning three years ago. A coronary, my mother said. The way to go, one-two-three, she said. Dot owned a condominium in Sarasota. The boys? I asked. What happened to her boys? An insurance broker, my mother said, and one has the store, and one is vice-president of a games factory.

Dot used to send me Christmas cards. I even found some of the old envelopes in a box in the back of the linen closet, they still had her address from Evanston. Didn't she put five dollars inside each card?

The last card I got from Dot came when I started college. I don't think I sent one to her. I was busy, I don't think I remembered.

They still had sororities at the State University when I was there. The closest I came to that kind of camaraderie was during my junior year when I shared a house on Market Street with three other girls. It was an ugly house, drafty and with a fearsome attic from which we regularly heard scraping noises. Mrs. Rochester, we decided. It's her, we'd shout. Get 'em, old girl! But we never went upstairs to investigate. In fact, we did nothing to that house—no coats of paint, no posters on the wall, and at the end of the year we all moved out.

One evening the three girls and I sat on the grime-smoothed chairs in the living room of that rented house. We drank beer, and I did Dot for those girls. The hand, I said, crept—yes, it did—it cre-ept up my leg heading straight for that garter. I mimed the actions. Oh God, one of the girls said, wiping her eyes, holding her sides.

Audrey and Elaine were eating dinner. I had made roast chicken, and everyone sat at the table comfortably picking the last shreds from the bones. Both girls were wearing jeans and old blouses. They didn't look alike, Audrey was thin and almost elegant, and Elaine, short and plump.

"I don't understand," my husband was saying, "why the two of you don't share an apartment. You could do with less room then. You're sisters. No strangers poking in your things."

"Why," Audrey said, "should a stranger poke in my things?—and why would I care?"

Audrey and Elaine exchanged glances.

That evening after my daughters had returned to their own apartments I found the checkbook unexpectedly as I packed my briefcase for the morning. I must have brought the checkbook home from work in a large manila envelope. It looked all right, it seemed to be intact. For safety I put it inside my overnight case, locked the suitcase and shoved it under the bed. I was content to know that inside that suitcase was the brown covered checkbook.

My husband came into the room as I was undressing. "Not a bad evening," he said. "The girls were fairly decent for a change. And the food was top drawer."

He began to unbutton his shirt. "What's that?" he said. "That paper on the floor?"

I bent over and picked the paper up. It was my birth certificate.

My husband laughed, full of food, benevolent. "You are helpless," he said. "You could not survive alone." He took the paper from my hands. "Legitimate," he read, "checked yes. City, Milwaukee."

"There was a mill," I whispered, "and by the mill there was a walk, and on the walk there was a key."

My husband embraced me, pulled me close, repeated my name.

Did he know who he held in his arms? *Conspirator.* Finders keepers. *Thief.* Losers weepers. *Girl with heart of stone.*

Tea Party

SARAH ROSSITER

THE FIRST THING Emma noticed when she opened the cottage door was the stillness. So quiet it was that she could hear one of Morgan's cows mooing in the back pasture over a mile away. Most days the wind blew, coming in from the Bristol Channel with such force that the trees along the channel cliffs grew sideways instead of straight and nothing could be heard but the moan of the wind and the waves breaking against the rocks. Not that there was much worth listening to in St. Donat's. On the rare windless day you could hear the College clock chime the hour or the occasional car passing through on its way to Swansea. No one ever stopped in St. Donat's and Emma couldn't blame them for that. There was nothing to stop for, not even a shop. Just the College, well hidden behind the castle walls, and outside, along the road, three houses, Morgan's farm, the tenant cottage, and the new college bungalow where the American lived.

The chickens scattered as Emma made her way across the yard to the small green door in the stone wall. She pulled the latch, and stooping, squeezed through the opening to stand on the edge of the road. She glanced across to see if the American might be watching, then looked both ways before crossing over. Though it was early yet for the cows to be brought home, Emma was taking no chances. It would not do for Owen to see her now. When she'd told him of the invitation the night before, at first he'd not believed her.

"She never! Making it up you are."

"I'm not!"

"The American is it then? The young one, looks like a stick?"

"Sweet looking she is."

"Sweet on me you mean. Every day I bring the cows by, she's at the window looking out. Fancies me she does."

"It might be you she fancies but it's me she's asked to tea."

"Whatever for? She's got her fancy friends up at College, doesn't she?"

"I wouldn't know I'm sure. But she was ever so friendly. I'll tell you what, she reminded me of Eleanor."

"Eleanor?"

"You know the one. The star of that American show, the soap opera, 'Day without End.' "

"You and that frigging telly. I've a mind to take it back to rental. And you're not to go to tea as well."

Emma had looked over his shoulder at the green mold around the kitchen window and hadn't said a word.

He had no way of stopping her but Emma knew what a noise he'd make if he caught her in the act. Not caring who heard either. So she looked both ways; there was nothing to be seen but puddles and cowpats. She crossed slowly, not wanting to appear too eager.

Rain was falling in a slow steady drizzle and Emma's mackintosh had long ago lost its waterproofing. Besides, it was so tight that she could no longer button up the front. She held the edges together as best she could but even so could feel the wet seeping through. Though she'd not weighed herself, Emma knew she'd gained at least a stone since they'd moved to St. Donat's the year before.

"If you'd do something besides watch the telly and eat sweets all day," Owen said.

"It's lonely I am, Owen. No one to talk to and not a car either."

"And what do you think I am then? Talking to Morgan's cows all day and another come evening."

"It would be lovely to have a car."

"Wouldn't it now? And I suppose you'd fancy a fridge and a gas cooker and a telephone too?"

"I wouldn't mind."

"My, such a lady I married and to think I never knew."

"It's important to broaden our horizons, Owen. Eleanor said so, just today."

Owen looked her up and down and laughed loudly.

"You've broadened all right!" he said.

Emma sucked in her stomach as she walked up the American's drive. The girdle helped but not enough. She was trying to walk gracefully but found it difficult when holding her breath and the black stiletto heels made her ankles wobble. The American opened the door before Emma could knock.

"I'm so glad you could come," she said, smiling.

"You're ever so nice to have me," Emma said, bobbing her head so that she could feel her little sausage curls dance.

As soon as Owen had left that morning, Emma had put up her hair, using every roller she had. It had been a morning of torture; not only were the rollers heavy but they pinched and pulled every time she moved. Still, when at last she removed them, she was struck by the feeling of weightlessness.

And she liked the way the curls framed her face, the look reminded her of Alice, Eleanor's best girlfriend on "Day without End." Eleanor herself had hair like the American's, straight as straw and the same color too. At least Emma supposed the color the same; it was hard to tell on the black-and-white telly.

"Come in out of the rain. Isn't the weather depressing?"

"It is and all," said Emma though she hadn't thought about it once all day.

They were standing in a large hallway with a shiny wood floor. Four doorways led off it as well as a stairway going up to a second floor. Emma only had time to peek through the closest doorway. She saw a large white refrigerator next to a large white cooker and a round yellow-topped table, the same primrose yellow as the linoleum on the floor. With the white ruffled curtains at the window it might have been Eleanor's kitchen on "Day without End."

"Here," said the American, "let me take your coat."

She stood watching while Emma shrugged herself out of the old gray mackintosh. Emma felt her cheeks growing hot even though underneath the mackintosh she was wearing a respectable black pullover and her new plum-colored miniskirt bought in Cardiff the Saturday before. Owen had been rude about the skirt, telling her she hadn't the legs and was too old besides. The salesgirl had objected, saying that she herself preferred "ample legs" like Emma's to the other legs one saw these days. Like bits of spaghetti she said they were. As for being too old, Emma herself had seen plenty who were older walking around showing their legs. She was only thirty-two. Emma handed her mackintosh to the American.

"I like your skirt," the American said. "What a pretty color."

Emma smiled. "Plum it's called. And yours is ever so nice as well." It was a miniskirt like Emma's but plaid, a checkerboard of pale reds and greens. "Christmas colors," said Emma.

The American laughed. "I hadn't thought of that. You're right."

When she turned to hang Emma's coat in the closet, Emma glanced at her legs. Long and thin they were but shapely too, not at all like spaghetti bits. Once she'd hung the coat, the American led Emma directly into the sitting room. Emma had hoped she might show her about the house first. When they had met on the road the day before, Emma, making conversation, asked her how she liked the new bungalow.

"It's a little too new," the American said.

"It is now?" said Emma, baffled.

"You know what I mean about new houses? They haven't been lived in and they're just shells really. It takes years for a house to develop a soul."

"Fancy that," said Emma, who hadn't a clue what she meant. But she didn't mind not understanding because all the time they were talking Emma could feel her horizons broadening.

Emma saw that the sitting room stretched the length of the house. Large and bright with red rugs on the floor and a picture window at either end. The back window looked over Morgan's pastures and the front looked across the road to Emma's cottage. Because of the wall surrounding the cottage only the second floor with its two narrow windows set in the steeply pitched slate roof could be seen. With the moss on the roof and the gaps in the chimney where the bricks had fallen out, the cottage looked as dreary outside as in.

Mortified, Emma turned her back on the view and sat on a couch set before the window. The American sat in an armchair facing her. Between them was a brightly polished table and to Emma's right, a slow burning fire in the grate. The room seemed very warm to Emma and the fire not half hot enough to throw out such heat.

"It's lovely and warm in here," she said, smiling at the American.

"Goodness, do you think so?" The American looked about, as if afraid someone might be listening, then turned to Emma. "I wouldn't say this to anyone from the College but you know, we were really surprised by the primitive central heating."

Emma blinked. The American leaned forward in her chair.

"I mean if it was an old house we'd understand but to build a new house with a heating system that depends on a coal stove in the kitchen. . . . " She shrugged, then smiled. "It's not that I'm complaining. It's really a very nice house. I just haven't gotten used to being cold all the time."

Emma had no idea how central heating was supposed to work. In the cottage they had a coal-burning Aga for cooking and heating and one small electric fire that they moved from room to room. It never did much good unless you sat right in front and then it burned the legs.

"Do you cook on it too then?" she asked.

"On what?"

"The coal stove."

The American laughed. "Heavens no! There's a regular stove in the kitchen, electric. I prefer gas, don't you?"

"I do and all," said Emma who had never cooked on anything but coal.

There was an uncomfortable silence. Emma knew that as the guest she should be making the conversation but all she could think of was how badly she wanted to see the rest of the house. She crossed her legs, hoping to appear at ease, but uncrossed them quickly when she noticed how high the skirt rose on her thighs. Even with her legs straight, she felt naked, which made her wish she had her coat to hold in her lap. The American had crossed her legs and if Emma had wanted, she could have seen right up to her panties. So instead she looked around the room. At the other end was a round dining table with six matching chairs and another small table that held the stereo. The white walls were hung with paintings and beneath them were white painted bookcases filled with books.

"My, it's a regular library you have," said Emma. "Did you bring the books with you from America then?"

"Oh no, we bought most of them here. They're much cheaper in this country, especially paperbacks." Leaning forward, she picked up a book from the coffee table and held it up for Emma to see. "This would have cost at least two dollars at home; here it's just two shillings, about fifty cents."

Emma looked at the book and felt the blush coming to her cheeks again. What a book to leave lying about for people to see. *Sons and Lovers* indeed! She never would have thought, from looking at her, that the American was the sort. Perhaps her husband then but even so. The American was looking at Emma, obviously waiting for her to speak. Emma cleared her throat.

"Fancy that," she said. "I expect your husband must need a good many books for his teaching."

"Well, yes, he does need some. But I'm afraid most of them are mine." Replacing the book on the table, she smiled shyly. "I have a thing about books," she said as if telling a secret.

Emma cleared her throat again. "Do you now?" she said.

The American nodded. "I need to read the way other people need to eat. Richard says it's avoidance."

Emma wished she hadn't mentioned eating because the word alone was enough to set her stomach grumbling.

"Everyone needs to eat," she said, "though my Owen, he never tires of telling me I eat more than my fair share." She patted her stomach. "I expect he's right and all."

"It's only because you're bored," she said, smiling at Emma so kindly that Emma couldn't help smiling in return.

Despite the book that lay on the table between them, she began to feel more comfortable. Lovely it was to have a friend who could understand. She settled herself back against the sofa and recrossed her legs.

"And how are you liking Wales then, Mrs. . . . ?"

"Robertson, but please, call me Lizard."

Emma's surprise must have shown because Lizard ducked her head, laughing. When she looked up again, Emma saw that her cheeks were bright pink.

"My real name is Elizabeth, Liz for short. But when I was little, everyone called me Lizard and I'm afraid the name stuck."

"What an interesting name then," Emma said politely, knowing that never, even under torture, could she call the American Lizard.

"No it's not. It's ugly. But, you know, I never really thought about it until

I came over here. No one uses nicknames here. So usually I introduce myself as Elizabeth, unless I'm feeling relaxed and then I forget."

Emma couldn't help wondering what the American was like when she wasn't relaxed. She'd never seen anyone twitch so, always twiddling with her hair or nibbling on her fingernails. She wriggled about in the chair too, crossing and uncrossing her legs, like a child who couldn't sit still. Not that Emma minded but she did find it surprising. She herself could sit motionless for hours at a time in front of the telly. The American, she supposed, was one of those high-strung types. On "Day without End" they were all a bit that way, crying and carrying on over trifles. Emma loved the way Eleanor cried. Unlike the others on the show, she cried quietly, like a real lady. Though Emma imagined both Eleanor and the American to be in their early twenties, Eleanor seemed older.

A lovely strong face Eleanor had, with sharp cheekbones, and eyelashes so long they made shadows on her cheeks. The American's face was thin and pale, the color of cream. A pretty face, but there was something, a certain softness perhaps, in the wide eyes, the small chin, the long fine hair that hung so straight down her back that made Emma think of a child. She had no eyelashes that Emma could see; she was not even wearing lipstick. The only color in her face came from a dusting of light brown freckles across the bridge of her nose.

Emma realized now that it had been foolish of her to assume that this American and Eleanor would be alike. She knew from watching the show that Americans could be as different from one another as the Welsh. But as Eleanor was fond of saying, there were two kinds of knowing, and the real knowing came from what she called "a learning experience." And this tea party with a real American was just that; Emma was learning through her own personal experience. And she was also pleased to discover that, while it would have been ever so exciting to have a friend as worldly as Eleanor, she was easier with this one.

All morning, as Emma sat in front of the telly, head weighted with rollers, she had imagined how it would be, the two of them sipping tea from fragile china cups as they discussed the complications of Eleanor's life. Emma was sure the American would be impressed with how much she knew about American living. "Oh, not much at all, really," Emma had planned to say modestly.

But now that she was here and as comfortable as she felt with her new friend, Emma could think of no way to casually introduce the subject of "Day without End." If only there were a telly in the sitting room, she could make a start by asking if it was color. But there wasn't and somehow it seemed forward to inquire if they had one in the bedroom. Suddenly Emma realized that she'd said nothing for ages. It was one of her failings, going off inside her head that way, and it drove Owen bonkers. She looked at the

American, who was staring at the fire, not seeming to mind the silence at all. Emma coughed politely, to attract attention.

"Your husband, is he liking to teach at College then?" she asked when the American looked up.

"Richard? Oh yes, I suppose." She began to fiddle with her hair. "He's busy; boarding schools are terrible that way. But then he likes being busy; he's very conscientious."

"And how about yourself then? I should think it is ever so interesting, being international. People to meet from all over the world."

"Actually they're mostly British. We're the only Americans."

"You must be ever so popular then!"

"Why is that?" the American asked, looking puzzled.

"Being American and all. Such an interesting country I've always thought."

Emma waited for the American to ask her what she found interesting and then she could begin to talk about "Day without End." But all the American did was say "Hmm" and stare out the window over Emma's head. Emma's stomach began to rumble again, the way it always did when she was nervous. She coughed to cover the sound, wishing more than ever there was something to nibble on. She had heard that American's didn't have tea, not as a meal anyway. She hoped this wasn't true. The room was much too warm and Emma was beginning to sweat. Besides, the heat was causing her feet to swell so that the ache in her toes was worse than before. She was wondering if she might slip the heels off under the table when the American suddenly spoke.

"Do you know what I like best about living here?"

"What's that then?" Emma said, startled.

"To look out the window at your house."

Emma couldn't help herself; she laughed. "You never!"

The American nodded. "It's got such character, those narrow little windows and that steep roof. It's like something out of a fairy tale. I bet it's wonderful inside."

Was she hinting for a visit? The very thought made Emma blush for shame.

"Terrible it is. Terrible. Moss growing on the walls and the roof leaking day and night."

"But those things can be fixed, can't they?"

"It's Morgan's place, not ours, and not a shilling will he spend."

"Oh, what a shame! Surely if you talk to him?"

Emma snorted. "Easier to talk to a stone. But never mind, it's moving we are, ever so soon, to one of the new council flats in Llantwit. Lovely they are with picture windows and all the mod cons."

The American looked sadly at Emma. "Oh, I'm sorry," she said.

Just at that moment the kettle began to whistle from the kitchen.

"I'll be right back. You make yourself at home," the American said, smiling at Emma from the doorway.

Emma took several deep breaths to calm herself. She should not, she knew, have told the lie about the council flat but she also knew that had the American asked her outright to visit the cottage, Emma, in all politeness, could not have refused. And it was not just the mold and the leaky roof that gave cause for shame but all of it, from Owen's mucky boots at the door to their few sticks of furniture to the chipped mugs. They had had two teacups once, ever so sweet with pink roses, and delicate too, thin as tissue. But Owen had thrown one against the Aga in a rage and Emma had dropped the other on the stone floor. No, Emma decided, better to die from disease than the shame of such a visit.

Emma had to admit that despite her feelings of friendship for the American, she still found her puzzling. Usually Emma took pride in her understanding of the people she met. Her Mum had always called Emma the "deep one," always said what a shame she'd not been able to stay in school past "O" levels. The trouble was Emma had never met anyone like this American, not even on the telly. What, for instance, did she mean by saying "I'm sorry" when Emma told her about the move to the council flat. Big and grand they were, modern as could be, set right on the main road next to all the shops, and the cinema only one street over.

The American returned with a large tray that she set down on the table between them.

"I'm so glad you could come," she said as she began to dish up the food.

And Emma realized then that the American had meant she was sorry Emma would be moving away, just when they'd found each other too.

"What a lovely tea then!" Emma said with so much feeling in her voice that the American looked up, startled.

It was a regular high tea with sandwiches and crisps, gherkins and biscuits, even a sponge. The American smiled as she handed Emma her plate.

"Why don't you start with this and then we can help ourselves to seconds."

She had given Emma a bit of everything, all neatly arranged on a gold-rimmed white plate.

"Fancy your going to the trouble of cutting the crusts!" Emma said as she picked up a dainty triangle of white bread.

"It wasn't any trouble. I hope you like watercress."

"My personal preference," she said, "though it's seldom I see it. My Owen now, he likes his fishpaste so that's what we get. Fishpaste or Marmite."

"Richard likes Marmite too. Isn't it awful?"

"It is and all. Nasty brown stuff, more like medicine than food, I'd say."

They smiled at each other. As Emma helped herself to another sandwich she noticed the American was only toying with her food, pushing it about on her plate with her finger.

"Don't mind me," she said when she saw Emma looking. "I'm never hungry at teatime."

"It's not a meal you have in America then," Emma said, pleased to be able to show off her knowledge.

"No. I was amazed to find people over here eating four meals a day."

"It's the boredom, I expect," said Emma.

"What?"

"What you said before, about eating being a way to pass the time and all."

"Oh. But everybody can't be bored, can they?"

"There's truth in that, I suppose," Emma said, taking another sandwich. Without the crusts, there was no more than two bites a triangle. "You must have ever so much to keep you busy with a car to take you places and interesting friends up at College."

She tried to chew more slowly but this was difficult as she was hungry.

"They're very nice, most of them. But they're busy, all the ones my age have little children."

"Children can be a terrible nuisance," Emma said, eyeing the teapot. Her throat was parched from the conversation.

"That's what Richard says. He says we should wait. But . . . "

She couldn't seem to find the words. Instead she shrugged her shoulders and stared into the fire.

"And right he is," Emma said kindly but firmly. "Oldest of nine I was and changing nappies before I could walk. Never again I said to my Owen and he agreed. Hard it is to get ahead in this world with babies holding you down."

"I suppose so, but . . . " she looked at Emma, shyly, and laughed, "I never knew days could be so long."

" 'Day without End,' " Emma said, pleased to have found an opening.

She popped a crisp into her mouth, something she hadn't dared do before because of the noise they made when chewed, and held it on her tongue to soften.

"I knew you'd understand," the American said. "That's just what it's like; days without end. Richard doesn't understand at all. He just gets cross."

"My Owen's the same, goes on and on he does. I suppose," she said casually, "you watch a good deal then?"

"Watch what?"

"Why, the telly. 'Day without End' and all."

The American looked puzzled. "I can't say that I do," she said. "I've never liked television much."

"Is that a fact?"

"I thought it would be better over here but it's mostly American stuff and the worst of it at that. Like 'Day without End.' Isn't that one of those soap operas?"

Emma cleared her throat. "I expect it is and all."

"The people at College watch the news and from it they get the impression that the States is nothing but muggings and racism and riots in the street."

"Oh but surely they know better than that then!"

The American smiled at Emma. "You'd think so, wouldn't you?"

"I would and all. Ever so lovely it is, I'm sure."

"You don't have to go that far," said the American laughing, and Emma laughed too, so as not to seem rude.

"Are you ready for tea?"

"Yes please," said Emma.

The American poured the tea into two white cups, as fragile as the ones Emma had imagined. It was a shame they would not be discussing "Day without End" but glad she was she'd not made a fool of herself by admitting she watched it.

The American held her teacup with the little finger extended and Emma did the same.

"What do you do, to keep busy?" the American asked.

Emma took several swallows of her tea before answering.

"Oh, I putter about. Bursar from College, he came by last week to offer me work but Owen said no to that, thank you but no; he wants me at home."

"That's sweet," the American said.

Emma stared at her to see if she was joking. "I wouldn't know about that," she said. "He likes his tea on time, he does."

"Richard eats most of his meals up at school."

"Lucky you are. Plenty of time to get off on your own."

"That's what Richard says."

"What's that then?"

"That I'm fortunate to have so much time on my hands and I should take advantage of it."

"And right he is too. Why, if I had a car, there'd be no stopping me. All I'd need is a friend for company." Emma, her cheeks flushed with warmth and pleasure, smiled at her friend while she waited for the invitation she knew was coming.

Perhaps, she thought, they could go for a spin this very afternoon. Drive right past Owen as he was bringing the cows home. Lovely little red Morris

Minor the American had and Emma could just imagine the look on Owen's face when he saw who was inside it. Emma waited but the American, instead of asking, stared at Emma without smiling. The look made Emma uncomfortable. Had she been too forward, made her wishes too plain. The American suddenly leaned towards Emma.

"What would you do if you had a car?" she asked, her voice quiet and curious.

"Why, what wouldn't I do! I'd get out, I would, away from all that." Emma waved her hand in the direction of the cottage. "I'd go to Cardiff one day, Swansea the next. With some experience I might drive to London on the motorway."

"And then what?"

Emma blinked. It occurred to her to wonder if the American was quite right in the head. Ashamed of such an unkind thought, instead of answering, she took a bite of sponge.

"This sponge is ever so nice," she said, forgetting to swallow first. The yellow crumbs sprayed onto her lap. "Oh dear," she said, ducking her head to dab at the crumbs with her napkin.

"No, really, I'm curious. What would you do when you'd finished driving around?"

"Why, I suppose I'd come home again, wouldn't I?" Emma said with a snap in her voice.

The American didn't mind; in fact from the way she was nodding her head up and down she seemed pleased with Emma's answer.

"That's right. That's the problem. No matter how much traveling I do, I can't get away. It doesn't matter where I am, I'm always trapped. The loneliness, it's inside, you see."

Her voice had gone quite thick and Emma realized with dismay that at any moment she might begin to cry. She would not, Emma knew, cry in ladylike fashion like Eleanor. Emma felt herself being torn in two; half of her wanted to stay with this strange new friend and give what comfort she could, the other half wanted to bolt for home. The gold clock on the mantel struck four. If she hurried she could catch most of "Day without End."

"It's been ever so pleasant," she said, starting to rise.

The American looked at the clock. "Heavens, is it four o'clock already?" Clearing her throat, she turned to Emma. "Your husband will be coming by with the cows in a minute."

"He will and all and I best be going. Likes his tea prompt he does."

Rising, the American went to stand by the window. Emma stood behind her, shifting her weight from one foot to the other in an attempt to lessen the pain in her toes.

"Thanks ever so," she said to the American's back. "And if it's company you'd be wanting when you're off in your car, I'd be happy to oblige."

"Look. Here he comes," the American said.

Emma, taking care to stand out of sight, watched as the cows passed between the two houses. They moved slowly, milling and mooing, their heads lowered, tails flicking at midges. Behind them walked Owen, a switch in his hand, his head bent forward against the rain. One cow stopped short and Owen whacked it hard on the rump, cursing in Welsh. Emma was glad for the Welsh but the noise of him was bad enough.

"Walks just like one of the cows he does," she said, embarrassed by the mud caking his Wellingtons, the slouch of his shoulders, his tangled, dark hair. "Could do with a haircut as well."

"Oh no!" said the American, turning to Emma. "I love the way he looks."

"Do you now?" Emma said, standing straight as she could and looking the American in the eye. Because the American was several inches taller, Emma had to look up but even so the American became agitated. She looked away from Emma, her cheeks red.

"Oh, I don't mean it like that! Not that he isn't good-looking; he is, very. But what I like is how natural he seems, so much a part of his surroundings. Maybe 'earthiness' is the best word to describe him."

Earthiness indeed, thought Emma as she moved towards the hall closet to fetch her mackintosh. Just wait till Owen heard that what the American fancied about him was the mud on his trousers. Insulting as it was to the both of them, Emma couldn't wait to tell him, just to see the look on his face. The American followed her into the hall.

"Do you know what I mean?" she said as Emma pulled on her coat. "It's the same way I feel about your house, a sense of belonging in a way that ours doesn't, and we don't either."

Emma, coat on at last, turned to face her.

"Thanks ever so. It was a lovely tea."

The American looked worried. "I haven't said anything wrong, have I?"

And from the tone of her voice, Emma knew that however insulting she had been, it had not been intentional. As she opened the front door, Emma smiled. "Not to worry," she said.

"Oh, I am glad!" the American said. "I knew you'd understand. I just knew."

There was no answer to that so Emma bobbed her head once before closing the door behind her. She walked quickly down the drive and across the road, knowing that if she hurried she could catch the last five minutes of "Day without End."

Shadow Bands

JEANNE SCHINTO

MIRA STEPPED CAREFULLY: she was being studied. She walked with exaggerated precision into her parents' kitchen. As purposefully as a blind girl, confident, unblinking, she stared straight ahead as if at some privileged vision.

Behind her, the boy—a slim brown child: Charlie Nicely from the household next door—followed her every gesture with eyes that were huge and black and liquid, clouded with a far-off pain, one he only anticipated, maybe: a future pain. Cautiously he moved with the rigid gait of a wounded soldier, obedient hands down by his sides, dark fingers pointed. He moved as if he thought he might be in danger of knocking something over—or waking someone up—with a sudden, unexpected motion, one that might surprise even himself.

Actually, there was nothing or no one to disturb. Mira's parents were not home, and any objects of real value had been placed well out of reach of children. Not only that, but the noise of adults drunkenly shouting was coming through the wall of the row house next door. Not party sounds, not festive—anyway, this was mid-afternoon—but the sounds of desperation none too cleverly disguised, the kind that people make when they know that no one is listening to them.

In that house, identical to Mira's parents' except that it recently had *not* been made brand-new, Charlie lived with his mother and grandfather and several other family members and friends—and maybe some enemies as well. There were so many of them, in fact, that no one could accurately count them; none of their neighbors could, that is. As for the Nicelys themselves (they were sometimes called the "Nasty Nicelys"), probably they just didn't bother. There certainly wasn't any need for them to count for the purpose of setting a supper table, for example, because their table never was set. Not that they even had a table. And everyone on the block, rich or poor, black or white, hoped that the Nicelys soon would take themselves and their lack of table manners elsewhere. "White Trash," they were pronounced by their neighbors—except for Charlie. Charlie *Brown* was his full nickname, given to him by the man he called "Granddaddy," because the child had a black man for a father, one, incidentally, whom he'd never seen. Brad Williams had been sent to jail for armed robbery six years ago, about the time of Charlie's birth. Since then, his mother'd had two more children—white—by Gary "Lurch" Shepherd: two more sons, Chubby (Gary, Jr.) and Day-Day (David), with permanently dirty faces and the blazing blue eyes of every Nicely, of the white ones, that is. And though some Nicelys eventually did leave—most notably (at least, most recently), Charlie's grandmother, Beverly Jean, who was born-again and living on a rocky farm outside Frostburg—some on the block were less hopeful than others about an imminent departure by the whole, extended Nicely clan; after all, the family, in one form or another, had been living in the rented house going on thirty-five years.

The kitchen of Mira's parents, who'd been living in the neighborhood just six months, was an enviable place: shining copper everywhere; the latest equipment, most of it unused. Mira's parents worked late into the evening, and usually already had eaten dinner with clients by the time they taxied home.

Mira's own suppers consisted mainly of sweets—calories that were adding to the young womanliness that had begun to envelop her. She ate in front of the flickering colors of the downstairs TV. She was lonely in her new school, a new city, in her new, uncongenial, "changing" neighborhood, and had taken to befriending Charlie expressly against her parents' wishes. They objected not only to the upbringing he was being given by the nearly toothless, twenty-year-old girl (his mother) he simply called "Vicky," but because Mira was more than twice his age.

For Mira's part, she knew she ought to look for friends among her peers; knew, too, that she should be looking down on the Nicelys. Ignore them and hope they'll go away, as everyone else on the block hoped. But she didn't. She loved to play lessons with Charlie. She spent most of her free time drilling him, teaching him things. She seemed to be preparing him for something; she didn't know what.

Mira pushed up her sleeves, revealing pink chubby arms, and took the greatest care in selecting for Charlie a piece of fruit from the bowl—his reward. "Want me to cut it up for you?" She held the apple in her palm for him to admire. In her other hand she held the knife. She began to use it even before Charlie had nodded.

"What did you have for supper last night?" Mira asked, handing him a slice. She was curious about everything that went on in his household. She asked him all kinds of questions, knowing it would be rude to ask them of someone other than Charlie.

"About a hunnert bowls of raisin bran," he replied. He had taken the fruit and begun to eat it without even looking at it. Mira surreptitiously sniffed and examined any piece of food offered to her in a home other than her own.

"Did the cockroaches get in it this time?" she asked him playfully. But he answered matter-of-factly.

"Nope. They stayed in the 'frigerator."

"And how do you think they get into the refrigerator in the first place, Charlie?"

He hunched his small shoulders. "The big ones open the door for the little ones?"

"What's your favorite meal? If you could have just one thing to eat for the rest of your life, and it had to be that, what would you choose?"

"Penny cakes."

"Does Vicky make them for you?"

Charlie shook his head. "Nope. Detox does." Detox was Stanley Nicely, his grandfather's brother.

After he'd eaten a slice or two more, he started back toward the dining-room table, where the playing cards were spread out. He had been able to divide them into the red and the black without trouble, but could see no difference between the club and the spade, the heart and the diamond.

Mira sat down across from him and watched his eyes work. They were two deep, round pools reflecting her whenever he glanced up to catch a helpful signal. He seemed to be able to take in a lot without moving his head. Yet, somehow, his eyes were unseeing too; he must have taught himself not to notice certain things, the better not to. Mira's eyes looked as if they did not know enough to avert themselves from anything.

"Let's play War," Charlie suggested brightly after a while—somewhat craftily, too.

"No," Mira said in her teacherly way, although she would have enjoyed a game of War. "I think we should keep trying to separate the suits."

"Thass too hard," Charlie insisted quietly.

"Never say never, Charlie. You can do it. Just look at each card. See this one?" She made the card snap. "How the sides are sharp and pointed? That's the diamond. And this one?" She snapped another. "With the rounded parts and a point at the bottom? That's the heart. Maybe we'll draw them later."

He lowered his eyes to the cards again. His obedience amazed Mira: how could he always be so good? It also made her slightly uncomfortable. He set himself to whatever task she gave him, without a sigh or a grimace or making any other kind of face, as surely Mira herself would have.

She suspected that he'd slept in his clothes: they were the same ones he'd worn yesterday. That proved nothing, but Mira liked to think that it did.

Besides, Pearl, a neighbor of them both—a black woman who worked as a nurse's aide at night—had remarked to Mira's father once, and Mira had overheard, that Charlie didn't even have a bed of his own. "He must sleep hung up by a nail in the corner, like an old raggedy coat," Pearl had said. And Mira had pictured him sleeping just that way until she had asked Charlie himself and he told her that he slept with his granddaddy on the living-room couch.

Of all the Nicelys besides Charlie, it was Charlie's grandfather, Roy, whom Mira saw most frequently, as he walked jauntily down the sidewalk, whistling an unrecognizable tune. He delivered packages for the liquor store on the corner in pants too short and a jacket too thin, never in a hurry. Licking his lips and adjusting his false teeth with his tongue to make a ready smile, he winked at Mira whenever they passed. She knew that he was dirty—round circles of hair had been eaten out of his scalp by something. And once she had seen him urinating without breaking his stride. That was the same day he called out to her from his porch as she left her house: "_Voulez-vous couchez avec-moi ce soir?_ I bet you didn't know I knew French, did you?" He came wobbly-legged down his porch steps and followed her down the sidewalk. "I know French, German, Italian, too. I was in all those places in the Navy. Shot a German _woman_. She didn't die, though."

"Don't get friendly with _any_ of them," Mira's parents gently had warned her. Still she had with Charlie, and made it a point to wave or nod whenever she passed by any of the others. Roy, Detox, and the third brother, Ernie— all three of them, skeletally thin with gaunt, red, wrinkled faces and blue eyes that looked seared, as if they had gotten too close a look at something— waved back, cordial enough, and so did Roy's many sons: Ricky, Mike, Steve, and Dirtball among them. And so did Lurch, who now lived in the house as well. But Mira never said anything more to them but "Hi," though if she were walking with her parents, she did not even say that, for invariably Roy (and any one of the others) conveniently would let a passing car catch his eye as their paths crossed.

"Don't you know a baseball diamond?" Mira urged Charlie, seeing that, though lucky guesses had helped him a little, he still had not been able to separate the cards correctly. "A heart-shaped box of candy?" Roughly she traced the symbols on the table while Charlie shrugged, looking smaller than usual; he was almost cowering. Then he collected himself and began to study the cards again, but in a way that let Mira know he was only pretending to try now.

"Okay, let's go outside in the garden and draw things," she sighed.

Charlie followed Mira with her sketch pads and coffee can full of colored pencils out into the bright sunny rectangle of her parents' back yard. In their house he moved so stiltedly—he was almost theatrically careful. In their garden he relaxed a little. They walked to the far end of the yard that had been planted in rows with vegetables, herbs, and flowers; they sat on the brick path with their backs against the garage that had been warmed by the sun.

Mira began to draw the window of the Nicelys' back bedroom on the second floor. It was broken and covered with the pages of a dirty magazine fastened with electrician's tape. She worked on this awhile, then decided she would draw both that window and the window of her own bedroom, the mirror image of next door. The two houses met in a peaked roof. One half of it—the Nicelys'—stood unpainted, crumbling; and the broken window was prominent. Mira's parents' half was painted a soft blue-gray with a shade pulled down exactly one-quarter of the way and a houseplant on the windowsill.

Someday, Mira thought, she'd do a drawing of the view *from* her window *down* into the two back yards, one so different from the other. The Nicelys used their back yard as a parking lot and garbage dump. Three cars were squeezed into it, end to end. At the head of this line, up against their house, a two-man-tall pile of garbage teetered. They threw their garbage—mostly brown shopping bags full of beer cans and fast-food wrappers—out of the back bedroom window every night. A rat the size of a small dog had tunneled in and lived beneath the mound. Charlie had seen it and its burrowed cave. Mira hadn't, but both she and Charlie could smell the rodent from where they sat, on this side of the fence.

"Yuck," Mira said, holding her nose.

"Lurch say he's gonna kill it with a baseball bat upside the head," Charlie said proudly of the man he sometimes referred to as his "father." He spoke of Lurch's proposal as if he were imparting world-important knowledge.

"Well, I wish he'd hurry up and do it, then."

"Dirtball say it's dead already—that's why it smells so bad!"

"Well, is it? I thought you said you saw it."

"I did! . . . Or maybe it was his mother," he added more quietly, backing down.

"Maybe."

"I won't go back there no more," Charlie confided, " 'cept walking on top of the cars."

"I don't blame you, but I bet Vicky doesn't like you making footprints on her car roof too much."

"She never sees me," he laughed somewhat nervously. The mention of his mother must have made him nervous. He got up and walked among the rows of vegetables, foot in front of foot carefully placed along the pathways of straw, just as Mira had shown him.

"I do it when she's not home," Charlie added. He bent down to look at a cucumber seedling. Sometimes, Mira thought, he does things solely to please me, because he senses the right thing to do, and then he does it, like a teacher's pet, never mind his true feelings and what he really wants to do. She watched him walk among the rows as cautiously as if he thought the soil were paper-thin and a step too heavy might break right through it.

"You could have a garden in your backyard, Charlie, if you cleaned it up," Mira said.

"What about the cars?"

"They could park them out on the street, like everybody else on the block."

"You park your car in your garage."

Mira had no rejoinder to this. She just watched Charlie in silence. He kept silent, too, until he added, almost to himself: "If Vicky had a garden, she'd grow things jess to step on 'em."

Mira was stung by this remark delivered as unbitterly as if it had been a compliment. She felt the truth of it, and the astuteness of Charlie.

She worked long and hard on her drawing, into the evening. She enjoyed the filling in of detail on opposite sides of the picture. Her parents were still at work; then, since it was a Friday, they were going with another couple to a movie and then would get something to eat.

Charlie had gone home at once when Vicky had called him to come and eat what she'd brought him. From her side of the fence Mira had heard her say to Charlie and his two half-brothers: "And you'd better eat every fucken bite!" Vicky never even looked at Mira, ever. A tall, skinny, sallow-skinned girl with bruise-colored eyes, the missing teeth—not all of them simply fallen out, but some of them knocked out or broken off at the gumline—she grumbled and grimaced, looking down, when she and Mira passed on the sidewalk. Vicky's most frequent destination was the pay phone outside the liquor store. It was while Vicky was on the phone that Mira successfully, unobtrusively, had read the tattoo on her arm. The word she had chosen, scrawled so unprofessionally a child might have done it, was *LOVE* in the same bruise color of her eyes.

Once, late at night, Mira had overheard Vicky and Lurch talking in the Nicelys' backyard. It sounded as if Lurch was planning to leave Vicky, and she was trying to talk him out of it. She reminded him of his sons. "I hope they die!" Lurch had retorted. "Well, I'd like to see how well you do out there in that big world all by yourself," Vicky had said. That seemed to end it, and Lurch evidently had stayed.

Now Vicky appeared to be pregnant again, and Mira wondered if it would be a girl this time. She didn't think Vicky would like a girl, but probably wouldn't let a little thing like the wrong-sexed child bother her much. Vicky seemed to sense an order to things, something beyond her control, and yet she was a part of it: she didn't fight it. Nothing to fight: she couldn't see it. Mira admired that in Vicky, despite everything else, including her treatment of Charlie. Mira, who felt she herself rightly belonged nowhere, even envied Vicky a little. All the Nicelys, except Charlie, truly belonged with each other.

Mira worked on her drawing until it was long past nine. She still wasn't finished when she heard noise and shouting on the street outside. It went on for quite a while, but she didn't get up to see what it was. She was used to disturbances made by the Nicelys. She half-expected Charlie to lift the mail slot in the front door—that was how he knocked—and ask to come in and tell her about it. But he didn't. And she didn't get up from the table to go look out the window until she saw the ambulance lights—red, silver, red, silver—racing around the room.

Police and police cars were everywhere, with lights and badges flashing. In the center of it all, a big black man was being bandaged, leaning up against a parked car like someone being frisked. Huge amounts of the whitest gauze were being wrapped around his middle. His head had already been wrapped in a turban of gauze by the ambulance attendants.

Several Nicelys were out on the sidewalk, shouting at the wounded man, making boxers' moves, but not getting up too close to him. Somewhere Roy had lost his false teeth, but still he was shouting the loudest: "I hope you die!" At this, the wounded man jerked up from the stretcher on which he had been laid and started to fight. The police restrained him, and they and the ambulance drivers eventually got him to lie back down.

Several police went into the Nicelys' house. From her window Mira could see that they all made sure to avoid a wide black pool on the sidewalk, just outside the Nicelys' gate: it glistened under the orange street lights. She watched from the window until the ambulance workers and all of the police were gone—and until it was finally, mysteriously, quiet next door. She waited a long time for Charlie to come over—to tell her what had happened. But his eyes never did appear in the rectangle of the mail slot, although several times she imagined she'd heard the squeak it made whenever he opened it.

She went to bed, and later on, heard her parents arrive home, coming in the back door from the garage. Mira didn't get up to say hello to them, or to say anything else; she pretended to be asleep. She wanted to keep wondering in the dark about the Nicelys. It wasn't the first time police had come to their door. Once, they came in the middle of the night to take Dirtball away for questioning. Mira heard them rumble up the stairs and bang on the back bedroom door, saying to him, "Be cool, now, man, be cool." The next day, no one seemed disturbed. They were all out on the front porch, as usual, drinking and laughing. Later, Dirtball returned—a big, pimply boy of nineteen with the expression on his face of a child who thinks he's outsmarted someone—telling stories. "And you know what they gave me to eat?" he asked no one in particular, swaggering in the Nicelys' dirt patch of a front yard. "A bologna sandwich! And I said to them, 'I don't eat no bologna sandwiches!' "

The Nicelys all had been so cheerful! If the same thing had happened to either of Mira's parents or to anyone they knew, they would have been somber and busy making phone calls for days. Mira fell in and out of sleep, wondering how the Nicelys' mood would be tomorrow. She felt strangely elated, almost happy, as if she had glimpsed something of rare privilege, a thing usually hidden, one of life's secrets, direct and real. Because she never had felt this way before, and because it was for such a peculiar reason, she decided it must be a feeling she would have more often as she got more grown up. She wondered if her parents would see that she was changed. So distant, murmuring in their cavernous bedroom down the hall—they were two tall strangers in her mind's eye tonight. They would never understand that she was actually happy to be living next door to the Nicelys.

The minute she awoke the next morning, she got dressed and tiptoed downstairs. She looked again at the sidewalk, and saw exactly what last night she had only supposed: that the black was not any black at all, but the bright red blood of a person. This excited her, made her feel special for living so close to such an event, such a family who would do such a thing.

She opened the door, stepped out into the brilliant sunshine falling at an angle across the porch, and stared at the splattered side of the parked car that the man had leaned up against while the ambulance workers had dressed him. The splashes of blood he had left behind were almost artistic, free and large, like a modern painter's marks. But the wide flat puddle of red on the sidewalk, where he must have lain before the ambulance arrived, just beyond the Nicelys' gate, was redder than any paint Mira had seen on either a house or a canvas. She stared at it a long while, fascinated. When a young black man walked by and expressed to her wordlessly his own excitement and wonder at the stain—over the noise of his suitcase-sized box of blaring music—she felt proud, but knew enough to keep it inside: on her face she wore a look of ponderousness and worry.

Mothers from the projects had a different reaction, and Mira took it as a personal insult. With their laundry in wire shopping carts, and little children trailing behind them, they scuffed by with a first and then a second disgusted glance at the stain under their feet, but not a third one backwards. They did not stop. They were not fascinated or amused. And they did not look at Mira standing with her feet apart on her front porch. They kept walking, finally not seeing at all—urban professionals—as the wheels of their carts squealed under the weight of large households' dirty clothes.

Mira wondered after these women disapprovingly. How was it that they had come to have such a lack of simple curiosity? How was it that they deliberately chose not to see? She kept her eyes on the spot, as if it were her duty, feeling important, even enjoying herself. She still was keeping her vigil when Charlie Brown came out onto his porch.

He wore the same rumpled clothes he'd worn now for three days running. He had lint and pieces of dust caught in his matted hair. She saw that one of his eyes was blackened, and that he looked frightened and upset, but was trying not to. She was glad he chose to hide it; if he didn't, it would spoil things. She wasn't pleased with his reaction, but she also felt sorry for the boy.

"Charlie, what happened to you?" she asked gently.

"Walked into a post, wasn't looken," he said, carefully rehearsed, and even someone who didn't think they knew him would have said that he was lying. He was much more somber than she'd ever seen him before. That wouldn't be fun. She didn't like him lying to her, either, but she'd forgive him this once, under the circumstances.

"The pig won a car," he added to Mira's thoughtful silence—she was back looking at the blood.

"What pig, Charlie?" She was annoyed. Did he think she could read his mind?

"In the cartoon!" he said, his small voice straining.

"I don't watch cartoons, Charlie, you know that," she snapped. She had told him many times that most cartoons were dumb, and supposedly he had finally agreed with her.

"That's why I'm tellen you!" he shouted.

"Shh!" she warned, pointing to his door and then to her parents'. She was annoyed at the shouting and surprised at it, too.

"Then it went out," he added in a lower voice, nearly a mumble.

"What went out? The cartoon?"

He nodded at his torn sneakers, which had many knots in the laces.

"Is your electricity shut off again?" Mira sighed.

In reply Charlie just looked across at the row of town houses on the other side of the street, squinting into the yellow sun. And Mira thought of the Nicelys groping around in their dark house tonight. It was interesting when the electricity was shut off during a storm, but this was something inconvenient, not interesting at all. What could Mira do about it? Nothing. Why couldn't the Nicelys just pay their bill? They seemed to have enough money for beer and cigarettes every day, she thought self-righteously. She felt like an adult, having such an opinion. Adult-like, too, was her next idea: Poor Charlie—so what would they, she and he, do today?

"Less play lessons," Charlie said demandingly, giving his foot a little stamp. But Mira said no. He couldn't come inside when her parents were at home. They wouldn't even like it, really, if the two of them just talked together outside.

"No, let's go for a walk," she said, as if this were something they always did, although they never had before. But she'd learned long ago from her parents, indirectly, that if the tone of voice you used was confident enough, it made your idea seem that way, too. Besides, she also had this newfound importance. "Yes, we'll go for a walk. You go tell Vicky you're going somewhere with me."

"She's sleepen."

"Well, then, go tell your granddaddy."

"He's sleepen, too!"

"Well, then, come on!" And they took off together down the street.

He ran and ran in circles around her, then ran far ahead and circled back. Mira, plump, out of shape, struggled to keep up, and marvelled at Charlie's energy and strength. His upper body appeared to remain stationary, while his muscular little legs whirred beneath him. He never moved with such freedom in Mira's parents' house or yard. Nor in his own back yard or in sight of anyone in his household. She began to think she didn't know him very well after all. Even the familiar shirt he wore looked strange against this new landscape of the streets leading downtown. The shirt was red with a silver patch made of duct tape smack in the middle of the back of it, like a target, where Vicky had touched it with a cigarette. Mira kept her eye on that patch—the sun made it appear to flutter like a silver bird following him—as she struggled along, her lungs and chubby knees aching.

Passing the temperature and time on the bank sign, she shouted after him, hoping to make a number lesson out of it, but her words were lost: Charlie was too far ahead to understand them, and wouldn't come back to listen to her explain.

He tore in and out of stores, creating suspicion. She followed close behind, pulling up her socks on the run. In the drug store he slowed, surveying the items on the shelves, while she bought a package of cough drops—this, just to show the glowering store manager that they did have some legitimate business in the place. Then Charlie ran up and told her proudly, in a loud voice, and in front of the cashier and several other customers waiting sleepily behind them in the line, that the last time he and Vicky had been here, she'd taken a chocolate bar from the display and given it to him to eat. "And she didn't pay for it or nothin'!" he beamed and then ran out the door. Mira, reddening, paid for her purchase and hurried away after him, thinking that the actions of members of his household were very often not precise and praiseworthy at all, and shouldn't be considered that way; and Charlie should know that: he should be told. But the boy was already far ahead of her up the street.

She followed him into the city park and up the grassy hill. It was the place that she had come with her class not too long ago to view an eclipse of the sun. They had been made to put their backs to it and look at its image projected through a pinprick in cardboard onto yet another piece of cardboard. Actually, it had only been an *annular* eclipse. Carefully she had been taught the distinction by Mr. Hammond, the bearded young science teacher, who smiled too much, who wanted too much for the students to like him, so they didn't. They did learn from him about penumbras, shadow bands, Baily's Beads, the corona—all in preparation for the viewing. But when the day finally came and they looked through their cardboard contraptions, they saw nothing even remotely spectacular. The skies had been overcast; then they'd further darkened, but otherwise . . . nothing. Mira was convinced that she would have seen *something* if she'd been allowed to look at the sun directly—at least she would have seen what there was to see of the sun that day: a large spot of glare in the bleak, gray sky, with furious clouds racing past it.

It was here on the grassy slope that Charlie finally rested. He threw himself down on the ground, and Mira sat, too; then she saw that they weren't alone.

Not far off was the couple she often noticed on her way to the school bus stop: a tall black man in an Army fatigue jacket and his girlfriend, who was white with red hair and always wore skirts that swept the sidewalk. They were never not together, and to her it looked as if they were clearly in love. The dreaminess of their eyes was certainly something to behold. Neither would ever hurt the other, she felt sure. Would they? Sometimes, when she saw them walking, she had to look closely to make sure that their eyes were open. They held hands, and each led the other along. Probably they lived in the park; probably they were junkies, Mira thought; but she admired them and their togetherness anyway, at least from a distance.

"Who *was* that man at your house last night, Charlie?" she asked, watching the man in the fatigue jacket eat popcorn from a bag that the girl held out to him. They were sitting on a blanket with many household items lined up on it with them. He did look like the man who'd been hurt last night at the Nicelys'—but it couldn't be the same person, could it? "Who was it?" she asked again.

The boy shrugged. "I don't know." He wouldn't look at her.

Mira smirked. He really was a poor liar. "You do too know who it was, Charlie!"

"No I don't!" he said into her face.

She flinched, but persisted: "Wasn't it your father?"

"Lurch?" The boy was confused by her.

"No! Your real father!"

He was silent, chewing his lip, looking away from her again, and she saw that his unhappy mood had returned. After a while, though, she saw that a new, diverting thought had crossed his mind; he said with glee, "Lurch got him in the back with a machete!"

"Who? That guy last night? That's awful, Charlie! Is he going to be all right?"

"Vicky got a machete in the shoulder down in Virginia! She was on TV!" he bragged.

"For fighting? On the news? That's bad, Charlie. That's not good. And it's not good that she took that candy bar in the drug store, or that Detox threw a bottle through that car window, or that Dirtball . . . "

In the middle of her speech Charlie got up and started running again, this time at a group of birds feeding on the grass.

"Charlie!" Mira got up and followed after him.

Four black crows big as cats flew into the trees caw-cawing, then folded their wings and glared down at them both, while Charlie flapped his arms, jumping up and down, futilely trying to touch the lowest tree limbs.

"Charlie!"

"What?"

"Don't do that!"

"Do what?"

"Scare the birds. They aren't doing anything to you!"

In response Charlie ran and leapt at them some more, circling the wide base of the tree.

To show indifference—that is, to hide her hurt and anger—Mira turned her back on him and looked up at the sun, full-face, eyes open. She stared boldly at it as long as she could, then had to glance away with her eye sockets aching, tearing, and her vision spotty. She nearly lost her balance. When she recovered herself, she looked around for Charlie. He was over by the junkies, and so were two black girls about Mira's age.

It looked as if the girls considered themselves to be very grown up, at least to Mira. What were they all talking about? Maybe the girls were asking the junkies for drugs. They were mildly overweight, like Mira, in their new spring dresses. They must have walked over from the projects. Maybe one of them had a baby at home. Maybe both of them did. Mira felt superior to them in many ways, but she also was intimidated by them.

"Charlie!" Mira called to the boy, who stood on the edge of the group's blanket, listening to them. He ignored her, and took some popcorn from the bag held out to him. But Mira decided not to be afraid. She took the path—a dusty path; no one had meant a path to be here, but the grass had been worn by many lazy walkers over the years, and now there was a diagonal cut right through the heart of the park. She walked straight over to Charlie and the others in the group, but stayed on the path.

"Charlie, Vicky's going to be mad when she wakes up and finds out that you're gone. You better come home with me now."

But the boy just kept eating the popcorn and listening to the man whose slowly worded sentence Mira had interrupted. Everyone else but Charlie was looking at her. Finally it was one of the black girls who spoke up: "Hey, white bitch, you leave this boy alone." She had a gravelly voice and the whites of her eyes were not white at all, but yellow.

"You take care your own babies," said the other black girl. The skin of her forehead was wrinkled and so was one of her forearms—burn marks.

Mira was indignant. "He's not my baby!"

"Well, why you actin' like you his momma, then?" the other one said, and they both moved closer to Mira, who was still standing firm on the path.

"I'm not."

"You get outa here, bitch! Go on, go on home!" the burned girl said and picked something up off the path.

"Come on, Charlie," Mira said, frightened now, but still holding her ground. Then she saw the two girls moving, shifting directions, darting like disturbed shadows. She smelled the sweet, sharp odors of their skin. She couldn't see where Charlie was anymore. Then the burned girl's hand came up close to Mira's face as she threw some grit into Mira's eyes.

She cried out for Charlie, groping, but found only strange arms and hands that pushed and pulled her and scratched at her cheeks and pulled her hair. A blow to her stomach knocked her breath out, and she couldn't even speak. She heard them laughing as she tried to catch her breath, gasping like a drowning person. She knew she must look ridiculous. She kept sipping at the air, never getting enough. Finally, then, she could scream, but she still couldn't see. She screamed and screamed, fascinated at how good it felt to take such deep breaths, then let it all out again. She rubbed the last of the grit from her eyes, and saw that the junkies still dreamed, the girls were gone . . . and so was Charlie.

She limped home, ignoring the stares. She knew her lip was swollen and her shirt bloodied, but she didn't care. She wore these as an emblem of something.

From the head of her block she could see that her parents were busy out on the sidewalk. Her father held the garden hose and was directing it at the stain outside the Nicelys' gate. Her mother was using a stiff broom to push the water into the gutter. As Mira approached, she watched the water flow red, then pink, all along the gutter to the drain, and her stomach turned queasy. Her parents were so intent on their chore, grim-faced and officious, they didn't even notice her. Later they would shriek and tear the explanations from her. But for now she sneaked up the steps of her porch, and caught sight of Charlie on his porch. He was crouched behind the wooden slats of the railing, watching her parents work. When he saw Mira, he stood and his black eyes flashed at her with hope. But the teeth of his smile looked too sharp to her now; Mira hurried past.

Rough Strife

LYNNE SHARON SCHWARTZ

Now let us sport us while we may;
And now, like am'rous birds of prey
. . . tear our pleasure with rough strife
Through the iron gates of life.
—Andrew Marvell

CAROLINE AND IVAN finally had a child. Conception stunned them; they didn't think, by now, that it could happen. For years they had tried and failed, till it seemed that a special barren destiny was preordained. Meanwhile, in the wide spaces of childlessness, they had created activity: their work flourished. Ivan, happy and moderately powerful in a large foundation, helped decide how to distribute money for artistic and social projects. Caroline taught mathematics at a small suburban university. Being a mathematician, she found, conferred a painful private wisdom on her efforts to conceive. In her brain, as Ivan exploded within her, she would involuntarily calculate probabilities; millions of blind sperm and one reluctant egg clustered before her eyes in swiftly transmuting geometric patterns. She lost her grasp of pleasure, forgot what it could feel like without a goal. She had no idea what Ivan might be thinking about, scattered seed money, maybe. Their passion became courteous and automatic until, by attrition, for months they didn't make love—it was too awkward.

One September Sunday morning she was in the shower, watching, through a crack in the curtain, Ivan naked at the washstand. He was shaving, his jaw tilted at an innocently self-satisfied angle. He wasn't aware of being watched, so that a secret quality, an essence of Ivan, exuded in great waves. Caroline could almost see it, a cloudy aura. He stroked his jaw vainly with intense concentration, a self-absorption so contagious that she needed, suddenly, to possess it with him. She stepped out of the shower.

"Ivan."

He turned abruptly, surprised, perhaps even annoyed at the interruption.

"Let's not have a baby any more. Let's just . . . come on." When she placed her wet hand on his back he lifted her easily off her feet with his right arm, the razor still poised in his other, outstretched hand.

"Come on," she insisted. She opened the door and a draft blew into the small steamy room. She pulled him by the hand toward the bedroom.

Ivan grinned. "You're soaking wet."

"Wet, dry, what's the difference?" It was hard to speak. She began to run, to tease him; he caught her and tossed her onto their disheveled bed and dug his teeth so deep into her shoulder that she thought she would bleed.

Then with disinterest, taken up only in this fresh rushing need for him, weeks later Caroline conceived. Afterwards she liked to say that she had known the moment it happened. It felt different, she told him, like a pin pricking a balloon, but without the shattering noise, without the quick collapse. "Oh, come on," said Ivan. "That's impossible."

But she was a mathematician, after all, and dealt with infinitesimal precise abstractions, and she did know how it had happened. The baby was conceived in strife, one early October night, Indian summer. All day the sun glowed hot and low in the sky, settling an amber torpor on people and things, and the night was the same, only now a dark hot heaviness sunk slowly down. The scent of the still-blooming honeysuckle rose to their bedroom window. Just as she was bending over to kiss him, heavy and quivering with heat like the night, he teased her about something, about a mole on her leg, and in reply she punched him lightly on the shoulder. He grabbed her wrists, and when she began kicking, pinned her feet down with his own. In an instant Ivan lay stretched out on her back like a blanket, smothering her, while she struggled beneath, writhing to escape. It was a silent, sweaty struggle, interrupted with outbursts of wild laughter, shrieks and gasping breaths. She tried biting but, laughing loudly, he evaded her, and she tried scratching the fists that held her down, but she couldn't reach. All her desire was transformed into physical effort, but he was too strong for her. He wanted her to say she gave up, but she refused, and since he wouldn't loosen his grip they lay locked and panting in their static embrace for some time.

"You win," she said at last, but as he rolled off she sneakily jabbed him in the ribs with her elbow.

"Aha!" Ivan shouted, and was ready to begin again, but she quickly distracted him. Once the wrestling was at an end, though, Caroline found her passion dissipated, and her pleasure tinged with resentment. After they made love forcefully, when they were covered with sweat, dripping on each other, she said, "Still, you don't play fair."

"I don't play fair! Look who's talking. Do you want me to give you a handicap?"

"No."

"So?"

"It's not fair, that's all."

Ivan laughed gloatingly and curled up in her arms. She smiled in the dark. That was the night the baby was conceived, not in high passion but rough strife.

She lay on the table in the doctor's office weeks later. The doctor, whom she had known for a long time, habitually kept up a running conversation while he probed. Today, fretting over his weight problem, he outlined his plans for a new diet. Tensely she watched him, framed and centered by her raised knees, which were still bronzed from summer sun. His other hand was pressing on her stomach. Caroline was nauseated with fear and trembling, afraid of the verdict. It was taking so long, perhaps it was a tumor.

"I'm cutting out all starches," he said. "I've really let myself go lately."

"Good idea." Then she gasped in pain. A final, sickening thrust, and he was out. Relief, and a sore gap where he had been. In a moment, she knew, she would be retching violently.

"Well?"

"Well, Caroline, you hit the jackpot this time."

She felt a smile, a stupid, puppet smile, spread over her face. In the tiny bathroom where she threw up, she saw in the mirror the silly smile looming over her ashen face like a dancer's glowing grimace of labored joy. She smiled through the rest of the visit, through his advice about milk, weight, travel and rest, smiled at herself in the window of the bus, and at her moving image in the fenders of parked cars as she walked home.

Ivan, incredulous over the telephone, came home beaming stupidly just like Caroline, and brought a bottle of champagne. After dinner they drank it and made love.

"Do you think it's all right to do this?" he asked.

"Oh, Ivan, honestly. It's microscopic."

He was in one of his whimsical moods and made terrible jokes that she laughed at with easy indulgence. He said he was going to pay the baby a visit and asked if she had any messages she wanted delivered. He unlocked from her embrace, moved down her body and said he was going to have a look for himself. Clowning, he put his ear between her legs to listen. Whatever amusement she felt soon ebbed away into irritation. She had never thought Ivan would be a doting parent—he was so preoccupied with himself. Finally he stopped his antics as she clasped her arms around him and whispered, "Ivan, you are really too much." He became unusually gentle. Tamed, and she didn't like it, hoped he wouldn't continue that way for months. Pleasure lapped over her with a mild, lackadaisical bitterness, and then when she could be articulate once more she explained patiently, "Ivan, you know, it really is all right. I mean, it's a natural process."

"Well I didn't want to hurt you."

"I'm not sick."

Then, as though her body were admonishing that cool confidence, she did get sick. There were mornings when she awoke with such paralyzing nausea that she had to ask Ivan to bring her a hard roll from the kitchen before she could stir from bed. To move from her awakening position seemed a tremendous risk, as if she might spill out. She rarely threw up—the nausea resembled violent hunger. Something wanted to be filled, not expelled, a perilous vacuum occupying her insides. The crucial act was getting the first few mouthfuls down. Then the solidity and denseness of the hard unbuttered roll stabilized her, like a heavy weight thrown down to anchor a tottering ship. Her head ached. On the mornings when she had no classes she would wander around the house till almost noon clutching the partly eaten roll in her hand like a talisman. Finishing one roll, she quickly went to the bread-box for another; she bought them regularly at the bakery a half-dozen at a time. With enough roll inside her she could sometimes manage a half-cup of tea, but liquids were risky. They sloshed around inside and made her envision the baby sloshing around too, in its cloudy fluid. By early afternoon she would feel fine. The baby, she imagined, claimed her for the night and was reluctant to give up its hold in the morning: they vied till she conquered. She was willing to yield her sleeping hours to the baby, her dreams even, if necessary, but she wanted the daylight for herself.

The mornings that she taught were agony. Ivan would wake her up early, bring her a roll, and gently prod her out of bed.

"I simply cannot do it," she would say, placing her legs cautiously over the side of the bed.

"Sure you can. Now get up."

"I'll die if I get up."

"You have no choice. You have a job." He was freshly showered and dressed, and his neatness irritated her. He had nothing more to do—the discomfort was all hers. She rose to her feet and swayed.

Ivan looked alarmed. "Do you want me to call and tell them you can't make it?"

"No, no." That frightened her. She needed to hold on to the job, to defend herself against the growing baby. Once she walked into the classroom she would be fine. A Mondrian print hung on the back wall—she could look at that, and it would steady her. With waves of nausea roiling in her chest, she stumbled into the bathroom.

She liked him to wait until she was out of the shower before he left for work, because she anticipated fainting under the impact of the water. Often at the end she forced herself to stand under an ice cold flow, leaning her head way back and letting her short fair hair drip down behind her. Though it was torture, when she emerged she felt more alive.

After the shower had been off a while Ivan would come and open the bathroom door. "Are you O.K. now, Caroline? I've got to go." It made her feel like a child. She would be wrapped in a towel with her hair dripping on the mat, brushing her teeth or rubbing cream into her face. "Yes, thanks for waiting. I guess this'll end soon. They say it's only the first few months."

He kissed her lips, her bare damp shoulder, gave a parting squeeze to her toweled behind, and was gone. She watched him walk down the hall. Ivan was very large. She had always been drawn and aroused by his largeness, by the huge bones and the taut legs that felt as though he had steel rods inside. But now she watched with some trepidation, hoping Ivan wouldn't have a large, inflexible baby.

Very slowly she would put on clothes. Selecting each article seemed a much more demanding task than ever before. Seeing how slow she had become, she allowed herself over an hour, keeping her hard roll nearby as she dressed and prepared her face. All the while, through the stages of dressing, she evaluated her body closely in the full-length mirror, first naked, then in bra and underpants, then with shoes added, and finally with a dress. She was looking for signs, but the baby was ivisible. Nothing had changed yet. She was still as she had always been, not quite slim yet somehow appearing small, almost delicate. She used to pride herself on strength. When they moved in she had worked as hard as Ivan, lugging furniture and lifting heavy cartons. He was impressed. Now, of course, she could no longer do that—it took all her strength to move her own weight.

With the profound sensuous narcissism of women past first youth, she admired her still-narrow waist and full breasts. She was especially fond of her shoulders and prominent collarbone, which had a fragile, inviting look. That would all be gone soon, of course, gone soft. Curious about how she would alter, she scanned her face for the pregnant look she knew well from the faces of friends. It was far less a tangible change than a look of transparent vulnerability that took over the face: nearly a pleading look, a beg for help like a message from a powerless invaded country to the rest of the world. Caroline did not see it on her face yet.

From the tenth to the fourteenth week of her pregnancy she slept, with brief intervals of lucidity when she taught her classes. It was a strange dreamy time. The passionate nausea faded, but the lure of the bed was irresistible. In the middle of the day, even, she could pass by the bedroom, glimpse the waiting bed and be overcome by the soft heavy desire to lie down. She fell into a stupor immediately and did not dream. She forgot what it was like to awaken with energy and move through an entire day without lying down once. She forgot the feeling of eyes opened wide without effort. She would have liked to hide this strange, shameful perversity from Ivan, but that was impossible. Ivan kept wanting to go to the movies. Clearly, he was bored with her. Maybe, she imagined, staring up at the bedroom ceiling through slitted eyes, he would become so bored he would abandon her and

the baby and she would not be able to support the house alone and she and
the baby would end up on the street in rags, begging. She smiled. That was
highly unlikely. Ivan would not be the same Ivan without her.

"You go on, Ivan. I just can't."

Once he said, "I thought I might ask Ruth Forbes to go with me to see the
Charlie Chaplin in town. I know she likes him. Would that bother you?"

She was half-asleep, slowly eating a large apple in bed and watching
Medical Center on television, but she roused herself to answer. "No, of
course not." Ruth Forbes was a divorced woman who lived down the block,
a casual friend and not Ivan's type at all, too large, loud and depressed.
Caroline didn't care if he wanted her company. She didn't care if he held her
hand on his knee in the movies as he liked to do, or even if, improbably, he
made love to her afterwards in her sloppy house crawling with children. She
didn't care about anything except staying nestled in bed.

She made love with him sometimes, in a slow way. She felt no specific
desire but didn't want to deny him, she loved him so. Or had, she thought
vaguely, when she was alive and strong. Besides, she knew she could sleep
right after. Usually there would be a moment when she came alive despite
herself, when the reality of his body would strike her all at once with a
wistful throb of lust, but mostly she was too tired to see it through, to leap
towards it, so she let it subside, merely nodding at it gratefully as a sign of
dormant life. She felt sorry for Ivan, but helpless.

Once to her great shame, she fell asleep while he was inside her. He woke
her with a pat on her cheek, actually, she realized from the faint sting, a
gesture more like a slap than a pat. "Caroline, for Christ's sake, you're
sleeping."

"No, no, I'm sorry. I wasn't really sleeping. Oh, Ivan, it's nothing. This
will end." She wondered, though.

Moments later she felt his hands on her thighs. His lips were brooding on
her stomach, edging, with expertise, lower and lower down. He was
murmuring something she couldn't catch. She felt an ache, an irritation. Of
course he meant well, Ivan always did. Wryly, she appreciated his
intentions. But she couldn't bear that excitement now.

"Please," she said. "Please don't do that."

He was terribly hurt. He said nothing, but leaped away violently and
pulled all the blankets around him. She was contrite, shed a few private tears
and fell instantly into a dreamless dark.

He wanted to go to a New Year's Eve party some close friends were
giving, and naturally he wanted her to come with him. Caroline vowed to
herself she would do this for him because she had been giving so little for so
long. She planned to get dressed and look very beautiful, as she could still
look when she took plenty of time and tried hard enough; she would not

drink very much—it was sleep-inducing—and she would not be the one to suggest going home. After sleeping through the day in preparation, she washed her hair, using something she found in the drugstore to heighten the blonde flecks. Then she put on a long green velvet dress with gold embroidery, and inserted the gold hoop earrings Ivan bought her some years ago for her twenty-fifth birthday. Before they set out she drank a cup of black coffee. She would have taken No-Doze but she was afraid of drugs, afraid of giving birth to an armless or legless baby who would be a burden and a heartache to them for the rest of their days.

At the party of mostly university people, she chatted with everyone equally, those she knew well and those she had never met. Sociably, she held a filled glass in her hand, taking tiny sips. She and Ivan were not together very much—it was crowded, smoky and loud; people kept moving and encounters were brief—but she knew he was aware of her, could feel his awareness through the milling bodies. He was aware and he was pleased. He deserved more than the somnambulist she had become, and she was pleased to please him. But after a while her legs would not support her for another instant. The skin tingled: soft warning bells rang from every pore. She allowed herself a moment to sit down alone in a small alcove off the living room, where she smoked a cigarette and stared down at her lap, holding her eyes open very wide. Examining the gold and rose-colored embroidery on her dress, Caroline traced the coiled pattern, mathematical and hypnotic, with her index finger. Just as she was happily merging into its intricacies, a man, a stranger, came in, breaking her trance. He was a very young man, twenty-three, maybe, of no apparent interest.

"Hi. I hear you're expecting a baby," he began, and sat down with a distinct air of settling in.

"Yes. That's quite an opening line. How did you know?"

"I know because Linda told me. You know Linda, don't you? I'm her brother."

He began asking about her symptoms. Sleepiness? Apathy? He knew, he had worked in a clinic. Unresponsive, she retorted by inquiring about his taste in music. He sat on a leather hassock opposite Caroline on the couch, and with every inquisitive sentence drew his seat closer till their knees were almost touching. She shifted her weight to avoid him, tucked her feet under her and lit another cigarette, feeling she could lie down and fall into a stupor quite easily. Still, words were coming out of her mouth, she heard them; she hoped they were not encouraging words but she seemed to have very little control over what they were.

"I—" he said. "You see—" He reached out and put his hand over hers. "Pregnant women, like, they really turn me on. I mean, there's a special aura. You're sensational."

She pulled her hand away. "God almighty."

"What's the matter? Honestly, I didn't mean to offend you."

"I really must go." She stood up and stepped around him.

"Could I see you some time?"

"You're seeing me now. Enjoy it."

He ran his eyes over her from head to toe, appraising. "It doesn't show yet."

Gazing down at her body, Caroline stretched the loose velvet dress taut over her stomach. "No, you're right, it doesn't." Then, over her shoulder, as she left their little corner, she tossed, "Fuck you, you pig."

With a surge of energy she downed a quick Scotch, found Ivan and tugged at his arm. "Let's dance."

Ivan's blue eyes lightened with shock. At home she could barely walk.

"Yes, let's." He took her in his arms and she buried her face against his shoulder. But she held her tears back, she would not let him know.

Later she told him about it. It was three-thirty in the morning, they had just made love drunkenly, and Ivan was in high spirits. She knew why—he felt he had her back again. She had held him close and uttered her old sounds, familiar moans and cries like a poignant, nearly forgotten tune, and Ivan was miraculously restored, his impact once again sensible to eye and ear. He was making her laugh hysterically now, imitating the eccentric professor of art history at the party, an owlish émigré from Bavaria who expounded on the dilemmas of today's youth, all the while pronouncing "youth" as if it rhymed with "mouth." Ivan had also discovered that he pronounced "unique" as if it were "eunuch." Then, sitting up in bed cross-legged, they competed in making up pretentious scholarly sentences that included both "unique" and "youth" mispronounced.

"Speaking of 'yowth,'" Caroline said, "I met a weird one tonight, Linda's brother. A very eunuch yowth, I must say." And giggling, she recounted their conversation. Suddenly at the end she unexpectedly found herself in tears. Shuddering, she flopped over and sobbed into her pillow.

"Caroline," he said tenderly, "please. For heaven's sake, it was just some nut. It was nothing. Don't get all upset over it." He stroked her bare back.

"I can't help it," she wailed. "It made me feel so disgusting."

"You're much too sensitive. Come on." He ran his hand slowly through her hair, over and over.

She pulled the blanket around her. "Enough. I'm going to sleep."

A few days later, when classes were beginning again for the new semester, she woke early and went immediately to the shower, going through the ritual motions briskly and automatically. She was finished and brushing her teeth when she realized what had happened. There she was on her feet, sturdy, before eight in the morning, planning how she would introduce the topic of the differential calculus to her new students. She stared at her face in the mirror with unaccustomed recognition, her mouth dripping white foam, her dark eyes startled. She was alive. She didn't know how the miracle had happened, nor did she care to explore it. Back in the bedroom she dressed quickly, zipping up a pair of slim rust-colored woollen slacks with satisfaction. It didn't show yet, but soon.

"Ivan, time to get up."

He grunted and opened his eyes. When at last they focused on Caroline leaning over him they burned blue and wide with astonishment. He rubbed a fist across his forehead. "Are you dressed already?"

"Yes. I'm cured."

"What do you mean?"

"I'm not tired any more. I'm slept out. I've come back to life."

"Oh." He moaned and rolled over in one piece like a seal.

"Aren't you getting up?"

"In a little while. I'm so tired. I must sleep for a while." The words were thick and slurred.

"Well!" She was strangely annoyed. Ivan always got up with vigor. "Are you sick?"

"Uh-uh."

After a quick cup of coffee she called out, "Ivan, I'm leaving now. Don't forget to get up." The January air was crisp and exhilarating, and she walked the half-mile to the university at a nimble clip, going over her introductory remarks in her head.

Ivan was tired for a week. Caroline wanted to go out to dinner every evening—she had her appetite back. She had broken through dense earth to fresh air. It was a new year and soon they would have a new baby. But all Ivan wanted to do was stay home and lie on the bed and watch television. It was repellent. Sloth, she pointed out to him more than once, was one of the seven deadly sins. The fifth night she said in exasperation, "What the hell is the matter with you? If you're sick go to a doctor."

"I'm not sick. I'm tired. Can't I be tired too? Leave me alone. I left you alone, didn't I?"

"That was different."

"How?"

"I'm pregnant and you're not, in case you've forgotten."

"How could I forget?"

She said nothing, only cast him an evil look.

One evening soon after Ivan's symptoms disappeared, they sat together on the living-room sofa sharing sections of the newspaper. Ivan had his feet up on the coffee table and Caroline sat diagonally, resting her legs on his. She paused in her reading and touched her stomach.

"Ivan."

"What?"

"It's no use. I'm going to have to buy some maternity clothes."

He put down the paper and stared. "Really?" He seemed distressed.

"Yes."

"Well, don't buy any of those ugly things they wear. Can't you get some of those, you know, sort of Indian things?"

"Yes. That's a good idea. I will."

He picked up the paper again.

"It moves."

"What?"

"I said it moves. The baby."

"It moves?"

She laughed. "Remember Galileo? *Eppure, si muove.*" They had spent years together in Italy in their first youth, in mad love, and visited the birthplace of Galileo. He was a hero to both of them, because his mind remained free and strong though his body succumbed to tyranny.

Ivan laughed too. "*Eppure, si muove.* Let me see." He bent his head down to feel it, then looked up at her, his face full of longing, marvel and envy. In a moment he was scrambling at her clothes in a young eager rush. He wanted to be there, he said. Caroline, taken by surprise, was suspended between laughter and tears. He had her on the floor in silence, and for each it was swift and consuming.

Ivan lay spent in her arms. Caroline, still gasping and clutching him, said, "I could never love it as much as I love you." She wondered, then, hearing her words fall in the still air, whether this would always be true.

Shortly after she began wearing the Indian shirts and dresses, she noticed that Ivan was acting oddly. He stayed late at the office more than ever before, and often brought work home with him. He appeared to have lost interest in the baby, rarely asking how she felt, and when she moaned in bed sometimes, "Oh, I can't get to sleep, it keeps moving around," he responded with a grunt or not at all. He asked her, one warm Sunday in March, if she wanted to go bicycle riding.

"Ivan, I can't go bicycle riding. I mean, look at me."

"Oh, right. Of course."

He seemed to avoid looking at her, and she did look terrible, she had to admit. Even she looked at herself in the mirror as infrequently as possible. She dreaded what she had heard about hair falling out and teeth rotting, but she drank her milk diligently and so far neither of those things had happened. But besides the grotesque belly, her ankles swelled up so that the shape of her own legs was alien. She took diuretics and woke every hour at night to go to the bathroom. Sometimes it was impossible to get back to sleep so she sat up in bed reading. Ivan said, "Can't you turn the light out? You know I can't sleep with the light on."

"But what should I do? I can't sleep at all."

"Read in the living room."

"It's so cold in there at night."

He would turn away irritably. Once he took the blanket and went to sleep in the living room himself.

They liked to go for drives in the country on warm weekends. It seemed to Caroline that he chose the bumpiest, most untended roads and drove them as rashly as possible. Then when they stopped to picnic and he lay back to bask in the sharp April sunlight, she would always need to go and look for a bathroom, or even a clump of trees. At first this amused him, but soon his amusement became sardonic. He pulled in wearily at gas stations where he didn't need gas and waited in the car with folded arms and a sullen expression that made her apologetic about her ludicrous needs. They were growing apart. She could feel the distance between them like a patch of fog, dimming and distorting the relations of objects in space. The baby that lay between them in the dark was pushing them apart.

Sometimes as she lay awake in bed at night, not wanting to read in the cold living room but reluctant to turn on the light (and it was only a small light, she thought bitterly, a small bedside light), Caroline brooded over the horrible deformities the baby might be born with. She was thirty-one years old, not the best age to bear a first child. It could have cerebral palsy, cleft palate, two heads, club foot. She wondered if she could love a baby with a gross defect. She wondered if Ivan would want to put it in an institution, and if there were any decent institutions in their area, and if they would be spending every Sunday afternoon for the rest of their lives visiting the baby and driving home heartbroken in silence. She lived through these visits to the institution in vivid detail till she knew the doctors' and nurses' faces well. And there would come a point when Ivan would refuse to go any more—she knew what he was like, selfish with his time and impatient with futility—and she would have to go alone. She wondered if Ivan ever thought about these things, but with that cold mood of his she was afraid to ask.

One night she was desolate. She couldn't bear the loneliness and the heaviness any more, so she woke him.

"Ivan, please. Talk to me. I'm so lonely."

He sat up abruptly. "What?" He was still asleep. With the dark straight hair hanging down over his lean face he looked boyish and vulnerable. Without knowing why, she felt sorry for him.

"I'm sorry. I know you were sleeping but I—" Here she began to weep. "I just lie here forever in the dark and think awful things and you're so far away, and I just—"

"Oh, Caroline. Oh, God." Now he was wide awake, and took her in his arms.

"You're so far away," she wept. "I don't know what's the matter with you."

"I'm sorry. I know it's hard for you. You're so—everything's so different, that's all."

"But it's still me."

"I know. I know it's stupid of me. I can't—"

She knew what it was. It would never be the same. They sat up all night holding each other, and they talked. Ivan talked more than he had in weeks. He said of course the baby would be perfectly all right, and it would be born at just the right time, too, late June, so she could finish up the term, and they would start their natural childbirth group in two weeks so he could be with her and help her, though of course she would do it easily because she was so competent at everything, and then they would have the summer for the early difficult months, and she would be feeling fine and be ready to go back to work in the fall, and they would find a good person, someone like a grandmother, to come in, and he would try to stagger his schedule so she would not feel overburdened and trapped, and in short everything would be just fine, and they would make love again like they used to and be close again. He said exactly what she needed to hear, while she huddled against him, wrenched with pain to realize that he had known all along the right words to say but hadn't thought to say them till she woke him in desperation. Still, in the dawn she slept contented. She loved him. Every now and then she perceived this like a fact of life, an ancient tropism.

Two weeks later they had one of their horrible quarrels. It happened at a gallery, at the opening of a show by a group of young local artists Ivan had discovered. He had encouraged them to apply to his foundation for money and smoothed the way to their success. Now at their triumphant hour he was to be publicly thanked at a formal dinner. There were too many paintings to look at, too many people to greet, and too many glasses of champagne thrust at Caroline, who was near the end of her eighth month now. She walked around for an hour, then whispered to Ivan, "Listen, I'm sorry but I've got to go. Give me the car keys, will you? I don't feel well."

"What's the matter?"

"I can't stop having to go to the bathroom and my feet are killing me and my head aches, and the kid is rolling around like a basketball. You stay and enjoy it. You can get a ride with someone. I'll see you later."

"I'll drive you home," he said grimly. "We'll leave."

An awful knot gripped her stomach. The knot was the image of his perverse resistance, the immense trouble coming, all the trouble congealed and solidified and tied up in one moment. Meanwhile they smiled at the passers-by as they whispered ferociously to each other.

"Ivan, I do not want you to take me home. This is your event. Stay. I am leaving. We are separate people."

"If you're as sick as you say you can't drive home alone. You're my wife and I'll take you home."

"Suit yourself," she said sweetly, because the director of the gallery was approaching. "We all know you're much bigger and stronger than I am." And she smiled maliciously.

Ivan waved vaguely at the director, turned and ushered her to the door. Outside he exploded.

"Shit, Caroline! We can't do a fucking thing anymore, can we?"

"You can do anything you like. Just give me the keys. I left mine home."

"I will not give you the keys. Get in the car. You're supposed to be sick."

"You big resentful selfish idiot. Jealous of an embryo." She was screaming now. He started the car with a rush that jolted her forward against the dashboard. "I'd be better off driving myself. You'll kill me this way."

"Shut up," he shouted. "I don't want to hear any more."

"I don't care what you want to hear or not hear."

"Shut the hell up or I swear I'll go into a tree. I don't give a shit anymore."

It was starting to rain, a soft silent rain that glittered in the drab dusk outside. At exactly the same moment they rolled up their windows. They were sealed in together, Caroline thought, like restless beasts in a cage. The air in the car was dank and stuffy.

When they got home he slammed the door so hard the house shook. Caroline had calmed herself. She sank down in a chair, kicked off her shoes and rubbed her ankles. "Ivan, why don't you go back? It's not too late. These dinners are always late anyway. I'll be O.K."

"I don't want to go anymore," he yelled. "The whole thing is spoiled. Our whole lives are spoiled from now on. We were better off before. I thought you had gotten over wanting it. I thought it was a dead issue." He stared at her bulging stomach with such loathing that she was shocked into horrid, lucid perception.

"You disgust me," she said quietly. "Frankly, you always have and probably always will." She didn't know why she said that. It was quite untrue. It was only true that he disgusted her at this moment, yet the rest had rolled out like string from a hidden ball of twine.

"So why did we ever start this in the first place?" he screamed.

She didn't know whether he meant the marriage or the baby, and for an instant she was afraid he might hit her, there was such compressed force in his huge shoulders.

"Get the hell out of here. I don't want to have to look at you."

"I will. I'll go back. I'll take your advice. Call your fucking obstetrician if you need anything. I'm sure he's always glad of an extra feel."

"You ignorant pig. Go on. And don't hurry back. Find yourself a skinny little art student and give her a big treat."

"I just might." He slammed the door and the house shook again.

He would be back. This was not the first time. Only now she felt no secret excitement, no tremor, no passion that could reshape into lust; she was too heavy and burdened. It would not be easy to make it up—she was in no condition. It would lie between them silently like a dead weight till weeks after the baby was born, till Ivan felt he could reclaim his rightful territory. She knew him too well. Caroline took two aspirins. When she woke at three he was in bed beside her, gripping the blanket in his sleep and breathing heavily. For days afterwards they spoke with strained, subdued courtesy.

They worked diligently in the natural childbirth classes once a week, while at home they giggled over how silly the exercises were, yet Ivan insisted she pant her five minutes each day as instructed. As relaxation training, Ivan was supposed to lift each of her legs and arms three times and drop them, while she remained perfectly limp and passive. From the very start Caroline was excellent at this routine, which they did in bed before going to sleep. A substitute, she thought, yawning. She could make her body so limp and passive her arms and legs bounced on the mattress when they fell. One night for diversion she tried doing it to Ivan, but he couldn't master the technique of passivity.

"Don't do anything, Ivan. I lift the leg and I drop the leg. You do nothing. Do you see? Nothing at all," she smiled.

But that was not possible for him. He tried to be limp but kept working along with her; she could see his muscles, precisely those leg muscles she found so desirable, exerting to lift and drop, lift and drop.

"You can't give yourself up. Don't you feel what you're doing? You have to let me do it to you. Let me try just your hand, from the wrist. That might be easier."

"No, forget it. Give me back my hand." He smiled and stroked her stomach gently. "What's the difference? I don't have to do it well. You do it very well."

She did it very well indeed when the time came. It was a short labor, less than an hour, very unusual for a first baby, the nurses kept muttering. She breathed intently, beginning with the long slow breaths she had been taught, feeling quite remote from the bustle around her. Then, in a flurry, they raced her down the hall on a wheeled table with a train of white-coated people trotting after, and she thought, panting, No matter what I suffer, soon I will be thin again, I will be more beautiful than ever.

The room was crowded with people, far more people than she would have thought necessary, but the only faces she singled out were Ivan's and the doctor's. The doctor, with a new russet beard and his face a good deal thinner now, was once again framed by her knees, paler than before. Wildly enthusiastic about the proceedings, he yelled, "Terrific, Caroline, terrific," as though they were in a noisy public place. "O.K., start pushing."

They placed her hands on chrome rails along the table. On the left, groping, she found Ivan's hand and held it instead of the rail. She pushed. In surprise she became aware of a great cleavage, like a mountain of granite splitting apart, only it was in her, she realized, and if it kept on going it would go right up to her neck. She gripped Ivan's warm hand, and just as she opened her mouth to roar someone clapped an oxygen mask on her face so the roar reverberated inward on her own ears. She wasn't supposed to roar, the natural childbirth teacher hadn't mentioned anything about that, she was supposed to breathe and push. But as long as no one seemed to take any notice she might as well keep on roaring, it felt so satisfying and necessary. The teacher would never know. She trusted that if she split all the way up to her neck they would sew her up somehow—she was too far gone to worry about that now. Maybe that was why there were so many of them, yes, of course, to put her back together, and maybe they had simply forgotten to tell her about being bisected; or maybe it was a closely guarded secret, like an initiation rite. She gripped Ivan's hand tighter. She was not having too bad a time, she would surely survive, she told herself, captivated by the hellish bestial sounds going from her mouth to her ear; it certainly was what her students would call a peak experience, and how gratifying to hear the doctor exclaim, "Oh, this is one terrific girl! One more, Caroline, give me one more push and send it out. Sock it to me."

She always tried to be obliging, if possible. Now she raised herself on her elbows and, staring straight at him—he too, after all, had been most obliging these long months—gave him with tremendous force the final push he asked for. She had Ivan's hand tightly around the rail, could feel his knuckles bursting, and then all of a sudden the room and the faces were obliterated. A dark thick curtain swiftly wrapped around her and she was left all alone gasping, sucked violently into a windy black hole of pain so explosive she knew it must be death, she was dying fast, like a bomb detonating. It was all right, it was almost over, only she would have liked to see his blue eyes one last time.

From somewhere in the void Ivan's voice shouted in exultation, "It's coming out," and the roaring stopped and at last there was peace and quiet in her ears. The curtain fell away, the world returned. But her eyes kept on burning, as if they had seen something not meant for living eyes to see and return from alive.

"Give it to me," Caroline said, and held it. She saw that every part was in the proper place, then shut her eyes.

They wheeled her to a room and eased her onto the bed. It was past ten in the morning. She could dimly remember they had been up all night watching a James Cagney movie about prize-fighting while they timed her irregular mild contractions. James Cagney went blind from blows given by poisoned gloves in a rigged match, and she wept for him as she held her hands on her stomach and breathed. Neither she nor Ivan had slept or eaten for hours.

"Ivan, there is something I am really dying to have right now."

"Your wish is my command."

She asked for a roast beef on rye with ketchup, and iced tea. "Would you mind? It'll be hours before they serve lunch."

He brought it and stood at the window while she ate ravenously.

"Didn't you get anything for yourself?"

"No, I'm too exhausted to eat." He did, in fact, look terrible. He was sallow; his eyes, usually so radiant, were nearly drained of color, and small downward-curving lines around his mouth recalled his laborious vigil.

"You had a rough night, Ivan. You ought to get some sleep. What's it like outside?"

"What?" Ivan's movements seemed to her extremely purposeless. He was pacing the room with his hands deep in his pockets, going slowly from the foot of the bed to the window and back. Her eyes followed him from the pillow. Every now and then he would stop to peer at Caroline in an unfamiliar way, as if she were a puzzling stranger.

"Ivan, are you O.K.? I meant the weather. What's it doing outside?" It struck her, as she asked, that it was weeks since she had cared to know anything about the outside. That there was an outside, now that she was emptied out, came rushing at her with the most urgent importance, wafting her on a tide of grateful joy.

"Oh," he said vaguely, and came to sit on the edge of her bed. "Well, it's doing something very peculiar outside, as a matter of fact. It's raining but the sun is shining."

She laughed at him. "But haven't you ever seen it do that before?"

"I don't know. I guess so." He opened his mouth and closed it several times. She ate, waiting patiently. Finally he spoke. "You know, Caroline, you really have quite a grip. When you were holding my hand in there, you squeezed it so tight I thought you would break it."

"Oh, come on, that can't be."

"I'm not joking." He massaged his hand absently. Ivan never complained of pain; if anything he understated. But now he held out his right hand and showed her the raw red knuckles and palm, with raised flaming welts forming.

She took his hand. "You're serious. Did I do that? Well, how do you like that?"

"I really thought you'd break my hand. It was killing me." He kept repeating it, not resentfully but dully, as though there were something secreted in the words that he couldn't fathom.

"But why didn't you take it away if it hurt that badly?" She put down her half-eaten sandwich as she saw the pale amazement ripple over his face.

"Oh, no, I couldn't do that. I mean—if that was what you needed just then—" He looked away, embarrassed. "Listen," he shrugged, not facing her, "we're in a hospital, after all. What better place? They'd fix it for me."

Overwhelmed, Caroline lay back on the pillows. "Oh, Ivan. You would do that?"

"What are you crying for?" he asked gently. "You didn't break it, did you? Almost doesn't count. So what are you crying about. You just had a baby. Don't cry."

And she smiled and thought her heart would burst.

The Girl Who Loved Horses

ELIZABETH SPENCER

I

She had drawn back from throwing a pan of bird scraps out the door because she heard what was coming, the two-part pounding of a full gallop, not the graceful triple notes of a canter. They were mounting the drive now, turning into the stretch along the side of the house; once before, someone appearing at the screen door had made the horse shy, so that, barely held beneath the rider, barely restrained, he had plunged off into the flower beds. So she stepped back from the door and saw the two of them shoot past, rounding a final corner, heading for the straight run of drive into the cattle gate and the barn lot back of it.

She flung out the scraps, then walked to the other side of the kitchen and peered through the window, raised for spring, toward the barn lot. The horse had slowed, out of habit, knowing what came next. And the white shirt that had passed hugged so low as to seem some strange part of the animal's trappings, or as though he had run under a low line of drying laundry and caught something to an otherwise empty saddle and bare withers, now rose up, angling to an upright posture. A gloved hand extended to pat the lathered neck.

"Lord have mercy," the woman said. The young woman riding the horse was her daughter, but she was speaking also for her son-in-law who went in for even more reckless behavior in the jumping ring the two of them had set up. What she meant by it was that they were going to kill themselves before they ever had any children, or if they did have children safely they'd bring up the children to be just as foolish about horses and careless of life and limb as they were themselves.

The young woman's booted heel struck the back steps. The screen door banged.

"You ought not to bring him in hot like that," the mother said. "I do know that much."

"Cottrell is out there," she said.

"It's still March, even if it has got warm."

"Cottrell knows what to do."

She ran water at the sink, and cupping her hand drank primitive fashion out of it, bending to the tap, then wet her hands in the running water and thrust her fingers into the dusty, sweat-damp roots of her sand-colored hair. It had been a good ride.

"I hope he doesn't take up too much time," the mother said. "My beds need working."

She spoke mildly but it was always part of the same quarrel they were in like a stream that was now a trickle, now a still pool, but sometimes after a freshet could turn into a torrent. Such as: "Y'all are just crazy. Y'all are wasting everything on those things. And what are they? I know they're pretty and all that, but they're not a thing in the world but animals. Cows are animals. You can make a lot more money in cattle, than carting those things around over two states and three counties."

She could work herself up too much to eat, leaving the two of them at the table, but would see them just the same in her mind's eye, just as if she'd stayed. There were the sandy-haired young woman, already thirty—married four years and still apparently with no intention of producing a family (she was an only child and the estate, though small, was a fine piece of land)—and across from her the dark spare still young man she had married.

She knew how they would sit there alone and not even look at one another or discuss what she'd said or talk against her; they would just sit there and maybe pass each other some food or one of them would get up for the coffee-pot. The fanatics of a strange cult would do the same, she often thought, loosening her long hair upstairs, brushing the gray and brown together to a colorless patina, putting on one of her long cotton gowns with the ruched neck, crawling in between white cotton sheets. She was a widow and if she didn't want to sit up and try to talk to the family after a hard day, she didn't have to. Reading was a joy, lifelong. She found her place in *Middlemarch*, one of her favorites.

But during the day not even reading (if she'd had the time) could shut out the sounds from back of the privet hedge, plainly to be heard from the house. The trudging of the trot, the pause, the low directive, the thud of hooves, the heave and shout, and sometimes the ring of struck wood as a bar came down. And every jump a risk of life and limb. One dislocated shoulder—Clyde's, thank heaven, not Deedee's—a taping, a sling, a contraption of boards, and pain "like a hot knife," he had said. A hot knife. Wouldn't that hurt anybody enough to make him quit risking life and limb with those two blood horses, quit at least talking about getting still another one while swallowing down painkiller he said he hated to be sissy enough to take?

"Uh-huh," the mother said. "But it'll be Deborah next. You thought about that?"

"Aw, now, Miss Emma," he'd lean back to say, charming her through his warrior's haze of pain. "Deedee and me—that's what we're hooked on. Think of us without it, Mama. You really want to kill us. We couldn't live." He was speaking to his mother-in-law but smiling at his wife. And she, Deborah, was smiling back.

Her name was Deborah Dale, but they'd always, of course, being from LaGrange, Tennessee, right over the Mississippi border, that is to say, real South, had had a hundred nicknames for her. Deedee, her father had named her, and "Deeds" her funny cousins said—"Hey, Deeds, how ya' doin'?" Being on this property in a town of pretty properties, though theirs was a little way out, a little bit larger than most, she was always out romping, swimming in forbidden creeks, climbing forbidden fences, going barefoot too soon in the spring, the last one in at recess, the first one to turn in an exam paper. ("Are you quite sure that you have finished, Deborah?" "Yes, ma'am.")

When she graduated from ponies to that sturdy calico her uncle gave her, bringing it in from his farm because he had an eye for a good match, there was almost no finding her. "I always know she's somewhere on the place," her mother said. "We just can't see it all at once," said her father. He was ailing even back then but he undertook walks. Once when the leaves had all but gone from the trees, on a warm November afternoon, from a slight rise, he saw her down in a little-used pasture with a straight open stretch among some oaks. The ground was spongy and clotted with damp and a child ought not to have tried to run there, on foot. But there went the calico with Deedee clinging low, going like the wind, and knowing furthermore out of what couldn't be anything but long practice, where to turn, where to veer, where to. stop.

"One fine afternoon," he said to himself, suspecting even then (they hadn't told him yet) what his illness was, "and Emma's going to be left with nobody." He remarked on this privately, not without anguish and not without humor.

They stopped her riding, at least like that, by sending her off to a boarding school, where a watchful ringmaster took "those girls interested in equitation" out on leafy trails, "at the walk, at the trot, and at the canter." They also, with that depth of consideration which must flourish even among those Southerners unlucky enough to wind up in the lower reaches of hell, kept her young spirit out of the worst of the dying. She just got a call from the housemother one night. Her father had "passed away."

After college she forgot it, she gave it up. It was too expensive, it took a lot of time and devotion, she was interested in boys. Some boys were interested in her. She worked in Memphis, drove home to her mother every night. In winter she had to eat breakfast in the dark. On some evenings the phone rang; on some it was silent. Her mother treated both kinds of evenings just the same.

To Emma Tyler it always seemed that Clyde Mecklin materialized out of nowhere. She ran straight into him when opening the front door one evening to get the paper off the porch, he being just about to turn the bell or knock. There he stood, dark and straight in the late light that comes after first dark and is so clear. He was clear as anything in it, clear as the first stamp of a young man ever cast.

"Is Deb'rah here?" At least no Yankee. But not Miss Tyler or Miss Deborah Tyler, or Miss Deborah. No, he was city all right.

She did not answer at first.

"What's the matter, scare you? I was just about to knock."

She still said nothing.

"Maybe this is the wrong place," he said.

"No, it's the right place," Emma Tyler finally said. She stepped back and held the door wider. "Come on in."

"Scared the life out of me," she told Deborah when she finally came down to breakfast the next day, Clyde's car having been heard to depart by Emma Tyler in her upstairs bedroom at an hour she did not care to verify. "Why didn't you tell me you were expecting him? I just opened the door and there he was."

"I liked him so much," said Deborah with grave honesty. "I guess I was scared he wouldn't come. That would have hurt."

"Do you still like him?" her mother ventured, after this confidence.

"He's all for outdoors," said Deborah, as dreamy over coffee as any mother had ever beheld. "Everybody is so indoors, He likes hunting, going fishing, farms."

"Has he got one?"

"He'd like to have. All he's got's this job. He's coming back next weekend. You can talk to him. He's interested in horses."

"But does he know we don't keep horses anymore?"

"That was just my thumbnail sketch," said Deborah. "We don't have to run out and buy any."

"No, I don't imagine so," said her mother, but Deborah hardly remarked the peculiar turn of tone, the dryness. She was letting coast through her head the scene: her mother (whom she now loved better than she ever had in her life) opening the door just before Clyde knocked, so seeing unexpectedly for the first time, that face, that head, that being. . . . When he had kissed her

her ears drummed, and it came back to her once more, not thought of in years, the drumming hooves of the calico, and the ghosting father, behind, invisible, observant, off on the bare distant November rise.

It was after she married that Deborah got beautiful. All LaGrange noticed it. "I declare," they said to her mother or sometimes right out to her face, "I always said she was nice looking but I never thought anything like that."

II

Emma first saw the boy in the parking lot. He was new.

In former days she'd parked in front of nearly any place she wanted to go—hardware, or drugstore, or courthouse: change for the meter was her biggest problem. But so many streets were one-way now and what with the increased numbers of cars, the growth of the town, those days were gone; she used a parking lot back of a cafe, near the newspaper office. The entrance to the lot was a bottleneck of a narrow drive between the two brick buildings; once in, it was hard sometimes to park.

That day the boy offered to help. He was an expert driver, she noted, whereas Emma was inclined to perspire, crane and fret, fearful of scraping a fender or grazing a door. He spun the wheel with one hand; a glance told him all he had to know; he as good as sat the car in place, as skillful (she reluctantly thought) as her children on their horses. When she returned an hour later, the cars were denser still; he helped her again. She wondered whether to tip him. This happened twice more.

"You've been so nice to me," she said, the last time. "They're lucky to have you."

"It's not much of a job," he said. "Just all I can get for the moment. Being new and all."

"I might need some help," she said. "You can call up at the Tyler place if you want work. It's in the book. Right now I'm in a hurry."

On the warm June day, Deborah sat the horse comfortably in the side yard and watched her mother and the young man (whose name was Willett? Williams?), who, having worked the beds and straightened a fence post, was now replacing warped fence boards with new ones.

"Who is he?" she asked her mother, not quite low enough, and meaning what a Southern woman invariably means by that question, not what is his name but where did he come from, is he anybody we know? What excuse, in other words, does he have for even being born?

"One thing, he's a good worker," her mother said, preening a little. Did they think she couldn't manage if she had to? "Now don't you make him feel bad."

"Feel bad!" But once again, if only to spite her mother, who was in a way criticizing her and Clyde by hiring anybody at all to do work that Clyde or the Negro help would have been able to do if only it weren't for those horses—once again Deborah had spoken too loudly.

If she ever had freely to admit things, even to herself, Deborah would have to say she knew she not only looked good that June day, she looked sexy as hell. Her light hair, tousled from a ride in the fields, had grown longer in the last year; it had slipped its pins on one side and lay in a sensuous lock along her cheek. A breeze stirred it, then passed by. Her soft poplin shirt was loose at the throat, the two top buttons open, the cuffs turned back to her elbows. The new horse, the third, was gentle, too much so (this worred them); she sat it easily, one leg up, crossed lazily over the flat English pommel, while the horse, head stretched down, cropped at the tender grass. In the silence between their voices, the tearing of the grass was the only sound except for a shrill jay's cry.

"Make him feel bad!" she repeated.

The boy looked up. The horse, seeking grass, had moved forward; she was closer than before, eyes looking down on him above the rise of her breasts and throat; she saw the closeness go through him, saw her presence register as strongly as if the earth's accidental shifting had slammed them physically together. For a minute there was nothing but the two of them. The jay was silent; even the horse, sensing something, had raised his head.

Stepping back, the boy stumbled over the pile of lumber, then fell in it. Deborah laughed. Nothing, that day, could have stopped her laughter. She was beautifully, languidly, atop a fine horse on the year's choice day at the peak of her life.

"You know what?" Deborah said at supper, when they were discussing her mother's helper. "I thought who he looks like. He looks like Clyde."

"The poor guy," Clyde said. "Was that the best you could do?"

Emma sat still. Now that she thought of it, he did look like Clyde. She stopped eating, to think it over. What difference did it make if he did? She returned to her plate.

Deborah ate lustily, her table manners unrestrained. She swabbed bread into the empty salad bowl, drenched it with dressing, bit it in hunks.

"The poor woman's Clyde, that's what you hired," she said. She looked up.

The screen door had just softly closed in the kitchen behind them. Emma's hired man had come in for his money.

It was the next day that the boy, whose name was Willet or Williams, broke the riding mower by running it full speed into a rock pile overgrown with weeds but clearly visible, and left without asking for pay but evidently taking with him in his car a number of selected items from barn, garage, and tack room, along with a transistor radio that Clyde kept in the kitchen for getting news with his early coffee.

Emma Tyler, vexed for a number of reasons she did not care to sort out (prime among them was the very peaceful and good time she had been having with the boy the day before in the yard when Deborah had chosen to ride over and join them), telephoned the police and reported the whole matter. But boy, car, and stolen articles vanished into the nowhere. That was all, for what they took to be forever.

III

Three years later, aged 33, Deborah Mecklin was carrying her fine head higher than ever uptown in LaGrange. She drove herself on errands back and forth in car or station wagon, not looking to left or right, not speaking so much as before. She was trying not to hear from the outside what they were now saying about Clyde, how well he'd done with the horses, that place was as good as a stud farm now that he kept ten or a dozen, advertised and traded, as well as showed. And the money was coming in hard and fast. But, they would add, he moved with a fast set, and there was also the occasional gossip item, too often, in Clyde's case, with someone ready to report first hand; look how quick, now you thought of it, he'd taken up with Deborah, and how she'd snapped him up too soon to hear what his reputation was, even back then. It would be a cold day in August before any one woman would be enough for him. And his father before him? And his father before him. So the voices said.

Deborah, too, was trying not to hear what was still sounding from inside her head after her fall in the last big horse show:

The doctor: You barely escaped concussion, young lady.

Clyde: I just never saw your timing go off like that. I can't get over it.

Emma: You'd better let it go for a while, honey. There're other things, so many other things.

Back home, she later said to Emma: "Oh, Mama, I know you're right sometimes, and sometimes I'm sick of it all, but Clyde depends on me, he always has, and now look—"

"Yes, and 'Now look' is right, he has to be out with it to keep it all running. You got your wish, is all I can say."

Emma was frequently over at her sister-in-law Marian's farm these days. The ladies were aging, Marian especially down in the back, and those twilights in the house alone were more and more all that Deedee had to keep herself company with. Sometimes the phone rang and there'd be Clyde on it, to say he'd be late again. Or there'd be no call at all. And once she (of all people) pressed some curtains and hung them, and once hunted for old photographs, and once, standing in the middle of the little-used parlor among the walnut Victorian furniture upholstered in gold and blue and rose, she had said "Daddy?" right out loud, like he might have been there to answer, really been there. It had surprised her, the word falling out like that as though a thought took reality all by itself and made a word on its own.

And once there came a knock at the door.

All she thought, though she hadn't heard the car, was that it was Clyde and that he'd forgotten his key, or seeing her there, his arms loaded maybe, was asking her to let him in. It was past dark. Though times were a little more chancy now, LaGrange was a safe place. People nearer to town used to brag that if they went off for any length of time less than a weekend and locked the doors, the neighbors would get their feelings hurt; and if the Tylers lived further out and "locked up," the feeling for it was ritual mainly, a precaution.

She glanced through the sidelight, saw what she took for Clyde and opened the door. There were cedars in the front yard, not too near the house, but dense enough to block out whatever gathering of light there might have been from the long slope of property beyond the front gate. There was no moon.

The man she took for Clyde, instead of stepping through the door or up to the threshold to greet her, withdrew a step and leaned down and to one side, turning outward as though to pick up something. It was she who stepped forward, to greet, help, inquire; for deep within was the idea her mother had seen to it was firmly and forever planted: that one day one of them was going to get too badly hurt by "those things" ever to be patched up.

So it was in outer dark, three paces from the safe threshold and to the left of the area where the light was falling outward, a dim single sidelight near the mantelpiece having been all she had switched on, too faint to penetrate the sheer gathered curtains of the sidelight, that the man at the door rose up, that he tried to take her. The first she knew of it, his face was was in hers, not Clyde's but something like it and at Clyde's exact height, so that for the moment she thought that some joke was on, and then the strange hand caught the parting of her blouse, a new mouth fell hard on her own, one knee thrust her legs apart, the free hand diving in to clutch and press against the thin nylon between her thighs. She recoiled at the same time that she felt, touched in the quick, the painful glory of desire brought on too fast—looking back on that instant's two-edged meaning, she would never hear about rape without the lightning quiver of ambivalence within the word. However, at the time no meditation stopped her knee from coming up into the nameless groin and nothing stopped her from tearing back her mouth slathered with spit so suddenly smeared into it as to drag it into the shape of a scream she was unable yet to find a voice for. Her good right arm struck like a hard backhand against a line-smoking tennis serve. Then from the driveway came the stream of twin headlights thrusting through the cedars.

"Bitch!" The word, distorted and low, was like a groan; she had hurt him, freed herself for a moment, but the struggle would have just begun except for the lights, and the screams that were just trying to get out of her. "You fucking bitch." He saw the car lights, wavered, then turned. His leap into the shrubbery was bent, like a hunchback's. She stopped screaming suddenly. Hurt where he lived, she thought. The animal motion, wounded, drew her curiosity for a second. Saved, she saw the car sweep round the drive, but watched the bushes shake, put up her hand to touch but not to close the torn halves of the blouse, which was ripped open to her waist.

Inside, she stood looking down at herself in the dim light. There was a nail scratch near the left nipple, two teeth marks between elbow and wrist where she'd smashed into his mouth. She wiped her own mouth on the back of her hand, gagging at the taste of cigarette smoke, bitterly staled. Animals! She'd always had a special feeling for them, a helpless tenderness. In her memory the bushes, shaking to a crippled fight, shook forever.

She went upstairs, stood trembling in her mother's room (Emma was away), combed her hair with her mother's comb. Then, hearing Clyde's voice calling her below, she stripped off her ravaged blouse and hastened across to their own rooms to hide it in a drawer, change into a fresh one, come downstairs. She had made her decision already. Who was this man? A nothing . . . an unknown. She hated women who shouted Rape! Rape! It was an incident, but once she told it everyone would know, along with the police, and would add to it: they'd say she'd been violated. It was an incident, but Clyde, once he knew, would trace him down. Clyde would kill him.

"Did you know the door was wide open?" He was standing in the livingroom.

"I know. I must have opened it when I heard the car. I thought you were stopping in the front."

"Well, I hardly ever do."

"Sometimes you do."

"Deedee, have you been drinking?"

"Drinking . . . ? Me?" She squinted at him, joking in her own way; it was a standing quarrel now that alone she sometimes poured one or two.

He would check her breath but not her marked body. Lust with him was mole-dark now, not desire in the soft increase of morning light, or on slowly westering afternoons or by the nightlight's glow. He would kill for her because she was his wife. . . .

"Who was that man?"

Uptown one winter afternoon late, she had seen him again. He had been coming out of the hamburger place and looking back, seeing her through the streetlights, he had turned quickly into an alley. She had hurried to catch up, to see. But only a form was hastening there, deeper into the unlit slit between brick walls, down toward a street and a section nobody went into without good reason.

"That man," she repeated to the owner (also the proprietor and cook) in the hamburger place. "He was in here just now."

"I don't know him. He hangs around. Wondered myself. You know him?"

"I think he used to work for us once, two or three years ago. I just wondered."

"I thought I seen him somewhere myself."

"He looks a little bit like Clyde."

"Maybe so. Now you mention it." He wiped the counter with a wet rag. "Get you anything, Miss Deb'rah?"

"I've got to get home."

"Y'all got yourselves some prizes, huh?"

"Aw, just some good luck." She was gone.

Prizes, yes. Two trophies at the Shelby County Fair, one in Brownsville where she'd almost lost control again, and Clyde not worrying about her so much as scolding her. His recent theory was that she was out to spite him. He would think it if he was guilty about the women, and she didn't doubt any more that he was. But worse than spite was what had got to her, hating as she did to admit it.

It was fear.

She'd never know it before. When it first started she hadn't even known what the name of it was.

Over two years ago, Clyde had started buying colts not broken yet from a stud farm south of Nashville, bringing them home for him and Deborah to get in shape together. It saved a pile of money to do it that way. She'd been thrown in consequence three times, trampled once, a terrifying moment as the double reins had caught up her outstretched arm so she couldn't fall free. Now when she closed her eyes at night, steel hooves sometimes hung through the dark above them, and she felt hard ground beneath her head, smelt smeared grass on cheek and elbow. To Clyde she murmured in the dark: "I'm not good at it any more." "Why, Deeds, you were always good. It's temporary, honey. That was a bad luck day."

A great couple. That's what Clyde thought of them. But more than half their name had been made by her, by the sight of her, Deborah Mecklin, out in full dress, black broadcloth and white satin stock with hair drawn trimly back beneath the smooth rise of the hat, entering the show ring. She looked damned good back of the glossy neck's steep arch, the pointed ears and lacquered hooves which hardly touched earth before springing upward, as though in the instant before actual flight. There was always the stillness, then the murmur, the rustle of the crowd. At top form she could even get applause. A fame for a time spread round them. The Mecklins. Great riders. "Ridgewood Stable. Blood horses trained. Saddle and Show." He'd had it put up in wrought iron, with a sign as well, Old English style, of a horseman spurring.

("Well, you got to make money," said Miss Emma to her son-in-law. "And don't I know it," she said. "But I just hate to think how many times I kept those historical people from putting up a marker on this place. And now all I do is worry one of y'all's going to break your neck. If it wasn't for Marian needing me and all . . . I just can't sleep a wink over here."

("You like to be over there anyway, Mama," Deborah said. "You know we want you here."

("Sure, we want you here," said Clyde. "As for the property, we talked it all out beforehand. I don't think I've damaged it any way."

("I just never saw it as a horse farm. But it's you all I worry about. It's the danger.")

Deborah drove home.

When the workingman her mother had hired three years before had stolen things and left, he had left too on the garage wall inside, a long pair of crossing diagonal lines, brown, in mud, she thought, until she smelled what it was, and there were the blood-stained menstrual pads she later came across in the driveway, dug up out of the garbage, strewed out into the yard.

She told Clyde about the first but not the second discovery. "Some critters are mean," he'd shrugged it off. "Some critters are just mean."

They'd been dancing, out at the club. And so in love back then, he'd turned and turned her, far apart, then close, talking into her ear, making her laugh and answer, but finally he said: "Are you a mean critter, Deedee? Some critters are mean." And she'd remembered what she didn't tell.

But in those days Clyde was passionate and fun, both marvellously together, and the devil appearing at midnight in the bend of a country road would not have scared her. Nothing would have. It was the day of her life when they bought the first two horses.

"I thought I seen him somewhere myself."

"He looks a little bit like Clyde."

And dusk again, a third and final time.

The parking lot where she'd come after a movie was empty except for a few cars. The small office was unlighted, but a man she took for the attendant was bending to the door on the far side of a long cream-colored sedan near the back fence. "Want my ticket?" she called. The man straightened, head rising above the body frame, and she knew him. Had he been about to steal a car, or was he breaking in for whatever he could find, or was it her coming all alone that he was waiting for? However it was, he knew her as instantly as she knew him. Each other was what they had, by whatever design or absence of it, found. Deborah did not cry out or stir.

Who knew how many lines life had cut away from him down through the years till the moment when an arrogant woman on a horse had ridden him down with lust and laughter? He wasn't bad-looking; his eyes were beautiful; he was the kind to whom nothing good could happen. From that bright day to this chilly dusk, it had probably just been the same old story.

Deborah waited. Someway or other, what was coming, threading through the cars like an animal lost for years catching the scent of a former owner, was her own.

("You're losing nerve, Deedee," Clyde had told her recently. "That's what's really bothering me. You're scared, aren't you?")

The bitter-stale smell of cigarette breath, though not so near as before, not forced against her mouth, was still unmistakably familiar. But the prod of a gun's muzzle just under the rise of her breast was not. It had never happened to her before. She shuddered at the touch with a chill spring-like start of something like life, which was also something like death.

"Get inside," he said.

"Are you the same one?" she asked. "Just tell me that. Three years ago, Mama hired somebody. Was that you?"

"Get in the car."

She opened the door, slid over to the driver's seat, found him beside her. The gun, thrust under his crossed arm, resumed its place against her.

"Drive."

"Was it you the other night at the door?" Her voice trembled as the motor started, the gear caught.

"He left me with the lot; ain't nobody coming."

The car eased into an empty street.

"Go out of town. The Memphis road."

She was driving past familiar, cared-for lawns and houses, trees and intersections. Someone waved from a car at a stoplight, taking them for her and Clyde. She was frightened and accepting fear which come to think of it was all she'd been doing for months, working with those horses. ("Don't let him bluff you, Deedee. It's you or him. He'll do it if he can.")

"What do you want with me? What is it you want?"

He spoke straight outward, only his mouth moving, watching the road, never turning his head to her. "You're going out on that Memphis road and you're going up a side road with me. There's some woods I know. When I'm through with you you ain't never going to have nothing to ask nobody about me because you're going to know it all and it ain't going to make you laugh none, I guarantee."

Deborah cleared the town and swinging into the highway wondered at herself. Did she want him? She had waited when she might have run. Did she want, trembling, pleading, degraded, finally to let him have every single thing his own way?

(Do you see steel hooves above you over and over because you want them one day to smash into your brain?

("Daddy, Daddy," she had murmured long ago when the old unshaven tramp had come up into the lawn, bleary-eyed, face blood-burst with years of drink and weather, frightening as the boogeyman, "raw head and bloody bones," like the Negro women scared her with. That day the sky streamed with end-of-the-world fire. But she hadn't called so loudly as she might have, she'd let him come closer, to look at him better, until the threatening voice of her father behind her, just on the door's slamming, had cried: "What do you want in this yard? What you think you want here? Deborah! You come in this house this minute!" But the mystery still lay dark within her, forgotten for years, then stirring to life again: When I said "Daddy, Daddy?" was I calling to the tramp or to the house? Did I think the tramp was him in some sort of joke or dream or trick? If not, why did I say it? Why?

("Why do you ride a horse so fast, Deedee? Why do you like to do that?" *I'm going where the sky breaks open.* "I just like to." "Why do you like to drive so fast?" "I don't know.")

Suppose he kills me, too, thought Deborah, striking the straight stretch on the Memphis road, the beginning of the long rolling run through farms and woods. She stole a glance to her right. He looked like Clyde, all right. What right did he have to look like Clyde?

("It's you or him, Deedee." All her life they'd said that to her from the time her first pony, scared at something, didn't want to cross a bridge. "Don't let him get away with it. It's you or him.")

Righting the big car into the road ahead, she understood what was demanded of her. She pressed the accelerator gradually downward toward the floor.

"And by the time he realized it," she said, sitting straight in her chair at supper between Clyde and Emma, who by chance were there that night together; "—by the time he knew, we were hitting above seventy-five, and he said, 'What you speeding for?' and I said, 'I want to get it over with.' And he said, 'Okay, but that's too fast.' By that time we were touching eighty and he said, 'What the fucking hell—' excuse me, Mama, '—you think you're doing? You slow this thing down.' So I said, 'I tell you what I'm doing. This is a rolling road with high banks and trees and lots of curves. If you try to take the wheel away from me, I'm going to wreck us both. If you try to sit there with that gun in my side I'm going to go faster and faster and sooner or later something will happen, like a curve too sharp to take or a car too many to pass with a big truck coming and we're both going to get smashed up at the very least. It won't do any good to shoot me when it's more than likely both of us will die. You want that?'

"He grabbed at the wheel but I put on another burst of speed and when he pulled at the wheel we side-rolled, skidded back, and another car coming almost didn't get out of the way. I said, 'You see what you're doing, I guess.' And he said, 'Jesus God.' Then I knew I had him, had whipped him down.

"But it was another two or three miles like that before he said, 'Okay, okay, so I quit. Just slow down and let's forget it.' And I said, 'You give me that gun. The mood I'm in, I can drive with one hand or no hands at all, and don't think I won't do it.' But he wanted his gun at least, I could tell. He didn't give in till a truck was ahead and we passed but barely missed a car that was coming (it had to run off the concrete), and he put it down, in my lap."

(Like a dog, she could have said, but didn't. And I felt sorry for him, she could have added, because it was his glory's end.)

"So I said, 'Get over, way over,' and he did, and I coasted from fast to slow. I turned the gun around on him and let him out on an empty stretch of road, by a rise with a wood and a country side road rambling off, real pretty, and I thought, Maybe that's where he was talking about, where he meant to screw hell—excuse me, Mama—out of me. I held the gun till he closed the door and went down in the ditch a little way, then I put the safety catch on and threw it at him. It hit his shoulder, then fell in the weeds. I saw it fall, driving off."

"Oh, my poor baby," said Emma. "Oh, my precious child."

It was Clyde who rose, came round the table to her, drew her to her feet, held her close. "That's nerve," he said. "That's class." He let her go and she sat down again. "Why didn't you shoot him?"

"I don't know."

"He was the one we hired that time," Emma said. "I'd be willing to bet you anything."

"No, it wasn't," said Deborah quickly. "This one was blond and short, red-nosed from too much drinking, I guess. Awful like Mickey Rooney, gone and gotten old. Like the boogeyman, I guess."

"The poor woman's Mickey Rooney. You women find yourselves the damnedest men."

"She's not right about that," said Emma. "What do you want to tell that for? I know it was him. I feel like it was."

"Why'd you throw the gun away?" Clyde asked. "We could trace that."

"It's what I felt like doing," she said. She had seen it strike, how his shoulder, struck, went back a little.

Clyde Mecklin sat watching his wife. She had scarcely touched her food and now, pale, distracted, she had risen to wander toward the windows, look out at the empty lawn, the shrubs and flowers, the stretch of white-painted fence, ghostly by moonlight.

"It's the last horse I'll ever break," she said, more to herself than not, but Clyde heard and stood up and was coming to her.

"Now, Deedee—"

"When you know you know," she said, and turned, her face set against him: her anger, her victory, held up like a blade against his stubborn willfulness. "I want my children now," she said.

At the mention of children, Emma's presence with them became multiple and vague; it trembled with thanksgiving, it spiralled on wings of joy.

Deborah turned again, back to the window. Whenever she looked away, the eyes by the road were there below her: they were worthless, nothing, but infinite, never finishing—the surface there was no touching bottom for—taking to them, into themselves, the self that was hers no longer.

The Interpretation of Dreams by Sigmund Freud: A Story

DANIEL STERN

"ALWAYS A THREESOME," she said. "Two men and a woman. Except that one man, the one with previous rights in the matter, is always dead."

"I hate this nickel analysis," he said.

"I can't help it. When it gets neat is when it feels true. You don't have to *do* anything about it. It's just that it's like a murder mystery with a series of imaginary murders. If you marry two widows there are two dead men in the background."

This is how it went after his second wife was bitten on the finger by a squirrel. Dickstein had a feeling things would change, and not for the better. It was a three-month situation: meeting, wooing, marrying and up to New York for a new life. She was fourteen years younger than he and nothing besides falling in love and marriage had been decided; would she work at her music, at a job, have a baby, have two babies? In the meantime, it was a muggy August and against his wishes—though he hadn't examined them or actually expressed them—she had been marking time taking a course at the N.Y.U. Summer School: *Dream, Myth and Metaphor.*

The day had been warm and after class she'd lingered in a small rainbow of sunlight and offered one of the peanuts she was shucking and munching to a begging squirrel. She was a Georgia girl and the peanut habit died hard.

Fortunately, after the animal nipped her and drew blood a sharp Park attendant netted the squirrel. The rabies test was negative but they put the little bastard to sleep anyway. Leaving Sharon in bed for a few days with shock and a bandaged hand.

"You're mad at me," she said to Dickstein.

"Surprised," he said. "What happened to your country girl smarts? You don't feed New York squirrels from your hand."

"Well, how would I learn that in Chapel Hill?"

He snapped a portable dinner tray in place and tried a laugh. "I always thought that course was dangerous."

"How so?"

He shut up fast. There was no decent way he could tell her how he'd felt the day she came back from the class with a paperback copy of Frued's *Interpretation of Dreams*. Tell her what? That if he'd wanted to marry somebody who could rattle off about latent and manifest content, who could play peekaboo with symbols and wish-fulfillment and repression he wouldn't have waited until he was thirty-nine to remarry. He could have tied up with any of the smart-ass, over-educated, under-serious women he'd spent most of his life with.

Sharon was wonderfully articulate without being glib. She had the Southern gift for language flow without the little chunks of undigested information—okay, call it knowledge—that was the conversation he'd grown up with and hated. He couldn't tell her any of this because it would come out upside down. The truth of it was in intangibles: the intelligence of her smile, the quick wit that sparkled questions the night he'd lectured to a dozen students who'd swallowed a snowstorm just to hear him compare Schubert and Keats.

"They both go from major to minor keys and back again very quickly," she'd said. Not a question or academic comment: a fragment of song. Just what he was in need of: idea-tossed, song-hungry. "I mean," he said, "that I expected you to start poking at yourself with the new tools of psychology."

"Instead," she said, "I'm poking at you."

"Can you have wine?" he asked. "I forgot what the doctor said."

Sharon shivered against her pillow. "He didn't say. I'll have a glass, thank you. Listen, you knew I was a widow, right off."

"You told me instantly. With all the appropriately Southern Gothic details."

"Gothic! It was a hunting accident. Everybody in our part of Georgia hunts. But you didn't tell me your first wife—Alma—was a widow until—for God's sake, last week!"

"It didn't seem important. It's all of three months, not our Golden Wedding anniversary. Both men died natural deaths—one, sickness, one a shooting accident—both men were considerably older than the woman. Now you know what I know."

Dickstein filled the bowls with linguine and shared the wine.

"Two widows," she sighed.

"I'm damned if I know why I didn't tell you sooner. But you didn't notice anything odd until New York University and Sigmund Freud told you it was worthy of thinking about."

He set down an amazement of utensils, any which way on the trays. It was not like him and he noted it.

"It gave me the shivers," she began . . .

"What did?"

"Reading the dream book. I think you have to read things at the right moment for them to get to you. I must have read Freud at school. I took all the right courses. I graduated. I took a year of graduate school."

"You were doing music, not psychology."

"But reading this now in class it gave me the eerie feeling that everything is connected."

"Overdetermined . . . "

"Please don't be just clever," she said. "I'm wounded and I'm trying to track something down. I got shaky in class and that's why I wasn't careful in the park . . . It wasn't a change in the way I think—I wasn't born yesterday. It was a weird change in the way I *feel* about the way I think."

"Let me see; is that oozing?"

"Looks the same. I've been bitten before."

"Not in Washington Square Park. City animals are more dangerous."

She ate carefully with her left hand.

"I'm talking about the sensation of strangeness—just thinking that causes and connections run through everything like the bloodstream through the body."

"Did you think everything was random, till yesterday?"

She laughed. "I *felt* that way till yesterday. Then, sitting on the bench with the bag of peanuts I got distracted, the wet heat, I'm used to more hot and dry in August, and I began to think about you and Alma and me and Joshua and widows and husbands and fathers and wives and mothers, and it was more like a dream than *thinking* and I fed this squirrel and I must have done it in a funny way because I've fed them a million times before and nothing every happened and he bit me."

Dickstein didn't know why the memory appeared for delivery at that moment. It was not a buried one, was right at hand. Rather, it showed up at that instant to help deal with Sharon who sounded shakier every minute.

"To give you a dose of strange," he told her, "you're not my second widow. You're my fourth. You're living with a regular Bluebeard in reverse."

And he told her of being puppy-young, meeting the war-widow with the long legs at a fund-raising chamber music evening, and about his family's terror.

His father, Doctor Dickstein, the Gynecologist/Philosopher and his Big Moment in Paternal Wisdom.

"A woman whose husband has died and who marries a younger man puts too much of a burden on the boy. And don't forget: she'll always be comparing you to him."

So he was shipped out to Stanford instead of finishing at Columbia and fell in love, for a time, with a California aerospace widow. Nothing glamorous like a test-pilot crash; just an equipment explosion.

"It's not funny," Sharon said; she was purplish from trying not to laugh. His intent was distraction and seemed to be succeeding. She was slipping into her country accent as she did when she felt easier. She wasn't a modern West Side of New York Sharon; her full name was Rose-a-Sharon. "I grieved so much," she said, "when Joshua died. I was mad, too, 'cause I hated hunting."

"We're not talking about how it feels when your husband dies. We're talking about how much more connective tissue there is here than even you thought of."

She wasn't laughing anymore. "Four," she murmured. "A daytime dream of *the* dream. The older man who possesses your woman, first, dies, but you didn't kill him. You just get to have *her*. Over and over again. My God. Doesn't that count as murder and possession of the spoils?"

What he couldn't bring himself to bring up was what would seem to be the underlying strategy. He saw all these men as brutal, himself as tender; they were heedless of their women, he was concerned; they took what they wanted, he asked or waited for the moment to ripen.

When Dickstein envisioned those hunting trips of Sharon's husband, Joshua, he imagined some kind of secret, violent sex mixed in with the country satisfactions of blood sport. He'd never asked her about such things and she'd not offered much beyond a black mustache, six-foot-three height and a paper mill business. Questions of fidelity were not included in the data. But when he recalled his father's caution, he welcomed the comparison. Not only were they dead and he alive: *he was molded to offer precisely what they lacked. That was his enterprise!*

But he wasn't going to bring up all that and reinforce this dream-book talk. Instead, he poured the wine more freely than usual and the astonishment turned festive. Sharon was pretty in what she called her sick-time-of-the-month robe, though only her finger bled. They laughed again at her fears of the 'uncanny' connections in the mind. (Freud, he told her, had written a famous letter in which he claimed an absence of any such 'uncanny' feelings; more about religion than psychology, though.) And she promised never to feed squirrels in the city, again—and she grew coy and sensual, drinking more and eating less, holding her injured hand out into the air as she caressed him with the other and it seemed like a nice idea to eat dinner in the bedroom at times and afterwards she asked him if she were the more precious of the prizes he'd won from the dream-murder of all those father/lovers; and he kissed her mouth as answer and evasion and she grew most Southern and promised to at least consider dropping the class since something about it bothered him, if he would take her to Turkey at Christmas-time. (Had had absolutely no interest in things Turkish.)

She wondered aloud if they'd made a baby; and he wondered, silently, thinking he could be a husband and a father and could die, like all the others, leaving his lovely Rose-a-Sharon for . . . who?

Late that night he woke, his head frantic from too much wine. In the bathroom he stared at the mirror and thought of his father's face for the first time in many months: square-immigrant tough where Dickstein's was second-generation soft-nurtured; perfunctory and commanding with his sullen, witty wife, where Dickstein was the one who provided attentions and the occasions for laughter. He remembered the early childhood Saturday visits to Dr. Dickstein's office, the women waiting patiently, obediently, and the chrome and the stirrups . . . and remembered, too, years later, how amazed he was that the old man should be at the mercy of the pain and fears which came with final illness. He'd never seen his father at the mercy of anything, before.

Dickstein's eyes blazed in the bathroom mirror with the awful knowledge that there were no more of these imposing older men to die and leave him their women to take for his own. He would be forty in three months, he thought and listened to Sharon's regular hiss of breath. Now, he was at the top of the ladder: an uncomfortable, precarious position.

There she lay, the next widow, unsuspecting; in spite of her squirrel-wisdom, in spite of N.Y.U. and Freud. Because she was young and easy in her skin and had been bereaved only by a rifle, not by time and entropy.

"Peasant pleasures," his father would have said, with irony, about people who died in hunting accidents. He'd sent himself through college and sold insurance to help pay for Medical School. These successes entitled him to a loftiness toward those less educated and less successful. Including, on occasion, his wife and son. But now Dickstein, staring into the mirror, saw mirror-images hard to ignore. He, too, had become a Doctor Dickstein, though only a Ph.D. shadow of the real thing: no chrome, no stirrups, not even a white coat.

Like his father he always had at least three major activities. (The old man lectured, did the first television medical education series along with his regular practice. Dickstein taught English, lectured when asked and edited a journal.) The income and prestige were not comparable but the restless multiple activities had similar outlines.

He searched in the mirror for some of the older man's features he could recognize and endow with the qualities he admired. What he thought of as a Hungarian mouth, he saw, eloquent, romantic.

"The better for talking out of both sides at the same time," Doctor Dickstein had said, laughing his runaway laugh. Dickstein, too, laughed nonstop, large and loud. For years he'd felt his father's heavy laughter aimed at him. The truth was, he suspected, that it was aimed at everyone, the good doctor included.

But that was all gone. It was utterly quiet in the night. He sat on the closed commode and leaned his flushed face against the tile of the sink.

"The top of the ladder," he whispered. And now it was not some young woman waiting to greet him. It was his father, waiting where vanished fathers wait for sons.

The disturbing image mixed with the wine in his gut in a surprise of nausea. He vomited into the sink with an energetic heave. It lasted several minutes and then he fell asleep wedged against the sink, the water still running.

Sharon found him about ten minutes after dawn. He was slumped over the sink. When she touched his shoulder instead of jumping he woke gradually, her lovely cloud of yellow-reddish hair swimming into vague then focused view. Her eyes and cheeks looked slept-in, striated, rumpled.

She had to pee and he tottered to his feet and waited. When she finished she washed the sink and sat him down again and washed his face with her good hand. He had the convalescent's quiet gladness that she was present, that she had found him, that he had found her.

She would undoubtedly survive him. That was in the natural order of things. But, first, for as long as possible, they would survive together. He would be her loving husband, father, friend, teacher: wise, sensual, patient; knowing that, like all teachers, he was temporary.

And for himself, he would learn to ward off the inevitable, to slow down the dance of death. It was time to become his own father: forgiving, intelligent, always remembering that he had once been young and lost and now was found.

A new arrangement.

The bathroom smelled of vomit and Sharon sprayed something lilac into the air and gave him something mint to rinse his mouth with and kissed him and stumbled back to bed and sleep.

Dickstein sat there a moment. He had never felt so lucky in his life.

It was like a dream.

Mourning

ROBERT TAYLOR, JR.

Jesse James had a wife
Who mourned for his life. . . .

I *1876-1881*

He's a blue-eyed handsome man but he makes you worry. She watches him ride away, his linen duster flying and the dust swirling up behind him, and she thinks: this is to be my portion. A skillet. Little Jesse crying. Mary moaning. This plank floor and these thick windows, the bright fire, the distant trees. Zee, he says, I'm going. She knows, has known long ago. He comes in and paces. He wrings his hands. He stares, his blue eyes glazing over, then commencing to blink.

Stay here with me, she says.

Zee, I have got to go.

She knows, but regrets. Zerelda, his mother and her aunt and namesake, also regrets.

I see he's gone again, she says.

Yes, he's gone again.

Say where?

He never says.

No. He wouldn't.

She walks her mother-in-law to the door. The trees sway and clouds move across the sky as though in a great rush to get someplace else. The clouds look like great dark hands, big fists. She closes the door, fixes the latch, turns to her children, who are hungry, one crying, one tugging at her hand.

In Saratoga they ride out the long boulevard in a grand phaeton, past the mansions with the wonderful turrets and spacious porches, the driver sitting tall and rigid in front of them in a narrow-brimmed, flat-topped gray hat that she is certain will blow away in one of the warm gusts of wind but that remains firmly in place while she almost loses the scarf she's tied so carefully in a broad bow around her neck. Jesse wears the dark suit he's purchased in New York City. Quiet, he sits as rigid as the driver, his hands folded in his lap. You would think he sat in church, listened to a sermon. Wouldn't it be wonderful, she wants to say, to live in a home such as one of these. She sees herself moving from room to room, her silk gown rustling, Jesse in the parlor with his newspaper, his cigar, the children in the playroom two floors above, watched by a selfless nursemaid. She loves little Jesse, sweet Mary, but can she help it if she sometimes desires her husband, wants him all alone to herself, the way it used to be?

But of course it has never been as it should be. Not even now, in this fine carriage, is it as it should be. Look at him. What is he thinking, what is he feeling. Shouldn't she know, have some inkling. Why does he so seldom speak, take her into his confidence. There has been a time—but no, there hasn't been a time. Nothing has been provided. She must grasp, she must always be pulling at him, at life itself. He has no self. Don't his actions say as much? She believes everything she has ever heard about him. He is an outlaw, a thief. He has nothing of his own, not even a name.

At the baths the woman helps her down into the warm water. She thinks of Jesse, wonders what he thinks as he feels the water's warmth. No doubt nothing. Probably he thinks nothing at all, a secret even to himself. Is the water warm enough, the woman asks. It is very warm. Warm and calming. She lowers herself into it. I might drown, she thinks. I might let my head come with my body down into the water. Then I would be the mystery.

Aunt Zerelda waves the stump of her right arm as though it were a stick. Zee, she says, men are all the same. Even my dear Dr. Samuel, why, he's no more with me sometimes than my dead father, just a memory of himself in the flesh. There's much we must resign ourselves to.

Little Jesse jumps at his grandmother when she comes, and Zee thinks he will knock her over surely, for he's a growing boy, heavy as sin, but Ma Zerelda clasps her good arm around him and lets him hang onto the other and together they stagger towards the high-back rocker. Tell me about the Pinkertons, he says. Tell me how they blew off your arm, Nanna. He has his father's tact, as well as his blue eyes and the same shuffling gait. Mary looks like her grandmother in the eyes, their sockets set back as if for better safety, and like her father in the mouth, the lips small in proportion to the chin and nose and customarily drawn tight. When I grow up, she says frequently, I'm going to marry a rich, rich man and live in a big house with tall trees all around it so that nobody can ever find us.

I won't think about him, she tells herself. He is dead to me and I will go on with my life. And she rides into town, the children left with their grandmother. She rides in the little cabriolet Jesse has brought her from St. Louis, rides with her head high, her hands tight around the thick reins. I'm permitting myself to be seen, she thinks. I want the gentlemen on Messanie Street to turn their heads when I pass. There goes a fine-looking woman, I want them to say, tipping their high-crowned hats.

He says it was the war that changed everything. That is what he used to say, his voice lowering so that it doesn't sound like a voice, the vowels firm as fruit fresh-picked. Before the war, he says, a man had a chance. There was rich farms, prosperous towns, and for them of a mind to seek fortune in other climes there was California and the promise of gold.

California. Hasn't his father gone to California. Left his mother behind with three young children. Gone and found nothing, sent nothing back. In fact never heard from again. And all this *before the war.*

Oh, he could be tiresome sometimes. Lord, yes. Before the war! Before the war indeed. Before the war as well as during it he was a boy, no man at all, hardly out of knee britches when the redlegs start their raiding and the Federals their burning, scarce eighteen when Lee surrenders. But with two years of fighting with Quantrill's raiders, he points out, his blue eyes fierce and rapidly blinking, as if he suddenly sees the whole war again, everything all at once, the fire and the bloodshed, himself in the midst of it, pistols brandished and smoking. *I'm with child,* she tells him, and off he goes, not saying where, climbing onto the big horse, and she lies there alone in the bed and thinks maybe he is only a dream, everything that has happened to her since she has left the home of her parents in Kansas City a dream, this house on the hill, these children who survive and those poor dead twins, this child in her womb tinier surely than a finger, all a dream. She will wake up and there he will be, a man with Jesse's eyes—only they will not blink like his do. Unflinching, this man looks deep into her eyes and says, You are my life. Let me be yours. A lover to love, this one. An outlaw, perhaps, but alive, hidden in her heart.

Hotter, she tells the attendant. I want the water hotter. I want it steaming hot. And then he says, It's time, Zee. It's time we moved on. The baths make her feel as though she might live a life, after all, of perfect loveliness, in warmth, submerged but breathing fine. It's time, he says, and they are on the train again, headed south, the land through the windows passing as if it were in fact another kind of river, swift and dangerous to cross, whose dirt you might drown in.

She is with child, the fourth time in their marriage. When Jesse and Mary learn to walk, they move so like their father that she expects them to come to her any minute, say, Now it's time. We have got to move on. We don't know when we'll be back. They will not, she is certain, ever be able to stay put, doomed with a double dose of the blood that dooms their father, their uncle. Getting even takes a long time, at least a life. Young, lying wounded in her father's house, he tells her what has happened. They found me in the cornfield, he says. They was Jim Lane's men, come looking for Quantrill. Frank'd been riding with Quantrill, and I guess they found that out and so naturally came to us. But we wasn't saying a word. I lit out for the fields, nary a thought in my head about what fate I was leaving behind for my dear mother. I tore through them fields, run through the corn rows, and all the time I hear the horses tromping over the stalks and know it ain't no escaping. They get me down there all right, but I swear they'll pay. I'll be harder to find next time.

He could've been a preacher like his runaway daddy, yes, he could if he could only preach on the wrongs done to him and to his brother and to his beloved maimed mother. On that subject he might speak for hours and keep your attention.

She has heard him sing hymns, a pure and lovely tenor, when he comes to visit her, his cousin Zerelda Mims of Kansas City, and takes her to the Baptist Church, later to ride with her to the river, the Missouri, wider and bluer in those sweet summers before the war, with tufts of columbine and chicory spread across its banks like decoration put there for their pleasure alone. I am a family man, he tells her later, courting her while she nurses his war wound. I want to be a husband to a good woman, a loving father. Do you think that is possible, Zee. Can you see your way to helping me. Lord, how could any woman resist, him there in her bed, lying so peaceful between her sheets, the blue comforter tucked beneath his chin, his blue eyes always filling with tears, and not a single complaint, not once a word about the pain she knows he's feeling, his lung, the doctor says, punctured clean through by a Federal's bullet, a fingertip shot away.

Mama, she says, I think I love him.

Lord help us, her mama says.

II *1882*

She doesn't look forward to the visits from Frank and Annie. In his tight suit with the black bow tie, the pin-striped trousers, the shiny boots, Frank talks like a schoolteacher, puffing his big cigar and looking at her as if amused with something, as if he finds her stupid, comical. And how, he asks, is the little mama. Annie glides through the doorway as if pretending to be a swan. She is a plump woman with large hands and feet, given to the wearing of pearly brooches above her commodious breast and many thick rattling crinolines beneath her bell-shaped skirts. Hello, Zerelda-dear, she says. It's *so* good to see you again. Frank sits in the rocker, creaking and puffing, in his schoolteacher's tight collar.

We been through hell and high water, Jesse says. Frank's the only man in the world I trust. He'll never betray me, Zee, not Frank, not for any sum of money. I don't know why you don't like him better.

She tries to. She tries to make conversation with him. And what, she asks him, pouring hot coffee into the delicate cup, do you think will ever become of the Indians? The subject interests her. It is a topic of interest in the East, she has noted, as well as in the West. The Easterner's point of view, she has observed, differs sharply from that of the Westerner. Is there room for all the tribes in the Indian Territory? Is it right that they should all be moved there—and can they really be guaranteed permanent asylum anywhere. Grant's policy was perhaps radical, though idealistic to be sure, but what will a man like Arthur do with the mess Hayes left. Frank has no opinions. He quotes her Shakespeare—he *says* it's Shakespeare. He reckons things will work out. He puffs his cigar, sips his coffee. Maybe, he says to Jesse, you and me'd best step into the other room. Ladies, will you excuse us for a moment.

Have you heard, Annie says, leaning forward in her chair, what the Indians do with the white women they capture.

She has read accounts, has Annie, true-life accounts, and the things they say will make your blood boil. Savages. Why, it's ridiculous to even think that a wild Cheyenne such as them that raid in Kansas will ever turn Christian. They are savage through and through, and the only solution to the problem is to show them we won't stand for any more of their outrages.

At least she has an opinion. As for herself, why, listen, what if you *were* captured by a savage Cheyenne, Annie. What would you do. Be honest now.

What would I do! Fight tooth and nail for my freedom, of course. I'd not give in. I'd run. I'd escape.

Would you. Well. I think I might not. Not if my brave had enough passion in him. Not if he wanted me so badly that he couldn't bear the thought of life without me and would hold onto me whether I loved him in return or not.

Oh, certainly, Zee, but I don't think that's the way it is, at least not in the accounts I've read.

Accounts! Why you don't think a woman is going to speak of such pleasure when she's recaptured by her family, do you. Would you? No. You'd have to protect *their* honor, save their pride. Or else be treated as the lowest of the low. No, I don't place much faith in the accounts.

Really, Zee? Don't you.

She shakes her head. Little Jesse pulls at her skirt. Mayn't he please go in the room where his daddy and Uncle Frank are? Mary sits in the middle of the room, legs crossed in front of her, her rag doll, a present from Ma Zerelda, flat on its face being whipped vigorously. Indian children would be quiet, well-behaved, trained from an early age to do their share. The air in the dark

tipi would be sweet and leathery, her brave's eyes dark brown and unflinching, his touch, as he draws her to him, gentle.

She hasn't wanted this return. Missouri, he tells her, is our home, but she's
been happy in Tennessee, as happy, at any rate, as she has ever been since
their marriage. The death of the twins brings him closer to her for a time, and
he begins to take an interest in farming. Then it's: We must return to
Missouri. It is time. I feel it in my bones. There's no use arguing. When he
brings up his bones, she knows it's no use quarreling, he's made up his mind,
he's got to go.

What surprises her is the feeling of warmth she has. The Mississippi
seems to move with the same pace and thickness as her blood. She feels
steady, calm. Perhaps, she thinks, it *is* right, this return of the family to
Missouri. How white the rocks that rim the hills, how thick and swirling the
snow-washed grass in the valleys, how stately the rows of willow and
cottonwood along the creekbanks, bark shining in the late winter sunlight
like fine silk stretched tight and brushed perfectly clean. Then, at last in St.
Joseph, bold in the spring sun, she walks past the storefronts along
Messanie Street. *Mrs. Howard. I am Mrs. Howard of Lafayette Street.*

The house on the hill commands a view of St. Joseph, the Missouri River,
and all of Kansas beyond. Home, she thinks, yes, he's right this time. This is
our home. A child will be born here. It is 1882. The world is not the same as
when Jesse lies wounded in my father's house and talks so foolish of
families. Because it wasn't possible then—even I must have known that it
wasn't possible to live in peace, not for him nor for me, not then, not in those
times.

Merchants smile pleasantly, offer assistance. They are not suspicious.
Why should they be. We are at last living the life we have planned for
ourselves. She tells him she is with child and he kisses her hand, clasps it
almost with tenderness. Mr. and Mrs. Thomas Howard, of Lafayette Street,
St. Joseph, Missouri.

But then he goes. He rides off alone, leaving before daybreak, returns in a
week, two weeks, a month, she doesn't know. His mother sits in the rocker
by the fire, the chair not moving, and talks to her of burdens and injustices
while the children loll about on the floor, calm as dolls for a change, drawing
stick figures on their slates.

Things get worse, the old woman says, waving her stump, before they get
better. I raised them up to be good boys, my Frank and my Jesse. They
never gave me heartache such as my Susan did. They are gentlemen. I raised
them up to be gentlemen. But they have no peace, while Susan, who has
shamed her mother and her brothers more than once, prospers in Texas with
that scoundrel Parmer. Lord a-mercy.

In the middle of March the chill winds give way to warm breezes from the south and the rain falls like mist. When the gray has gone, she takes the children to the river. We'll have a picnic, she tells them, with Aunt Annie and your cousin Bob. But the river's high and muddy, the banks thick with briars and silt. Annie sees a snake. And so they have their picnic lunch in the yard of the house on the hill. We can see the river anyway, says Annie. Who needs to be close to it.

When Jesse comes back it is the eve of April and the Ford boys come with him. Well, he says, you're swelling up just fine, but she's in no mood for sweet talk. She needs love and knows there's no getting it from him, not anymore, not ever, though it breaks her heart to think it. Where is she to get it, if not from her husband. She looks at her children and they seem not hers, some other woman's, and the child within her might be rock. She remembers, she tries to imagine the moments when his touch thrilled, his glance warmed. There was a gentleness, a tenderness. It was trust, she remembers, trust that we had. When, now, might that have been.

What do you think, Annie asks, of that Charley Ford.

Not at all, she says. I don't think of him at all.

Have you noticed the way he looks at me? Zee, he gives me the shivers.

Stop ogling him. Stop flirting with him, Annie.

Zee! You're one to talk.

They sit in the straight chairs by the south window, the dark curtains drawn back, the morning sun streaming through the panes. It is a warmth, she thinks, but not the warmth I need. She has lost that warmth, just when she believed she had it back, lost it as sure as she has lost her youth. When she hears the gun, she thinks it is the sound of her soul breaking loose from its skin. She closes her eyes, a girl again in Old Missouri, Missouri before the war, waking to the sound of the mourning dove, the footsteps of her father, birds, so many of them, singing in the trees, beautiful, something fine and beautiful, her mother calling, Zee! Zee! and now the sun lighting up everything, Jesse her cousin, her lover, on his way to pay her a secret visit, him just a boy trying to look like a man by strapping that big pistol around his waist and letting the fuzz above his sweet boy's lips stay, blonding in the sunshine, curling ever so slightly at the corners of his mouth, where the cheeks soften and the chin drops like it wants speech, a tongue and mouth of its own. What has happened. What in God's name has happened. Zerelda, they're calling her name, but isn't it his mother they want and not his wife. It's always somebody, Shepherds or Hiteses or Cumminses or Liddils or Ryans, who could keep track of them, these mean-eyed men with their guns and their grins, their matted hair, their small teeth. Pleased to meet you, Ma'am. She is sure. How does he know, her blue-eyed Jesse, who he can trust. This one, no. This one, yes. And Frank, Frank forever.

What has happened. A gunshot or a slamming door. Jesse doesn't slam a door, leaves a room quietly, enters in silence. He is there or he is not and in either case you think that is the way it will always be, his presence all one with his absence, eternal his comings and goings. And so it is not like him, she thinks, rising from her chair, to go so noisily. Perhaps it is thunder. Perhaps nothing at all, her soul, her bursting heart, her wild imagination, her unsettled mind.

Charley Ford, what have you done.

No. It's Bob that's done it. Bob, my brother Bob Ford. Yonder he goes. Zerelda, you musn't look.

He seems to embrace the wall, her Jesse, the red coming on the back of his head like another set of lips that she might more conveniently kiss while the other pair, those pale thin ones she remembers always drawn tight like stays, squeeze against the skin of the room. Oh, she'll look, all right. She sees him lying there, for sure not wanting her, wanting no one to hold him back, a secret and safe, you bet, her Mr. Howard, gone for good.

Interviews with Insufficiently Famous Americans

JOHN UPDIKE

The Counsellor

ONE FEELS REASSURED, in the presence of the counsellor. There are those humming brown elevators that lift you toward his firm, and that stunning receptionist whose face is as soaked in powder as a Turkish Delight used to be in sugar, before the candy manufacturers began to feel the pinch. And then, his view! All of the metropolis seems encapsulated in his windows, like a town in a spherical paperweight—the spires, the bridges, the penthouses, the traffic jams, the harbor, all there, twinkling. He rises in a cascade of pin-stripes. His face is so clean and rosy it looks skinned. He is broad-shouldered, and not exactly four-dimensional, but making more of the three dimensions than the rest of us do: he *bulks*. "Fill me in," he says, "on the problem."

While being filled in, he leans back in his chair and presses his fingertips together. They must teach that in law school—a variant of prayer, with the eyes open. He does not take a note. For he has summoned in another lawyer, younger, less bulky, to take notes, on a yellow legal pad held on his gaunt young knee. One feels, of course, wretched, fetching one's clinging shreds of the organic world—life, that begins in the bursting of membranes and ends with a relaxation of the sphincter muscle—into such impeccable presences, such well-groomed offices. Since childhood, one has been told that there can be no squaring of the circle, but one hopes of the counsellor that he can cube an egg, and a scrambled egg at that. He leans forward, touches the desktop with his elbows, lets his slow silence bulk him larger, and at last offers, "There may be a way around that."

One could cry in gratitude.

With manicured hands he outlines in the air a program of counter-terror, writ responding to writ, tort (from *tortus*, crooked) nullifying tort. There may be depositions taken. The demeanor of the judge cannot be foreseen. You want to call a bluff, but you don't want to call it to the point where it *feels* called. In a situation involving X, Y, and Z, who is to say that Z will prove rational, and not do the self-destructive thing? This is still a free country, with great opportunities for self-destruction. There are variables. Variables cost money. Show me a free variable, I'll show you totalitarianism. In a nation of laws not men, brinkmanship prevails from sea to shining sea. *Et cetera, sub rosa, entre nous.*

A twinkling maze of imponderable possibilities has arisen above the counsellor's glass desktop. One feels driven outward, from one's petty fate to general considerations of an abstract and ramifying nature. One asks,

Q.: What is justice?
A.: Depends on the state. Justice in Delaware is mere mischief in South Dakota. Alabama, who knows? Had a client last week who was made to look pitiable in Alabama. This same fellow came up smelling like roses in Maryland. *Non serviam*, I say.
Q.: Do you feel you are providing an essential service?
A.: I service human foolishness. If foolishness were non-essential, it would have faded away aeons ago, with the hand-held flint chopper. *Requiescat in pace*, chopper.
Q.: Let me put it another way. Do you feel that the noble intent of the law is always commensurately served by its minions?
A.: Define me a minion. We build on air. All of us. We build on air. When the Pilgrims landed at that there rock, this was lawless forest. From here to Big Sur, lawless forest. Now we've got such a structure the average man can't go two hours without committing a misdemeanor. I don't say that's good. I don't say that's bad. I say that's a fact. Out of this fact some fortunate few of us have generated an industry. Out of some other fact our worthy colleagues at the bar have generated a contrary industry. It all comes out in the locker room, where they polish your shoes while you shower. Define me a minion, I'll give you a misdemeanor. *Sic semper tyrannis*. You follow me?
Q.: I'm getting there. Can you estimate how much this lecture has cost me?
A.: It would be ill-advised to comment at this time.
Q.: Can you tell me if you think we have a case?
A.: It would be premature to venture a comment this far down the road.
Q.: In general, *sub specie aeternitatis*, what are my chances?
A.: All I can say at this juncture is *Nihil ab nihilo, de profundis*. Best of luck to you and yours. I've really enjoyed our conversation. [One stands to go.] Here, let me show you these Polaroids of my wife and kids. Cute as buttons, huh? The house in the background, we bought it for seventy grand in 1967, it would go for two hundred big ones now, easy; and that leaves us an acre out back to retire on. Keep your nose clean, your powder dry, your

chin up. Have a stick of Juicy Fruit, foul stuff but it saved my sanity when I gave up smoking ciggyboos. If that ain't your cup of tea, take a lick of the receptionist on your way out. Ha-ha-ha. Ha-ha-ha-*ha*.

At the hourly rate his counselling commands, each "ha" has cost 12½¢.

The Widow

Q.: NICE PLACE you have here.
A.: I try to keep it up. But it's hard. It's hard.
Q.: How many years has it been now?
A.: Seven. Seven come September. He was sitting in that chair, right where you are now, and the next minute he was gone. Just a kind of long sigh, and he was gone.
Q.: Sounds like a pretty good way to go. Since we all have to go sometime.
A.: That's what everybody said. The minister, the undertaker. I suppose I should have been grateful, but if it had been less sudden, it might have been less of a shock. It was as if he *wanted* to go, the way he went so easy.
Q.: Well. I doubt that. But it's you I'm interested in, you in the years since. You look wonderfully well.
A.: Ever since I stopped taking the pills. These doctors nowadays, they prescribe the pills, I honestly believe, to kill you. I was having dizzy spells, one leg seemed to be larger than the other, my hands felt like they were full of prickers . . . it all stopped, once I stopped taking the pills.
Q.: And your . . . mental state?
A.: If you mean do I still have all my buttons, you'll have to judge that for yourself. Oh, I'm forgetful, but then I always was. I know if I stand in the middle of the room long enough it'll come to me. It's like the sleeping. At first I used to panic, but now if I wake up at three in the morning I just accept it as what my body wants. Trust your body, is the moral of it all, I suppose.
Q.: By mental state I meant more grief, loneliness, sense of self, since . . . you became a widow.
A.: Well, first, there's the space. No, first, there's the ghosts. Then there's the space.
Q.: Ghosts?
A.: Oh yes, right there. All the time. Talking to me, telling me to put one foot in front of the other, not to panic. Rattling the latches at night. As certain as you're sitting there. Many a time I've seen it rock by itself.

Q.: Perhaps I should change chairs.

A.: Oh no, sit right there. People do all the time.

Q.: After the ghosts, space?

A.: An amazing amount of it. Amazing. I never noticed the sky before. Seventy years on earth and I never looked at the sky. Just yesterday, there were clouds in it with little downward points, like a mountain range seen upside down, or a kind of wet handwriting, it looked ever so weird, I can't describe it properly. And the trees. The way the trees are so patient, so *themselves*, gathering their substance out of air—it sounds silly, in words.

Q.: So you would say then that since your husband's passing your life has taken a turn toward the mystical?

A.: Not mystical, *practical*. The income tax, for instance. I do it all myself, federal and state. I never knew I had it in me to enjoy numbers. And people. I have friends, of all ages. Too many at times, I take the phone off the hook. I think what I meant about the space before, it's space you can arrange yourself, there's nobody pushing at you with *his* space, nobody to tell you you're crazy when you're weeding the peas at four in the morning and start singing.

Q.: You often sing to yourself?

A.: I'm not sure.

Q.: I don't mean to pry—

A.: Then don't pry.

One must be prepared, in interviewing the elderly, for these sudden changes in mood, for abrupt closure of access. Human material rubbed so thin by longevity resembles a book whose pages in their tissue fineness admit phrases from the next page or, in their long proximity *en face*, have become scrambled inky mirrors one of the other. Paranoia is the natural state of a skidding organism. Volatility is the inevitable condition of angels. The widow's face, so uncannily tranquil and spacious before, has grown hard and narrow as a gem that is cutting the transparent interface of the interview. One must return to scratch:

Q.: But, er, ma'am, prying wasn't—I mean, what we want to do here, your testimony is so positive, so unexpectedly so, that we want to bring to the widest possible audience . . . uh, its great value in this era of widows, to all those others who find themselves alone.

A.: You are not alone. You are not. Not.

The Undertaker

THE MAN IS SO YOUNG, is what strikes one forcibly. As if only the dead should bury the dead, we are startled by his downy cheeks, his supple puppyish bulk, his handshake limp and damp and silken as the handshakes of the very young are. Inherited the kit and caboodle—six downstairs rooms wired for Musak and a basement full of coffins—from his father, probably. Or maybe the old man is stashed around the corner, coiled to cinch the deal.

But he never shows, it is the young man we must deal with. He wears the correct suit of lugubrious blue, and his voice is right, that strange *timbre* undertakers achieve, not quite deep enough to be ministerial nor high enough to be eunuchoid, but pitched in between, and resistless as a mountain stream of salad oil, onflowing but tranquil; nothing will ripple it. What they must see, these childlike blue eyes gliding through these rooms whose wallpaper holds faint veins of silver. Joy-riders decapitated. The last twisted husks of alcoholic ruin. Plump churchwomen turned skeletal by cancer. Beaming former athletes dyed purple in the final fit of asphyxia. Nobody should have to see such things. Who can begrudge him his fleet of Cadillacs outside in the parking lot, and the lambskin-lined Maserati he keeps for his private use, on weekends?

He responds to questions sympathetically, perceiving the interviewer as a kind of mourner, to be handled with care.

Q.: Do you enjoy your work?
A.: I'm not sure "enjoy" is right. Work it is. I had wanted to be a florist. My father runs a greenhouse. My uncle took me on here instead.
Q. (*the inevitable joke, delivered quickly*): Well, you plant in both cases.
A. (*unsmiling*): It's human-relations work mostly. The craft angle of it anybody could learn in six months. It's the dealing with the relatives, the newspapers, even the old fogeys who control the cemetery lots, that is gratifying to me. That part of it you never get a hundred-percent grip on.
Q.: Do you have a basic philosophy for dealing with the—the survivors?
A.: Neutral
Q.: Neutral?
A.: I try to maintain neutrality. I take the cue from them. If they want to crack jokes, I know a few. If they want to have hysterics, we got soundproofing in the walls. Open coffin, closed coffin, public viewing, private service, scatter the ashes—it doesn't faze us. We're at your service. Last winter we had an old lady who wanted to be hung in a tree as food for the birds, but the state doesn't allow it. Scattering the ashes isn't so popular in some localities, either. What people don't realize, there can be *bones*.

Teeth, too. Do it at sea, sometimes the receptacle floats, and you should keep the tide charts in mind. That's the kind of problem that's gratifying to me, one that tests your general knowledge.

Q.: Have you read any Jessica Mitford?

A.: That's the lady said we worked short hours and overcharged.

Q.: 'Fraid so.

A.: With all due respect, I don't think the lady quite got a grip on the extent of the service we have to provide. Door to door, so to speak. Deathbed to grave. Once the deceased becomes the deceased, he's on our hands entirely. That's quite an—

Q.: Undertaking?

A.: You said it. Also there's the sociological aspect. We try to leave the fabric intact, with one thread snipped out. Who's there when that nasty bit of work needs to be done? Not Miss Mitford.

Q.: Right. In conclusion, might we see your—receptacles?

They are beautiful. Big baby's cribs, lined with baby blue, pink, peach, lemon. A little sea of them down there, below ground level. Marine metaphors flock to the swimming consciousness. These caskets are boats, calked and mortised and varnished for a long row in black water. Of course they will be rowed, not wind-driven or motor-propelled. *Row, row, row your boat:* we began in first grade by singing that round, and went on to *Michael, row the boat ashore, Hallelujah.* Charon used to pole his skiff of stiffs across the Styx, but this is an age of self-service; you row your own. The undertaker, down here in his watery cave of treasure, amid the silent waves of curved mahogany and plumped-up satin, with frills or without, has grown even more boyish, broad, erect, and translucent; his blue eyes reflect an inner sky, and one remembers where one has seen him before. On the deep imagined sea. He is Billy Budd.

A Lesson in the Classics

GLORIA WHELAN

WALTER MILLER, paper and pencil in hand, awaited the English couple's order. "The shrimp in lemon sauce," he addressed their indecision, "is a cold dish. The shrimp Theseus is baked with feta cheese and a tomato sauce. Theseus, you will recall, came here to Crete to kill the Minotaur. He was the father of Hippolytus by the Queen of the Amazons. Later he married Phaedra. . . . " He tried to keep his tone light, gossipy, but the eyes of the couple glazed over as his students' eyes often had when he had tried to impart to them the differences between genuine and spurious dipthongs or the reasons the Ionic alphabet triumphed over the Attic. He sighed. There was, after all, little difference between his former position as professor of classical languages and his present one as maitre d' of the Poseidon.

The young couple, pale and delicate as two spring shoots, shivered in their flimsy holiday clothes. The early spring evenings in Agios Nikolaos could be cool. Winter snows still lay in crumpled folds on Mt. Dikti's summit and the winds sweeping in from the Aegean were the temperature of a properly chilled white wine.

After the couple settled for the shrimp Theseus, Professor Miller moved on to a table of Germans who began giving their order in a pastiche of pidgin English and Greek. When Professor Miller replied in his pedantic German, they lapsed gratefully into their own tongue, even teasing him a little, accusing him of learning his German from *Faust*, which was true.

The Cafe Poseidon looked out over the harbor to the nearby island of Spinlonga where an imposing Venetian fortress had once enclosed a colony of lepers from Crete. Professor Miller wondered what it would be like to be exiled at the threshold of one's home: he, at least, had the grace of distance. Directly in front of the café a row of fishing boats lay at anchor, painted in primary colors, their decks heaped with saffron-colored nets. Beyond the boats and the island were sea and mountains. Before his retirement he had lived for thirty years in a small college town in a prairie state. The sea and the mountains appeared to him a kind of boast or excess on the part of the Maker.

Professor Miller carried his orders to the kitchen. The taking of the orders and the settling of bills were his only responsibilities. The waiters, Evangelos and Stephanos, did the rest. They were aided by Evangelos' two schoolgirl cousins, Maria and Olga, who hovered about the tables like mute butterflies, emptying ashtrays, brushing away crumbs, and giggling helplessly (Maria) or fleeing in panic (Olga) when a customer made a request of them.

The chef greeted him cheerfully, "Professor, the moussaka is from lunch and if you don't push it, it will be for lunch tomorrow." The farmer who delivered the eggs and cheese was having an ouzo. Professor Miller could smell the pungent mix of licorice from the drink and dung from the farmer's boots.

"Professor," the farmer said, "are you from New Jersey? I have a brother in New Jersey who cleans rugs. You call him up and in five minutes he's there with his machine." Professor Miller tried to explain more than a thousand miles lay between New Jersey and his own state, but the farmer refused to believe anything in America was beyond his brother's grasp. As the professor left the kitchen the farmer called after him, "You let me know when you're ready to go home, I'll send some cheese back for my brother. He'll take care of your rugs, cheap."

Professor Miller could not say when he would go home. He had first come to the Café Poseidon as a patron, choosing an outdoor table where in his loneliness he might have for company the people strolling along the sidewalk and the cars coming and going in the street. He and his wife, Connie, had planned the trip to Greece to celebrate his retirement as head of the classical language department at the small college where he had taught Greek and Latin to a dwindling number of students: the ones going on to the seminary. Students these days were romantics who refused to hear the interminable history of man's bungling. They preferred to believe in a world where charity and love prevailed and why should they not? At the denominational college, the students lived their lives in the company of good people, people who would willingly work against their own interest for the sake of a friend or a principle. From this they posited the rest of the world.

Professor Miller thought himself more sophisticated than the other members of the faculty, adopting for himself the role of ambassador from a wider, larger world; teaching the New Testament, but slipping in a little Aeschylus and even Aristophanes and then worrying that he was introducing the apple into Eden.

When three months before he and Connie were to leave for Greece, Connie had died, Professor Miller had decided to give the trip up, only to reconsider, alarmed by the way the objects in his home had grown leaden and immobile: the dregs from his pipe stayed in the ashtray, a strata of soiled shirts and socks waited on the bedroom chair, even the airy tiers of used

Kleenex that mounded alongside his bed would not disappear. When Connie had been alive all these things had vanished the moment he put them down. With Connie gone he had been afraid to settle into a chair or lie on his bed for fear, he, too, would remain rooted.

And so he had set off on the trip conscientiously retaining in his itinerary Connie's preferences for settings rich in botany. His colleagues had envied his opportunity to follow in Paul's footsteps but his own interests centered on the archaeological sites, especially the realms of the doomed Atreus and Pelops families whom he knew so well from his years of teaching and whose penchant for misfortune had always seemed to him at once fascinating and perverse.

In Athens, in Delphi, and Mycenae, rising early, climbing in and out of the tour busses, there had been little time for loneliness. He found his days full of confirmation. It was all there: the Stoa of Zeus where Socrates had paced, chivvying his students; the mottled, rose and gray rocky mound of the Aeropagus where Paul preached, with indifferent success, to the Athenians; the great lion gates inside which Clytemnestra awaited Agamemnon, dagger in hand. He had climbed to the amphitheater atop the ruins of Delphi and looking out over gray-green olive groves and flowering Judas, had seen like a revelation the line stretching straight—Yahweh, Zeus, Agamemnon, Socrates, Paul. He has been right to fight the faculty, right to reject the word "pagan," right to insist on teaching it all. He took to having a glass of wine with his dinner feeling a mischievous relief that in these foreign parts he was free of the faculty's censorship.

On that first visit to the Poseidon, he had overheard one of the waiters trying unsuccessfully to explain to an Englishwoman why he was unable to serve the woman's small son fresh milk. The professor, who had conscientiously studied modern Greek in preparation for his trip, excused himself for intruding and translated for the Englishwoman the waiter's explanation that in Greece all was rock and drought. Where there was little pasture, there would be few cows.

Returning to dine at the Poseidon the evening before he was to leave Crete, he had again come to the waiter's aid. A French family wanted mineral water in place of the carafe of water that had been brought to their table. Grateful for the professor's help, the waiter, whose name he later learned was Evangelos, had presented Professor Miller with a bottle of Demestica, explaining that their matire d', who understood these various languages, had left for Athens and a job in his uncle's restaurant. Evangelos was a beautiful young man with a fine body that might have been sculpted by Phidias and tousled black curls. There was a sensuality about him and a certain sleek, pampered look that suggested to the professor the boy spent much of his time with women who were devoted to him. At the same time he had an ingratiating bonhomie which Professor Miller, who had not had the opportunity to make friends with a Greek on the trip, appreciated. When Evangelos said laughingly to the professor, "Why don't you apply for the job of maitre d'?" Professor Miller had been pleased rather than insulted at the little joke.

That night he had returned to his hotel room and begun to pack his clothes. He was still tipsy from the bottle of wine and the packing did not go well. He sank down on his bed and smiling foolishly said aloud, "Beware of Greeks bearing gifts." He had not been drunk since his junior year at college when he and his roommate, now the pastor of a large congregation in Minneapolis, had stolen a bottle of his grandfather's schnapps.

He thought of the musty smell that would greet him when he returned to his silent, empty house. Only that morning he had received a letter telling of a late spring blizzard rolling across the prairie. He decided he did not want to leave Greece with its sun and its hillsides that had grown gold with blossoming brooms and heathers. Yet he did not wish to stay on alone at his hotel with no one to talk with and nothing to occupy him. Furthermore, his funds were dwindling.

The next morning he had walked over to the Poseidon and asked to see the owner. Evangelos, who was sitting over a cup of coffee in the empty restaurant, slowly thrust out his legs and stretched his arms like a cat who has been sleeping in the sun. He grinned at the professor. "Her office is just down the street," he said, "but you won't find her in for another hour. She likes her bed." He winked.

Professor Miller sat on the stony beach and watched enviously as an older couple rubbed one another's shoulders with suntan lotion. When an hour had passed he walked down to the office Evangelos had pointed out. He found the proprietor of the restaurant, Madame Papoulias, also managed a real estate firm and a travel agency. When he was admitted to her office Professor Miller saw that although she was at least ten years younger than he, her features were ancient. He had seen the same face with its classic straight nose and dark oval eyes that tilted ever so slightly, peering out at him from Minoan murals in the museum at Iráklion. He felt he was entering another time.

As if the woman could read his mind, she had said, "You want to see the less well-known ruins—Phaestos or perhaps Petsofás or Zákros—someplace where a little still remains for the imagination. You think the Englishman Evans went too far with his reconstructions at Knossos: all that plaster and concrete offends you. I have a tour just for scholars like yourself and this early in the season I can give you a very good price."

He had been taken aback. It was not as a scholar that he wished to present himself. "I'm afraid that is not why I am here." She had spoken to him in

English but he replied in Greek. "I would like to be considered for the position of maitre d' at your restaurant, Madame. I must admit to having been a college professor all my life—although as a student I did wait on tables in a dormitory. However, I speak English, Greek, Italian and German. My French is rudimentary, but the French do not expect nor want others to speak their language well. I am reliable and will not ask for much in the way of a salary."

Madame Papoulias had laughed out loud. The professor with his stilted Greek and fussy manners was a gift from the gods. The night before, two customers had refused to pay after Evangelos had botched their orders. In her mind she had already dressed the professor in the sea-blue jacket that was the uniform of her Poseidon employees. With his silver hair and fine carriage he would give the restaurant dignity. Evangelos needed a little keeping-down as well, he was taking too much for granted. She hired the professor on the spot and at considerably less than she would have had to pay her competitor's maitre d' whom she had been planning to lure away. She also rented the professor a small studio apartment at only a slightly higher rent than she could have had from English tourists. The English infuriated her by taking long daily showers which exhausted the water reservoir.

Professor Miller had seen she was taking advantage of him but he did not mind. He was relieved to find himself in capable hands.

The next evening, compressed into a jacket that was too tight around his waist and with the menu memorized in four languages—the work of a few hours—Professor Miller embarked upon his new profession. He imagined how horrified the faculty at his college would be were they to learn what he was doing, but he told himself there was nothing undignified in overseeing the serving of food. The disciples had done it. The waiters, Evangelos and Stephanos, were won over at once. Unlike the last maitre d' or any maitre d' of their memory, the professor scrupulously divided with them his tips. If they thought him a fool for doing so, they kept it to themselves.

Professor Miller was delighted with his small whitewashed room with its four arched windows that looked out onto the pebbled beach and the sea. The room was furnished with two narrow beds, a chest of drawers, a rough wooden table and chairs, and a soiled flokati rug that crouched on the floor like a matted sheep. A light bulb shaded by a cheese basket illuminated the room, imprinting an intricate lattice on the whitewashed wall. The room was equipped with a small refrigerator and a hot plate. Dishes had to be washed in the bathroom sink. The supply of water from the bathroom faucets was limited, but there was always an inch or so of water on the stone floor from a leak, whose source, like a hidden spring, he could never discover.

Each morning Professor Miller went first to the bakery for a cake-like bread seeded with raisins and then on to the square to buy oranges and a creamy sheep's cheese, *myzithra*, which he learned to eat as the Cretans did, with honey. After breakfast he boarded one of the buses that traveled between the villages. Some days he would take the coastal road, getting off at the seaside and walking for miles along the rocky shore, gazing out at the sea. He would not have been surprised to see the Argo heave into view.

Other days he chose the road that wound up the mountain to the Lassithi plateau, passing through villages that clung like swallow's nests to the mountain. Each house had a roof piled high with drying brush to fuel the winter fires and a yard with rosebushes and goats. The rosebushes in the impoverished villages puzzled him. He had never thought of roses as a necessity.

Leaving the bus he would wander out onto the meadows of the plateau noting the flora for Connie's sake: pink anemones, lavender columbine, red poppies, and one day, a miniature white cyclamen with delicate swept-back petals, like a child's pale face turned to the wind. There were apple and almond orchards and fig trees whose immature fruit were like small green amphorae. One morning he watched transported, as the villagers set the sails on the thousands of windmills. For a moment as the acres of canvas billowed out, he thought the whole plain would levitate.

In letters to his friends at the college, Professor Miller explained he was staying on to do some translating, which, he told himself, was not really a lie. Each morning about the time he used to leave for his first class, he caught himself thinking of the college: the long corridors that reeked from their nightly applications of ammonia and disinfectant, the worn linoleum floors and blemished walls, the students wearing T-shirts with pictures of Kierkegaard (seminary students) or C. S. Lewis (literature majors). He supposed the postcards he sent would be tacked up on the bulletin board next to requests for roommates (neatness counts, charismatic preferred) and appeals to support missionaries aspiring to Uganda or Zaire.

He asked himself if in all his years of teaching he had made an impression on any of these students? He supposed so, for graduates had regularly returned to visit him. After a half-hour's desultory conversation about the student's new life and the pursuits of his classmates, the student would fall silent and stare into space. Absorbing what? The books on his shelves? His faith? His love? Professor Miller shuddered. At the end of a half hour, or hour if there were a greater need, the student apparently replenished, would leave. Professor Miller sighed over these memories and told himself he must not look back. But looking forward was no better.

By late afternoon he was at the Poseidon for his dinner before going on duty. It was a pleasant time. Around the table they were a family. This evening Evangelos had teased, "You've got a woman. I see you get on the bus every day. Her husband goes off to the fields and you sneak in for a little party." He made a quick, obscene gesture which the professor did not understand. Olga and Maria blushed. The chef had reproved Evangelos, "You're not one to talk, a young rooster like you spending your nights with an old stewing hen." At this Olga and Maria had a fit of giggling.

Lately Madame Papoulias had been joining them for dinner. Professor Miller was uncertain about her marital status. At first he had thought her a widow for she invariably wore black, but she had explained, "It is only for a cousin, and one I never got on with, but the Church expects you to wear mourning for three years. As you grow older, you are always in black." Her black sweater and skirt were comforting to Professor Miller who could not stop thinking of his wife. The black clothes were an outward confirmation of his inward state.

Madame Papoulias was a woman with a sensuous appetite and ate as though she were putting food to some use for which it was not intended. This evening she had come early and prepared *lagós*, hare, for them. Professor Miller watched with alarm as she lifted the delicate bones to her mouth and stripped off their meat. She must have borne a personal grudge against the small animal. When she caught him staring at her, he hastened to compliment her on the stew. She replied that she could do much better and invited him to her apartment for lunch the following Sunday.

In the intervening days he struggled with a growing sense of guilt, thinking it might be unsuitable for him to call at the apartment of Madame Papoulias. He had noticed the hungry way she had looked at him. Yet how often he and Connie had visited the homes of their fellow faculty members on Sunday afternoons, listening to classical recordings, enjoying a potluck dinner and always—for it was Sunday—ending the day with a short devotional service. Perhaps the Greeks had a similar tradition?

He was reassured when Madame Papoulias, a picture of suffering dignity, greeted him in her usual black clothes. But when he discovered he was to be the only guest, he grew uneasy and looked nervously about for clues as to what might happen to him. The apartment was furnished with cumbersome Victorian tables and chests rooted like thick trees to the floor. On the walls were Kalim rugs and Cretan embroideries. The most prominent spot was given to an enormous television set. Arranged in front of the set were a pile of brightly colored cushions. Professor Miller thought the apartment a bit Gypsyish.

"There is no reason we should both be alone on a Sunday afternoon," Madame Papoulias said. It was late in May and hot weather had come. Sultry air found its way through the closed shutters and mingled but did not mix with the cool air the thick walls had trapped in the night.

She poured him a glass of *tiskoudía* which he knew to be Cretan gin. Like a character in the hackneyed plot of a spy story he covertly reconnoitered the potted palms for one where the gin might be disposed of while his hostess was out of the room. Something warned him he must keep a clear head.

"Tell me," she said, "why an educated man like yourself has taken such a job, though God knows it was a blessing for me."

"I wanted to stay on here for a while. I've grown fond of your island. And to be truthful, I didn't want to go back to an empty house." He explained about Connie, embarrassed to be mentioning her name in this woman's apartment.

"You are welcome to keep me company anytime. I don't eat enough when I cook for myself. Just see how thin I'm getting." She pushed in her stomach and threw out her ample chest.

Professor Miller felt his face grow red and reached for the gin.

After lunch they sat side by side on the cushions in front of the television set watching a soccer match from Athens. Madame Papoulias, an enthusiast, nudged him with her elbow and grabbed at his thigh in her excitement. The game, incomprehensible to Professor Miller, dragged on. For a moment he nodded. She put her hand over his and suggested, "You needn't go in to the Poseidon. Evangelos can manage for one night."

The professor hastened off.

By July the water in the reservoirs was at a precarious level. Scorching winds blew open the door and windows of Professor Miller's apartment. It was too hot to wander in the fields and the reflection of the sun on the water made him giddy. He took to reading in his room until noon and then proceeding to Madame Papoulias' apartment for lunch, taking with him a basket of figs. They dined on cheese and salads. For dessert they ate figs. Professor Miller watched squeamishly as the juice from the ripe fruit ran down Madame Papoulias' chin.

She spoke to him of the property she owned: on Koundourou Street, on Atlandithos Square, even a little house on the Plastira which looked out onto Lake Voulismani. "The view is superb, but the roof needs a bit of repair. My sister's son is working on it. He is a fisherman but he hasn't had his boat out all month. There aren't enough fish to pay for the gasoline. I don't understand it. The whole sea and there are no fish. It's another curse on Crete. We are an unlucky island."

Professor Miller demured, "I doubt there is a more beautiful place on earth—the sky, the mountains," he made a little halting gesture with his hand to indicate expanse, "the sea, whether there are fish in it or not."

"How happy I am to hear you, an American, say that. What I want is to find a way to get your people over here. The English and the Germans are the only ones who come. They have money, but they don't spend it. The Americans don't have the money, but they spent it anyhow."

Professor Miller was not accustomed to speak of money. The faculty at his college was poorly paid—as anyone should be, their president pointed out, who embarked on a life of witness. The few businessmen he knew were alumni of the college whom he had met while a member of the college gifts committee. He knew them only in the context of their wishing to give money away.

Madame Papoulias mistook his silence. "You are a deep one," she said. "I have decided you are working at the Poseidon to learn the restaurant business. Now that you are retired you are going back to the States and open a Greek restaurant. You are here to learn my little secrets." She waggled a finger at him.

For a moment he was charmed by the ridiculous idea and then, of course, denied it.

One afternoon when no breeze came through the shutters and even the lettuce leaves on the salad plates were limp, Madame Papoulias insisted Professor Miller remove his shoes and trousers and take a nap in her large mahogany bed. "You have to follow the custom of the country," she said, relaxing the knot on his tie and then turning her back to him so that he might fiddle with her zipper. "In this weather you cannot remain on your feet all night if you don't take a little rest during the day." She lay beside him in a bra and petticoat of some slippery pink material. They were too small for her so that her flesh appeared even more abundant. He was being offered a second helping before he had begun on the first.

When her warm hand slipped into the fly of his shorts quick as a mouse into its hole, he wanted to grab his clothes and run. The word fornicator sounded in his head like a siren. Only a week before he had read in an Athen's newspaper of a woman tourist from Australia and a married man from Athens who had been discovered in bed together and sent to jail. But running away would surely be an insult to Madame Papoulias. As they had all of his life, his manners prevailed.

Wherever he touched Madame Papoulias her soft, moist flesh clung to him. What if as a punishment, he worried, their bodies were eternally bonded? Unlike his own God who was merely strict, the Greek gods were capricious, as well, and might take precedence here?

Afterwards he wondered if he were expected to whisper words of love but she spoke instead of the villas and small hotels she would someday buy and refurbish. "The cost of fuel will rise in England and Germany. It will become colder and colder for those people. They will flock to Crete. These grateful people will pay large sums for the warmth of our sun. Her voice was husky with desire, but whether for him or for her future holdings, he could not say.

One afternoon she told him how it had been during the war. The day the Germans had parachuted into Crete, she had been thirteen. She had looked up to see the sky full of white sails. "The sails of the windmills," she said, "to you are beautiful, but all I think of when I see them are the white sails in the sky when the Germans came down upon us."

At night as he lay alone in his own bed, pleasantly tired from an evening's work at the Poseidon, Professor Miller thought of Paul scourging the Corinthians for their lasciviousness. But the next day he would return to Madame Papoulias' apartment. It was not her flesh that brought him, for it had become an embarrassment to him that on most days he was capable of little more than companionship. He was attracted to Madame Papoulias' easy familiarity with tragedy and her ability to survive it. Her father had been accused by the Germans of sabotage. She and her mother had seen him taken off to be executed. During the occupation, many people in their village had starved. Yet, here she was, triumphantly alive and flourishing, seeing opportunity in the disaster of nations growing cold.

Each time her warm skin grafted itself to his body, one or more of life's abrasions healed over. Each time he entered her, he felt himself floundering in a great sea, while bit by bit, the flotsam and jetsam of her vigor accumulated around him, so that at last he had enough to cling to, enough to bring him safely to shore. He watched her secretly, afraid he would find her growing weaker, fading as her strength flowed into him. But, no, she remained as indomitable, as robust as ever. Gradually, he found his thoughts creeping beyond Connie's death and his retirement. Exposed to the high sun of this woman, the shadows of his own sorrow grew shorter.

October was mild and pleasant but nothing green remained. The vegetation on the hillsides had withered and crisped. Everything had been harvested. The countryside was used up. Each day there were fewer tourists. Stephanos had been let go for the season. Olga and Maria had returned to school. Lying in bed with Madame Papoulias one afternoon he asked her if it was not time for him to leave as well. In her dresser mirror he could see the two of them stretched out like twin effigies on some ancient tomb. The effigy that was Madame Papoulias abruptly sat up.

"But November is our best month," she pleaded, "the sea still holds the warmth of the summer. With the tourists gone, the island is ours again. Forgive me for saying so, but what do you have to go back to? If you want a restaurant (Professor Miller had not been able to disabuse her of the idea), why not stay here? Send for your money. I know a way to get it into the country. It will go farther here. With your capital, we can make the Poseidon a first-class restaurant and next door there is a little hotel for sale. We could go in together." She padded over to the dresser and pulled some papers from a drawer. "Look, I have figured out how much you would have to put in. I promise you'll get your money back ten times over.

"You will tell me what Americans like, what they must have to make them comfortable. But of course, we cannot make them *too* comfortable. They like to brag a little about being in a primitive country. Isn't that so? In exchange for American dollars we will make them a little comfortable and a little uncomfortable—you will tell me how much of each. You can write to your friends at the college and urge them to come. We will give them special rates."

Professor Miller saw that all those afternoons when they had been lying together, she had been planning how he might be used. This did not disturb him. He was relieved to find he had not been alone in his need. What alarmed him was a vision of Professor Schuler, who taught Old Testament history, or Professor Liebig, who taught Christian ethics, and the head of the college, President Riess, lounging about on Madame Papoulias' cushions or gathered about her large mahogany bed observing Madame in her slippery petticoat and himself in his white shorts. He told himself he must leave at once.

That evening in the restaurant, Evangelos said, "I suppose you'll be going soon, Professor, like all the tourists." There was an unexpected note of satisfaction in his voice.

The Professor, goaded by Evangelos' tone and unhappy at being lumped with the tourists, began to ask himself if he had to leave. When he was finished for the evening, instead of going to his room, he walked along the sea, dismayed that for all its expanse, a plane could carry him over it in no time and not only through space, but through time as well. It would take him away from this ancient place that was the work of centuries to a countryside that was raw with its newness. A thin edge of rose and turquoise was separating sky from sea when he decided he would sell his house. He need not even go home where he would be sure to lose his resolve. He knew a lawyer who would take care of the business for him. With the money from the sale he and Madame Papoulias would open the hotel and, of course, they must marry. He recalled Jackie Kennedy's wedding to Onassis. On the day of their marriage would Madame Papoulias at last be allowed to discard her black clothes for a white dress? The President's widow had looked charming with a wreath of flowers in her dark hair. Perhaps Madame Papoulias would wear a similar wreath.

Professor Miller, pleasantly startled by his boldness, decided to go to Madame Papoulias' at once and tell her his news. He hurried past empty cafés and silent houses. Her street was approached by a flight of steep stairs and as he reached the top he was breathing very fast, but whether from excitement or exhaustion, he could not say. As he paused for a moment to catch his breath he looked tenderly at Madame Papoulias' house. The white walls were stained with the spreading rose of the sky. Blue shutters covered the windows. The small balcony was crowded with pots of sprawling geraniums. He thought with pleasure, this will be my home soon. The idea gave him great satisfaction. The house he had left behind in the prairie state disappeared from his mind as a child forgets his old neighborhood and runs eagerly out across unfamiliar lawns to greet new friends. At that moment the door of Madame Papoulias' home opened and Evangelos stepped out. One hand was smoothing down his dampened curls, the other was making a little adjustment in the fit of his trousers. He saw Professor Miller and walked without hesitation toward him. Evangelos put an arm lightly around the professor who had neither the pride nor the presence to step away. The expression on Evangelos' sleep-swollen face was intimate and conspiratorial like someone in a secret fraternity who at last had been permitted to identify himself to a fellow member. "I don't mind, Professor. We have a saying here, 'When the wine is good, you keep it for yourself; when it grows a little sour, you are glad to share it.' "

Professor Miller waited until Evangelos was out of view and then he descended the stairway into the street below. In the bakery a man was sliding trays of bread onto the counter top. A few chairs in the cafés were already occupied by old men who wished not to be alone in the first hours of the day. He hurried on to his apartment and with shaking hands began to fold his clothes into tidy packages and place them into his suitcase.

In the evening when she appeared at the restaurant to inquire where he had been all afternoon, he told Madame Papoulias he had been making preparations to leave the next day. She did not seem surprised, only sulking a little because he had not made the arrangements for his flight through her travel agency. "I could have used the commission on the tickets as well as another," she said.

Professor Miller saw he had traveled too far. For the first time in many months he wished himself back among the good people.

CONTRIBUTORS

Alice Adams is the author of a number of novels and short story collections, including most recently *Superior Women* (a novel) and *Return Trips* (stories). Her short fiction has been included many times in the annual O. Henry Awards anthology. Born in Virginia, she now lives in San Francisco.

Margaret Atwood, the distinguished Canadian writer, is the author of a number of books of fiction, poetry, and criticism. Her most recent novel is *The Handmaid's Tale.* She lives in Toronto.

Joe David Bellamy, former editor of *Fiction International,* has recently published stories in *Prairie Schooner, Kansas Quarterly,* and *The North American Review.* He teaches at St. Lawrence University in Canton, New York.

Pinckney Benedict, recipient of the Henfield Foundation's Transatlantic Review Award, is enrolled in the graduate writing program at the University of Iowa. "Town Smokes" is his first nationally published short story. His home is in Lewisburg, West Virginia.

Leigh Buchanan Bienen is a criminal defense attorney and an advocate for women. A resident of Princeton, she has published books and articles on the law; and fiction and literary criticism in *Epoch, The Mississippi Review, Transition,* and elsewhere.

Paul Bowles is the author of a number of highly acclaimed novels, including *The Sheltering Sky* and *Let It Come Down.* His most recent collection of short stories was *Midnight Mass.* He lives in Tangier, Morocco.

Barry Callaghan, the editor of *Exile,* is a distinguished Canadian poet, fiction writer, and translator. His books include *The Hogg Poems and Drawings* and *The Black Queen Stories.* His short fiction has appeared in the United States, Canada, and England (regularly in *Punch* as well as in successive issues of *The Punch Book of Short Stories*). He teaches at York University in Toronto.

Margaret Drabble, one of the most widely acclaimed of contemporary English novelists, is the author of *The Realms of Gold, The Needle's Eye, The Ice Age,* and other works.

Margareta Ekström, the winner of many literary awards in her native Sweden, is a novelist, short story writer, diarist, and poet. She has published nine volumes of short fiction in Swedish; the first collection of her stories to be published in English was *Death's Midwives,* Ontario Review Press 1985. She lives in Stockholm.

Abby Frucht's stories have appeared in *Agni Review, Epoch,* and elsewhere. She lives in Oberlin, Ohio.

Carlos Fuentes, the distinguished Mexican writer, has published a number of books of fiction, the most recent being *Burnt Water* (stories) and *The Old Gringo* (a novel). He teaches part of the year at Harvard University.

Tess Gallagher, poet and fiction writer, has published stories in *The New Yorker, The Missouri Review, The North American Review,* and elsewhere. Her most recent books are *Willingly* (poems) and *The Lover of Horses* (stories). She teaches at Syracuse University.

Reginald Gibbons, the editor of *TriQuarterly,* is a poet, fiction writer, critic, and translator. His most recent book is *Saints* (poems). He lives in Evanston, Illinois.

William Goyen is the author of numerous works of fiction, including the novels *House of Breath* and *Arcadio,* and *Had I a Hundred Mouths: New & Selected Stories 1947-1983.* Born in Trinity, Texas in 1915, he divided his time in later years between New York and Los Angeles, until his death in 1983.

William Heyen is the author of a number of books of poetry, including *Noise in the Trees, The Swastika Poems,* and *Erika.* He lives in Brockport, New York, where he teaches at the State University. "Any Sport" is his first published story.

Josephine Jacobsen has published many books of poetry and fiction, including *A Walk with Raschid* (stories) and *The Chinese Insomniacs* (poems). A new collection of stories, *Adios, Mr. Morley,* is forthcoming. She lives in Baltimore.

Greg Johnson, author of the recent *Emily Dickinson: Perception and the Poet's Quest,* has published essays, reviews, fiction, and poetry in *The Georgia Review, Southwest Review, Virginia Quarterly Review,* and many other journals. A resident of Atlanta, he has taught most recently at Emory University.

Maxine Kumin, poet, short story writer, and novelist, won the Pulitzer Prize for her poetry in 1973. Her most recent books are *Why Can't We Live*

Together like Civilized Human Beings (stories) and *The Long Approach* (poems). She livers in Warner, New Hampshire.

Joyce Carol Oates is the author of a number of books of fiction, poetry, and essays, including most recently the novel *Marya: A Life* and the short story collection *Raven's Wing*. She lives in Princeton, New Jersey, where she teaches at the University and helps edit *The Ontario Review*.

Bette Pesetsky, of Dobbs Ferry, New York, is the author of a story collection, *Stories up to a Point*, and two novels, *Author from a Savage People* and *Digs*.

Sarah Rossiter has published short fiction recently in *The Massachusetts Review, The North American Review*, and elsewhere. She makes her home in Weston, Massachusetts.

Jeanne Schinto's stories have appeared in *Ascent, Cimarron Review, Confrontation*, and elsewhere. She lives in Lawrence, Massachusetts.

Lynne Sharon Schwartz, of New York City, has published several novels, the most recent *Disturbances in the Field*. Her short stories are collected in *Acquainted with the Night*.

Elizabeth Spencer's novels include *The Voice at the Back Door, The Light in the Piazza*, and *The Snare*. *The Stories of Elizabeth Spencer* was published in 1981. A former resident of Montreal, she teaches at the University of North Carolina in Chapel Hill.

Daniel Stern is the author of nine novels, the most recent *An Urban Affair*. A collection of his short fiction will be published this year. A resident of New York City, he has been a visiting professor at Wesleyan University.

Robert Taylor, Jr. has published stories in *The Agni Review, Georgia Review, Prairie Schooner*, and elsewhere. His latest book is *Fiddle and Bow*. He grew up in Oklahoma and now lives in Pennsylvania, where he teaches at Bucknell University.

John Updike, the author of numerous works of fiction, poetry, and literary criticism, was awarded the Pulitzer Prize in 1982 for his novel *Rabbit Is Rich*. His most recent titles are *The Witches of Eastwick* and *Roger's Version* (novels) and *Trust Me* (short stories), forthcoming in the spring of 1987.

Gloria Whelan, of Oxbow, Michigan, has published stories in *The Virginia Quarterly Review, Michigan Quarterly Review*, and elsewhere.